BLINDMAN'S
BLUFF

BLINDMAN'S BLUFF

FAYE KELLERMAN

HarperCollins*Publishers*

HarperCollins*Publishers*
77–85 Fulham Palace Road,
Hammersmith, London W6 8JB

www.harpercollins.co.uk

Published by HarperCollins*Publishers* 2009

1

First published in the USA by
William Morrow, an imprint of HarperCollins*Publishers*

A catalogue record for this book
is available from the British Library

ISBN: 978-0-00-729563-0

This novel is entirely a work of fiction.
The names, characters and incidents portrayed in it are
the work of the author's imagination. Any resemblance to
actual persons, living or dead, events or localities is
entirely coincidental.

Set in Sabon by Palimpsest Book Production Limited,
Grangemouth, Stirlingshire

Printed and bound in Australia by
Griffin Press

To Jonathan:
forever my inspiration

BLINDMAN'S BLUFF

ONE

AH, FANTASY: the stuff of life.

As he dressed for work, he looked in the mirror. Staring back at him was a handsome man around six feet four . . .

No. That was way too tall.

Staring back at him was a six-foot-one, devilishly handsome angular man with a surfer mop of sun-kissed hair and preternatural blue eyes, so intense that whenever any woman looked at him, she had to avert her eyes in embarrassment.

Well, the eyes part was probably true.

How about this?

In the mirror, staring back at him was an angular face topped by a nest of curly, dark hair and a shy smile that made women swoon— so boyish and charming, yet masculine at the same time.

He felt his lips turn into a smile, and he raked fingers through his own curly locks, which were on the thin side—not thinning, but not a lot of weight to the fibers. Pulling up on the knot of his tie, he eased it into the folds of his collar and felt the fabric: deluxe, heavy silk handpainted with an array of colors that would go with almost anything randomly chosen from his closet. As he tucked his shirttail into his pants, his hands ran over the rises and falls of a six-pack courtesy of crunches and weight lifting and a very strict eating regimen. Like most bodybuilders, his muscles craved protein, which was fine as long as he trimmed the fat. That was why whenever he looked in the mirror, he liked what he saw.

More like what he imagined he saw.

DECKER WAS GENUINELY perplexed. "I don't understand how you got past the voir dire."

"Maybe the judge believed me when I said I could be objective," Rina answered.

Adding artificial sweetener to his coffee, Decker grunted. He had always taken his java straight up, but of late he had developed a sweet tooth, especially after a meat meal. Not that dinner was all that heavy—skirt steaks and salad. He liked simple cooking whenever it was just the two of them. "Even if the judge shamed you into serving, the public defender should have booted your attractive derriere off the panel."

"Maybe the P.D. believed that I could be objective."

"For the last eighteen years, you've heard me piss and moan about the sorry state of the justice system. How could you possibly be objective?"

Rina smiled behind her coffee cup. "You're assuming I believe everything you tell me."

"Thank you very much."

"Being a detective lieutenant's wife has not leeched all rationality from my brain. I can think for myself and be just as rational as the next person."

"It sounds to me like you want to serve." Decker took a sip of his coffee—strong and sweet. "More power to you, darlin'. That's what our jury system needs, smart people doing their civic duties." He gave her a sly smile. "Or it could be that Mr. P.D. enjoys looking at you."

"It's a she and maybe she does."

Decker laughed. Anyone would enjoy staring at Rina. Over the past years, her face had grown a few laugh lines, but she still cut a regal pose: an alabaster complexion tinged with pink at the cheekbones, silken black hair, and cornflower-colored eyes.

"It wasn't that I *didn't* want to get out of it," Rina explained. "It's just that past a certain point, if you want to be excused, you have to start lying. Saying things like 'no, I can't ever be objective,' and that makes you sound like a doofus."

"What's the case?"

"You know I can't talk about it."

"Ah, c'mon!" Decker bit into a sugar cookie, home baked courtesy of his sixteen-year-old daughter. Crumbs nested in his mustache. "Who am I going to tell?"

"An entire squad room perhaps?" Rina replied. "Do you have any court appearances in L.A. coming up?"

"Not that I know of. Why?"

"I thought maybe we could meet for lunch."

"Yeah, let's get crazy and spend those fifteen dollars a day the courts give you."

"Plus gas, but only one way. Indeed, serving on a jury is not the pathway to riches. Even selling blood pays more. But I am doing my public duty and as one employed to protect and serve, you should be grateful."

Decker kissed her forehead. "I'm very proud of you. You're doing the right thing. And I won't ask you about the case anymore. Just please tell me it isn't a murder case."

"I can't tell you yes or no, but because you have seen the worst of humanity and have a very active imagination, I will tell you not to worry."

"Thank you." Decker checked his watch. It was past nine in the evening. "Didn't Hannah say she'd be back home by now?"

"She did, but you know your daughter. Time is a fluid concept with her. Want me to call her?"

"Will she answer her cell?"

"Probably not, especially if she's driving . . . Wait. That's her pulling up."

A moment later, their daughter came barreling through the front door, lugging a two-ton knapsack on her back and carrying two paper bags filled with groceries. Decker relieved her of the backpack, and Rina took the food.

"What's all this for?" Rina asked.

"I'm having a few girlfriends over for Shabbos. Other than what I bake, we don't have anything good in the house anymore. Do you want me to put the groceries away?"

"I'll do it," Rina said. "Say hello to your father. He's been worried about you."

Hannah checked her watch. "It's ten after nine."

"I know I'm overprotective, I don't care. I'll never change. And we don't have junk in the house, because if it's there, I eat it."

"I know, Abba. And being as you pay all the bills, I respect your wishes. But I'm only sixteen and this is probably one of the few times in my life that I'll be able to eat junk without gaining massive amounts of weight. I look at you and I look at Cindy and I know I'm not always going to be this thin."

"What's wrong with Cindy? She's perfectly normal."

"She's a big girl like I am, and she watches her weight like a hawk. I'm not at that point yet, but it's only a matter of time before my metabolism catches up with me."

Decker patted his belly. "Well, what's wrong with me?"

"Nothing's *wrong* with you, Abba. You look great for . . ." Hannah stopped herself. *For your age* were the unspoken words. She kissed his cheek. "I hope my husband will be as handsome as you."

Decker smiled despite himself. "Thank you, but I'm sure your husband will be much handsomer."

"That would be impossible. No one is as handsome as you are and with the exception of pro athletes, hardly anyone is as tall as you. It gets a tall girl down sometimes. We either have to wear flats or tower over most of the class."

"You're not that tall."

"That's only because to you everyone is short. I'm already taller than Cindy and she's five nine."

"If you're taller, it's not by much. And there are many boys over five nine."

"Not Jewish boys."

"I'm a Jewish boy."

"Not Jewish boys who are still in high school."

Decker liked that. It meant she'd have to wait until college to find a boyfriend. Hannah noticed the subtle smile. "You're not being very sympathetic."

"I'm sorry I gave you the Big T gene."

"That's okay," Hannah said. "It comes with its benefits but also its detriments. When you're tall and thin and dress nicely, people think you're trying to be a model and that you don't have a brain in your head."

"I'm sure you get lots of sympathy from your friends about that."

"I don't tell my friends that, I'm telling you." She looked at the dining room table. "Did you like the cookies?"

"Too much. That's precisely why I don't want junk in the house."

"Enjoy the cookies, Abba," Hannah told him. "Life is short even if you're not."

IT STARTED AS a soft tinkling in the background of her dream until Rina realized it was the phone. Marge Dunn was on the line and her voice was a monotone.

"I need to speak to the boss."

Rina regarded her husband. He hadn't changed positions since falling asleep four hours ago. The nightstand clock said it was almost three in the morning. Because Peter was a lieutenant, he didn't get many middle-of-the-night calls. The West Valley didn't teem with crime, and his elite squad of homicide investigators usually fielded whatever mayhem happened in the wee hours. Murders were rare, but when they occurred, they were usually nasty. But even nasty did not necessitate waking up the Loo at three in the morning.

A sensational story was another animal altogether.

Rina rubbed goose bumps on her arm, then gently shook him awake. "It's Marge."

Decker bolted up in bed and took the phone from Rina. His voice was still heavy with sleep. "What's going on?"

"Multiple homicide."

"Dear God—"

"At last count, there were four murdered and one attempted homicide. The survivor—a son of the couple murdered—is on his way to St. Joe's; he was shot but he'll probably live."

Decker stood up and grabbed his shirt, buttoning it while he spoke. "Who're the victims?"

"For starters, how about Guy and Gilliam Kaffey—as in Kaffey Industries."

Decker gasped. Guy and his younger brother, Mace, were responsible for most of the shopping malls in Southern California. "Where?"

"Coyote Ranch."

"Someone broke into the ranch?" He tucked the phone underneath his chin and talked as he slipped on his pants. "I thought the place was a fortress."

"I don't know about that, but it's gigantic—seventy acres abutting the foothills. Not to mention the mansion. It's its own city."

Decker remembered a magazine feature someone had done on the ranch a while ago. It was a series of compounds, although the main quarters were big enough to house a convention. Along with the numerous other buildings on the ranch, there were the requisite swimming pool, hot tub, and tennis court. It also had a kennel, a riding corral big enough for Olympic equestrian courses, a ten-stall stable for the wife's show horses, an airstrip long enough for any prop plane, and its own freeway exit. About a year ago, Guy Kaffey made a bid to purchase the L.A. Galaxy after the team had secured David Beckham, but the deal fell through.

As Decker recalled, there were two sons and he wondered which one had been shot. "What about all the bodyguards?"

"Two in the guardhouse at the front and both of them dead," Marge answered. "We're still searching. There's something like ten different structures on the property. So there may be more bodies. What's your ETA?"

"Maybe ten minutes. Who's down there now?"

"About a half-dozen squad cars. Oliver called in Strapp. Only a matter of time before the press gets wind."

"Secure the property. I don't want the press messing up the crime scene."

"Will do. See you soon."

Decker hung up and made a mental checklist of what he'd need— a notepad and pens, gloves, evidence bags, face masks, magnifying glass, metal detector, Vaseline, and Advil, the last item not for forensic use but because he had a pounding headache, the result of being awakened from a deep sleep.

Rina said, "What's going on?"

"Multiple homicide at Coyote Ranch."

She sat up straight. "The Kaffey place?"

"Yes, ma'am. No doubt, it's going to be a circus by the time I arrive."

"That's horrible!"

"It's going to be a nightmare in logistics. The place is around seventy acres—absolutely no way to totally wall off the area."

"I know, it's tremendous. About a year ago, they did a showcase home there for some kind of charity. I heard the gardens were absolutely magnificent. I wanted to go but something came up."

"Doesn't look like you'll get a second chance." Decker opened the gun safe, took out his Beretta, and slipped it into his shoulder harness. "That's a terrible thing to say but I make no excuses. Dealing with the press in high-profile cases brings out the bastard in me."

"They've called the press at three-fifteen in the morning?"

"Can't stop death and taxes—and you can't stop the news." He gave her a peck on the top of her head. "I love you."

"Love you, too." Rina sighed. "That's really sad. All that money is a deadly magnet for leeches, con artists, and just plain evil people." She shook her head. "I don't know about being too thin, but you certainly can be too rich."

THE ONLY GOOD thing about being called in the early hours of the morning was ripping through the city sans traffic. Decker zipped through empty streets, dark and misty and occasionally haloed by streetlamps. The freeway was an eerie, endless black road fading into fog. In 1994, the Southland had been pummeled by the Northridge earthquake, a terrifying ninety seconds of doomsday that had brought down buildings and had collapsed the concrete bridges of the freeways. Had the temblor occurred just a few hours later during the morning commute, the casualties would have been tens of thousands instead of under a hundred.

The Coyote Road off-ramp was blocked by two black-and-whites, nose to nose. Decker displayed the badge around his neck to the police officers, and it took a few minutes for the cars to part to allow him forward. One of the cops directed him to the ranch. It was a straight shot—no turnoffs anywhere—and the packed dirt road seemed to go on for about a mile before the main house came into view. Once it did, it grew like a sea monster surfacing for air. The outdoor lights had been turned on to the max with almost every crevice and crack illuminated, giving the place a theme park appearance.

The mansion was Spanish villa in style and, in its own blown-up way, harmonious with the surroundings. The final height was three stories of adobe-colored stucco with wood-railed balconies, stained-glass windows, and a red Spanish tiled roof. The structure sat on the rise of a man-made knoll. Beyond the mansion were vast, empty acres and the shadows of the foothills.

About two hundred yards into the drive, Decker saw a parking lot filled with a half-dozen squad cars, the coroner's van, a half-dozen TV vans with satellites and antennas, several forensic vans, and another eight unmarked cars, and there was *still* room to spare. The media had set up shop, with enough artificial illumination to do microsurgery because each network and cable TV station had its own lighting, its own camera and sound people, its own producers, and its own perky reporter waiting for the story. The mob longed to be closer to the hot spot, but a barrier of yellow crime scene tape, cones, and uniformed officers kept them corralled.

After showing his badge, Decker ducked under the tape and walked the distance to the entrance on foot, passing meticulously barbered mazes of boxwood elms outlining the formal gardens. Inside the shrubbery were different groupings of spring flowers, including but not limited to roses, irises, daffodils, lilies, anemones, dahlias, zinnias, cosmos, and dozens of other types of flora he didn't recognize. Somewhere close by were gardenias and night-blooming jasmine, infusing death with a sickly sweet fragrance. The flagstone walkway cut through several rows of blooming citrus. Lemon trees, if Decker had to make a guess.

Two officers were guarding the front door. They recognized Decker and waved him through. The interior lights were also on full blast. The entry hall could have been a ballroom in a Spanish castle. The floor was composed of heavy planks of old, hardened wood—irregular with a patina that no contrived distressing could manufacture. The ceiling soared and was lined with massive beams that had been carved and embellished with petroglyphs, the cave figures looking like something found in the Southwest. The walls were festooned with layers of gilt paneling and held museum-sized tapestries. Decker would have probably kept gawking, enraptured by the sheer size of the place, had he not caught the eye of a uniform who motioned him forward.

Proceeding down a half-dozen steps, he walked into a living room with double-height ceilings and more painted beams. Same hardwood on the floor, only most of it was covered with dozens of authentic-looking Navajo rugs. More gilt paneling, more tapestries along with enormous art canvases of bloody battles. The room was furnished with mammoth-sized couches, chairs, and tables. Decker was a big guy—six four, 220-plus pounds—but the scale of his surroundings made him feel positively diminutive.

Someone was talking to him. "This place is bigger than the college I attended."

Decker regarded Scott Oliver, one of his crack Homicide detectives. He was in his late fifties and carried his age very well, thanks to good skin and repeated rounds of black hair dye. It was almost four in the morning, yet Oliver had dressed like a CEO at a board meeting: black pin-striped suit, red tie, and a starched and pressed white shirt.

"It was only community college, but the campus was still pretty big."

"Do you know the square footage?"

"A hundred thousand, give or take."

"Man oh man, that is . . ." Decker stopped talking because words were failing him. Although there was a uniformed officer at each doorway, there were no evidence markers on the floor or on the furniture. No one from CSI was busy dusting or dabbing. "Where's the crime scene?"

"The library."

"Where's the library?"

"Hold on," Oliver told him. "Let me get my map."

TWO

T HE LABYRINTHINE HALLWAYS should have confounded any ordinary burglar's escape route. Even with printed directions, Oliver made a couple of wrong turns.

Decker said, "Marge told me there were four bodies."

"We are now up to five. The Kaffeys, a maid, and two guards."

"Good lord! Signs of a robbery? Anything ransacked?"

"Nothing so obvious." They continued down endless foyers. "No single perpetrator, that's for certain. Whoever did this had a plan and a gang of people to carry it out. It *had* to be an inside job."

"Who reported the crime? The injured son?"

"I don't know. When we got here, the son was being loaded into the ambulance and was out of it."

"Any idea when the shootings occurred?"

"Nothing definite, but rigor has started."

"So between four and twenty-four hours," Decker said. "Maybe the contents of the stomachs can narrow it down. Who's out from the morgue?"

"Two coroner investigators and an assistant coroner. Turn right. The library should be through the double doors ahead."

As soon as he walked inside, Decker felt a tinge of vertigo brought on by not only the gargantuan size of the room, but the lack of corners. The library was a rotunda with a domed ceiling of steel and glass. The curved walls were covered by black walnut paneling and bookshelves and floor-to-ceiling tapestries of mythological creatures gamboling in the forests. There was a walk-in fireplace big enough to contain a raging inferno. Antique rugs sat atop the oceanic wooden floor. Lots of furniture: sofas and love seats, tables and chairs, two grand pianos, and lamps too numerous too count.

The crime scene was a story in two parts. There was action near the fireplace and action in front of a tapestry of a gorgon devouring a young lord.

Oliver pointed to a spot. "Gilliam Kaffey was sitting in front of the fireplace, reading a book and drinking a glass of wine; Dad and son were having a conversation in those two club chairs over there."

His finger was aimed at a grouping of two brown leather, nail-studded chairs where Marge Dunn was working in front of the man-eating gorgon. She was talking animatedly to one of the coroner's investigators wearing the standard morgue issue: a black jacket with the identifying yellow lettering on back. Dunn saw Decker and Oliver and motioned them forward with a gloved hand. Marge's hair had grown a little longer in the past few months, probably at the urging of her newest boyfriend, Will Barnes. She had on beige pants, a white shirt, and a dark brown cable-knit sweater. Rubber shoes on her feet. Decker and Oliver made their way over to the crime scene.

Guy Kaffey was on his back in a pond of blood with a gaping gorge in his chest. Tissue and bone had exploded over the man's face and limbs and what hadn't spilled onto the floor was splattered on the better part of the tapestry, giving the hapless lad and his plight unasked-for verity.

"Let me get you orientated." Marge reached into her pocket, removed a map, and unfolded it. "This is the house and we are right . . . here."

Decker took out his notepad and glanced around the windowless room. When he commented on it, Marge said, "I was told by the surviving maid that the artwork here is very old and sensitive to direct light."

"So someone else besides the son survived the attack?" Decker asked.

"No, she came in and discovered the bodies," Marge said. "Her name is Ana Mendez. I have her in a room guarded by one of our men."

Oliver said, "We also need to interview the groundskeeper and the groomsman. They're also being guarded by L.A.'s finest."

Marge said, "All of them in separate rooms."

"The groundskeeper is Paco Albanez—maybe around fifty-five—who's worked here for about three years." Oliver checked his notes. "The groomer is Riley Karns. He's around thirty. I don't know how long he's been here."

Decker said, "Do you know who called the crime in?"

Marge said, "We're sorting that out. The maid said that someone called an off-duty bodyguard and maybe he called 911."

"It was the maid who found the surviving son lying on the floor," Oliver said. "She thought he was dead."

"Who is the off-duty bodyguard that she supposedly called?" Decker asked.

"Piet Kotsky," Marge told him. "I spoke to him on the phone. He's coming in from Palm Springs. It works like this . . . I think. The bodyguards stay on-site only when they're working. They work in twenty-four-hour shifts, rotating through eight people. There are always two bodyguards in the main house and two men manning the guardhouse located at the entrance gate of the property. Both of those guys are dead. Gunshot wounds to the head and chest. All the camera equipment and closed-circuit TVs are smashed and destroyed."

"Names?" Decker asked.

"Kotsky doesn't know who was on duty tonight, but he said once he sees them, he can identify them."

"What about the two guards in the main house?"

"They appear to be missing," Marge said.

"So two guards missing and two guards murdered."

Marge and Oliver nodded.

"Oliver mentioned a murdered maid?"

"In the servant's bedroom downstairs."

"And how did Ana Mendez manage to dodge the bullet?"

"She was off tonight," Oliver said. "Her story is that she had re-turned to the ranch around one in the morning."

"How'd she get back? No public transportation for miles."

"She has a car."

"She didn't notice the lack of guards in the guardhouse?"

Marge said, "She went around through the back gate at the ser-vice entrance. No guards are routinely stationed there. Ana has a gate access card. She gets in, parks her car, and goes into her room. She sees the body and starts screaming for help. At this point, it gets a little muddy. She apparently went upstairs and found the other bodies."

"She went upstairs without knowing if there were still people in the house?" Decker asked.

"I told you, her story's a little confusing. Once she saw the bod-ies, she called Kotsky and he reported the crime . . . I think."

"I'll talk to her again. She's Spanish speaking?"

"She is, although her English is pretty good."

Decker said, "On to the guards. Do you know who arranges their schedules?"

Oliver said, "Kotsky makes the assignments but doesn't arrange them. That's done by a man named Neptune Brady who is the Kaffeys' head bodyguard. Brady has his own bungalow on the grounds, but for the past few days, he's been visiting his sick father in Oakland."

"Has anyone contacted him?"

"Kotsky called him up and told us that Brady chartered a jet and should be here soon." Marge paused. "We did take a brief peek in-side his bungalow just to make sure no one else was dead. I didn't rifle through his room. We'll need a warrant to do that."

"Let's put in for one in case Brady's uncooperative." Decker looked around the room. "Ideas on how this played out?"

Oliver said, "Gilliam was sitting in front of the fireplace, sipping wine and reading. Marge and I think that she went down first. She's still slumped on the couch, her book is a few feet away, covered in blood. See for yourself."

Decker walked over to the scene. Sprawled on the couch were the remnants of a beautiful woman. Her blue eyes were open and blank, and her blond hair was matted with caked blood. The woman's torso had been nearly bisected at the waist by several shotgun blasts. It was sickening, and Decker involuntarily averted his eyes. There were some things he'd never get used to.

"This is carnage," he said. "We'll need lots of photographs because our memories aren't going to be able to process all of this information."

Marge continued, "The disturbance of someone entering the room must have drawn the attention of the father and son. We figured they went down next."

Oliver said, "There are two Kaffey sons. The one who was shot was the older one, Gil."

"Does he have immediate family who need to be notified?" Decker asked.

"We're working on it," Oliver said. "No one's called any police station to ask about him."

"What about the younger brother?" Decker asked.

Marge said, "Piet Kotsky told me that the younger son's name is Grant and he lives in New York. So does Guy's younger brother, Mace Kaffey."

"Who is also in the business," Oliver pointed out. "Both of them have been notified."

"By who? Kotsky? Brady?"

Marge and Oliver shrugged ignorance.

"Back to the crime scene," Decker said. "Any idea what Guy and Gil were doing?"

Oliver said, "They could have been talking business, but we didn't find papers."

Marge said, "Guy Kaffey probably stood up and saw what was happening to his wife. Then he was blown backward. The son was a little quicker and started running away when the bullets caught him. He went down a few feet away from one of the doors out of here."

"And the shooters didn't bother to check to make sure he was dead?"

Marge shrugged. "Maybe something distracted the shooters and they fled."

Decker said, "We have one, two, three . . . six doors in the room. So we could have a band of shooters with each one coming in from a different door and overwhelming the couple. Any idea of what could have sent a posse of murderers out of the ranch without finishing off the son?"

Oliver shrugged. "Maybe an alarm, although we haven't decoded the system yet. Maybe the maid coming into the house. But she didn't see anyone leave."

Decker thought a moment. "If everyone was drinking and relaxing, it probably wasn't too late: after dinner but early enough for a nightcap—around ten or eleven."

"Around," Marge said.

"And the groomer and the groundskeeper," Decker said, "were they in the house when you arrived?"

"Yes."

"You said that they live here?"

Oliver said, "In the bungalows on the grounds."

"So how did they find out about the murders? Did someone get them or were they awakened by the noise or . . ."

The two detectives shrugged.

"We're going to be camped out here for a while." Again, Decker massaged his aching head. "Let's let CSI, the photographers, and the coroner investigators do their things here in the library. We've still got a couple of other crime scenes and witnesses to interview. Where are the other bodies?"

Marge showed him the area on her map. Decker said, "I could use one of those."

Oliver gave his to the boss. "I'll get another one."

"Thanks," Decker said. "You two take over the other crime scenes, and I'll talk to the witnesses, especially the Spanish speakers. I'll see if we can piece together a time frame and a chain of events."

"Sounds like a plan," Marge said. "Ana is in this room." She showed him on the map. "Albanez is here and Karns is here."

Decker marked the rooms on the map. Then he wrote each name on the top of a piece of paper in his notebook. There were a slew of players. He might as well start the scorecard.

CURLED UP IN a chair, Ana Mendez had just about disappeared. She seemed to be in her late thirties and was diminutive in size—under five feet—with almond skin stretched over a broad forehead and pronounced cheekbones. Her mouth was wide, her eyes round and dark. Her hair had been clipped into a pageboy, giving her face the appearance of someone staring out the window with two black drapes on the side and her short bangs being the valence curtain.

The maid had been sleeping, but woke up when Decker walked into the room. She rubbed her eyes, swollen from crying and squinting in the bright artificial light. He noticed that her white housekeeper's uniform was smeared with brown stains and made a mental note to give the clothing to CSI.

Decker asked her to start from the beginning. This was her story.

Ana's day off went from Monday evening to Tuesday evening. Usually she returned to the ranch earlier in the evening, but last night was a special function at her church, including a short midnight prayer service. She left afterward, around 12:30, and drove back to the ranch, arriving around an hour later. The mansion was entirely enclosed with heavy, wrought-iron fencing that had spikes on top, so most of the gates were unguarded. She had a card key for the gate closest to the kitchen. After she entered the premises, she drove to the service lot, parking her car behind the kitchen. She walked down a flight of steps to the service wing and used her bedroom key to get inside the building. When Decker asked about an alarm, she told him that the servants' quarters was alarmed, but it wasn't connected to the main house. The mansion had its own security system. This way, the help could go in and out without disturbing the Kaffeys' safety system.

Her eyes swelled with tears when she described what she saw in the bedroom. She had turned on the light and there was blood everywhere—on the walls, on the carpet, on the two twin beds. But the worst part was Alicia: she was lying on her back and wasn't moving. Her face had been shot off. It was horrible. Terrifying. She started screaming.

The next part of her story was mixed with giant sobs. She ran upstairs: the interior stairs that led to the mansion's kitchen. Normally the kitchen door was locked at midnight to prevent anyone using the servants' entrance from coming into the main house. But not tonight. Ana distinctly remembered flying into the kitchen and screaming for the missus.

But no one answered.

When Decker asked her about the mansion's alarm going off when she went into the kitchen, Ana couldn't remember. She had been hysterical, and she apologized for her hazy memory.

Decker thought she was doing pretty well.

She discovered the Kaffeys in the library—first the men, then the missus. No one was moving so she thought they were all dead, including Gil. She had watched enough television to know that she shouldn't touch anything.

Still screaming, she ran outside. She was alone and the grounds were dark and spooky. She knew where Paco Albanez's bungalow was because she was friendly with the groundskeeper. But to get to Paco's bungalow, she had to walk by the pool, cross over the tennis courts, and go through the fruit orchards. Riley Karns lived closer to the main house. Even though she didn't know him well, she woke him up. He told her to stay in his quarters while he looked around. Around fifteen minutes later, Riley came back with Paco Albanez and the three of them tried to figure out what to do. They knew they had to call the police and since Riley spoke English, he volunteered. He told Paco and her to wait in his bungalow while he made the calls. Then he left. He came back about thirty minutes later with two policemen. The officers brought the three of them into the house and separated them. The policeman said that people would be talking to her. First it was the lady policewoman. Now it was him.

The story was a straightforward narrative. She didn't seem overly addled nor did her words seem rehearsed. When she was done, she looked up at Decker forlornly and asked when could she leave? When he told her she needed to stay for a little while longer, she burst into tears.

Decker patted her hand and left to interview Riley Karns.

The groomsman was a tiny man with a strong grip and an even stronger English accent. His elfin features were set into a weathered face and his complexion was wan from horror as well as lack of sleep.

He had worked with horses for years—as a jockey, as a trainer, and as an equestrian jumper or doing dressage in horse shows. His job not only included tending to the horses and dogs, but also teaching Gilliam Kaffey basic equestrian skills. He wore dark sweats that appeared to be smudged with stains. When Decker asked if had changed his clothing tonight, he answered no. Karns's account dovetailed with Ana's story. He filled in Ana's missing minutes— the half hour or so that she was alone with Paco Albanez in Karns's bungalow.

Karns admitted that his first call should have been 911, but he wasn't thinking so clearly. Instead, he had rung up Neptune Brady— the Kaffeys' chief of staff. Karns knew that Brady was up north in Oakland visiting his father but he called him anyway. When the two of them connected, Neptune told Karns to call 911 immediately, then to ring up Piet Kotsky and have him get over to the ranch to find out what the hell went wrong. Brady told him that he was going to try to charter a private jet to get the hell down to L.A. He'd call Kotsky once his travel plans were firmed up. Brady also told Karns that he'd notify the family.

Karns simply did as he was told. He called 911, then he called

Piet Kotsky who said he'd leave right away, but it would take him three hours to get to the ranch. An ambulance arrived about five minutes later, then the police came. He took a couple of officers over to his bungalow where Ana and Paco were staying. The police took them inside and separated them.

Paco Albanez was in his fifties—a mocha-complexioned man with gold eyes, gray hair, and a white handlebar mustache. He was built low to the ground with a barrel chest and thick forearms. He, like Ana, had worked for the Kaffeys for about three years. He didn't have much to add to the mix. Karns woke him up with a start, told him to get his clothes on, and that a terrible tragedy had happened to the family. He was half asleep, but as soon as he saw how upset Ana was, he woke up pretty quickly. He stayed with Ana until the police arrived. His recitation also seemed on the up-and-up.

Decker left the interviews with many unanswered questions. Among them:

1. Why was the door to the kitchen unlocked?

2. Did the killers come through the staff quarters, murder the sleeping maid, and access the house through the kitchen? If so, who let them in?

3. Did the alarm go off when Ana went into the kitchen? And if it didn't, who turned it off?

4. Who possesses keys to the main house besides the family?

5. Who knows the alarm code besides the family?

6. Who was the first one to realize that Gil Kaffey wasn't dead?

7. And, finally, why didn't the murderers make sure that Kaffey was dead?

There were housekeepers, guardhouse guards, mansion guards, a groundskeeper, a groomer, Piet Kotsky, and Neptune Brady. And this was Guy Kaffey's personal staff. Decker could only imagine how complicated it would get when he got into the business—a corporation that employed thousands. The manpower devoted to such a high-profile case would be staggering. In his mind, he saw a bursting case file filled with a forest's worth of felled trees. In recent months, their substation had started using paper from recycled pulp.

Go green.

Better than red: the predominant color of the evening.

THREE

THE TWO VOICES were deep and demanding. From the back, Decker noticed the bald guy first, garbed in loose-fitting chinos and a bomber jacket. He was thick necked and broad shouldered and appeared to be packing around 250 pounds of pure muscle. His companion had a head of thick black hair and wore gray slacks and a blue blazer. He was taller and leaner but also powerfully built. If they were football players, one would have been a tackle, the other a quarterback.

From the snippets of conversation, they appeared to be irate at the police. First they had been stopped like common criminals at the off-ramp, grilled like they'd done something wrong. And now Marge was refusing to let them see the crime scene. Though his favorite sergeant didn't require help, Decker went over to investigate.

Marge made quick introductions: Piet Kotsky and then Neptune Brady. Kotsky was flushed, with sweat dripping off a protruding forehead. His eyes were big and deep-set, and his skin was tightly drawn over prominent cheekbones. His complexion was jaundice in color—the hue of mummified skin.

Brady was younger, in his early to mid thirties. His lean face had spent a lot of hours in the tanning salon. He had pale blue eyes, thick lips, and tightly curled dark hair. His arms were folded across his chest, his hands big and adorned with several gold rings. His chin jutted forward when he spoke. "Are you in charge?" Without waiting for a response, he said, "What the fuck happened?"

Decker said, "We're still gathering information—"

"Do you know it took me about twenty minutes just to convince the idiots at the off-ramp that I actually had a reason to be at the ranch! Don't you guys communicate with one another?"

Decker took a step backward, giving them both some space. "What can I do for you, Mr. Brady?"

"For starters, how about some answers?"

"As soon as I have them, I'll pass them along. I'd like to ask you some questions." He turned to Marge. "Why don't you take Mr. Kotsky to one of the studies and interview him there, Sergeant."

"What is this?" Brady's nostrils flared. "Divide and conquer?"

"We're not the enemy, Mr. Brady. And I need information." Decker checked off items on his fingers. "We need a list of everyone who works at the house either full- or part-time. How many people are in the house at night at any one time? Who was supposed to be working last night? Who lives on the properties? Who lives off the properties? How long has each employee been working for the Kaffeys? Who has access keys? Alarm codes? Who hires? Who fires? Mundane information like that."

Brady shuffled his feet. "I can help you. First, I'd like to see what happened."

Marge said, "Mr. Kotsky, why don't you come with me and let Lieutenant Decker and Mr. Brady conduct their business."

Kotsky looked at Brady, who nodded. "Okay. Go into the east study."

Marge said, "Where's that on the map?"

"Piet will show you."

After they had gone, Brady said, "I need to see what happened."

"No one sees the victims unless it's been cleared by the coroner's investigators. We're in charge of the death scene, but they're in charge of the bodies."

"Bureaucracy!" Brady spat out. "No wonder the police don't get anything done."

Decker stared at him. "We get things done, but because we want to do them right, we're careful. Do you think Mr. Kaffey would let anyone inside the boardroom at his company just for the asking?"

Brady said, "The difference is I'm a taxpayer and I pay your salary."

Decker managed to keep a flat face. "Mr. Brady, you're not going anywhere any time soon because you have to wait for the family. So rather than twiddle your thumbs and be irritated, you might as well cooperate. You'd look a less suspicious in my eyes if you did."

"You suspect me?" When Decker didn't answer, Brady said, "I was hundreds of miles away." When Decker still didn't respond, Brady grew irate. "I've worked for Mr. Kaffey for years. I don't need this shit!"

"Sir, anyone who has had anything to do with the Kaffeys is a potential suspect right now. That's just the nature of the beast. If I didn't have a suspicious mind, I'd be a very bad detective."

Brady clenched his fists, and then slowly let his fingers relax. "I'm still in a state of shock."

"I'm sure you are."

"You have no idea . . ." His voice dropped a few notches. "I was in the middle of dealing with my own father's heart attack. Now I have to deal with the remaining family members. Do you know how fucking dreadful it was to make that phone call to Grant Kaffey? To tell him that his parents and brother are dead?"

Decker regarded the man. "Gil Kaffey's in the hospital, sir. He isn't dead."

"What?" Brady's eyes got wide. "Riley Karns told me he was dead." After an awkward pause, he muttered out loud, "Thank God for that." A cynical laugh. "Now the family's going to think that I'm a fucking moron!"

"Why don't you let me deal with the family?"

"The family's safety was my concern and I fucked up." His eyes suddenly pooled with tears. "I didn't have anything to do with this, but you're right to suspect everyone. What do you want to know?"

"For starters, how does your security work?"

"It doesn't, obviously." Brady bit his lip hard. "This is going to take a while."

"How about we find a private room and you can explain it to me."

"I can manage a room," Brady told him. "Lord knows there're enough of them—and then some."

THE SPOON WAS going around and around in the cereal bowl. Hannah was not interested in breakfast, nor was she interested in going to school. But while breakfast was somewhat optional, education was mandatory.

Rina said, "Why don't I make you a bagel and you can eat it in the car?"

The teenager pushed red locks out of her blue eyes. "I'm not hungry."

"You don't have to eat it. Just take it."

"Why?"

"Humor me, okay?" Rina picked up the cereal bowl and put an onion bagel in the toaster. "Get your stuff. We need to go."

"What's the hurry?"

"I have jury duty. I'm going to need at least an hour to make it there on time."

"Poor Eema. Not only does she have to suffer the vicissitudes of her sullen daughter, she's stuck with eleven other unlucky souls in smoggy downtown L.A."

The bagel popped up. Rina gave it a schmear of cream cheese and wrapped it in foil. "I'm not complaining. Let's go."

Hannah hoisted up her two-ton backpack. "What case are you working on?"

"I can't talk about it."

"C'mon. Who am I going to tell? Aviva Braverman?"

"You're not going to tell anyone because I'm not going to tell you." She checked her purse—more of a tote bag than a fashion statement. It contained a paperback book on Abigail Adams and today's *Los Angeles Times*. The murders had made the headlines. She pulled out her keys, set the alarm, and locked the door behind them.

"It's ridiculous that they didn't throw you off," Hannah told her. She put on her seat belt. "Abba's not only a cop, but a lieutenant."

Rina started the motor. "I have a mind of my own."

"Still, he influences you. He's your husband." Hannah unwrapped her bagel and started nibbling away. "Mmm . . . good." She adjusted the satellite radio until she found a station playing spine-jarring rock. "What's for dinner?"

Rina smiled to herself. Hannah was on to another topic. Like all teens, she had the attention span of a gnat. "Probably chicken."

"Probably?"

"Chicken or pasta."

"Why not pasta with chicken?"

"I can make pasta with chicken." Rina turned to her. "You can also make pasta with chicken."

"You make it better."

"That's nonsense. You're an excellent cook. You're just shunting it to me."

"Yes, I am. In a few years, I'll be away at college and then you won't have anyone to cook for anymore. You'll miss these days."

"I have your father."

"He's never home, and half the dinners you cook for him wind up in the warming drawer. Why do you bother?"

"Someone sounds resentful."

"I'm not resentful, I'm just stating fact. I love Abba, but he just isn't home very much." She bit her thumbnail. "Is he going to make it to my choir performance tonight?"

"Your performance is tonight? I thought it was tomorrow."

"Oh, Mrs. Kent changed it. I forgot to tell you."

"If your performance is tonight, Hannah, are you even going to eat dinner at home?"

"No, I guess not," Hannah said. "Is Abba going to make it?"

"He's made it to your last two performances. I'm sure he'll be there . . ." She thought about the morning news. "Unless something dire comes up."

"Something dire like murder?"

"Murder is very dire."

"It isn't really. What difference does it make? The person's already dead."

It was clear that Hannah was in her own narcissistic world. There was no use in trying to reason with her. Instead, Rina changed the radio station to oldies. The Beatles were singing about eight days a week.

"I love this song!" Hannah turned up the volume knob and sat back contentedly, eating her bagel, humming along while tapping her toes.

All resentment toward her father seemed to have dissipated.

The attention span of a gnat was sometimes a good thing.

WALKING INTO THE courtroom, he was glad he'd taken extra time to make sure his tie was properly knotted and his shirt collar had the right amount of starch. With his shoulders erect and a jaunty stride, he owned the world.

He had a gift.

Like a composer with perfect pitch, he had what he called perfect sound. Not only could he translate words and decipher speech—the minimum requirements for his job—but equally as important, he could code nuances and know everything about that person's background, often after just a few sentences. He could tell where the person grew up, where the person's parents grew up, and where the person was currently residing.

Of course, he could discern simple things like race and ethnicity, but who among the living could also zero in on social class and educational level in a single breath? How many fellow human beings could detect whether the person was happy or sad—no biggie there—

but also whether he or she was angry, peeved, jealous, annoyed, wistful, sentimental, considerate, empathetic, industrious, and lazy? And not by what they said, but how they said it. He could distinguish between nearly identical regional American accents, and he had a magic ear for international accents, too.

In his world, there was no need for visuals. The eye was a deceptive thing. He'd been given an otherworldly gift, not to be squandered on trivial things like a parlor game.

Name that accent.

People were such assholes.

His PDA buzzed. He fished it out of his pocket and pushed a well-worn button. The machine read the text message aloud in a staccato electronic voice: "See U for usual lunch." He turned off the handy-dandy portable and stowed it back in his pocket. The time was twelve-thirty, the place was a sushi bar in Little Tokyo, and the date was Dana.

The day was shaping up to be a good one. Taking his seat on the bench, he adjusted his designer sunglasses, turned his head in the direction of the jury box, and flashed the good citizens of Los Angeles a blinding smile of perfectly straight white teeth.

Showtime!

AFTER RECEIVING INSTRUCTIONS from the judge not to talk about the case, the jury filed out of the courtroom.

The woman in front was named Kate and that's all that Rina knew about her. She looked to be in her thirties with pinched features, clipped blond hair, and hoop earrings dangling from her earlobes. She turned to Rina and said, "Ally, Ryan, and Joy are going to the mall. You want to join us for lunch?"

"I brought a sack lunch, but I'd love to sit with you. Anything to get out of this building."

"Yeah, who's really in jail?" Kate smiled. "I'm going to use the little girls' room, and Ryan and Ally have to make a couple of phone calls. We're all meeting outside in about ten minutes."

"Sounds good." As Rina pushed open one of the double glass doors of the criminal courthouse, a blast of furnace air hit her face, and the roar of traffic filled her ears. The asphalt seemed to be melting with heat waves shimmering in the smog. The only shade in the area was provided by the multistory buildings—not much shadow in the noonday sun—and a row of hardy trees that seemed pollution resistant.

She dialed Peter's cell expecting to leave a message. She was delightfully surprised when he picked up.

"How's it going?" she asked.

"I'm still alive."

"That's a good thing. Where are you?"

"I'm with Sergeant Dunn and we're headed for St. Joseph's hospital intensive care unit. Gil Kaffey is out of surgery."

"That's good news. I read the story this morning, although I'm sure it's out of date already. You've got your hands full."

"As always."

"I love you."

"I love you, too."

"Am I going to see you anytime soon?"

"Eventually I'll have to sleep."

"Do you think you'll make it to Hannah's choir recital?"

A pause. "When is it again? Tomorrow at eight?"

"It's actually tonight at eight. The choir teacher changed the date and Hannah forgot to tell me."

"Oh boy." Another pause. "Yes, I will make it; however, I will not vouch for my appearance or my hygiene."

Rina felt relieved. "I'm sure that all Hannah wants is to see your face."

"That will happen. Just do me a favor. Poke me in the ribs if you see my eyes start to close. How's it going over there in beautiful downtown L.A.?"

"Summer is upon us." She wiped sweat off her forehead with the back of her hand. "I shouldn't have worn my sheytl today. It's too hot for a wig."

"Take it off. I won't tell."

Rina smiled. "So I'll meet you at school?"

"That would make sense."

"Should I bring you dinner?"

"That would also make sense. Gotta run. The sterile hallways and the antiseptic smells of St. Joe beckon, but don't be jealous of my good time. I'm sure you have your own party planned within the vaunted walls of justice."

"Actually, we've got some camaraderie going on. A group of us are going to the food mall for lunch across the street from the court-house."

"Well, aren't you the fortunate daughter."

"We're doing our civic duty for fifteen dollars a day. Even LAPD pays more than that."

"Want to switch places?"

"Not on your life. I prefer the living to the dead."

FOUR

IT TOOK MARGE and Decker nearly forty-five minutes to make it to the hospital in light traffic. Had Gil Kaffey been conscious during the ambulance ride, he would have had a lot of thinking time. What would he remember? Sometimes in traumatic incidents, retrograde amnesia set in: nature's inoculation against further pain.

St. Joe's medical complex consisted of the medium-sized hospital in four wings and an equal number of professional office buildings. It took a few passes to find an open parking space, and it was a tight squeeze at that. Marge maneuvered the Crown Vic with aplomb, and within a few minutes they were showing their badges at the nurses' station that manned the glassed-in intensive care unit. Before they were permitted inside, they needed to get Kaffey's doctors to sign them in. It took about twenty minutes to locate one of Kaffey's surgeons.

The doctor in charge, named Brandon Rain, was a beefy man in his thirties with broad shoulders and ham-hock forearms. He gave them an update. "Kaffey is heavily sedated. His body has gone through a terrible ordeal, so not more than a few minutes."

"How bad is it?" Decker wanted to know.

"The bullet cracked through a couple of floating ribs and caused some bleeding. It took him a while to get here and that area is very vascular. A little more central and the slug would have hit the spleen. He would have bled out." The surgeon's pager sprang to life. He checked the window on his cell. "I've got to run. Not more than a few minutes."

"Got it," Decker said.

"Have you heard from the family?" Marge asked.

"Not yet, but I'm sure I will," Rain told her. "Did you happen to notice the Kaffey building when you came in?"

"I did," Decker said. "I take it the family holds some sway?"

"Let me put it this way," Rain said. "They're charitable people. They're also moneyed people. In this economy, that's a winning combination."

GIL KAFFEY HAD tubes in his nose, tubes in his arms, and tubes in his stomach. His face was bruised and swollen, his eyes were bloodshot, and his lips dry and cracked. Marge had pulled up his picture on her laptop and the man in front of them bore no resemblance to the good-looking, self-confident guy on the computer screen. Kaffey's heart rate was steady, and an arm cuff inflated every ten minutes to get a BP reading. Gil was conscious but was very groggy. Decker wasn't looking for a lengthy interview. All he wanted was a name. It was the first question he asked.

Do you know who shot you?

No one was surprised when Kaffey shook his head no. His heart rate jumped as he tried to speak. "Four . . ."

The ICU nurse tossed the detectives a meaningful glance. "Just a few minutes."

"Got it," Decker said. "Did you say *four*, Mr. Kaffey?" When Gil nodded, he said, "Were there *four* people who attacked you?"

Kaffey shook his head. "For an . . ."

They waited. Nothing else came and Kaffey closed his eyes.

Decker said, "Do you mean the number four?"

Another shake. "For . . . in."

Decker said, "Foreign? As in foreign-speaking?"

Kaffey's heart rate quickened and his eyes opened slowly. He gave them a nod.

"The people who attacked you weren't speaking English."

Another nod.

"Do you know the language?" Marge asked him.

"No . . . dark . . ."

"Dark?" Marge repeated. "The room was dark?"

A shake of the head.

Marge tried again. "The men who attacked you were dark complexioned?"

Again the eyes opened. Another nod.

"Were they black?"

"No . . . dark . . ."

"Dark," Decker said. "Dark like Hispanic or maybe Mideastern or Mediterranean?"

A nod.

"But you didn't recognize the language they were speaking?"

No answer.

Marge asked him, "How many men do you remember?"

"May . . . be . . . three . . . four . . ." The eyes closed. "Tired."

The nurse broke in. "He's due for some pain medications. I need to call in the doctor." She rang a bell. "You should probably go now."

"You're the boss." Decker handed the nurse several cards. "When he's a bit more awake, please call us. I know that his health is paramount, but the more information we have, the better our chances of solving the crime."

"See . . ." Gil said.

Marge and Decker whipped their heads in Kaffey's direction.

"See what?" Marge asked.

He shook his head. "See . . . yes."

The detectives waited for more.

"Yes . . . see."

Decker smoothed his mustache, his version of stroking a beard. He did it when he was thinking hard. "Do you mean *sí* like the Spanish word for yes?"

"One of them." Labored breathing. "I heard him say *sí*."

RINA TOOK HER roast beef sandwich from a plastic baggie. It was on an onion roll with lettuce, tomato, and pickles.

Joy eyed it enviously. "That looks good."

"Want a bite?" Rina offered.

"No, I have my fast food. What would my system do without all that added sodium?"

The mall was an enclosed series of multiple fast-food outlets designed to appeal to the teeming mass of humanity that the city employed. Although ripe with the smell of cooking oil and meat, it was air-conditioned and on days where the mercury was hovering in the nineties, one could put up with a bit of stale grease.

They were a motley crew. Joy was a secretary for a metal recycling company. She was in her sixties, chunky with dyed red hair and rouged cheeks. Ally had just graduated from community college with a major in communications and was excited about her upcoming twenty-first birthday party. Everyone on the jury was invited. Ally's dark hair had a blond chip running down the middle like a skunk. Ryan was in his late thirties, married with three boys. He was a contractor and was happy to get off the job for a couple of days. He had been working on a big house and the clients were driving him crazy. Kate was the sole woman in a house of former air force men. Her two boys were now in their thirties and worked as pilots for FedEx. Her husband had put in thirty years with United Airlines.

"We went on a lot of great vacations," Kate said.

"I bet," Rina said. "We took an Alaskan cruise last year. It was heavenly."

"Alaska's beautiful," Ryan said. "I try to go fishing every summer up there."

"Salmon fishing?"

"You got it."

Joy said, "Aren't you worried about grizzly bears?"

"You go fishing when there's lots of fish. When the grizzlies are busy eating fish, they don't bother you."

Joy said, "Did you see that awful documentary where the guy and his girlfriend got attacked and were eaten by a grizzly bear?"

"Ugh," Ally said. "When was this?"

"Several years ago," Rina said.

Ryan said, "They are wild animals. You've got to have respect."

"Ugh!" Ally repeated.

"Probably not as yucky as today's headlines," Joy said. "Did you read about what happened at that huge mansion in the Valley?"

"Coyote Ranch," Ryan said. "The Kaffeys. They're major developers."

"I was sick when I read that. . . . It's just horrible! Three people dead!"

Joy was just a font of distasteful news. And she delivered it with such glee. Rina didn't bother to correct her on the body count. Keeping one's mouth shut was always a good option.

"They must have had an elaborate alarm system," Joy went on. "It had to be an inside job."

Kate said, "I certainly wouldn't want to be on that jury. I'd hang the bastards." She turned to Rina. "Where does your husband work?"

"In the West Valley."

"Oh . . . okay."

Joy's eyes widened. "So it's your husband's district?"

"Yes."

"Is he involved?"

"I think all of the West Valley is involved. The victims are high-profile people. It's going to get a lot of attention."

Joy leaned over. "What do you know about it?"

"The same as you do: what I've read in the morning papers."

Ally smiled. "She's going mute."

Rina smiled back and took a bite of her sandwich. Then she changed the subject. "Does anyone know who that guy in the spectator seating is?"

"The guy with the shades and the Tom Cruise smile?" Kate said. "Who is he?"

"I don't know, but he's been in and out of the courtroom since the voir dire."

"Maybe he's a reporter," Ally suggested.

Kate said, "I haven't seen a notepad."

"Lots of 'em use tape recorders. That's what I did when I had to do interviews for journalism."

Kate shrugged, "Maybe."

"It's a little weird," Joy said. "He just sits and smiles at us. Is he trying to intimidate us or something?"

"I don't know," Rina said. "Every time I sneak a glance at him, he's straightening his tie or wiping lint off his suit. He dresses nicely. He obviously cares about his appearance."

Ryan said, "Tell you one thing. He isn't involved with manual labor. Soft hands."

"Maybe he's like a private attorney," Joy said. "The guy on trial can use someone better than that schlump he has."

"Yeah, he is pretty schlumpy," Ally said.

Kate said, "We probably shouldn't be talking about the case."

"We're not talking about the case," Joy said, "just the schlumpy attorney."

"Still, Kate has a point," Rina said. "So what's the guess on who Mr. Smiles is?"

Shrugs all around.

"I just hope he's not a stalker," Ally said quietly.

"He's a little out in the open to be a stalker," Rina said.

Joy said, "I once had a stalker. Some guy at work. Wouldn't leave me alone."

Ally said, "What did you do?"

"I repeatedly told him to bug off. When he wouldn't, I threw coffee in his face." When the group stared at her, dumbfounded, Joy said, "It was lukewarm. But I made my point. He never bothered me again."

"You're tough," Ryan said. "Tougher than my clients."

Joy patted his hand with maternal affection. "I may be a grandma, but that still doesn't mean you can mess with me."

Ally said, "Did you bring up the stalker at the voir dire when they asked about experience with crime?"

"Nah, I didn't bring it up. It wasn't a crime really. Just bad behavior. Hell, if they eliminated people based on bad behavior, the system wouldn't have anyone left for jury duty."

FIVE

SINCE IT WAS L.A., the scene might have been a generic opening shot for any of the many hospital shows that had graced the small screen over the years. Men were shouting orders as they rushed down the hallways with anxious nurses in tow. Except in this case, the guys weren't in scrubs but suits and ties with an entourage of walking-around guys. The nurses were barking commands at the executive group, but the men clearly weren't listening. Someone mentioned calling security.

The crew charged past Marge and Decker as the detectives exchanged glances.

"The Kaffey family?" Marge asked.

Decker answered, "Maybe we should intercede before someone throws them out."

"Not likely being as we're in the Kaffey Emergency Services Building." Marge watched the confrontation in front of the ICU. "We should put a guard in front, Loo. We don't know if the family is involved. Maybe they've come back for unfinished business."

"Absolutely." Decker took in a deep breath and let it out. "Let's go."

They walked over to the sizable assemblage, the voices loud and demanding. The revolt was led by a young man in his twenties, backed up by an older man in his late fifties. Decker weaved himself into the hubbub. "Can I help someone?"

The young man glared at Decker with furious eyes. He was medium sized with a thick swatch of sandy hair. If Decker squinted hard enough, he could see some common fraternal features with Gil.

"Who the hell are you?"

"Detective Lieutenant Peter Decker, LAPD. This is Detective Sergeant Marge Dunn. She's from Homicide." He held out his hand. "Are you Grant Kaffey?"

The eyes narrowed. "Let me see some ID."

Decker opened the billfold, and both the young and older man scrutinized the badges. When they were satisfied, the older one said, "What the hell is going on?"

"How about some introductions first? We'd like to know who we're talking to."

The older man spoke up. "Mace Kaffey. I'm Guy's brother." He ran his hand over a face shadowed with grief, fatigue, and grizzle. "This is Grant Kaffey. We want to talk to Gil."

"Gil is very heavily sedated right now. He was wounded—"

"How bad?" The younger one looked horrified. "Was he shot?"

"He was shot."

"Oh God," Mace exclaimed.

Decker said, "How about if we find a quiet room and get some coffee? Sergeant Dunn and I will try to bring you up to speed."

"When do I get to see my brother?" Grant demanded.

"That's not my decision, Mr. Kaffey, that's up to the doctor." Decker turned to one of the nurses. "Can we get an empty room here?"

The head nurse—a stout woman with a stern expression named Jane Edderly—came charging into the commotion. "There are way too many people here. It's blocking the hallways."

Grant said, "Harvey, get us some coffee. Engles and Martin, you two stay here with us. The rest of you wait downstairs." Upon hearing orders, the underlings scattered. The younger Kaffey was still glaring at Decker. "I want to see my brother now!"

Decker turned to the head nurse. "Can you page Dr. Rain, please?"

"He's in surgery," Jane huffed.

"Do you know when he'll be out?"

"I have no idea! You're still blocking the aisles."

Grant started to speak, but Decker held up a hand. "Nurse Edderly, this is Grant Kaffey and Mace Kaffey. They've just undergone a terrible shock—the loss of Grant's father and mother and Mace's beloved brother and sister-in-law. I need to talk to them. Surely there's an empty room in the Kaffey building where we could talk."

Jane's eyes widened. She finally got it. "Let me look and see what's available."

"Thank you, I appreciate your cooperation." Decker turned to the men. "I'm very sorry for your losses. Tragedy of this kind just defies words."

Mace Kaffey ran his hands over a haggard face—exhausted eyes and deep-set wrinkles. The man was portly. "What happened?"

"We don't have all the details right now. As soon as we find a room, I'll fill you in on what I do know."

"Goddamn ranch!" Grant started pacing. "Too many fucking people going in and out. Impossible to keep track of all of them. I *told* my father that."

"How many people were under your father's personal employ?" Marge asked.

"Huh?" Grant stopped pacing. "At the ranch?"

"Yes, sir."

"Who knows? Too many people with too many keys. It's just ridiculous!"

Decker said, "I heard that the staff was vetted pretty carefully."

"Whatever that means! Who does private security anyway? They're either losers who couldn't make it into the police or ex-policemen who were thrown out for being on the take. Or with Dad, it was reformed delinquents who tugged on his misguided heartstrings."

Again, Marge and Decker exchanged glances.

Nurse Jane Edderly had returned. "We found a room for you. Please follow me."

"Thank you for helping out," Decker said.

Grant said, "Yeah, thanks for giving me a room in my family's building after a six-hour emergency flight to tend to my murdered parents. Thanks a whole fucking load, Nurse Edderly!"

The nurse glanced at him but remained silent.

Mace put a hand on Grant's shoulder, but he shook it off. The space was small but roomy enough for the four of them to sit while Grant's remaining two lackeys had to stand. Within a few minutes, everyone was drinking bad coffee. Mace looked defeated, but Grant was still on youthful fire.

"When can I see my brother?"

"Mr. Kaffey..." Decker paused. "Would you mind if I called one of you by your first name since both of you are Mr. Kaffey?"

"Call me Mace," the older man said.

"I frankly don't care what the fuck you call me. Just tell me what's going on. And who do I have to screw to see my brother?"

Marge said, "We saw your brother about twenty minutes ago. He was in a lot of pain, so the doctor upped the sedation. He's out of it. Your seeing him is not a police decision but a medical one."

"Then get the doctor over here!"

"I tried to have him paged," Decker said. "He's in surgery."

"Grant, let's just hear what the police have to say," Mace told him.

Marge turned to Grant. "You're right in several respects about the ranch's security. There was an obvious breach. Two of the guards were homicide victims, but there are two others who were on duty who're missing. We're working with a man named Neptune Brady. Do you know him?"

Mace said, "Neptune has been under Guy's employ for a while... first in the business and then he took him as his personal head of security."

"Why?" Grant asked. "Do you suspect him?"

"Just gathering information," Decker repeated. "What did Brady specifically do in the business?"

"I'm not sure," Mace said. "I'm East Coast–based."

Grant said, "He's a licensed private detective. He did some free-lance work. There were some numbers not adding up in the accounting office—embezzling. Dad put Neptune on the cases and he did good work. So Dad being Dad offered him a full-time job at the Coyote Ranch as head of security at an exorbitant salary."

"He was a generous guy?" Marge asked.

"Generous one minute, a tightwad the next. You never knew how his pocketbook would swing. Dad was paying Neptune a fortune, but Dad insisted that was how you kept them loyal."

"Do you get along with Mr. Brady?"

Grant said, "Neutral. We don't have much to do with each other."

"What about you?" Marge asked Mace.

"I barely know him. You think he did it?"

"We're just gathering information," Marge said. "You said something about your dad hiring delinquents?"

"What are you talking about?"

"You mentioned that your father hired security guards who were former delinquents."

"Yeah, Gil mentioned something about that to me. Is someone going to check up on my brother?" Grant looked at his two underlings. "Joe, find out what's happening with Mr. Kaffey."

After the assistant left, Decker said, "Can you help me sort out the specifics of the company? For starters, how many people does Kaffey Industries employ?"

"At the height of the real estate boom, maybe a thousand," Grant told him. "Now we're down to around eight hundred. Six fifty on the West Coast, and Mace and I got about a hundred and fifty working for us."

"You're real estate developers?" Marge asked.

"Primarily," Grant said.

"Shopping malls?"

"Primarily."

Decker said, "Have you two always worked on the East Coast?"

"Dad decided to expand about ten years ago. At first, we were commuting bicoastally. Then we decided to relocate."

"My wife's from New York," Mace said. "She jumped at the opportunity to move back east. Guy still came out every month. Not necessary for him to do so, but my brother has a hard time delegating. Grant can back me up on that."

"Dad's a workaholic," Grant told him. "He not only keeps long hours, he expects everyone else to keep long hours."

"Is that a problem?" Marge asked.

"Not with us, because we're three thousand miles away," Grant said. "My brother gets the brunt end. Dad accuses us of being soft because we have a life. But that's just Dad being Dad." Tears formed in his eyes. "Dad came from humble beginnings."

"We both did," Mace said with a bristle. "My father came over from Europe with nothing. He opened a small appliance repair shop back when people still repaired things. He was frugal and saved and managed to buy a couple of apartment buildings. Guy and I parlayed our dad's holdings into an empire."

Grant gave his uncle a hard stare and then turned his irritation on Decker. "What does this have to do with his murder?"

"Just trying to get a feel for your family, Mr. Kaffey. It helps to know some background. I'm sorry if you find the questions intrusive."

Marge stepped in. "Was your father having problems with anything specific? Maybe the embezzling accountant?"

"He was actually an account executive," Mace said. "Milfred Connors. I think there was talk of a lawsuit, but Guy paid him off."

"Son of a bitch," Grant said. "He steals and then he threatens to sue."

Marge wrote down the name. "So why pay him off?"

"Because it's easier than a protracted legal battle," Mace told her.

Grant said, "We had enough lawsuits going already." He backtracked. "Nothing out of the ordinary. Some we initiated. Some were initiated against us."

Mace said, "What about Cyclone Inc., Grant? They were really pissed when we pulled the permits for the Greenridge Project." He turned to Decker. "They've been impeding the project for years. We finally got all the permits and approvals, so they don't have a leg to stand on."

Decker said, "Why is Cyclone Inc. pissed at you?"

Grant said, "They own the Percivil Galleria and Bennington Mall—both of which have been around for twenty or thirty years. Bennington was knocked for a loop by the Woodbury Commons—one of the busiest outlet malls in the country. But Percivil was doing all right because it's across the Hudson where there isn't competition."

"Then we came on the scene," Mace said. "Kaffey is developing a state-of-the-art mall that's going to blow the Galleria out of the water."

Grant said, "Not only will it include almost every chain and luxury goods store, we're in the process of developing a resort hotel with two Tumi Addams–designed golf courses."

Mace said, "One indoors, one outdoors."

"Golf year-round. Plus we've signed on with some of the country's best chefs to open up restaurants."

"Wow," Marge said. "That would blow any existing mall away."

"Exactly!" Mace crowed.

Decker asked, "Where exactly is the development?"

"Upstate New York in Clarence County surrounded by some of the most beautiful land that ever existed," Mace said. "The area is filled with ecological nuts, but we did our due diligence. We've filed all the necessary environmental impact reports. The whole project is going to be green."

"Cyclone's been raising a stink about graft and corruption," Grant said. "Totally unfounded accusations. Assholes! They've already sicced the county tax assessors on our books. We came away clean. We've got nothing to hide!"

"Who's the CEO of Cyclone?" Decker asked.

"Paul Pritchard." Grant paused. "He's an asshole, but murder?"

Mace said, "Our project will kill his last profitable mall, Grant. Pritchard's a bastard, and I wouldn't put anything past him." He turned to Decker. "Check him out."

"We will," Marge said. "Getting back to the more immediate, does Gil live near your father?"

"Gil lives in L.A. Dad lives on the ranch and in Palos Verde Peninsula. The company is headquartered in Irvine."

Decker raised an eyebrow. "Not so far from Palos Verdes but far from Coyote Ranch."

"That was the purpose," Grant said. "When Dad wanted to get away, he wanted to get away. Initially he bought the property for Mom and her horses, but Dad came to love it. Mostly they entertained at the Palos Verdes house, but every so often they'd give a party at the ranch." His eyes looked far away. "One winter"—a laugh—"Dad got some snow machines and provided skiing on several man-made runs. The party lasted an entire weekend. That was something else."

"Was the ranch's security beefed up for the weekend?" Marge asked.

"Probably. That would be Neptune Brady's bailiwick. He knew the ins and outs of the ranch better than my parents. Fuckhead! How the hell did this happen? He's the one you should be questioning, not me."

Decker said, "He's on our radar. So far, he's been cooperative."

Grant became agitated. "Where the fuck is that doctor? I want to see my brother!"

"Let me go check on it," Marge said.

"Good idea." Decker turned to the men. "Thank you both for being so forthright at this very difficult time."

"Fucking nightmare!" Grant tried to pace, but there wasn't much floor space. Talking business had seemed to calm him down, giving him something else to think about. The minute he was brought back into his current tragedy, he was perched on the edge of an explosion. And who could blame him?

Decker said, "Do you think that the Greenridge Project will go through in the wake of this tragedy?"

"Absolutely," Mace said stiffly. "One thing has nothing to do with the other."

"It's just that Guy was the CEO, and a project of that magnitude is a mammoth enterprise. It sounds like the biggest shopping mall that Kaffey has developed."

Grant said, "It'll be difficult, but we can carry out Greenridge without Dad as long as Gil can take care of the rest of Kaffey." He shook his head. "God, that's a huge load."

Mace said, "It'll be hard to handle anything without Guy, but we can manage if we work together. We're not just business associates, we're family."

Decker regarded Guy's younger brother. His pep talk sounded forced—maybe trying to convince himself he was up to the job. Marge came back into the room. "Dr. Rain is just out of surgery. He'll see you both in his office as soon as he's cleaned up. Nurse Edderly will be happy to take you to his office."

Grant punched a fist into his palm. "I don't want anything to do with that bitch!"

"I'll be happy to take you," Marge said.

"Thank you," Mace said. "Are you staying with us?"

"We need to get back to the ranch." *To the crime scene,* Decker thought. "I also want to check out these two men you mentioned— Paul Pritchard and Milfred Connors."

"Connors was a low-level con man," Grant said. "He's a nothing."

"Sometimes it's the nothings who get pissed off," Mace told him.

"Exactly," Decker said. "Here are some business cards, gentlemen. Call me anytime."

"And here's my card," Grant countered. "That's a business number. You can call it anytime. If it's important, you can leave your number and I'll be paged."

"Thank you," Decker said. "Uh . . . just one last question. Do either of you know Spanish?"

"What?" Mace said.

"What's that about?" Grant asked.

"A lot of people who work at the ranch are Hispanic. In California, Hispanics do a lot of construction work. Just wondering if you and your dad and your brother can communicate with them directly."

"Of course we visit the job sites, but we don't talk directly to the men," Mace told him.

"Why would we do that?" Grant asked. "That's why we employ foremen."

SIX

ONCE BEHIND THE wheel, Marge got comfortable in her seat and spoke while adjusting the mirrors. "I'd love to see the company's financials on Greenridge, especially in this current climate. Sounds like something that was born in real estate boomland and is currently moribund in bustville."

"Maybe they already had the financing for the project."

"Something that big, including a hotel? That's a cool billion, right?"

"Too many zeroes and I get confused." Decker opened a bottle of water and chugged half of it. "Even if I had the financials, I wouldn't even begin to know how to interpret something that complicated."

Marge started the motor and drove out of the underground lot. "Do you think that the project might have something to do with the murders?"

"It's worth checking out, but I don't expect anything." Decker closed the cap. "Let's concentrate on what we do know."

"We have murdered guards and we have missing guards. Sounds like an inside job."

"Two things come to mind," Decker said. "An inside robbery job that was botched or an inside job where the guards were used in a murder for hire."

"In which case, we need to look deeper into the family."

Decker said, "What did you think of Grant?"

"Intense. He did most of the talking for his uncle."

"What do you think about Mace?"

"Not as much intense. We didn't know Guy Kaffey, but from today's conversation snippets, I'd say that younger brother Mace grew up under the shadow of Guy."

Decker said, "Grant's also the younger brother and you just described him as intense."

"Yeah, he's aggressive. But maybe Gil is even more aggressive. All I'm saying is that if Guy and Mace clashed, we both know who'd come out ahead. I wonder if Guy Kaffey was as enthusiastic on the Greenridge Project as Mace and Grant are."

"Guy was about to pull the plug and the two New Yorkers weren't happy with his decision?"

"My thoughts exactly," Marge said. "But even if that were the case, would that generate enough anger and hostility in Grant for him to kill his parents?"

Decker said, "We don't really know how Grant feels about his parents. There could have been a lot of playacting going on."

"True that," Marge said. "Interesting that you didn't ask if there was enough anger and hostility for Mace to kill a brother."

"Cain and Abel," Decker said. "The very first chapter. There are four recorded people on the newly minted universe and bam, one brother shoots the other because of jealousy. What does that say about the human race?"

"Doesn't say too much for us or for the Big Cheese in the sky," Marge noted. "Any police chief who ran a major city with a 25 percent homicide rate would get his ass canned in an eye blink."

THE MAN CALLED into the witness box was Hispanic.

No surprise there.

The entire afternoon had been a parade of Hispanics from the plaintiff—a beefy guy with tattoos—to the defendant—another beefy guy with tattoos. Rina could sum up the assortment of alleged assaults and batteries in one word.

Alcohol.

All the participants had been drunk at the time, both the ladies as well as the gents. Normally the melee would have been forgotten about the next day, but the police happened to be cruising by when the slugfest had been in full force. The cops managed to arrest whoever didn't scatter fast with the unlucky remaining souls blaming each one for starting the incident. Witnesses had suddenly come down with bad memories caused by cold feet.

The current participant in the witness box proved to be no exception.

At least, the jury finally figured out who Smiling Tom Cruise was.

When the first witness was called to the stand—a Hispanic woman in her fifties wearing a red miniskirt and with permanently inked eyebrows and a mane of long black hair—Smiling Tom, who had been sitting in the gallery, whipped out an electronic device. Walking slowing toward his destination, Tom held a small PDA in his hand, listening intently to something through an ear pod. When he reached the witness box, Tom turned off the radio and pulled out the earphone, stowing both in his front pocket.

The group exchanged glances and shrugged.

He sat himself directly behind the witness, his head leaning over the hoochie mama's shoulder. The witness seemed to enjoy his presence, turning to him and gracing Mr. Sunglasses with a wide, white smile. For once, Tom didn't smile back.

The case continued and Tom's purpose became clear.

He was a translator.

To call him a translator was an understatement.

What Tom did was act out the testimony. He was a one-man stage show, his voice rising and falling, imparting each phrase with the exact amount of emotion required. If there was an Oscar for translators, Sunglasses Tom would have won it hands down.

As the afternoon hours passed, the witnesses' recollections got more faint and indistinct and Arturo Gutierrez, now being grilled mercilessly by a hard-driving prosecutor in a red power suit, was more of the same. Although he did remember punches being thrown, he couldn't tell who threw the punches. Maybe the plaintiff hit the defendant, but maybe the defendant hit the plaintiff. The witnesses were tentative on the stand, and the only one having a good time seemed to be Tom.

By the time the prosecution rested and the defense was due up, it was time to go home. After receiving their orders not to talk or discuss the case with anyone, the jury slowly and silently filed out of the courtroom as the bailiff looked them over one by one by one. Rina was reminded of the metaphor used on the holiday of Rosh Hashanah, the Jewish New Year's. God judges all his people as they pass under him one by one—as if he were counting a flock of sheep.

Once in the hallway, the group made a break for the elevators.

Joy turned to Rina. "We're going out for drinks. Wanna come?"

"My daughter has a choir recital."

"When?" Kate asked.

"Around seven-thirty."

"We're only going out for about an hour."

"Maybe tomorrow," Rina said. "It's going to take me a little time to get home, and I want to pack dinner for my husband. I'm meeting him at the recital."

Joy said, "Well, aren't you the nice wife!"

"Sometimes when he's working big homicides and he's been up for about twenty hours, he forgets to eat."

No one spoke and the elevator doors opened and the group got out.

Ally said, "What do you think Smiling Tom was doing with his PDA?"

"I thought about that, too," Rina said. "Maybe going over testimony before he translated it. Whatever he was listening to, it had to have been sanctioned by the court. No one would be that brazen to approach the witness box listening to music."

"Good call," Ryan told her.

Joy said, "He looks pretty damn brazen to me."

"Yes, he was rather theatrical." Rina opened the double glass doors to freedom. "I'm on for lunch tomorrow."

"Great," Kate said. "We'll see you then. Wish your husband good luck."

"Yeah, pump him for some juicy details," Joy interjected.

"He's pretty tight-lipped, but I'll do what I can."

Joy was pleased with Rina's answer. She added, "And as long as you're packing something for him, pack something for me. Whatever you ate this afternoon looked a hell of a lot better than the swill I had."

ALTHOUGH RINA WAS early, Peter was earlier. While all the other parents were crowded toward the front, Peter had chosen a seat in an empty back row, sitting straight up with his head back, his eyes closed, and his mouth slightly open. She climbed over the folding chairs and gently shook his shoulder. He gave a snort at the same time his eyes popped open. "What?"

Rina took out a sandwich. "Here."

Decker rubbed his eyes and stretched. "Hi, darlin'." He leaned over and gave her a peck on the cheek. "Do you have something to drink? My mouth feels like cotton."

"Caffeinated or decaf?"

"Doesn't matter. I won't have any trouble sleeping tonight."

She handed him a can of Coke Zero. "It's turkey and pastrami on a baguette."

"I'm starved." Decker took a bite. "It's delicious. Thank you."

"You haven't eaten?"

"No." He popped open the Coke Zero and downed the entire can, and immediately Rina handed him a caffeine-free Diet Coke. "I think I'm dehydrated."

"I also have water if you want."

"A little later, thanks." He finished half the can. "How was your day in criminal justice?"

"Fine. How was yours?"

"Awful."

"The murders are all over the news."

"So I've heard."

"Some guards were killed as well?" Rina asked.

Decker nodded and finished the Coke. "I must thank Hannah for getting me out of the squad room. I left in a hurry. Things are a mess."

"Are you going back?"

"Probably. I'd like to finish some of my paperwork and strategize."

Rina knew from experience that multiple murders mean multiple, multiple suspects. "Are you awake enough to drive, Peter?"

"I'm fine." He smiled to prove the point. "Really, I'm fine. I was probably out for around twenty minutes. I feel remarkably refreshed."

"One of my fellow jurors wants to know all the juicy details of the Kaffey homicides."

"Tell her to read the papers."

"I shall." Rina took Peter's hand. "I'm glad you made it to the concert. Hannah made a point of asking about you."

"Lord only knows why. She hides herself as much as possible in the back row. I wouldn't even notice her except that she's tall. She never has any solos. Does the teacher have something against her?"

"Mrs. Kent is Hannah's biggest fan."

"So why doesn't she ever have a solo?"

"I don't think she wants one. She likes to see her father in the audience. It makes her feel like you care."

Decker shrugged. "I keep wondering with the kids, including Cindy who is in her midthirties, how long will I have to jump through hoops just to prove I love them?"

"Oh, I don't know . . ." Rina shrugged. "Probably the rest of our lives."

SEVEN

DECKER WAS DEAD to the world from twelve midnight until six-thirty the next morning when the alarm rang out. The bed was empty, but he heard noises coming from the kitchen. He showered and shaved and dressed and walked into the break-fast room at seven where coffee was already brewing.

"Good morning," Rina said. "How do you feel?"

"Not too bad." He poured a cup of java from the drip machine and took a sip. "Wow, that's good. Do you want me to wake up the princess?"

"I've already done that. She's in a good mood."

"What's the occasion?"

"You. She told me—and I quote—'It was really nice for Abba to show up. I know he must be swamped at work.'"

"That's lovely." A pause. "How long do you think her appreciation will last?"

"In the short run, it won't last very long at all. But in reality, it'll last a lifetime." Rina kissed his cheek. "I'll take her to school on my way to court."

"That would be great." He checked his watch. "I need to go. I'll stick my head in the lion's den and say good-bye."

"This morning, you'll probably have more of a lamb than a lion."

"Whatever I get is fine." He put down his mug. "She's a good girl. She's my baby and I love her dearly. If I'm a safe target for some of her frustration, so be it. If God'll just keep her safe, I'll take all those slings and arrows."

OLIVER KNOCKED ON the doorjamb and without waiting for an invitation, he walked into Decker's office. He had a mug of coffee in one hand and was holding a sheet of paper in the other. The man looked positively drained.

"Get any sleep last night, Oliver?"

"A couple of hours, but I'll be all right." He handed Decker a neatly typed up paper that resembled a family tree. "I've outlined Kaffey Security 101. If you look at the top of the sheet, I have Neptune Brady in the starring position because he's the head honcho. Then I branch off."

"Well done," Decker said.

"Not too bad for a zombie." Oliver smiled. "I divided it into two categories—guards at the ranch and personal bodyguards. Personal bodyguards—which I've abbreviated as PBG—are or were used mainly when Guy and Gilliam went out in public—restaurants, charity functions, business functions, parties. At least one PBG was with them at all times."

"What about if they went out individually?"

"Don't know about Gilliam, but there was definitely one on Guy. When no one was home, the security guards, or SG, watched the properties. So far I got fourteen names, but you can see there's overlap. Rondo Martin, Joe Pine, Francisco Cortez, Terry Wexford, Martin Cruces, Denny Orlando, Javier Beltran, and Piet Kotsky worked as personal bodyguards and security guards."

Decker regarded the paper. "You've crossed off Alfonso Lanz and Evan Teasdale. Those are the dead guards, right?"

"Yep."

"And these circled names—Rondo Martin and Denny Orlando—they're the missing guards?"

"Right again. No luck locating them yet, but we've been doing some hunting. When we went to pay a visit to Denny Orlando's apartment, his entire family was there, waiting for Denny to come home. Marge and I talked to the wife for a while. She described Denny as a good husband, a good father—they have two kids—and said it's not like Denny to up and disappear."

"That means nothing."

"I agree. He still needs to be probed, but you get that initial feeling about a person. Sometimes it's wrong but more often than not, it's right. We didn't find anything that points Denny in the direction of hit man. When we asked Brady about him, he seemed stunned. Denny always impressed Brady as a straight shooter. He's a deacon in his church."

"So was BTK."

"Yeah, I know, but I think we all agree that this probably isn't the work of a serial killer."

"What about the other one—Rondo Martin?"

"Brady was equally shocked, but of course, he has to be. He can't admit to us that he hired a psycho."

"You think he's a psycho?"

"He's a former deputy sheriff from Ponceville—a small farm community in central California. Brady wasn't sure how Rondo heard about the position for the Kaffeys, but he called Brady and told him he was interested in private security work. The pay was better and he was looking for something different. He was interviewed, went through a probationary period, and then was hired full-time. Moved down to L.A. with no strings attached."

"Hmmm . . ."

"Exactly. He lives in an apartment in the North Valley. When we went to his place, no one was home, but we got the keys from his landlord. His place, while not exactly stripped cleaned, was pretty damn bare. His car was also gone—an '02 Toyota Corolla—metallic blue. We've got an APB out on it."

"What about Orlando's car?"

"His wife took him to work. Martin was supposed to take him back home."

"So what are your thoughts?"

Scott ticked off his fingers. "Orlando and Martin were both involved. Martin was involved and shot Orlando. Orlando was involved and shot Martin. Neither was involved and both bolted because they were scared."

"What about prints? You pulled up a lot of them."

"We're checking them out."

"You have prints for Martin and Orlando?"

"Orlando, I don't know. We've put in a request at Ponceville for Martin's prints. He must have had a set to work in law enforcement."

"What about the other guards?" Decker asked.

"We're running through them one by one. We made phone contact with Terry Wexford, Martin Cruces, and Javier Beltran so we're on our way to eliminating them. Let me recap the way the system works."

Decker sipped coffee at his desk. "Shoot."

"There are always four security guards working at the ranch when Gilliam and Guy are in residence—two at the guardhouse and two inside the house. The men work twenty-four-hour shifts and are relieved by a new set of guards the next day. Sometimes individuals from the next group might come in a little early. So theoretically, it's possible to have as many as eight guards on the property at any one time."

"All right." Decker did some instant calculations. "That means— on average—a security guard works every third day."

"Around that." Oliver finished his lukewarm coffee. "The security guards don't live on the properties, but there are a couple of staff bungalows with empty beds if one of them is too tired to go home or comes in early."

"How many bungalows?"

"Two each with four cots and a TV for the staff, plus a separate bungalow for Neptune Brady. Both Kotsky and Brady told me it's not unusual to have a couple of men resting while waiting for their shift to start."

"Do the guards have keys to get into the property?"

"Gate keys but not house keys. There's a house keycard check system that Brady has in place."

"How does that work?"

"Each incoming guard is required to check out the keycard from an outgoing guard. There's a sign-in sheet and a sign-out sheet that includes time and date. The sheet for the night of the murder is missing, but that doesn't mean too much. Brady had the schedule for who was supposed to be on. We know who was murdered and we know who is missing."

"That's not much of a system—a sign-up sheet."

"You said it. Ripe for abuse, but it worked well for a number of years. Brady told me he was very diligent in counting the keycards, and they are next to impossible to duplicate. None were missing from the lockbox, but of course two keycards are gone, probably taken by the two missing guards."

"What a way to live," Decker said. "Rarified to be sure, but that comes with a price."

"Ain't that the truth," Oliver said. "Coyote Ranch is kind of the California version of Versailles. And we all know what happened to Marie Antoinette."

THE SECOND DAY of testimony was more of the same.

More forgetful people with Smiling Sunglasses Tom doing a bang-up acting job in the translation department. While the deputy D.A. gave off the professional look—navy pin-striped suit, white blouse, sensible pumps—the defense attorney was a schlub—stooped shoulders and a comb-over of unruly gray hair. His suit was too short in the sleeves, but too big on his bony frame. The crux of his case was that the arresting officers couldn't really see who punched whom and therefore his client should be exonerated.

The P.D. called up the young officer for the cross, and although the uniform wasn't the sharpest tool in the box, he seemed credible. The officer saw the defendant punch the plaintiff in the face. It was as simple as that. To Rina, the trial wasn't a total waste of the jurors' time, but it was proving to be not an efficient use of time. No one complained when the panel was dismissed for the lunch break.

Ryan was meeting a friend for lunch, so this afternoon it was just the girls. In a hope to steer the conversation away from the Kaffey murders, Rina had made extra sandwiches on homemade challah bread and was spending most of her time giving the women the recipe.

"I thought challah had to be braided," Joy said.

"Obviously not, since we're eating square slices," Kate said. "Wow, this is good. I love the olives and sun-dried tomatoes. It works really well with the salami."

"Thank you," Rina said. "In answer to your question, Joy, no, it doesn't have to be braided, although the braid is traditional on Friday night. On the Jewish New Year's through the holiday of Sukkoth, it's round. There's also something called a pull-apart challah that's also round."

"What's that?" Kate was taking notes.

"You make individual balls of dough around the size of a lime and pack them tightly into a round pan."

"Same recipe?"

"Same recipe. When it bakes, all the dough coalesces into one round loaf, but you can still see the individual sections. People use it because when you say the blessing over the bread, you pull apart the sections for your guests and it's a nice presentation."

Joy said, "Someone once told me that you burn part of the dough or something. Or did I get it wrong?"

"No, you didn't. You do burn a small section of the dough. That's the part called challah, actually. We do it to commemorate a different time when the Jews had the temple and burned flour sacrifices to God. But you can only do it if you've used a certain amount of flour. You don't take challah on a single loaf unless it's gigantic. Sometimes if I'm in the mood, I make a big, big batch and freeze some of the dough between the first and second rise so I can take challah, but that's for another day."

"Do you also bake?" Ally inquired.

"I do. I find it very good therapy."

Joy said, "You must have a lot of time on your hands with your husband busy solving murders."

"Less than you think," Rina said. "Peter mostly works a desk job."

"But not always, like right now." Joy almost licked her lips. "So what's going on with the Kaffey murder?"

"I know as much as you do," Rina told her. "Peter doesn't talk about his current cases. Sorry, but I don't have the inside dope."

"I think you're just being coy." Joy sat back in her chair and folded her arms.

"I'm not being coy. I just don't know more than what I read."

"How long do you think it'll take to solve it?" Ally asked.

"I wouldn't even hazard a guess," Rina said. "Peter's worked on cases that were solved within twenty-four hours, and the flip side is the cold cases that have been going on for years."

"Anything good?" Joy asked.

"What kind of a question is that?" Kate said. "I'm sure it's all very tragic."

Rina smiled. "You know, Joy, when Peter and I first got married, I tried to pry stuff out of him because I was as curious as you are. Now, to me his job is just a job. It pays the bills, and sometimes it gets in the way of doing what we want to do. I mean, you're married. What do you and your husband talk about?"

"My husband's a CPA," Joy said. "What are we going to talk about? Tax deductions?"

Rina paused, but there was a twinkle in her eye. "You know, I just inherited some paintings that might be of significant value. Do I have to pay a gift tax on them or only if I sell them?"

"I'm a respiratory therapist. Why would I know about that?"

"That's the point, Joy," Kate said. "She's a teacher. What does she know about murder?"

"Yeah, but there's a big difference," Joy said. "When Albert starts talking about numbers, it puts me to sleep."

Rina said, "I have the opposite problem. When Peter starts talking about the evils of mankind, it keeps me awake."

EIGHT

L EANING AGAINST THE wall, he slowly unwrapped a peanut power bar, his brain absorbing the cacophony of clatter. It was nearing the time when the courts reconvened and that meant noise coming at him from all directions. Across the way, two women were discussing bread recipes. One was from the Michigan area. She was older, in her sixties judging by the rhythm and deliberation of her speech. The second was a young Valley girl with a cowboy twang, reminding him that once California was the Wild West.

The din increased as the crowd filed in.

To his right was a woman who was on the Fernandez trial. He had heard her voice as the jury panel left the room even though she had been whispering. As he overheard her speak into her cell, he knew instantly that she was talking to her husband or a boyfriend. Although her language was clean and innocuous, her tone was full of sexual innuendo. The way she laughed and riposted. He imagined her to be a map of sensual curves. She sounded like she was clearly born and bred in L.A.

He took a bite of his bar and waited for court to resume, the noise level growing exponentially as people congregated in the courthouse hallway, sound waves bouncing off the hard interior surfaces. The open space had cement floors and wooden walls without a stitch of carpeting or upholstered furniture to absorb the racket. The only things to sit on were butt-breaking benches. He didn't feel like sitting. He sat around enough as it was.

If he paid attention, he could hear well.

To his left were two Hispanics: one from Mexico and the other from El Salvador. They were speaking in what they thought were hushed tones, but his ear was so attuned to the nuance of speech, they might as well have been shouting through a loudspeaker. They were jabbering on in rapid-fire Spanish about the news, specifically the horrendous murders in the West Valley. He had heard several different renditions of that story about the billionaire developer, his wife, and his son gunned down in their multiacre ranch.

How freakin' ironic was that? All that money and the poor schmuck couldn't buy himself some loyal security. But that was the problem with money. It attracted all sorts of misfits and cretins, but usually small-time con artists didn't murder. In his limited experience, homicides of big shots were done by other big shots—respectable people in deep shit with something dear to lose.

He continued to eavesdrop on the Spanish conversation and chuckled to himself. The two bozos kept calling Guy Kaffey, the slain billionaire, Señor Café—which translated into English as Mr. Coffee. Like the guy was a small appliance. As the men continued to talk, their voices dropped a notch. To him, it was strange that the two men were attempting a private conversation, but they clearly needed to talk. He could hear the urgency in their voices. And they probably had to be in these hallowed hallways—as witnesses, defendants, or plaintiffs. People didn't hang around for the commissary food.

There were strict rules for jurors on overhearing conversation revolving around current cases. That kind of eavesdropping could influence outcome. But he felt there was nothing wrong with listening in on casual conversation.

The woman on his right had hung up her cell phone. She sounded like she was now going through her purse. Her rifling was almost drowning out the Spanish conversation, which was becoming so inaudible that he was actually straining to make out the words. Not that their yapping was important to him, but now it was a point of pride.

Like the limbo song—how low can you go?

They were still talking about the Kaffey murder, and something about the intensity of the conversation drew his interest. Ever so slightly, he turned his head in the direction of the sound to absorb a couple more decibels. His ears perked up as it became clear that the men were speaking about the killings from personal knowledge.

The Mexican was talking about a man named José Pinon who had gone missing, and *el patrón*, the boss, was looking for him in Mexico.

"Because he fucked it up with the son," the Mexican told the El Salvadorian.

"*¿Qué pasa?*" El Salvadorian asked. What happened?

The Mexican's voice was full of contempt. "He ran out of bullets."

"*Ay . . . estúpido!*" the El Salvadorian said. "*So why didn't somebody else finish him off?*"

"'Cause José's a retard. He says he asked Martin to do it, but me? I don't hear nothing about that. I think he's covering his own stupid ass and he can kiss that good-bye. Martin is really pissed."

The El Salvadorian said. "*Martin es malo.*"

Martin is bad.

"*Muy malo,*" the Mexican said, "*pero no tan malo como el patrón.*"

But not as bad as the boss.

The El Salvadorian agreed with that assessment. He said, "*José es un hombre muerte.*"

José is a dead man.

"*Realmente absolutamente muerte,*" the Mexican added. "*Hora para que el diga sus rezos.*"

Really dead. Time for him to say his prayers.

He heard a bailiff call out a jury panel, and the men stopped talking. The woman with the throaty voice had closed her purse and was walking away from him. Immediately, he turned on his handheld radio and began to follow her as she moved to the other side of the hallway. After a few moments, when he felt they were sufficiently far enough away from the two Hispanics, he took a big step forward and tapped her on the shoulder.

Abruptly, Rina turned around and found herself face-to-face with Sunglasses Tom. "Yes?"

"Excuse me," he said. "My name is Brett Harriman and I work for the courthouse as a translator. I believe you're on the panel of one of my cases." When she didn't answer him, he said, "I want to assure you that what I'm about to ask of you has nothing to do with that case."

Rina stared at him and waited for him to continue.

"Um . . . this is awkward." He paused. "I know that this sounds really odd, but could you do me a favor?"

Finally she spoke. "It depends on what it is." Rina sized up the man. Brett Harriman née Smiling Tom seemed nervous. She couldn't see his eyes under the sunglasses, but his demeanor was jumpy.

He dropped his voice to a whisper, but he still sounded like an actor. "Please, please. Whatever you do, don't stare at the spot that I'm going to ask you to look at. And whisper, okay?"

Rina paused. "What on earth is going on?"

"I'm getting to that. The spot where you were standing just a few moments ago talking on your cell. A few feet away are two Hispanic men talking . . . don't stare at them."

"I'm not—"

"Without staring at them and acting as casual as you can, can you describe them to me?"

Involuntarily Rina glanced at the men, then turned her eyes away. When she looked back up, the two men were deep in conversation and hadn't appeared to notice her. She sneaked in a few passing looks and returned her questioning eyes to Tom/Brett, who wasn't reacting to her perplexity.

And when it finally occurred to her *why* he was acting so stoic, she almost hit her head and said, *Duh!* The indoor sunglasses should have been a giveaway, but he had always moved so seamlessly and without any help.

Tom Cruise/Brett Harriman was blind.

She wanted to ask him about it, but that would have been rude. Instead, she whispered, "Why do you want to know about the men?"

He whispered back, "Just describe them to me, please."

Rina took a quick snapshot. The men looked to be in their twenties, ordinary in size with the one on the right being slightly bigger than the one on the left. Bigger had on a black polo shirt. Smaller, who was doing most of the talking, was garbed in a Lakers' T-shirt. They both had shaved heads and tattoos on their arms, but the drawings were not professionally done. The homemade ink embedded under their skin looked more like discoloration rather than human artwork—a snake, a tiger head, a B12—someone was a vitamin nut.

Rina said softly, "I realize you're sight impaired, but why do you want to know what those two men look like?"

"I'd rather not say."

"I'm sorry, but if you want me to help, you have to tell me what you're after."

"It's personal . . ." Harriman heard the bailiff call group 23. "Forget it! That's my panel, I've got to go." He softened his voice. "It's all probably nonsense anyway."

He turned on his handheld radio, put an ear pod in his ear, and walked away, leaving Rina confused and curious. She managed to sneak in another sidelong glance at the men. What arm was showing wasn't overly muscular, but they did have meaty hands. They had on jeans and rubber-soled shoes. If she had to guess, she'd say that they probably worked construction.

When they announced her panel, Rina lined up with the rest of her group outside the courtroom, and they began their number countdown to identify who was present. They were missing juror number 7 who was chronically late, and the panel collectively groaned. Ally, Joy, and Kate came over to Rina.

Joy said, "What were you talking to Smiling Tom about?"

"Just passing the time." Rina's lie was smooth.

"I think he likes you," Ally said.

"Why not?" Kate said. "Just look at her."

"He's blind." When the three women stared at her, she said, "Or visually impaired. He uses that little radio as a homing device, kind of like an electronic cane."

"Ah . . ." Kate said. "That makes sense. I knew something was off."

"He just walked up to you and told you he was blind?" Ally said.

"No, but up close you can tell."

"How?" Joy asked.

"The way his head rolls when he talks to you . . . the way he rocks back and forth." Actually, he didn't do any of those things, but it sounded like something a blind person might do. "I spoke to him for about thirty seconds."

"Why'd you speak to him?" Joy wanted to know.

"He asked me for the time. After I answered him, he asked if this was my first time working with the criminal justice system. I told him that my husband was a police officer. Then he remembered me and my voice from the voir dire, that I was the one with the detective lieutenant husband. And then they called his jury so he had to go. And that was that." Rina gave the group a forced smile. "I was about to give him my challah recipe, but I didn't have a chance."

No one laughed.

Juror 7 showed up out of breath and apologized profusely for his tardiness. With his presence accounted for, the bailiff opened the door to their courtroom and the group began to file in. Her new circle of friends were looking at her with bemusement and skepticism.

Maybe she hadn't lied as well as she thought.

DECKER HANDED NEPTUNE Brady a copy of Oliver's guard list. Not only had Scott included the duties of each security officer, but he had also managed to find out who, if any, had a police record; a surprising number of them did. Most of the offenses were misdemeanors, but there were a half-dozen felonies among the twenty-two names: eight more added to the original list of fourteen.

Decker took in Brady's face. It was clear that the head of Kaffey Personal Security hadn't slept in a very long time. He raked a hand through a nest of black greasy curls.

"Look it over and see if you have anything to add."

Brady's blue eyes yo-yoed up and down the sheet. "Looks pretty good."

"How'd you manage to employ so many men with records?"

"Not me, Lieutenant." Brady sighed. "Kaffey had a soft spot for the disenfranchised."

"Yeah, Grant Kaffey said something about Guy hiring delinquents, but I can't believe you went along with it." Decker pointed to a name. "This isn't spray painting. This guy, Ernesto Sanchez, has two aggravated assaults—"

"Look at the dates. The convictions are years old. He went through rehab years ago and got his life back together. There's nothing more pious than a reformed drunk. Guy was involved in all sorts of bleeding-heart programs for the socially disadvantaged. It was horseshit, but when Guy got in those kinds of moods, I just did what he told me."

Brady's blue eyes were bloodshot. He had changed from his original clothes to a freshly laundered blue oxford button-down shirt and a pair of designer jeans. He kept playing with the collar on his shirt.

"The social consciousness was part of it. The other part was that Kaffey was a tightass and I was on a budget. These guys worked *cheap*."

"You're telling me that a man as rich as Guy Kaffey would hire felons because they worked cheap?"

"*Exactamente, mi amigo!*" He sighed again and ran his hands down his face. "The ranch is vast and the acreage bleeds into public trails. That kind of isolation comes with a price. Despite all the fences and the barbed wire and the alarms, the place has dozens of ways to get in and dozens of ways to get out. You need an army to really secure every exit and entrance and Kaffey wasn't willing to pay for it. He'd give me names and phone numbers and I'd say, Sure, boss."

"There are twenty-two names on this list. That's a pretty big posse."

"They didn't all work at once," Brady explained. "And the turn-over was high. I needed a posse just to keep the system going. Kaffey told me we didn't need geniuses, just bodies. Usually there were only four guards per shift. Guy was happy with that arrangement most of the time."

"So when wasn't he happy with the arrangement?"

Brady paused. "Sometimes he felt vulnerable. When he was in those kinds of moods, I'd have as many as a dozen men roaming the property."

"What about on the night of the murders?"

"Four guards were contracted to work. If Kaffey had asked for more guards, he didn't call me up and tell me to arrange it."

"Maybe he knew you were busy with a sick father and didn't want to disturb you."

Brady's laugh was bitter. "You think that consideration for his employees was ever a factor with Kaffey?"

"He let you go to Oakland to nurse your father back to health."

"At the time, my father was an inch away from dying. He had no choice. I was going even if it cost me my job."

"Yet he let you stay up in Oakland an extra week."

"That wasn't Guy Kaffey, that was Gil Kaffey. Not that Gil isn't a shark, but he can be human. Guy was loud, abrasive, and demand-ing. Then like that"—he snapped his fingers—"he'd be the nicest, most generous man on earth. I never knew which Guy would show up. His moods were random."

"I've pulled up a few of the most recent articles on Gil. As of nine months ago, he wasn't married. Is that still the case?"

"Gil is gay."

"Okay." Decker flipped through some of the articles and skimmed the text. "Doesn't mention anything about that in anything I've read."

"Where'd you get the articles from?"

"*Wall Street Journal . . . Newsweek . . . U.S. News & World Report.*"

"Why should they mention Gil being gay? He's a hard-nosed businessman, not head of the Gay and Lesbian Alliance. He keeps a low personal profile."

Decker said, "Does he have a partner?"

"No. He had a partner for about five years, but they broke up about six months ago."

"Name?"

"Antoine Resseur. He used to live in West Hollywood. I don't know what he's doing now."

"Why'd they break up?"

"I don't know. That wasn't my business."

"Let's get back to your business. Did you do security for Gil as well as Guy?"

"No, because Gil didn't want me to. He owns a seven-thousand-square-foot midcentury house in Trousdale and had it outfitted with a state-of-the-art security system. Occasionally, I've seen him with a bodyguard, but most of the time he flies below the radar."

"Were Guy and Gilliam Kaffey your only employers?"

"Yes. It's a full-time job and then some. For as little sleep as I got, I should have been a doctor." Brady rubbed his forehead and shook his head. "I was always asking Guy for more money, not for myself but in order to hire a better caliber of guys. I must have told Kaffey a thousand times that a little bit more money can go a long way. All those millions . . . what else is money for?"

"Maybe he took a hit in the market."

"The unemployment rate has skyrocketed. He could have had his pick of the litter in legitimate guards. Why choose losers on purpose?"

"Hard to understand," Decker said.

"Impossible to understand, but that was Guy. One minute he was totally cavalier about his personal safety, then he'd suddenly become totally paranoid. I could understand the paranoia. What I didn't get was the laissez-faire attitude. You're a *target*. Why skimp on your own safety?"

A thought came into Decker's head. "Was he on any psychiatric medication?"

Brady said, "Talk to his doctor."

"He was manic-depressive?"

"It's called bipolar disorder." Brady tapped his toe. "This could get me fired . . ." Then he laughed. "Like I'm not in deep shit already?"

Decker waited.

Brady said, "It's like this. When Guy was in one of his . . . expansive moods, he'd talk about his condition to anyone who'd listen. About how his wife wanted him to take his lithium and he didn't want to do it."

"Why not?"

"Guy claimed that when he was on lithium, it did stabilize him. It lifted him out of his lows. The problem was it also sliced the tops off his highs. He said he couldn't afford to have his highs chopped off. His highs allowed him to take chances. His highs were what made him a billionaire."

NINE

THE PRESS DEBRIEFING had gone well, although Strapp had little time to spend basking in his close-up. He came into Decker's office without knocking and shut the door with more force than needed. Decker looked up from his desk while Strapp kicked out a chair and sat down.

"Upstairs has decided that this is too big for a single Homicide unit."

"I agree."

Strapp narrowed his eyes. "You *agree*?"

"We need a task force." Decker regarded Strapp in his navy suit, light blue oxford shirt, and red tie. The man's face was all angles, his body language tense—a cork waiting to pop. "What's the problem? They want to kick this downtown and have one of their own guys lead it?"

"That was the idea. I fought for you. I thought you'd want it that way."

Meaning *Strapp* wanted it that way. The station house had received a great deal of attention a few months ago when Decker and his Homicide detectives had solved a cold case reopened by a billionaire's promise of funds. Strapp was smelling money again from the remaining Kaffeys if his Homicide unit came up with the solve.

"I appreciate it, Captain, and I'd be happy to lead a full-time team."

"What's the minimum you can work with and still keep the department running?"

"Something this scope and size, I'd say eight people. Big enough to work the angles, but not too big to control."

"Start with six. If you need more, come to me." Strapp drummed Decker's desktop. "I got the commander to agree to have the case worked from West Valley. But you'll need to report daily to me so I can report back to the commander. How many detectives do we have on Homicide detail?"

"Seven full-time Homicide detectives, including Marge Dunn and Scott Oliver who are already involved. If I could have Marge, Oliver, and Lee Wang on it full-time, that would be a good start."

"Lee for the computer work?"

"For the computer work and for the financials. He's the only one patient enough to go through columns of numbers. That'll leave four Homicide detectives for the community." Decker shuffled through his roster of detectives. "From CAPS, I'd like Brubeck, Messing . . . and Pratt. They've all worked Homicide before. That's my six."

"That's seven counting you."

Decker said, "Also if you want me on this mostly full-time, somebody needs to help me with my own paperwork and the scheduling issues that come up."

"We can get a secretary for that."

"It's not just paperwork, it's psychology. I need someone familiar with the guys. How about Wanda Bontemps? She's worked with me before, she's computer savvy, and she can do the minutes of the task force meetings."

"That makes eight."

"Which is how many I said I needed," Decker answered with a smile.

Strapp got up. "Eight for now, Decker. We'll see about the future. I want a list of everyone chosen and their assignments. I also want a summary of the decisions made written up in triplicate—a copy for you, me, and the commander. You can fudge on your own paperwork, but I'm going to need something in writing for downtown."

"I understand, sir." Decker smiled. "You're only as good as your last report."

IT TOOK LONGER than expected to assemble the crew because Brubeck was out in the field and Pratt had an emergency dental appointment. When Decker finally got them all together, he had seven eager detectives. Marge had prepared a summary of the case, bringing the others up to speed. As she spoke, the newly assigned detectives wrote frantically with pens in their notepads, except for Lee Wang and Wanda Bontemps who took notes on their laptops.

Wynona Pratt appeared to be jotting down every word. A ten-year vet, she was in her forties, five feet ten with a thin and wiry frame. Her face was long and her straw-colored hair was cut shorter than Decker's. She had worked Homicide in the Pacific Division, and the feedback on her had been good. She had transferred to West Valley a couple of years ago and wound up in Crimes Against Persons—CAPS—while waiting for something to open up in Homicide. Until that happened, she did her job well and with efficiency.

In his early sixties, Willy Brubeck had talked about retirement for the last ten years. But when the time came to turn in his badge, he decided to give it one more year. Decker was glad to have him onboard. A thirty-five-year vet, Brubeck had worked Homicide in South Central for twenty years. When the last of five kids was finally out of the house, Willy and his wife, Daisy, opted for a smaller home in a less trafficked area in the San Fernando Valley.

Brubeck had a round face, sharp eyes, and mocha-colored skin that was often grizzled with white stubble by five in the afternoon. He had an easy laugh, and eating was one of his favorite pastimes:

five ten and 250—with high blood pressure. But Brubeck was philosophical. Life was for living, not for starving.

Andrew Messing had joined LAPD five years ago, moving out from Mississippi where he had worked Homicide for five years. Drew had a boyish face with a hand-in-the-cookie-jar grin. The man was twice divorced, and Decker thought he'd be a good fit because he lacked personal obligations. Oliver liked him. Of late, the two of them had taken to bar hopping with Scott using Drew as bait. Didn't hurt that Messing had the curly hair, a wide smile, and an "ah shucks" southern accent.

Lee Wang had infinite patience to sort through trivia and columns of numbers. The man was a third-generation cop as well as a third-generation American. He didn't speak a word of Chinese, although he spoke fluent Spanish: handy with the growing Latino community in the West Valley.

Decker knew Wanda Bontemps from her uniform days. He suspected that she'd rather be investigating than taking minutes, but she was pleased that he had chosen her to sub for him, putting her in a position of authority. Decker knew she wouldn't abuse it. She was now in her fifties, a stout black woman with short blond hair and penetrating eyes. Like Wang, she was a computer person, and among her many virtues was her ability to troubleshoot operating systems.

After Marge's summary, there were lots of questions, stretching the meeting time past the two-hour mark. Decker called for a ten-minute coffee break and when the group reconvened, he was standing in front of the whiteboard on which he had written a list of assignments that needed to be done.

He put down his coffee cup and said, "Item number one. We need to interview all the guards in Guy Kaffey's employ—either present or past. Find out what they were doing the night of the murder and recheck their background." Decker passed out a sheet of paper to everyone in the room. "This list does not contain the two missing guards on duty the night of the murders. They'll be dealt with individually. If, in your investigations, you find an additional name, let all of us know about it, understood?"

Nods all around.

"Scott Oliver has checked for priors. You can see that we've got some outright felons. According to Neptune Brady and Grant Kaffey, Guy Kaffey had a penchant for hiring rehabilitated gang members."

Simultaneous expressions of disbelief from "C'mon" to "That's bullshit."

"That's why everyone needs to be interviewed, and their alibis have to be ironclad. Some of these yo-yos are good candidates for hit men. I need a couple of people on this."

Brubeck was the first hand up, followed by Messing.

"Okay, Drew and Willy, you're on."

Decker passed additional papers, the cluster secured with a paper clip.

"This packet is all the forensics picked up at the scene so far. I think the Coroner's Office is almost done processing the victims' bodies. A partial list of evidence includes some partial and latent prints, hair, saliva, fluids, and skin cells. Drew and Willy, take a print kit with you during the interviews and see who'll let you print them. Also a swab kit for DNA. That's more expensive to process but easier to collect."

Messing's hand went up. "Question."

"Yep?"

"It was my impression that the victims were gunned down," Messing drawled. "What kind of saliva and fluids did you find of interest?"

"We found some cigarette butts and a toothpick. We're working on pulling DNA from that."

"Discarded paper cups are good for DNA collection when people refuse a swab," Messing said. "Do we get a coffee budget?"

"As long as you don't get anything with foam or chocolate." Decker turned to Wanda. "You don't have to put that little interchange in the minutes."

Wanda smiled. "I kinda figured that out."

"Moving right along . . ." Decker flipped through the packet. "It looks like we found two types of firearms: a Smith and Wesson Night Guard .38, probably model 315, and a Beretta 9 mm. I want to know the firearms each of the guards routinely used. Any questions?"

"I'm good," Brubeck said.

"Ditto," Messing said.

Decker said, "This is what we have so far. Dunn and Oliver are still pulling up evidence from the other buildings on the property so there could be more. This brings us to item number two."

He checked it off on the whiteboard.

"The grounds have not been combed. That's about seventy acres. We need someone to organize and lead a meticulous ground grid search. This should be done and carried out within the next twenty-four to forty-eight hours. Who's interested?"

"I'll do it," Wynona volunteered.

"It's yours," Decker said. "I'll give you eight uniforms on the day of the search. Let's set it up for the day after tomorrow, six in the morning. You'll need every photon of daylight you can grab. I'll be there, but I'll have to leave around five since it's a Friday. Also, you're probably not going to finish in one day. Any problems with working through the weekend?"

"Not with me. I can't speak for the people working with me."

Decker said, "Coordinate with Lieutenant Hammer and tell him that you'll need eight men to work over the weekend."

"I'll give him a call as soon as we're done."

"Do a grid search first. Then I need a drawing of the entire property with all the gates, doors, and fencing clearly marked. The place is enclosed, but with an area that big, there must be weak spots."

Wynona was writing as fast as she could. "Got it."

"On Sunday morning at six, I'll meet you at the main entrance and you can show me what you have. That way, when this team meets again on Monday, I'll have the results of your work for everyone."

He turned to Marge and Oliver.

"Okay, I understand that you two got permission to go through the main house and the staff quarters?"

Marge said, "We've got permission from Grant and Gil to go through the house—"

"You've talked to *Gil* since yesterday?"

"Talked to his lawyer," Oliver said. "Though we don't know anything specific, he's going on the assumption that the sons are set to inherit the ranch."

"Interesting. What else have you found out about the inheritance?"

"We're working on that," Marge said.

"When do you think you can actually speak to Gil directly?"

"His doctor said that someone can come by tomorrow for a few minutes."

"What time?"

"Whenever he's up," Marge said.

Oliver said, "We've gone through the main house and are working our way through Neptune Brady's place. Paco Albanez, the gardener, and Riley Karns, the horse guy, have given us permission to go through their places. There are a few other buildings that we need to comb. Most likely, we'll finish everything this weekend and can present our findings to everyone on Monday."

Pratt asked, "How many buildings are on the ranch?"

Marge turned to Oliver. "How many? Eight?"

"Nine."

"Any other questions?" When no one spoke, Decker said, "The next thing on the list is for you, Lee. I need you to pull up everything you can on the family—personal and business. Run through each family member, their spouse, their kids, their business associates. Also run through everything you can find on Kaffey Industries and on the Greenridge Project in upstate New York near the Hudson River. I also want you to find out everything you can about Cyclone Inc. and its CEO—Paul Pritchard."

Decker wrote the names on the whiteboard and explained the billion-dollar project currently headed by Mace and Grant Kaffey.

"I want everything looked at, no matter how trivial: any article, any analysis, any puff piece, any letter to the editor, any in-house publication—"

"Anything that will help get a feeling for the family and the business," Wang said.

"Exactly," Decker said.

"I did an initial Google search. Over two million hits. I could use some help."

"Volunteers?" Decker asked.

Wanda raised her hand. "I'm no PC whiz, but I can look up articles."

"Me, too," Messing said.

"Great." Decker continued on. "I also have a lead on a possible disgruntled employee, an account executive named Milfred Connors." Decker wrote the name on the whiteboard. "Connors worked as an accountant for Kaffey Industries and was caught embezzling by none other than Neptune Brady. That's all I know about the case. I'll talk to Brady; who wants Connors?"

"I'll do it," Brubeck said.

"It's yours, Willy," Decker told him. "Marge and I initially talked to Grant and Mace Kaffey. We'll follow up on them since no one's been ruled out."

Oliver said, "That's good. The rich only like to deal with the top dog."

"In that case, they'll probably try to go over my head," Decker said. "No matter. I'll handle them. I've been known to be diplomatic."

The room erupted into laughter.

"Hey, hey, hey," Decker shouted. "It's not that funny."

Wanda said, "Strike that from the minutes as well?"

"Please." Decker smiled. "I'll also get in touch with Gil's former boyfriend, a man named Antoine Resseur. Lee, if you could find out about him before I do the interview, it would be helpful."

"Not a problem. Could you write the name on the board?"

Decker complied. "Okay, one other interesting side note about the family. Guy Kaffey may have suffered from manic-depression now known as bipolar disorder. I don't know if it's relevant, but in a manic phase, maybe he threatened someone. Lee, when you look up articles, bear that in mind. I'll check it out with his doctor. Are we all together? Any questions?"

When no one raised a hand, Decker turned to Marge and Oliver. "After you're done with the evidence collection in the buildings, I want you two to go back and reinterview Brady, Kotsky, Riley Karns, Paco Albanez, and the surviving maid, Ana Mendez. Get their stories down. If you suspect they're playing loose and fast with the truth, get back to me. Anything new on the missing guards?"

Marge said, "We're in constant contact with Denny Orlando's family, nothing so far on Rondo Martin. We've got a couple of calls into the Ponceville sheriff's office. I think we might have to do a field—"

Brubeck broke in, "S'cuse me, but did you just say Ponceville?"

"I did," Marge said. "Why? What's going on, Willy?"

"My wife's family owns a farm about ten miles east of downtown Ponceville." Willy smiled. "Don't look so surprised. Blacks have been farming for centuries. Only difference now is we get paid for it."

Wanda said, "I know. Strike it from the minutes."

Decker said, "What do you know about Ponceville, Willy?"

"It's one of the bigger farming communities in California that hasn't been bought up by agribusiness. Hardworking people . . . mostly whites but a few blacks and lots of Mexican migrants. Whole town of 'em just outside the farms. Personally, I never heard of Rondo Martin, but if he's been working in Ponceville within the last twenty years, I can find out about him with a couple of phone calls."

"Do it."

" 'Course a trip would be better."

"I can probably get funding to go up there, but let's start with the phone calls."

Decker pointed to the next item on the whiteboard.

"Okay, someone needs to check out the murdered housekeeper— Alicia Montoya. It would seem that the intended victims were the Kaffeys, and she was collateral damage. But we can't make assumptions. When Dunn and I spoke to Gil, he indicated that Spanish might have been spoken during the murders. Maybe some jealous boyfriend of the maid thought she was having an affair and the Kaffeys were collateral damage."

Shrugs all around. No one was buying.

"I've been surprised before," Decker said. "Lee, you speak Spanish. Talk to Alicia's family."

"I could use a partner to make sure that my Spanish is up to snuff."

Pratt's hand went up. "I can't read Cervantes but I speak a decent street Spanish."

Decker said, "Okay, I've put both of you down for Alicia Montoya. We're down to the last item on the board: the tip line. So far I've fielded about twenty calls, but the numbers are bound to rise, especially if the family offers a reward."

Oliver groaned. "Then the numbers will go through the roof."

"Are they offering a reward?" Marge asked.

"I don't know, but I suspect they will because it looks good, if for no other reason. No matter how many tips come in, we'll need to check them all out."

Oliver said, "What about the walk-ins, Loo? We always get a couple of those."

"I'll take the walk-ins," Decker answered. "Let me remind all of you that we are public servants. We treat everyone with respect and dignity. When people talk, don't just go through the motions. Listen and listen carefully because we never know who or what is going to break the case wide open. Any other questions?"

No one spoke up.

"The meeting is officially over. You've got your lists, your papers, and your pens. More important, you've got your eyes, your ears, and your legs. Now let's go out and solve some homicides."

TEN

THE TWO COPS stationed outside Gil Kaffey's ICU room momentarily confused Decker because he had approved only one uniform. As he neared the area, he realized that the second sentry was actually a rent-a-cop. Seeing Decker approach, the men stopped their conversation, straightened up, standing with legs apart and arms behind their backs, and watched him suspiciously. Decker flashed his badge to the LAPD uniform—a fifties-plus man with salt-and-pepper hair named Ray Aldofar who had gone a little soft around the middle. The rent-a-cop's name tag said Pepper. He was young, fit, and short and had combative eyes.

"Gentlemen," he said.

"Lieutenant," Aldofar answered. He made the introductions to Pepper and called him Jack.

It was Decker's turn to be wary. "Who hired you to watch this room, Mr. Pepper?"

"Mr. Kaffey insisted on having someone from his private staff." His voice was officious.

"Which Mr. Kaffey?"

"Grant, Mace, and Gil."

Decker peered through the glass windows of ICU. Gil was sleeping and still hooked up to a number of tubular apparatuses. "Gil Kaffey is coherent enough to hire his own security?"

Aldofar stepped in. "I was here when they brought Jack in, Lieutenant."

"Who is *they*?"

"Grant Kaffey and a big guy named Neptune Brady. He's the head of Kaffey security."

"I know who Neptune Brady is."

Aldofar said nothing. Pepper said, "Mr. Kaffey and Mr. Brady hired me to do a job. I was cleared by hospital security."

"You weren't cleared with me." When Pepper bristled, Decker said, "I'm sure you're good at your job, but I'm investigating a multiple-murder homicide. I need to know who has access to Gil Kaffey and since you don't report to me, you may miss something that I need."

Pepper remained on the defensive. "The Kaffeys are entitled to hire me."

"Except if it interferes in a homicide investigation." *Meaning how do I know if Mace or Grant Kaffey were in on the murders?* Decker said to Aldofar, "I need to see that visitors' list."

The cop took out his notepad and flipped over several pages. "Here it is . . . everyone who's gone in and out of the room, just like you requested."

Decker took the list. Most of the visitors had been hospital personnel: Dr. Rain, attending doctors, and nurses. Family included Grant and Mace, who had come four times together. Grant had visited an additional four times by himself. Two times, Grant had brought along Neptune Brady, and Brady visited two more times alone. Antoine Resseur—Gil's ex—had come by two times. Since only approved people had been allowed access, there were no other visitors. There had been at least a dozen attempted flower deliveries to the hospital room and all of the ICU; the bouquets were forwarded to the family compound in Newport.

Decker gave the notepad back to Aldofar. "Keep your eyes open. Put me down on the list. I'm going in."

He looked at Pepper.

"I know you have a job to do, but so do I. Let's try to avoid stepping on each other's toes. It works to your benefit, sir, because I have bigger feet."

AS GIL'S EYES slowly opened, his face twisted in pain and he moaned. Within seconds, a young blond nurse named Didi was at his bedside injecting something into his IV line. "Demerol," she told Decker.

"Is it going to put him back to sleep?"

"It might."

Decker waited. Gil closed his eyes and opened them several times. After about ten minutes, he managed to look at him with lids halfway closed. "Do I know you?"

"Lieutenant Peter Decker of LAPD, Mr. Kaffey. I'm investigating what happened at the ranch. How do you feel?"

"Shit."

"I'm sorry."

As he pulled up a chair, Didi the nurse said, "Did you clear this with Dr. Rain?"

Gil said, "Leave him . . . leave him."

"Just a few minutes," Didi told Decker. "Just because he can talk doesn't mean he should."

"I won't tire him out," Decker said.

"You're . . . the head?"

"I'm leading the investigation, yes. We have a lot of people working on this, and anything you can tell me might help. "

"I feel . . . real . . . shit . . ." His head bobbed. "Shit."

"It hurts to be shot . . ."

Eyes opened and stayed that way. "You ever . . ."

"Yes, I've been shot. It hurts."

"Burns like shit."

"Yes, it does."

Gil's head bobbed. "They said *sí, sí* . . . I heard it."

Decker took out his notepad. "The men who attacked you spoke Spanish?"

"Yeah . . . *sí, sí.*"

"Do you speak Spanish?"

"No . . . just *sí, sí.*"

"Did you recognize any other words?"

"It happened . . . fast."

"I'm sure you were in total shock. How many people attacked you?"

Silence.

Decker said, "Sometimes it helps if you close your eyes and view it like a movie or a photograph in your head."

He closed his eyes. "I see one . . . two . . ." He was counting them in his foggy brain. "Three . . ." His face, pale to start, went ashen. "Flashbulb in my eyes . . . then bang . . . Bang, bang, bang!"

Beep, beep, beep went the monitor. Gil's heartbeat started to race.

"So fucking *loud*! Hurt my head!"

Didi, the nurse, said, "You're exciting him. You're going to have to leave!"

Gil was still talking, his eyes moving rapidly under closed lids. "Happened like . . ." He tried to snap his fingers and his eyes popped open. "My heart . . . pumping. I'm running away . . . I feel fire . . . I fall."

Didi was about to inject him with more Demerol, when he said, "Stop!"

Both she and Decker were taken aback. Gil spat out, "Get the . . . *bastards*!"

"We have the same goal, Mr. Kaffey," Decker said. "What about their faces? Can you describe any of them?"

The eyes closed partway. "One . . . two . . . three of them."

"You remember three people attacking you."

"Three people . . ."

"Can you describe them?" Decker asked.

Tears formed in Gil's eyes. "Bastards . . . the one with the gun . . . I saw the arm . . . he had tattoos."

"What kind of tattoos?"

"Beeexcel . . ." His eyes blinked, and the tears ran down his face.

"Pardon?"

"The letters . . . B . . . X . . . L . . . L."

Decker thought a moment. "Could it have been B-X-I-I with a capital I?"

"Maybe."

The Bodega 12th Street gang contained nasty, nasty men, most of them with origins from El Salvador and Mexico. It had originated in the Ramparts division years ago but had spread like a cancer into just about every state in the union. They numbered around fifty thousand loosely organized criminals. There were men at the top, but most of the bastards were drug runners and hard-core felons. It was one of the most violent gangs in the country.

Gil was one lucky sucker.

"He had B-X-I-I tattooed on his arm," Decker said. "Can you tell me which arm?"

Gil was breathing shallowly. "Right-handed. On his right arm."

"His right arm was exposed then?"

Gil didn't answer.

"He was wearing short sleeves?"

"Black T-shirt."

"Good," Decker told him. "Any other tattoos?"

"Black cat . . . with Spanish words. Something negro."

"*Negro* is black in Spanish. Can you close your eyes and see that arm . . . tell me the other word?"

Gil closed his eyes. "G . . . A . . ." He shook his head.

"Could it be G-A-T-O? *Gato* means cat. So *gato negro* would be black cat."

No answer. Gil's lids were closed with eyes moving underneath them.

"Do you see the man's face, Mr. Kaffey?"

"I . . . more tattoos . . ." He touched his neck. "A snake . . . B . . . 1 or something."

"B12?"

Gil opened his eyes. "You know tattoos?"

"I know a few gang tattoos. B12 and BXII are two of them."

"Gangs . . . Why?"

The most likely answer was that someone hired hit men from the Bodega 12th Street. But no assumptions. Not yet. "That's what we need to figure out. Did your parents keep a lot of valuables in the house?"

"There were . . . guards."

"Some of the guards are missing."

"Who?"

"Rondo Martin and Denny Orlando. Maybe others as well."

"Not Denny." A long pause. "Dad liked Rondo."

"Did you know the men?"

"Denny's good . . . Rondo is cold." Gil raised a tube-injected hand to his face. "Cold eyes."

"Good to know." Decker tried to keep him on track. "The tattoos are a big help. You saw the neck . . . can your eyes go up a little bit more to the face?"

Gil closed his eyes and was quiet for such a long time, Decker thought he had fallen back asleep. His voice was very soft. "Dark eyes . . . a rag on his head." A big exhale. He touched his chin. "A soul patch . . ." Another long period of silence. Tears were falling down his cheek. "Then the flash and my father . . ." More tears. "I started to run . . . I'm very tired."

Gently, Decker patted his arm. "We'll talk again when you're feeling better."

He closed his eyes. Decker waited until Gil was asleep. Lord only knew the dreams that awaited him.

AS THE ELEVATOR door opened, Dr. Rain stepped out. "Lieutenant."

"Dr. Rain." Decker skipped the elevator. "I just finished a brief conversation with Gil Kaffey. He was a lot more coherent than the first time I saw him."

"I hope you didn't tire him out. Gil needs to conserve his energy to heal." He checked his watch. "Try to keep your future interviews short."

"Nurse Didi called you?"

"She did, and it was the right thing to do."

"I'll be more aware," Decker told him. "Do you know who Guy Kaffey's primary physician was?"

"For any medical information, you'll have to consult with the family. I'm not at liberty to discuss that."

"I found out he was taking medication for bipolar disorder."

"I wouldn't know. Guy Kaffey wasn't ever my patient so I can't address that." They both heard his name being paged. "I've got to go, but really, Lieutenant, what relevance does something like that have to solving a homicide?"

"It helps to know as much about the victim as you can find out." Decker pressed the elevator down button. "They say dead men don't talk, but if you listen carefully, they sure as hell do."

THE FOLDER CONTAINED summaries of each member of the Kaffey clan. Wang said, "I felt an overview would help the both of us and maybe satisfy the brass until I can wade through all the hits. If I printed out all the articles, we'd totally deforest an entire South American country. "

"Can't do that. Not green and not PC." Decker looked at the first heading: Guy Allen Kaffey. Wang had included a brief bio on Guy, Gil, Grant, Gilliam, and Mace.

"These are the principal players in Kaffey Industries." Wang handed him a separate folder. "Mace has a son named Sean who's working at one of the big brokerage firms. I don't know why he's not in the family business—maybe he's an independent kind of guy—but as the oddball, he attracted my attention."

"Oddballs deserve a second look." Decker nodded. "Thanks.

This is a start. Send two copies to Strapp. What are you up to now?"

"Back to my Mac." Wang stretched. "No matter how ergonomic the setup is, I still leave with a sore back from sitting incorrectly, burning wrists from all the typing, and tired eyes from peering at a computer screen. Man was not meant to work a desk job."

"Tell me about it. Most of my last six years as lieutenant have been spent with my butt glued to a chair. But I'm not complaining."

"Neither am I. It's been a long time since I was in the line of fire. Sometimes I think I miss it, but I betcha I really don't."

Decker said, "When I actually get to do some genuine police work, it feels really good. Then I get shot or shot at and it cures me for a while."

"Yeah, the last one was a close one. What happened to the nut-case guy?"

"He's at Patton State."

"He took out the guy behind you, right?"

"He did. He meant to get the guy behind me. The man was definitely mental, but lucky for me, his aim was true."

COFFEE CUP IN hand, Decker sat down at his desk and picked up Lee Wang's summaries, making notes in the margins in his illegible scrawl.

Guy Allen Kaffey's date of birth put him at sixty. He was born in St. Louis, Missouri, to immigrant parents who had long been deceased. A terrible student, Guy had dropped out of high school at sixteen with no marketable skills. But as he told *Business Acumen Monthly,* "I could keep up a steady patter better than anyone on the planet. That meant I could be a disc jockey or a salesman."

He chose real estate. Flat broke, he began peddling houses shortly after leaving high school and within a year, he had amassed enough cash to start his own real estate firm. As he told the magazine, "My first employee was my sixteen-year-old brother, Mace. Like me, he was flunking high school, but when he dropped out, at least he had instant employment. Still, my parents couldn't figure out where they went wrong. It was more like where they went *right*."

Five years later, Guy Kaffey picked up from the Midwest and moved his operation to the Land of Opportunity, switching from residential to commercial real estate. At twenty-two, Guy had his first million in the bank. Three years later, he qualified as a multimillionaire. *Forbes* listed Kaffey as a first-time billionaire when he reached the advanced age of thirty.

At thirty-one, he met his wife, Jill Sultie, at the craps table in Vegas after asking the beautiful woman next to him to blow on his dice. That evening, he had walked away with a hundred grand in profit and asked if the beautiful woman would like to celebrate by joining him for dinner. Sparks flew that night. The affair was intense and four months later, they were married.

"It was kismet," Kaffey told e-zine CorporationsUSA.com. "She was recently divorced and I wandered in at exactly the right time."

At Guy's request, Jill changed her name to Gilliam so they could be G and G, or as Guy used to say when introduced, "We're two grand."

Two children followed: Gil seven months after the wedding and Grant two years later. The family was portrayed as cohesive, although Gil and Grant both had called Guy a "taskmaster."

The financial road to billions hadn't always been steady. There were dips and ditches and sometimes even trenches and foxholes. CEO Guy Kaffey nearly went out of business fifteen years ago due to a downturn in the real estate market, mismanagement, and embezzlement charges leveled at the president of the company and second in command, Mace Kaffey.

Decker sat up. As he underlined the sentence, he immediately thought of Milfred Connors, the accused account executive who was caught embezzling by Neptune Brady. Was there a connection between Connors and Mace Kaffey?

It appeared that the brothers were involved in litigation that lasted several years, and neither Mace nor Grant thought it important enough to mention. Maybe that was because things eventually resolved. Mace remained in the business, but no longer sat on the board of directors. He was given a new title of executive VP of East Coast Operations, that sector eventually operated by Guy's younger son, Grant. The rest of the summary dealt with the Greenridge Project, some analysts implying that it was Mace's last shot to redeem himself with the company.

If that was the case, Mace seemed to be on shaky grounds. From the start, Greenridge was plagued with problems. The location demanded several dozen environmental impact reports that resulted in many changes of plans. Eventually the project found a design that was approved, but the delays and the added costs coupled with the downturn in the economy and funding deficits had swelled the original budget by a factor of five. There was a quote from the *Journal of News and Business* about the Greenridge Project:

> *Isn't it time that Guy Kaffey do what he should have done years ago? Pull the plug on his dead-weight brother, Mace? Filial loyalty is an admirable trait, but a company—even a privately owned company—cannot be run on sentiment.*

If Mace went down with the Greenridge Project, what about Grant? Wasn't he part of it as well? If there were problems, why would Mace be the goat and not Grant?

The last paragraph of the synopsis was "An Insider's Look at Guy Kaffey" from PropertiesInc.com that was more about Guy the man than Guy the businessman. His friends spoke about Guy's exuberance: his foes described him as a hothead. He was well known for his outbursts, and his moods could turn at a moment's notice. Guy was described as bold and daring, but he was also detail oriented and meticulous.

Decker wondered how much of his outbursts had to do with his possible bipolar disorder. Did he sue his brother in a manic fit or was there just cause? Certainly it would seem that the charges were unjustified if Guy agreed to hire Mace back into the company.

Decker put Guy's summary down and moved on to Mace. There

wasn't anything too illuminating in the summary. Mace was a high school dropout. He worked for his brother. He moved out to sunny Cal with his wife, Carol, to work with Guy in Kaffey Industries. He had a son named Sean. Everything seemed to be hunky-dory with Mace until the embezzlement charges were leveled against him.

This time Lee Wang got specific. Mace Kaffey was accused of stealing five million dollars. Decker couldn't help it; he whistled out loud. There weren't any specifics on how the embezzling was done except to say that Guy got wind of the discrepancy during a routine inventory check and one thing led to another until he was forced to confront his brother. Mace vehemently denied the charges and even offered to hire a private detective to find out who the real culprit was. But Guy had his own sources.

The battle of the brothers lasted several years and during that time, the company's stock plummeted. The charges and counter-charges seemed equally matched until Guy prevailed. A month later, the case was settled. Guy retained the title of CEO, Gil Kaffey moved into the president spot, Grant was named in charge of East Coast operations, and Mace was shipped to upstate New York with a VP after his name.

Decker was confused. If Mace really was guilty of such blatant embezzlement, why would Guy retain him? Did Milfred Connors frame Mace for his theft? Or just as likely, did he take the fall for Mace's stealing? Perhaps the two of them schemed together. And what happened to the money? Was it ever at least partially recovered?

He wrote notes in the margin and moved on to the next genera-tion—Gil, thirty-two; Grant, thirty; and Sean, twenty-eight. Grant was the only married man; his wife was named Brynn and there was one child—a toddler boy. Gil was gay; Sean was still unmarried. All three boys had graduated from Wharton at the University of Penn-sylvania. Gil and Grant were immediately sucked into Kaffey In-dustries, but Sean struck out on his own. He had just graduated from Harvard Law and was doing case law and business law at a small university in the Northeast.

Definitely the smart one, Decker thought.

The last bio had to do with Gilliam Kaffey née Jill Sultie. She grew up as trailer trash. Somewhere along the way, she blossomed from a bony adolescent into a beautiful woman and got a job as a Las Vegas showgirl when she was just eighteen. A year later, she was sporting a rock on her finger courtesy of her first husband, Renault Anderson, and buying her mother, Erlene, her very first house with a foundation instead of wheels.

For a while, it seemed as if Jill had found the golden goose and she was living on twenty-four-karat omelets. Then life came crashing down, mainly due to Renault's philandering. The divorce was said to be amicable. She met Guy during a low period of her life. They clicked instantly, and like they say in the movies, the rest is history.

Rubbing his eyes, Decker checked the wall clock and realized he had been reading for over an hour. He got up and stretched, then peered through the glass walls of his office. He spotted Wang typing away on the computer and opened the door.

"Lee?" Wang looked up. "Do you have a moment?"

"Sure."

Decker told him to come inside and have a seat. "I finished your synopses. The family history reads like a soap opera script."

"Yeah, could you make up a name like Renault Anderson?"

"That's one for the books. I have a couple of questions about Mace Kaffey. There are these allegations of embezzlement against him, and then all of a sudden, the lawsuit's settled."

"Yeah, weird, huh?"

"More than weird. There had to be a backstory. I'm wondering if the accusations were related to the embezzlement charges leveled against Milfred Connors."

"Yeah, I thought about that, too. Maybe that's why the lawsuit was settled. Maybe Connors framed Mace and when he was made, Guy dropped the suit."

"But then why would Mace have been demoted if he were innocent? And if Mace wasn't innocent, why would Guy keep his cheating brother in any aspect of the business?"

"Maybe that was part of the settlement."

"But from talking to Mace and Grant, Mace is heavily involved in the multimillion-dollar Greenridge Project. Why would Guy keep him in something so costly, especially if he thought that Mace was embezzling?"

"Maybe it was Grant who was embezzling, Mace took the fall for him, and Guy put Mace back east to keep an eye on Grant."

Decker frowned. "Sort of a convoluted theory, but I'm open to anything. The Greenridge Project sounds like a big boondoggle." "You wrote Guy up as a hard-nosed business type. If something was flushing money down the toilet, I don't think Guy would hesitate to pull the plug."

"On Mace, for sure, but maybe not on Grant. Maybe the old man had a soft spot for his sons. I found a year-old interview with Mace's son, Sean, on Kaffey Industries. Sean said a lot of things, but one particular thing stuck in my mind. Sean said and I quote, 'My uncle has more than a soft spot for his sons. It's actually a blind spot.'"

ELEVEN

THEY STOOD TWENTY abreast, police officers interspersed with volunteers trained in this tedious aspect of protocol. All of them had a whistle around their neck and held a map in their hands. They were waiting for Wynona Pratt to give the signal—one long toot to begin and two short toots to stop. The detective had come down to the ranch several hours earlier to scope out Coyote Ranch. The vast acreage beyond the buildings and the riding corral was hard-packed terrain pocked with clumps of grasses, thorny briar, silver-leaf shrubs, purple sage, wild daisies, yellow dill weed, and chaparral, the land stretching out until it collided with the foothills. There the fauna climbed and joined forces with fragrant pines, eucalyptus, and stunted California oak, greening the mountainsides and shading the trails that cut through them.

Adjusting her sun hat, Wynona peered through UV-protected spectacles at the map in front of her. She had divided it into five sectors, and with a little luck they'd finish it today. She had dressed comfortably—cargo pants to hold extra items, a cotton T-shirt, and sneakers. Her fair skin necessitated that she slather on sunscreen, and she hoped sun damage would be limited to freckles. She held her hand aloft, then brought it down with a snap along with a long, shrill whistle. The line walked forward in a unit, eyes on the ground in front of them. The list of what they were looking for was long and varied—footprints, tire tracks, drag marks, bits of clothing, popped buttons, bloodstains, food and food wrappers—any kind of evidence that pointed to human contact with nature.

The morning was cool but warming quickly. The sun was unmasked in a clear sky, reflective against the red stone. The air was filled with spring insects that had hatched with the heat—gnats, flies, bees, wasps. Crows cawed lazily as a hawk circled high above, looking for its breakfast.

The search of the first sector lasted just a little over two hours with meager results—a scattering of various fibers and metals including pop-tops and bottle caps. More numerous were horse prints and desiccated horse shit. A volunteer found a shoe impression that was clear enough to merit an alginate cast. The rest of the search was slim pickings. They moved on to sector two and by the time that space had been combed, the crew was hot and tired and needed sustenance. During the twenty-minute allotment they had for lunch break, Wynona called Marge.

"How's it going inside?"

Marge said, "TMI." Too much information. "Everywhere we turn, we have blood or tissue or a footprint or hair or a bullet casing."

"If you have TMI, we're suffering from TLI."

"How far along are you?"

"We're about to start with sector three. I'll call you in a couple of hours."

The group resumed their hunt at two in the afternoon. At 4:14, someone sounded two quick toots and the row of searchers lurched to a stop. The whistle blower was a young police officer in his twenties named Kyle Groger. He called Wynona over.

"Take a look at that area, Detective, about twenty feet from here." He pointed to the spot. "It looks odd."

Wynona took off her sunglasses and stared at the ground, her eyes traveling forward until she saw what had caught Groger's attention. From a distance, the patch was indistinguishable from the surrounding area. Same color ground, same types of foliage, same pebble-strewn earth. Yet it looked distinctly different.

First of all, the eight-by-eight plot of ground had sunk into the earth, lower than the surrounding terrain by about an inch or so. There were also two big boulders on top. The environs supported many big rocks, but two in such close proximity was a little odd. Also the foliage on the plot wasn't faring well: around a dozen drooping sage plants, straw yellow grasses, and scattered daisies with limp petals. It could be that these particular plants had wilted in the heat except that the flora that surrounded the area was erect and hydrated.

She walked over to the spot and pulled up a sage plant. It gave way with relative ease, and the roots were soft and dried out. She dropped to a stoop and dipped a finger in the ground. The soil was compact, and not easy to dig into. It was then she noticed that the earth had been scored by hundreds of little lines running in all directions. She stared at them closely. It was as if someone was hitting the ground, tamping it down with a shovel over and over and over.

A homemade grave?

She stood up and searched for shoe or tire prints, but found nothing. She called Marge on her cell phone and asked her how it was going inside.

"Still slogging through the muck. What's going on?"

"I think there's something here that you should see."

WHILE WAITING FOR extra shovels and buckets, Marge assigned one of the CSI techs the official role of police photographer.

"Get all those little hash marks," she told him.

The day had been long and fruitful . . . overly so. The evidence inside the main house included several types of shoe treads, a couple of bloody finger- and palmprints, a number of bullet casings, loose fabric and hairs, and that wasn't counting the blobs and streaks of blood and massive tissue spatter. The identification of what belonged to whom was to be sorted out later. Marge was happy to take a break from the charnel house, and Pratt's call was a good excuse for a breather.

Oliver, on the other hand, was probably much happier working inside because it was air-conditioned. He said, "Summer is upon us."

"You can go back inside. I can handle this."

"Nah, I'll stick around." He wiped his forehead. "We can work inside all night as long as DWP doesn't turn off the electricity."

They were both looking at the caved-in spot. Marge said, "It's disturbed ground. That's a no-brainer."

"Big grave for just one man," Oliver said.

"So maybe it's more than one man," Marge said. "I think it was predug. If it was done spur of the moment, it would take too long to dig."

"Unless it's shallow."

"We're missing two guards. If they're in there, it can't be all that shallow. Plus someone took the time to put plants back in the soil. This was a planned thing, Scotty."

"But not planned too far ahead. Otherwise someone might have spotted a big hole in the middle of the property."

Marge said, "It's really far from the main house."

Oliver said, "I don't know . . . maybe."

"We'll know soon enough." Marge tented her eyes with her fingers and regarded the vast tract of land. Wynona's search crew had scattered but was still in whistle-blowing reach. Most of them were sitting in the few tiny patches of shade available, roasting their butts while drinking tepid water and fanning themselves with their hands or sun hats. A flick of the wrist told her it was almost five. Sunset was around seven-thirty.

Oliver said, "Do you think we can dig this up in two and a half hours?"

"Depends what's in there. If we find something, it's a crime scene. Then who knows?" Marge took out her cell. "I think I'll put in an order for lighting, just in case."

Wynona walked over to them. She had taken off her sun hat, and her short blond hair was wet and matted. She took out a tube of sunscreen and started rubbing it into her cheeks. "How many people do you think you'll need for the dig?"

"I could use maybe eight. Why? What do you need?"

"I still have a sector and a half left to comb. I probably won't finish the last one, but if I get going now, I can finish the rest of sector four before twilight."

"If I take six from your gang, how many would you have left?"

"Twelve with me. I can manage with that, but I'd like a few to be police officers."

"How many cops do you have?"

"Eight."

Marge said, "You take four, I'll take four."

"Sounds good." Wynona stowed her sunscreen back in her cargo pants. After making the assignments, she said, "I'll get started. Call me if you find something." She tooted her whistle and her group stood up, wiping dust and dirt from their bottoms.

Just as the shovels and buckets arrived, Marge's cell phone sprung to life. The boss was on the other end. He asked what was going on and after she explained the situation, Decker said he was coming down.

He said, "Take plenty of pictures of the area before you put spade to ground."

"Already done," Marge said. "Do you want to us to hold the digging until you get here?"

"No, start while you've got daylight. I've got to finish up something at the station house and it's taking a while. But I'll make it over."

His voice sounded tense. Marge said, "Is Steel Strapp giving you a hard time?"

"I wish."

"Yowzer, Pete! It must be bad. What's going on?"

"I'll fill you in later. It's not bad, but it is complicated."

Marge checked her watch. "It's getting close to Sabbath, Pete. If we don't find anything, it's not worth missing Friday night dinner. I'll call if I need you."

"Thanks for the offer, but this case is too big for me to take time off. Maybe God could rest after six days, but we mere mortals just aren't that talented."

MARGE'S CALL COULDN'T have happened at a worse time.

Although Decker disliked being late for Friday night dinner, usually when it happened, Rina insisted on waiting for him. But tonight Rina had invited several couples, so Decker gave her the go-ahead-without-me speech, knowing in his heart of hearts that the Coyote Ranch dig was going to last into the night.

But the dig wasn't the only thing on his mind.

His mother always told him that it was impolite to stare, but in this case, it didn't make a difference. So Decker studied the man sitting across his desk, taking in his well-manicured appearance.

Brett Harriman was nicely appointed. He wore an unstructured natural linen jacket over a blue button-down and designer jeans. His sandals showed off his manicured toes, which matched his manicured hands. His hair was dark and shaggy, his face long and lean. He wore dark shades that not only covered his eyes but most of his eyebrows. The only giveaway to his visual impairment was a slight swinging of his head that helped his ears zero in on sound stereoscopically.

Decker tapped his pen on his desktop. "First of all, Mr. Harriman, I want to thank you for coming in and sharing your information with me."

"It's Brett and no thanks are necessary. It's my obligation. If people didn't do jury duty, I wouldn't have a job." A few seconds ticked by. "Well, that's not true. When you're fluent in as many languages as I am, there's always work."

"How many languages would that be?"

"A lot. Mostly the romance and Anglo-Saxon languages."

"How'd you learn them?"

Harriman shrugged. "Some I studied, some I picked up on tapes. Finnish and Hungarian I learned with intense tutoring. Also I travel a lot. The only way to really learn a language is to hear and speak it." Another pause. "Are you asking me these questions to size me up, to get rapport, or because you're interested in me as a person?"

"Probably all three," Decker said.

"I'm not a nutcase. I've been with the courts for almost five years."

"How'd you come to work for the courts?"

"Another personal question?" Harriman gave Decker a white-toothed smile as he tilted his head to the right. "Aren't you trying to solve a murder?"

"Murders, actually. How'd you come to work for the courts?"

"A friend of mine who works downtown told me that the courts were hiring witness translators. Mostly for Spanish but other languages, too. I applied and that was that."

"They weren't bothered by your blindness?"

Harriman grinned. "I wore tinted glasses. I don't think they knew until later. Besides, they would never fire me. I help their federally mandated numbers in hiring the handicapped. I'm also damn good at my job!"

"Where were you working before the courts?"

"I was a patient translator for six different hospitals. The job was getting a little monotonous. How many times can you translate 'take two of these pills for regular bowel movements'?" The pause was awkward. "It was more than that. It was hard day after day delivering bad news."

"That's miserable."

"Depressing as hell. Lucky for me I never had to look at the eyes of a patient who just got the news. I sure as hell heard it in the voice. And it didn't take me long to learn if the doctor was feeding bullshit, letting the patient or the families cling to hope when I could tell by the nuances in his voice that Tia Anabel was a goner."

Decker said, "There's a police detective in the Netherlands. He's blind. They use him to decipher accents and voices—like terrorists.

He can tell the origin of the speaker even if he or she is speaking fluent and unaccented Dutch."

"Nobody speaks unaccented anything." Harriman rocked his head to the other side "There are always giveaways if you know what to listen for."

"Could you ever see?"

"I still can see. You see with your brain, not with your eyes. But there was a time I was sighted. I was five when I lost my sight from a rhabdomyosarcoma—bilateral tumors." He tapped his foot on the floor. "Are you interested in what I told you or do you still think that it's worthless?"

"You're confusing worthlessness with a healthy dose of skepticism. I'm very interested in what you've told me, Mr. Harriman. If you don't mind, let's go over it again."

The blind man gave an exasperated sigh. "It's Brett, and I told you everything I know. The story's not going to change."

"But maybe my perception will. Please?"

He waited a few moments, then he said, "I was standing around the waiting area of the courtrooms eating a power bar. Two Hispanic guys were talking about the Coyote Ranch murders. One of the guys was from Mexico, the other from El Salvador. They kept on calling the victim Mr. Café because Kaffey is coffee in Spanish. Then they segued into talking about a guy named José Pinon who had gone missing and that the boss was looking for him in Mexico. Are you writing this down *again*? I can hear your pen scratching."

Decker said. "Just squaring what I wrote the first time against what you're saying now. You said then that the Mexican was doing most of the talking."

"That's correct. The Mexican said that the boss was looking for José. He—the boss—was very mad at José because he fucked up. And he fucked up by running out of bullets." A pause. "Does that mean anything to you?"

Damn straight it does. José Pinon translates to Joe Pine. Decker said, "It could. Go on."

"So José ran out of bullets," Harriman said. "So the El Salvadorian asked the Mexican why someone else didn't finish him off. And the Mexican said because José is a retard. Then he said Martin was very angry. Both agreed that Martin was a very bad man, but not as bad as the boss—whoever that is. They also both agreed that José was a dead man. At that point, I felt very uncomfortable eavesdropping. The way that the two of them were speaking . . . it sounded authentic. When I got home that night, I looked up the murders on my computer . . . It's voice activated, in case you're wondering."

"I figured."

"The son . . . Gil Kaffey . . . he was shot but he survived. I may be assuming too much but I surmised that they had been talking about Gil Kaffey and that José hadn't made sure that Gil was dead." Harriman rolled his head in the other direction. "I'm just relating the information to you. Maybe it'll do you some good."

"I appreciate your coming in. You mentioned José's name as José Pinon. How about Martin?"

"Just Martin."

"Did he mention *Rondo* Martin?"

"Just Martin as far as I can recall."

"Okay," Decker said. "If you heard these men speak again, do you think you could pick them out from other El Salvadorians or Mexicans?"

"Like a vocal lineup?"

"Something like that."

"Have you ever done something like that before?"

"No. It might be a first with the courts. Do you think you could ID the voices?"

"Absolutely." Harriman seemed insulted. "Why? Do you have a suspect?"

"Right now what we have are lots of people of interest."

"No arrests then."

"If we had an arrest, your voice-activated computer would know about it. Is there anything else that you'd like to add?"

Harriman thought for a moment. "The El Salvadorian sounded like a smoker. That might narrow it down to a gazillion people."

"I appreciate your information."

"Does it help?"

Damn straight. "It might." Decker reread part of Harriman's statement. "What's my best option for getting hold of you in case I need to speak to you again?"

Harriman took out his wallet, pulled a card from one of its compartments. He handed it to Decker. "My business and cell number. And how do I reach you in case I think of anything else?"

Decker dictated the number while Harriman entered it into his PDA by voice. Then Decker said, "Thanks again for doing your civic duty. People like you make our lives much easier. I'll walk you out."

"No need." Harriman activated his locator. "I came in alone, I'll go out alone."

ON HIS WAY over to Coyote Ranch, Decker pondered what to do with the information. Without physical descriptions, the men were non-existent, but that didn't mean he didn't have options. His first call was to Willy Brubeck. "Hey, Detective."

"What's going on, Loo?"

"I'm on my way to a dig at Coyote Ranch." Decker explained what was going on there. "What was on your agenda today?"

"Five guard interviews today, hope to do at least that many to-morrow. One of them had to cancel, but the rest were cooperative. No radar tweaking. Four were pretty freaked by the murders, one was pissed that he was out of a job. All of them gave me a cheek swab."

"Good work. Have either Drew or you found Joe Pine?"

"Joe's on my list, but I haven't gotten around to him yet."

"Bump him up to the top. Also what about the embezzling account executive, Milfred Connors? Have you made contact with him?"

"We keep missing each other."

"Set something up with him ASAP, and I want to be there."

"What's up with him?"

Decker explained Mace Kaffey's alleged embezzlement and the charges brought by his brother. "I'm just wondering if Connors took the fall for him."

"Interesting theory. I'll give him another call."

"Good. Last, any word about Rondo Martin from your sources in Ponceville?"

"I haven't heard back."

"Push on Martin." Decker told him about his conversation with Brett Harriman. "I'll probably wind up sending you to Ponceville, but you need to make all your preparatory calls first."

"We're working on information from a blind guy?" Brubeck said.

"He can't see but he sure as hell can hear. The list of guards who worked for the Kaffeys isn't public knowledge, and this guy named two guards on the roster. That makes my antennas twitch. And even if the knowledge was public, he used the name *José Pinon*, not *Joe Pine*. Marge and Oliver are busy with the dig at the ranch. Take Rondo Martin off their hands, and give Joe Pine to Andrew Messing. The first thing we need is a set of prints."

"I'll push the Ponceville sheriff. His name is Tim England, but they call him T."

"I don't care what they call him, just call him up and get a set of prints. Have Drew check with Neptune Brady and see if they have a set on Joe Pine. Then run both of them through NCIC once you've got the prints."

"I hear you."

"You two are still going to need to talk to all of the guards, but let's go with what we have first. Especially with Rondo Martin, because he was on duty and now he's missing."

"Good luck at the ranch. Maybe you'll get lucky."

"Thanks." Decker hung up the phone and thought about being lucky. This meant that they would dig up something that had an impact on the case—like a dead person. So lucky was probably not the correct word. Maybe what he was hoping for was that maybe the dig wasn't a total waste of valuable time.

TWELVE

AS THE DAYLIGHT drew to a close, the sun's rays lengthened and turned the ranchland into a sheet of polished copper. Even peering through shades, Decker had to squint. Men were digging up parched ground, gingerly relocating mounds of pebbled soil. After the first inch, Marge explained, the earth gave way easily, and everyone suspected that there was something down below. She and Oliver had been sifting through the piles of dirt, making sure that nothing significant went unnoticed. So far, the yield was confined to beer bottle caps, soda cans, food wrappers, and cigarette butts.

"They've been collected for evidence," Marge said. "Should we need to, we can have the cigarettes sent for DNA testing to give us an idea about who's been out here."

Oliver added, "We found the butts below the dirt, so they didn't ride the wind to the spot. Someone dug this hole for a purpose."

"It stinks," Marge said. "Mostly from horseshit."

Decker agreed, although the smell was a tad nostalgic, reminding him of his days as a single man owning a ranch. He wouldn't want to go back, but the recollection was sweet. His nostrils also picked up skunk spray. He looked upward and saw a fleet of crows overhead. They cawed noisily, bothered by the posse below invading their wide-open space. There were also several raptors circling overhead, the up-tilt of their wings suggesting that they were carrion feeders as opposed to hawks that ate fresh kill.

Crows ate carrion as well.

Made him wonder. What did they know that he didn't?

The sun had dipped below the hills, crowning them in fiery gold. Dusk was starting to cover the remnants of natural illumination. Marge had set up a half-dozen spots powered by beefed-up truck engines. She'd need them soon, as daylight was becoming a fond memory.

With nothing better to do than to watch the buzzards, Decker decided to be useful. He slipped on a pair of latex gloves, crouched down, and began winnowing through a dirt pile. Though he needed to focus, his mind began to wander as the monotony of the task set in.

It was Sabbath and he should have been home with Rina, enjoying good food and laughter and company over a bottle of wine. He should have been home with Hannah who was only a year away from college. There was so little time left with her, because his experience dictated that once kids left, they came back different. The love was still there, but the relationship changed irrevocably. They were young adults merging into the fast lane of life.

Cindy had been financially independent for years, and since she married she was less in Decker's consciousness. She was Koby's responsibility, not his. Decker supposed he'd feel the same way once his other children settled down.

His older stepson, Sammy, was on his way. A sophomore in medical school, he was engaged to one of his classmates, a lovely young girl named Rachel whom he met by happenstance at a busy restaurant. Jacob, the younger stepson, was a neuroscience major at Johns Hopkins with an eye toward graduate school. He was still with his girlfriend, Ilana, the two of them dating steadily for the last two years.

Hannah Rose was the last stop before his barreling locomotive of child rearing came to an abrupt halt. His and Rina's only biological child together, Hannah and her march to maturity not only represented that inevitable milestone of empty nesting, but signified the years of their cemented marriage. While he looked forward to calling his time his own, he knew he'd miss her terribly and he'd fret every time he got that nuanced phone call that told him that all wasn't perfect in her life.

Just as the stars began to flicker overhead, Wynona Pratt and her band of searchers came in from the field. She spied Decker and brought him up to date, handing him a map of the areas recently combed.

"We're going to reconvene tomorrow at nine to go over the last sector. I'll do the entrances and the exits to the property at that time." Wynona kicked the ground softly. "If you're okay with it, I thought I might stick around to see what's going on."

"Grab a set of gloves and help us sieve through the dirt."

As the night darkened, Marge turned on the spots, casting hot white light on the dig. The crew worked steadily for the next hour. As the hole grew deeper, it gave off a hint of odor.

The crows had turned in for the night, but the buzzards still circled.

The stink, faint at first, grew steadily stronger until everyone could easily discern it as the smell of rot. A garbage dump? In areas this rural, the local trash wasn't picked up on a once-a-week schedule.

Another twenty minutes of digging passed until someone held up his shovel and announced that he had hit something hard. As a flurry of people gathered around the spot, another digger proclaimed he had come upon something as well. From that point on, the work was more carefully crafted, going from shovels to trowels in order not to disturb or mangle what lay beneath the ground. The physical positions had shifted from backbreaking spading to knee-straining squatting as the group systematically began to remove dirt.

The sky had become studded with twinkling lights. Crickets chirped, frogs croaked, and a distant owl hooted. Gnarled trees became frozen inky specters.

And still vultures flew overhead, bathing in the artificial lights.

Another hour passed before the ground started yielding its booty. Decker could make out several elongated skulls, large arcing ribs, and multiple femurs.

A reliquary of bones.

From the looks of it, it appeared that they had exhumed a horse grave.

The animals had been in the ground long enough for most of the flesh to deteriorate, although not completely. Decker could discern some musculature, hair, fur, and a couple of melting hooves. Still, the stink was disproportionately strong given the amount of remaining soft tissue. And the stench grew stronger as they began to uncover more material.

Decker allowed them to keep going until the smell became downright toxic. He ordered everyone to stop, step back, and take a few breaths of fresh air. He called over his detectives. "Obviously, we hit a horse grave. It's not unusual to bury a dead animal out here when you have so much land, but something's off. There's too much stink for the amount of remaining flesh. Any ideas?"

Oliver said, "It's more than one horse."

"About three horses, looking at all the bones," Wynona added.

"That's weird," Oliver said. "Burying three horses at the same time. What'd they do? Put a couple in cold storage until they had enough to fill the hole?"

"You know what's really weird?" Marge said. "If you bury a dead horse—just dump it in the ground—when you dig it up, it should look like a skeleton of a horse that you dumped. It should be in roughly the same position as when it was buried. But all these bones are strewn willy-nilly."

Decker said, "What if the horse skeletons were disturbed by human interference, specifically by somebody wanting to bury something underneath the equine bones?"

Marge said, "Like the bodies of our missing guards?"

Decker said, "Suppose one of the murderers knew about the grave because he saw it originally being dug. What better place to dump the bodies of the missing guards?"

Oliver said, "Certainly smells like recent death down there."

Decker said, "Let's get everybody gloved up and wearing face masks. Who has a camera?"

"I do," Marge said.

"Me, too," Wynona added.

"Good. Before we remove any horse bones, I want photographs of before and after. Then we'll start removing biological material, bone by bone. Each time we remove something, take a picture. If the smell gets worse, and I fear it will, we'll have to stop and call the M.E.'s office. At that point, we'll turn this over to professional exhumers."

"WHOEVER PUT HIM in the ground did you a favor." The field coroner was named Lance Yakamoto. In his thirties, he was around five feet nine inches, 140 pounds, with a long face and tawny-colored eyes that sloped upward. He was in his blue scrubs and a black jacket, the yellow lettering in back stating that he was from the Coroner's Office. "If the body would have been dumped in the open, the decomposition would have been a lot quicker. With all the carrion-eating birds, we wouldn't have much to work with."

Decker said, "When I find and arrest the culprit, I'll be sure to give my thanks for dumping him in the ground."

Yakamoto said, "I'm just saying fact."

"I know," Decker answered. "Anything you want to tell me?"

"No rigor, some lividity, lots of insect activity. Once we get the body up, we'll put the bugs in bags and hand them over to the entomologist. He can probably give you a better fix on how long it's been in there. From what I saw, my guess is that he's been there for a couple of days. That would square with your murders, right?"

"Right." Decker looked at the brightly illuminated pit. The

county had sent a quartet of techs in HAZMAT suits. They were at the bottom of the hole, figuring out the best way to slide the corpse into a body bag. Since it had been rotting for a few days, skin had begun to slough off. There was some residual bloat from the internal gasses, but most of that had settled down. Still, with careful handling, the detectives were able to make out the distinct features even though much of the face was black, distorted, and bug eaten. Both Marge and Oliver thought he might have resembled the pictures they had of Denny Orlando.

"Are we sure there's only one body down there?" Decker asked Yakamoto.

"No, we're not sure," the assistant M.E. responded. "Not yet."

Oliver said, "Smells ripe enough for two bodies."

Decker said, "If Rondo Martin's down there, my lead is shot." He told the three detectives about his meeting with Brett Harriman, trying to remember the story as well as he could without notes.

Oliver asked, "You believe this guy? I mean it's hard enough getting something substantial from *eye*witnesses, Loo."

"Just because he's blind and couldn't see them doesn't mean he didn't hear the conversation correctly," Decker said. "That's what he's trained to do. To use his ears, Scott. Anyway, how would he know that Rondo Martin is involved?"

"He's a missing guard," Marge pointed out. "His name might have been in the papers."

Wynona said, "How does he read the papers if he's blind?"

"He has a voice-activated computer that tells him the news," Decker told her. "I'll concede that maybe he read or heard about Rondo Martin. But Joe Pine? Whom he kept referring to as José Pinon. How'd he pull that rabbit out of a hat?"

Oliver had no answer. Marge said, "Have you checked him out?"

"He came in this afternoon after the courts had closed. I'll start calling people on Monday."

"Do you even know if he's really blind?" Oliver asked.

Decker grinned. "Are you asking me if I threw something at him to see if he would duck? No, Scott, I did not do that."

"So I repeat. How do you know he's really blind? You know how many crazies Wanda Bontemps has fielded on the tip lines, especially now that Grant Kaffey has offered a twenty-thousand-dollar reward?"

"That's all?" Decker said.

"Looks like Guy wasn't the only cheapskate."

Decker said, "Harriman may be loony, but right now I'm taking him at his word. Willy Brubeck is looking into Rondo Martin with his sources in Ponceville. Joe Pine was on Brubeck's guard list to check out, but so far he's a no-show. Drew Messing is working on locating him. Enough about Martin. What's happening inside the house?"

"Lots of evidence to process," Marge said.

"Fingerprints?"

"A lot of smears, but CSI lifted a few that might be helpful," Oliver said. "We still have to comb the auxiliary buildings. It's going to take a while."

Marge said, "Can we go back to Brett Harriman for a moment? He didn't give you any name for *el patrón*?"

"Nope," Decker said. "One of the men just said that he was worse than Martin—who was a very bad man."

Shouts from inside the hole announced that the corpse was fully contained in the body bag. The trick now was how to hoist out the bag. The pit was around four-plus feet in depth. It was possible to scale in and out of the cavity by foot, but it was much harder to surface while holding a corpse.

Decker squatted at the edge of the hole. From this vantage point, the stench was considerably stronger. "If the three of you can get the bag above your heads, our people here can grab the bag and place it on the gurney."

The HAZMAT crew considered the suggestion and deemed it possible. It took some careful maneuvering but when they finally managed to do it, the gang above was ready. Six men snatched the edges of body bag and put it on the gurney. Yakamoto unzipped the sack. "What do you think?"

Marge stared at the discolored and disfigured face. Worms were crawling in and out of the apertures of his eyes, ears, nose, and mouth. Some of the flesh had fallen off; some of it had been eaten. "It's hard to say for sure, but with a little imagination it could be Denny Orlando." She looked over at Oliver.

"I think it's Orlando, but maybe it's because I'm fixated on him."

"We've got DNA now." Yakamoto zipped him back up. "We'll find out soon enough."

THE SUN HAD crested over the horizon just as the last bits of all the biological material were removed from the grave. One body was disinterred. Rondo Martin was still missing. It was 5:26 in the morning. If Decker left within the hour, he could make it home in time to eat breakfast, shower, dress, and go to shul. He'd probably be the first one there.

Or he could go home and collapse.

Though his body screamed exhaustion, there are some days where spiritual nourishment takes precedent over sleep. Today just felt like that kind of a day.

"We're done," Marge finally told him. "I'm gone."

"If you're gone, I'm gone," Oliver told her. "We came together, remember?"

"I'm not leaving without you, Scotty."

"Wanna grab some breakfast? I have nothing in my refrigerator. I'm thinking IHOP. I'm in the mood for pancakes and cholesterol."

"That'll work." Marge turned to Wynona. "You want to meet us?"

"Might as well chow down and coffee up. I have to be back here at nine."

Decker waved them all good-bye. It took him another twenty minutes to finish up with his paperwork. By 6:15, he was in his car and alone with his thoughts. He started the ignition and as the car warmed up, he checked his messages on his cell.

There were three.

The first was from Rina at 7:02. She was just about to light candles and wanted to wish him a good Shabbos. She loved him and hoped to see him soon. Her voice immediately put a smile on his face.

The second call was at 8:26 last night.

"Hi, Lieutenant Decker, it's Brett Harriman. I don't know why I didn't mention this before . . . maybe I was too overwhelmed with everything to remember correctly. Anyway, I of course couldn't see the men talking beside me, but I did ask a woman next to me to describe them as discreetly as possible. She kept asking me why and I didn't want to tell her. I felt a little foolish, so I told her to forget about it. So she may have seen them and could give you a description.

"The problem is I don't know her name, but I recognized her voice from the voir dire and I know she was impaneled on one of my cases.

"I don't know if you can get the list of jurors from that case, but it's worth a try. I'm sure she'll remember me because we didn't have a typical conversation. We can talk more about this if you want. Give me a call. Bye."

Decker saved the call in the archives. Harriman was sounding a little like an attention seeker, feeding him information bit by bit. Or maybe he was after the reward. Before Decker returned the phone call, he'd check out Harriman's credentials to ensure the man didn't have a truth problem.

The last call came in at 10:38 last night.

"It's Brett Harriman again. The woman that I told you about. I just remember that in the voir dire, she told the judge that she was married to a police lieutenant. Maybe she was trying to get out of jury duty, but they still impaneled her. I don't think she mentioned LAPD, it could have been some other city, but how many wives of police lieutenants could there be who served on a jury panel in the last week? Could be you even know her. That's it. Bye."

The line disconnected.

Time passed in very slow increments.

Did she see them?

Did they see *her*?

It took a long time for Decker to throw the gear in drive and when he did, he noticed his hands were shaking.

THIRTEEN

HE CURSED BRETT Harriman the entire ride home.

You couldn't have asked someone else for a description? It had to be my wife?

Hypocritical of him because if it had been anyone else but Rina, he would have been making phone calls, trying to get that damn jury list.

Did he really think she was in danger? Be logical, he told himself.

First, the men couldn't have been too concerned if they'd been talking about the Kaffey case openly. Second, maybe Rina didn't give them anything beyond a quick glance. Third, even if they had been aware of her at the time, they'd probably forgotten about her since.

Damn it, Harriman.

As he rounded the corner, he saw his wife picking up the morning papers. She was wearing a robe and slippers and was holding a mug of coffee. Her hair was loose and flowed down her back, and his heart stopped in his chest.

Don't say anything.

Her lips formed an open smile when he pulled in the driveway next to the house.

Take a deep breath.

As he got out of the car, he tried to smile back. He feared that it came out forced, like a smile after a Lidocaine shot from the dentist.

"Welcome." Rina handed him the coffee mug. "It's got cream in it. You want me to give you a fresh black cup?"

Decker took a sip. "No, this is great, thank you." He brushed his lips against hers. "How was dinner?"

"Everyone says hello. I saved you some rack of lamb."

"I was thinking more along the lines of cottage cheese and fruit, but lamb doesn't sound half bad. Do you have the hot plate on?"

"I do. Want me to warm it up for you?"

Decker put his arm around his wife as they walked to the front door. "Sure. Live dangerously, I say."

"With or without home fries?"

"The works." They went inside the house, Decker following Rina into the kitchen. "You know when Randy and I were in high school, Mom always made us eggs, potatoes, and sausage for breakfast. As long as I drink orange juice, I'll just say it's a variation of what I used to eat as a kid."

"There you go."

"If you don't mind, I'd like to shower first. I smell like I've been around dead bodies."

"Dead *bodies*—as in more than one?"

"Just one."

"One is enough." She took the lamb out of the refrigerator and put it on the hot plate. "One is too much. Did you have an identity?"

"We think it's Denny Orlando, one of the two missing guards."

"Oh my. That's so sad." She searched in the fridge to find the home fries among the containers of leftover food. "What about the other one?"

"Rondo Martin. He's still missing. We checked every inch down there and didn't find any sign of him. Let me clean up and get dressed. We'll have breakfast together, and then we'll go to shul."

Rina turned to him, perplexed. "You want to go to shul?"

"I need some godliness in my life right now."

"Then I'll go with you. I'll wake up Hannah and see if she wants to come with us. It's still pretty early. I'll give her a little more time."

"Let her sleep. She doesn't have to go just because we're going."

"Ordinarily she probably wouldn't, but she's meeting Aviva for lunch. Are you sure you don't want to sleep, Peter?"

"Absolutely. Isn't there a guest rabbi this week?"

"There is." Rina lifted her dark eyebrows. "I've heard he's kind of long-winded."

"The longer the better. As soon as he opens his mouth, I'll be asleep."

ABSENCE MAKES THE heart grow fonder . . . or at least more talkative. On the mile walk to synagogue, Hannah informed her father of every single detail of her life for the past week. This friend and that friend and after a while, Decker's mind went to autopilot with well-placed uh-huhs whenever his daughter took a breath. Although the content was inane, her voice was music. He didn't care what she talked about as long as she was talking to him. When they approached the storefront house of worship, she gave Decker a quick peck on the cheek, then ran off with her friend before he could say an official good-bye. He watched the two girls embrace as if they were long-lost relatives. He was more than a little jealous.

Rina said, "It's amazing."

"What is?" Decker said.

"At no point during the diatribe did she realize that you were sleeping with your eyes open."

"I heard every word."

"You heard it like you heard the birds chirping." Rina kissed his cheek. "You're a wonderful father. Don't snore. I'll see you later."

The speech lasted for nearly an hour, allowing Decker a terrific catnap. When he was nudged in the ribs by Barry Gold after the sermon was over, he was actually able to stand up and concentrate on the Mussaf prayers. In honor of the guest rabbi, there was a kiddush. Most of the parishioners were grumbling about the length of the address, but not Decker.

"Best sermon I ever slept to," he told Rina as he ate a small Styrofoam cup's worth of chulent—the traditional meat and bean stew provided gratis after services.

"Lucky you." Rina popped a grape into her mouth. "The Millers just extended a last-minute invitation for lunch. I excused us on the grounds of your exhaustion."

"That's a fact. You ready to go?"

"I am."

As soon as they left the synagogue, Decker felt his heart race, his thoughts interlaced with anxiety. The two of them walked home hand in hand. He knew he should be making small talk, but his mind was elsewhere.

How do I bring this up? Before or after lunch? Before I sleep or after I sleep?

When they reached home, Decker had yet to figure out a game plan. He supposed the best way to approach the subject was with honesty. "Can I help you set up for lunch?"

"Are you hungry after eating all that lamb and chulent?"

"Not really, but you may be hungry."

"I'm still dairy. I'd be fine with a yogurt and a cup of coffee." She patted his hand. "Should I tuck you in?"

Decker plunked himself down on the couch. "I need to talk to you for a few minutes."

"Uh-oh."

"Nothing bad." He patted the cushion next to him for her to take a seat. "Just a few minutes."

"Sure." She snuggled next to him. "What's up?"

Decker took in a deep breath, then exhaled. "Okay . . . here's the deal. Yesterday around three in the afternoon, I got a visitor at the station house. He said he might have some relevant information about the Kaffey murders. Every time we get a tip, we have to take it seriously—even if it's from Aunt Edna who channeled the information from Mars. Sometimes substance is buried in the lunacy."

"I understand. What are you getting at, sweetie?"

"The tipster said he overheard a conversation between two men speaking in Spanish. He related this conversation to me and in it were some names that no outsider should have been aware of. So I'm listening pretty carefully."

"Okay."

"So he's telling me about this conversation between two Hispanic men, but there's a problem. The tipster can only hear them. He can't describe the men to me because he's blind."

"I could see where that would be a problem," Rina said.

"But he's aware that he might have overheard something important. So he asks a woman next to him to describe the men across the way. She asks him why and he won't say. She persists and he feels a little foolish, so he drops the issue. But later, he can't get the conversation out of his mind, so he comes to the station house."

"This is sounding a little familiar."

"A little?"

"More than a little."

"I was afraid of that."

Rina said, "I don't know the guy's name. He works as a translator for the courts. He's in his thirties—curlyish hair, long face, dresses pretty sharp."

"His name is Brett Harriman."

"How did he find out my name?"

"He didn't. He recognized your voice from the voir dire and said you were impaneled on one of his cases. He remembered you telling the judge that you were married to a police lieutenant. I filled in the blanks and hoped I was wrong."

"You're not."

Decker leaned back and ran his hands down his face. "Did you get a peek at the men, Rina?"

"I looked at the two Hispanic men that I thought he was referring to."

"A good look?"

"A decent look. He told me to be discreet."

"He did?"

"Yes, he specifically told me not to stare, so I didn't."

Decker exhaled. "Thank you, Brett. Did they notice you?"

"Probably not. So these two men are involved?"

"It sounds like they had inside information. So you don't think they noticed you?"

"I doubt it. It was right before the afternoon session began and there were lots of people milling around the hallways." Rina paused. "Would you like a description of the men?"

"It doesn't matter."

"It doesn't *matter*?"

"Even if you could positively identify them from the mug books, I still wouldn't have anything. He heard the conversation; you didn't, right?"

"Right."

"So . . . there we have it. You don't need to be involved."

"So why bring it up in the first place?" Rina asked him.

"I was just trying to get an idea whether or not this guy is legit."

"He definitely works as a translator for the courts."

"How reliable do you think Harriman is?"

"Me?" Rina pointed to her chest. "I couldn't tell you. The guy seems to know his languages. And he's *very* dramatic. We used to call him Smiling Tom—after Tom Cruise—because he wore sunglasses and was always flashing a big white grin. After hearing him translate, we all decided that he missed his calling as an actor."

"So you think he might be exaggerating?"

"I can't tell you that. Just that he plays his voice like an instrument. Some soloists are more subtle than others. Actually I didn't even know he was blind until he talked to me. He uses some kind of electronic locator to move about. He walks like anyone else."

Decker tried to look casual. "Okay. Thanks for helping out."

"That's it?"

"Just wanted to get a feel for the guy."

"Peter, I'd be happy to look through the mug books."

"What for? Even if you picked someone out, I couldn't haul him in. Like I said, Harriman heard the conversation, not you."

"You could ask them to come in voluntarily. If they didn't, that would tell you something. And once you got them in, maybe Harriman could recognize the voices."

"Harriman said he'd absolutely be able to recognize the voices. But I don't know if that would hold up in court."

"You said that Harriman mentioned names that only an insider would know about. And you're telling me that you're not interested in talking to these guys?" When Decker didn't answer, she said, "Let me look, Peter. Chances are I might not recognize anyone or they're not in there."

He remained silent.

Rina said, "Whoever did it shouldn't be walking free and clear. If it was anyone else other than Cindy, Hannah, or me, you'd be hounding them."

"That's probably true."

"All I'd be doing is looking at mug shots."

"It's not the looking at the mug shots I mind. It's the recognizing part that makes me nervous."

She laid her cheek on his arm. "Don't worry. I have a big, strong man to protect me. He has a gun and he knows how to use it."

HE AWOKE TO the sound of the phone ringing. When the door opened, letting in artificial light, he announced he was awake and sat up. Rina told him that Willy Brubeck was on the line and it sounded important.

Decker said, "What's up, Willy?"

"I just got off the phone with Milfred Connors. He's willing to talk to us."

"Okay." Decker turned on the nightstand lamp. "When?"

"Tonight. I told him we'd be there as soon as we could. He lives in Long Beach so we better get a move on it. Want me to pick you up?"

Decker's brain was still in a fog. He checked the nightstand clock. It was quarter to eight. He'd slept for seven hours. "Uh, sure. That sounds fine."

"That's good 'cause I'm right outside your door."

"You are?" Decker stood up and stretched. "I need about ten minutes to shower and dress. Come inside and wait."

"Sounds good to me. Tell me, Rabbi. Does your wife still bake?"

Decker laughed. "We've got some leftover layer cake. I believe it's chocolate. You can have as much as you want."

"Just a slice if you don't mind."

"Not at all. I'll ask her to put a pot of coffee on. We working dogs live on caffeine and sugar."

UNLIKE MOST COASTAL regions, Long Beach never commanded the spectacular real estate prices common in other So Cal beach communities, probably because the city's tenor was more industrial than resort. From the 405 south, Decker was offered a bird's-eye view of the refineries belching out smoke followed by acres of car lots. That didn't mean there weren't some nice areas: certainly the old downtown area with its hotels and the famous aquarium had been revamped to attract the tourists. Still, most of the residential areas were made up of modest homes when compared with other shoreline districts.

Milfred Connors lived in a small California-style bungalow—stucco exterior and red-tiled roof illuminated by a streetlamp. It was one story sitting on a bumpy lawn almost devoid of landscaping. The cracked walkway led up to a dilapidated porch. The light was on and Decker rang the bell. The man who answered was stoop shouldered and rail thin. He had wisps of gray tendrils atop his head and a long, drawn face. He appeared to be around seventy plus or minus five years. He had on a white shirt, slacks, and slippers.

He stepped aside so that the detectives could come into the house.

The living room was neat and spare, the furniture including a floral couch, a leather recliner, and a flat-screen TV sitting on a plywood bureau. Scarred wood floors but quarter sawn oak, Decker noticed. They were original to the house.

"Have a seat." He offered them the sofa. "Would either of you like some coffee or tea?"

"I'm fine," Decker said, "but thank you."

"Me too, thanks," Brubeck said.

"Then just give me a minute to get my tea." He disappeared and came back a minute later holding a steaming mug. He sat on his leather recliner but didn't recline. "Is the visit about the Kaffey murders?"

Decker said, "Yes, in a way."

"Horrible thing."

"Yes, it is." Decker paused. "You worked for the company for a long time."

"Thirty years."

"Ever get a chance to see Guy interact with his brother or his sons?"

"All the time."

"What would you say about their relationships?"

"Well, now . . ." Connors sipped tea. "Guy could be rough. But he could be nice, too."

"Did you get along with him?"

"I wasn't on the same plane. Guy Kaffey was up here." Connors extended his arm. "I was down here." The accountant lowered his arm.

"Yet you saw him all the time."

"He was always checking the books. Not just me, everyone. I was one of about twenty." There was a long pause. "You want to talk to me because I was fired for embezzling."

"We want to talk to a lot of people, but you did make the list."

"Lucky me." Connors took a sip of tea. "It isn't what you think. I was fired, but no criminal charges were ever filed against me."

"Yet you didn't protest the termination," Decker said. "You didn't file any wrongful suit against the company."

When Connors didn't answer, Brubeck pulled out his notebook and a pen. "Why don't you tell us what happened?"

"It's complicated."

"I'm sure it is." Decker took out his pad of paper and a pencil. "How about if you start from the beginning."

Connors took another sip of tea. "I worked for Kaffey for thirty years. Never asked anything from him, but he sure as hell asked a lot of me. Unpaid overtime, on-call twenty-four/seven, especially during tax time. I did it all without a complaint. But then my wife got sick."

Decker nodded.

"It was only me and my wife," Connors told him. "We never had kids. Lara was a preschool teacher so I suppose she got her kid fix by her job. And me, I'm a numbers person, not a people person. Lara made all the social decisions."

"That's usually the way it is with married folk," Brubeck said.

"Well, that was the way it was for us." He warmed his hands on the tea mug. "I went to work, I came home. Whatever Lara planned was okay by me." His eyes welled up with tears. "She died five years ago from the big C. I can't seem to move on."

"My sympathies," Brubeck told him.

"Must have been hard," Decker said.

"It was hell, Lieutenant. She was in pain constantly. Even doped up, she was in pain. It was a very long illness. We had insurance, but it didn't pay for everything. When regular medicine didn't work, we tried experimental things that insurance wouldn't cover. We ate through my paycheck, we ate through our savings. The next stop was selling the house. I couldn't do that to her, but I didn't want to give up on treatment either."

Decker nodded and asked him to go on.

"I swallowed my pride and asked Mace Kaffey if he could arrange a loan for me. I knew Mace better than Guy, and everyone at the company knew that Mace was an easier touch than Guy."

"How long ago was this?" Decker asked Connors.

"Maybe six years ago—at the beginning of the end." Connors let out a deep sigh. "Mace told me to write off the loan as an inventory expense. And he told me to cut the check for thirty thousand, that he'd take a little extra in case I needed more. The company does business with hundreds of suppliers so it wasn't hard to bury it somewhere. I knew it was wrong but I did it anyway. Two days later, I had cash in my pocket. I rationalized it by telling myself that I was just following the boss's orders. I had every intention of paying it back."

"How did you plan on doing that?" Decker asked.

"Doing freelance work. I told Mace that I'd pay back every cent, but he told me not to worry about it. Just get the wife better and then we'd talk. It sounded too good to be true, but I wasn't going to question him. Twenty thousand was a lot, but I knew I could make that amount up. The problem was . . ."

He put the mug down on an end table.

"It wasn't just twenty thousand. It was twenty thousand, then forty, then sixty. By the time she died, I was one hundred and fifty thousand in the hole. That's a lot of money to pay back considering that my life savings, my pension plan, and my wife's pension plan had been totally wiped out. I had nothing left to my name except the house."

Connors rubbed his eyes.

"I went to Mace to tell him that I was going to sell the house to pay back the loan and he told me to hold off and not to do anything rash. I wasn't going to insist." A long pause. "He also told me to keep on borrowing from the company for just a while longer. He said that there were other people in bad straits. I needed to keep at it a little bit longer. And for my effort, he'd knock off some of the loan money."

"And you went along with it," Decker said.

"I was in debt and he was my boss. If he said to keep doing it, I kept doing it. I did summon up enough nerve to ask him if it was okay with Guy."

"What'd he answer?" Brubeck said.

"He said that Guy skimmed off the top all the time. All in all I wrote about two hundred thousand dollars' worth of phony checks."

"And that was okay with you?" Decker said.

Connors looked at the detectives. "I had lived two years in hell and I was deep in debt. So whatever Mace said, I did and didn't ask questions. Anyway, the whole mess came to a head when the company got audited. That meant opening the books. The embezzlement was discovered, the IRS began to levy charges against Kaffey Industries, and a huge lawsuit ensued between the brothers. I thought I was going down with the ship, but Mace, Gold bless him, covered for me."

"How?" Brubeck asked.

"He told Guy that the discrepancies had to do with the increased cost of materials or something stupid like that. Guy didn't buy it. Hence the lawsuit. But no matter how bad it looked for Mace, he didn't rat me out to the authorities. I was really grateful."

Decker said, "Mr. Connors, Mace was accused of embezzling *five million* dollars. Your part in the scheme didn't amount to nearly that much."

Connors shrugged. "Maybe he had the same kind of arrangement with a few other accountants. I was just one of many."

"You were an account executive," Brubeck said.

"Like I said, there are around twenty account executives in the company. Each one is in charge of one project or another."

"If Mace was stealing from the company, why didn't Guy kick his brother out?"

"I can't say for sure, but I think Mace wasn't lying when he said that Guy skimmed off the top, too. Since Guy was the CEO, he was much more vulnerable to jail time for cheating the IRS than Mace was. It was probably cheaper for Guy to keep him on rather than to prosecute him."

Decker said, "So the two brothers settled and Mace was moved back east."

"Yes, sir," Connors answered. "And that was that."

"Except for one thing," Decker said. "You were caught embezzling money even after Mace left the West Coast."

Connors threw up his hands.

Decker said, "Would you care to explain?"

"No charges were brought against me."

"You asked Mace for another favor."

"I just told him, I'd rather put a bullet into my head than go to jail."

"And he covered for you."

He shrugged.

Decker said, "Would you care to explain to us what happened?"

"Simple. I got caught." Connors shrugged again. "Some habits die hard."

FOURTEEN

DECKER BROUGHT OVER a cappuccino and a croissant and placed it in front of Rina. He had set her up at his desk. "The croissant is from Coffee Bean. The cap's from around the corner. Half caffeinated with whole milk."

"Perfect." Rina took a sip. "All I need is the Sunday paper."

"You usually read the Sunday paper in bed wearing a robe."

Rina had put on a soft, flannel top and a loose denim skirt and had on sneakers. "I'm very comfortable, and this is a lot more fun than reading an *L.A. Times* article about murder and mayhem."

Decker placed three mug books in front of her. "Darlin', it doesn't get more murder and mayhem than this."

"True, but in this case, at least I'm *doing* something." She took a sip of the cappuccino. "Don't worry. I'll be fine."

Decker rubbed his temples. He was dressed in a polo shirt and a pair of slacks. Right now he felt scrubbed clean, but that wouldn't last long. The dust at the ranch was fierce. "When you're done with these, I've got about another dozen books sitting on a table right outside my office. Go through as many as you want or as few as you want. When you get tired, quit. Eyestrain is the enemy."

"Gotcha."

"And don't guess. I'd rather you say 'I don't know' than to take a stab in the dark."

"I understand. I don't want to lead anyone on a wild-goose chase." Rina flipped open the first page—six men in full face and profile, their vital statistics—height, weight, eye color, hair color, race, and distinguishing marks—underneath the photograph. "Hmmm . . . the men I saw had tattoos. I guess that's standard nowadays."

"All tattooed men aren't cons, but all cons have tattoos. But ink work is almost as good as a fingerprint. No two tattoos are exactly alike. What kind of tattoos did you see?"

"One looked like a tiger or it could have been a leopard; the other guy . . . I think he had a snake. There were also letters."

"Letters? You mean like ABC letters?"

"More like Xs. And some Ls, maybe."

"Could they have been Roman numerals?"

"Good call, Peter. They probably were."

"Do you remember seeing the Roman numbers XII?"

"Maybe. Why?"

Decker scooped up the mug books. "Let me start you off with some other books. It may be a more efficient use of your time."

"Which books?"

"Members of the Bodega 12th Street gang. They're often tattooed with BXII or just XII."

"I've heard about Bodega Twelve. They mostly do drug running. Would it make sense for them to know about the Kaffey murders?"

"If they committed the murders, it would make total sense."

"Why would they murder the Kaffeys?"

"Because Bodega 12th Street is filled with murderers. Plus, I found out that Guy Kaffey often hired rehabilitated gang members for security."

"Oh, come on!"

"I'm not lyin'. Brady said that Guy wanted them out of ideology, but also because they worked cheap. Ordinarily, I would have thought he was feeding bull, but Grant confirmed that Guy actually did hire former gang members. Sometimes people—especially very rich people—don't recognize their own mortality. Hold on, I'll be right back." He came back with two other mug books. "Start with these. Hopefully you won't find anyone who looks familiar. And if you do recognize a face, don't tell anyone except me about it."

THIS IS A list of all the bullets, shells, and casings we found on the property." Wynona Pratt was dressed in a short-sleeve cotton shirt and had on jeans and tennis shoes. "Almost all of the ammo was located in the northeast sector—number four—near and in four stacked bales of hay."

"Sounds like a target practice area."

"That would be my guess. We also found a rusty knife and some other sharp pieces of metal that might have been knives or shivs, but it appears that they haven't been touched in a long time. I've sent them to forensics. I'll be ripping through the bags of evidence this afternoon at the station house. It's cooler there."

"Good. Tell me about the exits and entrances."

"The ranch is surrounded by a double layer of barbed wire and seven-foot cyclone fencing. Nothing is electrified so it is possible to cut through the metal if you have a good pair of wire clippers and you're wearing thick, protective gloves. I found eight gates in and out of the property." Wynona rummaged through her folder and pulled out a sheet of paper. "I even drew you a little map."

Decker scanned the diagram.

She said, "The gates are solid metal except for the two back gates, which are made out of cyclone fencing and secured by padlocks. Wire cutters could take care of them."

"Did either of the padlocks look breached?"

"No."

"What about the fencing? Holes anywhere?"

"Nothing that's obvious, but I haven't gotten down and checked every inch of the perimeter." Wynona adjusted her hat. "I have a set of knee pads at home. I'll organize something tomorrow morning unless you want it done right now."

"Tomorrow is fine." Decker mopped his brow with a handkerchief. He could hear the dogs and the horses registering protest at the heat. "Who's watching over the animals?"

"I assumed it was the groomsman—Riley Karns. He was here yesterday."

"Is he here today?"

"Haven't seen him."

"Who let you inside the property?"

"Piet Kotsky. He said you told Neptune Brady that you don't want any private guards around until you've cleared them."

"I might have said that," Decker told her. "Does that mean Riley Karns isn't considered a guard? Because I certainly haven't cleared him."

Wynona shrugged. "Someone has to take care of the livestock."

"I'm going to poke around the stables . . . see if he's there."

"Take a mask. I betcha it stinks."

"I don't mind horse shit. In my younger days I had a ranch and stables. I used to ride all the time."

She cocked her hip and looked at him. "Is that a fact?"

"It is. I'm at home around horses. It's people that I find confusing."

THE STABLES HAD eight stalls and six of them were empty, but the straw had been recently changed. The two remaining horses—both looked like Morgans—were well fed and well hydrated. Decker left the stables through a half door that led to a paddock. Three animals were hooked up to an automatic horse walker—a contraption that looked like a giant umbrella frame without the canvas top. As the horses walked, the frame rotated like a carousel.

Riley was grooming a well-muscled mare with a deep brown coat and a white blaze down her snout, moving the rubber currycomb in a gentle circular motion to loosen up dirt. He glanced up when he heard Decker come into the area, but he continued working. Karns was a tiny man, but with a wiry frame that screamed jockey. He had thin brown hair that was combed across his brow and tiny facial features embedded in a craggy face covered with a sheen of sweat. He wore a black T-shirt, jeans, and work boots.

Decker said to Karns, "Nice-looking quarter horse."

"Not just any quarter horse. Her sire—Big Ben—was AQHA World Cutting Champion two times over. Won a purse of over a half million." Karns pursed his lips. "I used to ride him . . . Big Ben."

"Did Mrs. Kaffey buy the mare on your recommendation?"

"I don't make recommendations," Karns said. "I'm just hired help. But when I heard that Big Ben was siring a foal, I gave the missus a contact number. She fell in love with Zepher. Who wouldn't?"

"She looks young."

"She is young. Wait till she fills in."

"She's got good muscle."

"Great muscle."

Decker said, "So the Morgans came first?"

"The missus loved Morgans. She shows them all the time." Karns grew quiet. Then he said, "Horse shows bore Mr. Kaffey. So he decided that he'd try his hand at racing. That's how he came to buying Tar Baby . . . the black stallion. The first time I raced him, I knew he didn't have it. But I kept me opinions to meself."

"Smart man."

"I'm just hired help, sir." Karns trailed a finger over Zepher's topline. "Go ahead. Ask your questions, Governor."

"It's Lieutenant Decker."

"Whatever you say, Guv. Where'd y'learn about horses?"

"I used to keep horses. I like quarter horses. Versatile animals. On my way over here, I noticed Afghan hounds in the kennel; was Mrs. Kaffey the primary force behind them as well?"

"Yes, the missus loved her Afghans, but not Mr. Kaffey. He didn't allow any animals in the house. I think he was bitter."

"Why's that?"

" 'Cause he tried out some of his own dogs and it was a disaster."

"Let me guess. Greyhounds."

"Right you are, Guv." Karns shook his head. "Mr. Kaffey thought he could make money racing them. He could have, except he bought on the cheap. Any half-wit could see that those dogs didn't have it. The man didn't know a fig about animals."

"Or he didn't want to put out the cash to buy champions."

"True enough, Governor."

"Who owns the remaining animals now that Mr. and Mrs. Kaffey are gone?"

"I reckon it'll be the boys. They're the ones paying me to keep 'em healthy. The younger one, Grant. Yesterday, he asked me how he would go about sellin' them. I told him if that's what he wanted, I could help. He said he wanted to wait until his brother got better first, but if I could get some prices, that would be good. He also said to sell the dogs. That won't be hard. Some of them are champions." He looked at Decker. "You're not asking me this to buy a dog."

"That's true."

"So what do you want, Guv?"

"Your building isn't too far from the kennel."

"About five minutes."

"Did you hear the dogs barking on the night of the murder?"

"When Ana woke me up, I heard the dogs barking. Ana probably woke them up with her screaming."

"In the summer, my setter often slept with the horses. Every time I drove up to my ranch, she'd come barreling out to meet me, barking away." When Karns didn't respond, Decker said, "The kennel isn't all that far from the house. You'd think they'd sense a commotion going on and start barking up a storm."

"Maybe they did."

"But their barking didn't wake you up."

"I told you. Ana woke me up." He switched from the currycomb to the dandy brush and flicked away a cloud of dirt from the animal. "When I went to the house with her and Paco, I heard them barking. I reckon they could have been barking all along and I didn't know about it. I'm a deep sleeper." He stopped for a moment. "I don't have trouble sleeping like upper class do, Governor. It's because I do an honest day's work and my conscience is clean."

"Let me ask you this, Riley. If the dogs heard people walking by the kennel, do you think they'd start barking?"

"Probably."

"And do you think that barking would probably wake you up?"

"Maybe. But not that night, Guv, not that night." He looked at his watch and adjusted the automatic horse walker to a slower tempo. "If an intruder came in through the horse trailer gate, he'd probably wake up the dogs. But if he came in through the other side, I wouldn't hear a peep and neither would my pets. So if I was you, I would be guessing that the intruder didn't come through this area."

Decker switched to another topic. "Did you know that we found a body dumped in an old horse grave?"

"Hard not to notice all the commotion going on last night . . . or the night before. I forget. Cops are here all the time now."

"Someone had to dig up the grave beforehand to place the body that deep inside the hole. You didn't hear any noise from that either?"

"The grave is on the other side of the ranch, Governor."

"Did you know there was a horse grave on the property?"

"Of course," Karns said. "I dug it. People with big ranches do it all the time."

"You buried three horses at once?"

"Not all at once. The first one I dug was for Netherworld, then the next one was for Buttercream. I dug her grave right next to his. But then when Potpie died, I didn't feel like digging a whole new grave. That's a lot of work. So I just dug up the area between Netherworld and Buttercream and made one big hole and stuck her there."

"How long ago did the horses die?"

"Netherworld and Buttercream died about two years ago. Potpie died last year. It didn't smell that bad. The first two had already rotted by then."

"Anyone else know about the horse grave?"

"The missus knew about it. She said a little prayer each time one of her babies died."

"Anyone else besides Mrs. Kaffey?"

Karns's eyes darted back and forth. He said nothing.

Decker said, "It's not a trick question. Who else *alive* knows about the graves?"

At last he said, "Paco Albanez takes care of the grounds around here. He has a backhoe. I asked him if I could borrow it. He told me it was out of order and asked me why I needed it. When I told him I had to dig a grave for the horses, he said he'd help me dig the hole if I wanted."

"Anyone else help you dig the hole?"

"Just meself and Paco."

"How did you decide where to dig the hole?" Decker could see Karns gnashing his teeth together, a big bulge forming along his jawline. "Did someone tell you where to dig?"

"I don't want any problems, Guv."

"No problems, Riley. But I do need you to tell me who told you to dig the hole."

"The mister told me to dig the hole. Joe Pine was on duty that day. He told me where to dig it."

FIFTEEN

KARNS WENT BACK to his grooming. When Decker didn't disappear, he said, "That's all I know."

"What you know is a lot, Riley."

Karns made a point of exhaling loudly. "Why I didn't want to get into it."

"Riley, my friend, you are very much *into it* whether you like it or not. You were one of the first people at the crime scene, and now you tell me that you dug Denny Orlando's grave—"

"Horseshit!" Karns whirled around, his face flushed and his hands shaking. "I didn't dig *Denny's* grave. I dug a grave for the horses where poor Denny was found."

"Well, *someone* dug up that hole for Denny," Decker snapped back, "and it had to be *someone* who knew that the grave existed."

Karns spat on the ground, missing Decker's shoe by several feet. "I've been honest with you and now you're twisting me words so the murders are me fault or something. I have nothing more to say."

Decker decided on the cooperative approach. "If you are being honest, then I got a deal for you. Take a lie detector test."

"Those things are worthless."

"Not true," Decker told him. "It'll only work to your benefit. I can't use it against you if you don't pass, but if you do pass, I'll direct my energies elsewhere."

"I don't trust you, Guv. You'll probably get me to say things I don't mean."

"I won't be giving you the test." When Karns regarded him, Decker smiled. "And as far as saying things, the questions are yes/no. It's hard to put your foot in your mouth with one word answers."

Karns didn't answer right away. Though Decker reserved a large sector of his judgment until the facts verified the hunch, his gut feeling told him that Riley wasn't being deliberately evasive. It was more like Karns had a profound distrust for anything that required electricity.

"How about if I set it up?" Decker said. "If you change your mind, just let me know."

"I'll think about it," Karns answered. "Now I'd like to get back to me business in peace if you don't mind."

"Just a few more questions. The animals' corpses must have been very heavy. You had to have had help to lug them over to the grave."

"We did the grave first, Guv. Then we put them to sleep near the hole."

"Ah, that would make sense."

"You'd know it if you really had horses."

"I had horses but I never put them down. The vet always did it."

"Yeah, I figured you wouldn't get your hands dirty."

Decker ignored the snide comment. "And you're sure that you and Paco did all the digging by yourselves? If you've been honest until now, don't go blowing it on a simple question."

Karns lowered his eyes. "Maybe Pine helped, too. Why don't you call him up?"

"We can't find Joe. Any idea where he might be?"

"No, not me." Back to eye contact. "Go ask Brady. He's in charge."

That was Decker's next step.

THE HEAD OF Kaffey security picked up on the third ring, but the connection was lousy. "I can barely hear you, Lieutenant. Can you text me?"

Decker hated texting. His thumbs were too big for the phone's keyboard. He pulled the unmarked onto the shoulder just before the entrance to Coyote Ranch's freeway ramp. "Where are you?"

Static.

"I can't hear you."

"What about now? Can you hear me?"

"Better," Decker said. "Don't move. Where are you?"

"At the Newport Beach residence. Mace and Gr . . . (*static*) . . . hired me . . . an eye on the place and, more important, on *them*."

Decker wasn't sure he heard right. Grant continued to trust Neptune Brady even after Gilliam and Guy were murdered under his watch? He said, "I need to talk to you."

"I can't leave . . . (*static*) . . . promised . . . (*static*) . . . protect them."

"You're breaking up, Mr. Brady."

"Damn this reception."

"I heard that."

"I can't leave my post, Lieutenant."

"Then I'll come out to Newport."

"I'll ask Mace and Grant. If it's . . . (*static*) . . . it's okay by me. When . . . (*static*) . . . be here?"

"It'll take me at least a couple of hours."

". . . (*static*) . . . bosses don't mind, how about three?"

"Three would be perfect."

Brady might have tried to say good-bye, but all Decker heard was the crackle of white noise then silence.

AFTER MARKING THE mug books with Post-its, Rina turned to the first preselected page. "This guy here—Fredrico Ortez—he could be the slighter man of the two."

Decker said, "Could be or definitely?"

"It's either this guy or maybe this guy." She turned to another page. "This man here . . . Alejandro Brand, the guy with the scar. The two men look alike—at least in the mug shots."

They did resemble each other—shaved heads, narrow faces, small noses with broad nostrils, thick lips, and deep-set eyes. Under distinguishing marks, both had tattoos of animals: Brand had a snake on his arm, and Ortez sported a dragon on his chest. Other marks included XII and a B12 for Bodega 12th Street.

Rina said, "I thought they might be brothers except they have different last names."

"Didn't you tell me that one of the guys had a snake tattoo?"

"I did. Maybe you should take a closer look at Brand?"

"Maybe I will. What about the bigger of the two men?"

"Maybe this guy . . ." Rina showed him a picture. "Or maybe him or him. I'm less sure about that one." She closed the books. "To tell you the truth, after a while everyone begins to look alike. At the time, I could picture them in my head, but things fade. I just gave them a glance." She shrugged. "Sorry."

Secretly, Decker was relieved. "You did great. I'll copy down these names and see if we have any legitimate reason to bring them into the station house. And even if we don't have anything on them now, these guys are mess-ups. If I tailed them for an hour, I'm sure I could catch them doing something illegal."

"I could have been more precise if I looked a little harder, but he kept telling me not to stare . . . the blind guy . . . Harriman."

"He used good judgment."

"I don't know if I could pick them out of a lineup."

"You won't have to. If I can bring in these jokers on something else, I'll record the interview and send the tapes over to Harriman along with some similar tapes. He told me he could identify the voices. Let's see if he means it." Decker closed the mug books and stood up. "I have to go to Newport Beach. It's a long ride. Want to keep me company?"

"What's in New—Oh, that's the Kaffeys' main house. I suppose I could go look at the art galleries. See if there are any botanical paintings I want to add to our collection."

Decker frowned. "Two-thirds of the collection is sitting in closets. And we didn't pay for those. Why would you want more and pay for them?"

"I don't pay for anything, Peter. I cull. I talk about what I have, and the gallery owners talk about what they have. Sometimes I trade up and sometimes I trade down. It's kind of fun."

"My idea of fun would be to sell the collection and put the money in the bank."

"That is an option."

"But not yours. And that's why I'm a philistine and you're a connoisseur."

"You're not sentimentally attached to the paintings like I am. I see one painting and I think of Cecily Eden and how much fun the two of us had together talking about plants and gardens although I'm still mystified why she left her paintings to me and not her heirs."

"She knew you'd appreciate them and you do." He kissed the top of her head. "Let's get going. If I have a spare minute, I'll come with you to a couple of the galleries. It would give me great pleasure to see you dangle a Martin Heade in front of the wide-eyed art dealers."

THE FIFTY-MILE RIDE went quickly, enhanced by good conversation and the clear cerulean skies reflected in diamond-studded water. With the sloping hills ablaze with wildflowers to the east and the sandy shores that marked the western end of the continent, Newport and its environs had to qualify as one of the most geographically scenic places on the planet. Exquisite in its beauty, the berg was also exquisite in its price tag, one of those cases where if you have to ask, you can't afford it.

The area was teeming with traffic and tourists. The slowdown in the economy didn't seem to have affected this marina. It was stuffed with sailboats, speedboats, catamarans, cabin cruisers, and yachts of all sizes and shapes. Galleries, boutiques, and cafés seemed to be the businesses of choice. Decker dropped Rina in front of a gallery, then checked his map and headed out to residential territory.

The Kaffeys had named their mansion the Wind Chimes, and it sat behind wrought-iron gates that included a guardhouse replete with sentries, and a twelve-foot hedge that seemed to stretch for blocks. After conversing with one of the uniforms, he and his clunker car were allowed to tool down the sinuous driveway sur-rounded by a forest of pines, firs, sycamores, elms, and eucalyptus. He would have stopped to gawk, but there were too many guards who kept waving him forward. When he reached the pebbled motor court, the mansion came into view.

Decker's family had taken a family trip to the Biltmore in North Carolina when he was a kid and though he knew the place couldn't possibly be *that* big, it still appeared otherworldly. It appeared that Guy Kaffey had been copying the Biltmore's French Regency style. Like its model, it was fashioned from limestone and had multiple-peaked blue slate roofs with an abundance of gables and chimneys. He could have picked up more details but he was stopped by a pri-vate sentry. The man was squat and brutish looking and was pack-ing a Saturday night special. After checking out Decker's ID then radioing someone on his walkie-talkie, he decided that the LAPD cop passed muster. "Leave the car here. We'll take you up to the en-trance in a golf cart. And we'll keep your gun."

Decker smiled. "Leaving the car here is okay. Going up to the house in a golf cart is okay. Nobody touches my weapon."

More radioing and walkie-talkie conversation. Finally, the sentry said, "What are you carrying?"

"Standard-issue 9 mm Beretta. Is that Mr. Brady on the wire?"

The guard ignored him, but he must have been cleared. A few minutes later, Decker was winding his way past the house down a paved pathway that led through flower gardens, ferneries, orchards, a grape arbor, and a vegetable garden spilling over with a variety of tomatoes, pole beans, basil, squashes, and baseball-bat-sized Italian zucchini. The golf cart stopped at a gazebo with a roof that matched the house, and everyone got out. The spot overlooked an infinity pool that bled into the Pacific blue.

Dressed in a blue blazer with brass buttons, white linen pants, and rubber-soled boat shoes, Neptune Brady was surveying the ocean through a mounted telescope. He was chewing gum, his jaw clenching and relaxing, as he moved the tube across the expanse of water. Decker took in the view before he spoke. The house was situated on a bluff—about fifty feet above the water. There were dozens of boats in the foreground and a couple of commercial liners on the horizon. Waves were softly breaking, white foam licking the sand. From the bluff's height, it sounded like whispering winds.

Brady waved off his men with a flick of the wrist and within a few minutes it was just the two of them. He said, "I had this installed when the family first moved in." He was still peering through the lens. "Kaffey refused the fence off the bluff because he claimed it ruined the view."

"He had a point," Decker said.

"Yeah, but it's easier for someone to breech security." Brady looked away from the lens and regarded Decker full face. "Not that it stopped them at Coyote Ranch."

In the harsh sunlight, Brady had aged in just a few days: more wrinkles and more gray hair. His pupils were constricted, and his eyes appeared almost colorless. "I don't know how much time I can give you. I may have to leave abruptly."

"Where are Grant and Mace Kaffey?"

"At the hospital with Gil. He's doing better."

"Good to hear."

"Thank *God* he made it through." A heavy sigh. "I think it's finally dawning on me . . . the scope." He waited a beat. "It's coming to an end for me."

"What's coming to an end?"

"Everything. My business was taking care of Guy and Gilliam, and I failed."

"The family kept you on," Decker said.

His jaw went up and down as he stared at Decker. "What choice did they have?"

"They could have fired you immediately." *And the fact that they didn't is of interest to me.* "They chose not to."

"I think they're too dazed to make changes. Once Gil recovers, I'm going to get axed."

"What do you think went wrong?"

"It could be a thousand things. On the surface it looks like that once you found Denny, well . . . I guess everyone's pointing a finger at Rondo Martin. But I can't believe . . . I still think it had to be outsiders with inside information."

Thinking about Joe Pine, Decker asked, "Anyone specific in mind?"

Brady sat down on a bench and stared at the ocean. "There were lots of maids and people working the grounds: here at Wind Chimes and also Coyote Ranch. At least ten people a day roaming around, weeding or watering or planting. Who knows what conspiracies go on behind my back?"

"Did the same people work at both locations?"

"Mostly yes, but there's a lot of turnover. Guy would get angry and fire people, and then there'd be a whole new crop of workers."

"Did you vet everyone who worked for the Kaffeys?"

"I did background checks on anyone Guy asked me about. But I wasn't in charge of hiring and firing domestic help."

"Who was?"

"I don't know. It wasn't me."

"They never asked for your opinion?"

Brady's jaw began working overtime. "This didn't come from me, but I'm sure that some of their help didn't have green cards. Like I told you before, Guy was cheap. If all he needed was a body to pull out weeds, he'd go for the lowest price tag. Maybe Paco Albanez would know more. He's legal, by the way. I did the background check on him."

"Who hired Paco?"

"Guy."

"Who hired Riley Karns?"

"Gilliam. She put him in charge of all the animals—dogs and horses."

"Where'd she find Riley Karns?"

"She hired him away from one of the horse clubs where she used to show her Morgans. I did a background check on him and nothing turned up. He had a good reputation with the animals. Once he was a skilled jockey. He rode quarter horses."

"We'll get back to him in a minute," Decker said. "So you personally think the murders were the work of the hired help?"

"Someone on the inside. Not all of them . . . just a few bad apples."

"What about Rondo Martin? Is he a bad apple?"

"I personally screened him. He had worked for Ponceville for eight years. The place was a rural farming community so there wasn't much crime to begin with, but under Martin's reign whatever crime they had had gone down. Nothing about him waved a red flag."

"How long had he worked for you?"

"Two years."

"Why did he leave Ponceville?"

"I seem to remember him wanting a bigger city, but I might be mistaken. Look it up in his file. I gave it to one of your detectives. His name escapes me, but he was a sharp dresser."

It is said that the clothes make the man and nothing could be truer in this case. "That would be Scott Oliver. How well did you know Rondo Martin?"

"He showed up for work on time. He did his job well and without attitude."

"Did he speak Spanish?"

It took a moment before Brady processed the question. "Some of the guards were bilingual, but I don't know about Martin." He took in Decker's eyes. "I know how it looks, but you had your suspicions about Denny Orlando. Then he turned up dead."

"You think Martin is dead?"

"No idea."

"What about Joe Pine? Did he speak Spanish?"

Brady paused. "Yes, fluently. Why are you asking about him?"

"He's missing."

The pause lasted longer than it should have. "He's missing?" When Decker nodded, Brady shook his head. "He was one of Guy's rehabilitated gangbangers. I'm sure he has a record. I never liked him, but Guy was the boss."

Brady's PDA went off.

"Excuse me." The guard talked in hushed tones, then he said, "Right away." He turned to Decker. "Grant and Mace have returned from the hospital. They'd like a few words with you."

"That's fine. Riley Karns told me that he was one of the guys who originally dug the graves for the horses. He said that Joe Pine— who was on duty that day—told him where to dig it."

"That could be. Hold on." Brady spoke on the phone. "I need the cart A-sap." He stowed his phone in his pocket. "Usually, I had nothing to do with the horses but when one of them was sick . . . I think it was Netherworld, Guy told me that he didn't want to spend the money on cremation. He told me to find an out-of-the-way spot on the property and get rid of it. I think I did punt to Pine to find the spot." A pause. "I think I told him that if he needed help to ask Riley or Paco."

"So you didn't choose the spot?"

"No, but I knew the horses were buried somewhere around there." The man was sweating. He wiped his face with a handker-chief. "I'd like to remind you that I was five hundred miles away when the murders occurred."

That meant nothing. Decker said, "I need a list of everyone who knew about the grave. So far I have Karns, Paco Albanez, Joe Pine, and you. Anyone else?"

"I don't know, for goodness' sakes. It was at least a year ago."

"You're in charge," Decker said evenly. "You have to know these things."

Brady took a deep breath and let it out. "You're right. I'll find out."

"What do you know about Joe Pine?"

"Not much. When Guy said to hire someone, I did it. I think his family was from Mexico. He lives in Pacoima." Brady saw the golf cart pull up. "We'll talk later. Let's go see the bosses. Maybe they can help you out."

"Speaking of the bosses, I heard Greenridge was in deep trouble."

Brady glanced at the driver of the golf cart, who was making a big show of *not* paying attention. "I don't know anything about that. And if I were you I'd be careful with my innuendos. Since you don't know what you're dealing with, someone might take it the wrong way."

"Sounds like a threat, although I'm sure you didn't mean that."

"I meant it as cautionary words. Guy and Gilliam were protected by a league of people and look what happened. Let's go."

Brady sat next to the driver, Decker sat in back. With a slight little backlash, they were on their way. Neptune was right about one thing. Investigating crimes was dangerous work. That was Decker's job: to open doors without knowing what's on the other side. Most of the time, it was harmless. But all it took was one little misstep and the next thing you knew you were looking down the barrel of a shotgun.

SIXTEEN

THE GOLF CART stopped at the service entrance of Wind Chimes. Decker followed Brady through a series of hallways until the security man opened a set of double doors. Mace and Grant were waiting in an all-glass conservatory, its French doors wide open to allow in the fresh, briny air and the hypnotic song of the ocean waves. The space held several couches, chairs, and end tables, most of them holding vases of white and purple *Phalaenopsis* orchids, yellow cymbidiums, pink bromeliads, and assorted African violets. Shades had been lowered to cut the glare of the afternoon sun.

The men were drinking something over ice. Grant wore a white polo shirt, jeans, and sandals. His sandy hair had lightened and his skin had darkened in a couple of days courtesy of the California sun. Mace's dark complexion had turned a deep bronze. Stubble smudged his face except above his lip where sufficient hair had grown to be called a mustache. He wore a blue shirt with his sleeves rolled up, exposing the thick muscle of his arms. Gabardine pants covered his tree-trunk legs.

Grant extended his glass toward Decker. "Lemonade. Would you like a glass? Or are you the beer type?"

Beer = unrefined. "Lemonade sounds great, thank you."

"What about you, Neptune?"

"I'm fine, Mr. Kaffey, but thank you."

To Decker, Grant said, "Want a shot of vodka to go with?"

"Not when I'm working."

"Working on Sunday? That's dedication." Grant called a house-keeper and asked for an additional glass of lemonade. "Let's hope it's the real thing and not meant for show. I know you're under pressure."

Decker ignored the bait. "I heard your brother's doing better."

"Doctor says he'll be out in a week—very good news. I suppose you'll be pestering him with questions."

"Can't be dedicated unless you pester."

"Be delicate. He's still in shock. Maybe not the physical shock but . . . you know what I mean."

"I do. Where is he going to be staying?"

"He's going to his house. His ex-boyfriend will be with him as well as a full-time nurse."

"Your brother's ex is Antoine Resseur?"

"Yes. He's a good guy." Grant's eyes turned toward the ocean. "Dr. Rain said he anticipates a full recovery. He just has to be careful until his liver heals. Absolutely no alcohol. That's a bit of a pain."

Decker took out his notepad. "Does Gil drink a lot?"

"Social drinker like me. In fact . . ." Grant went over to a cabinet and added a shot of Bombay Sapphire to the lemonade. "You only live once."

A uniformed maid came in and gave Decker a glass of lemonade. He thanked her and said to Grant, "I have in my records that Gil lives in the Hollywood Hills."

"Oriole Way. I don't know the address, but it's a split-level, mid-century modern, which tells you nothing because most of the houses were built around that time."

"I'll get the address."

Grant's eyes moistened. "I got a call from the coroner. He said it'll be a few more days before . . ."

"These things take time," Decker said. "I'm sorry."

"Life goes on," Grant said. "We're having a small service tomorrow, and then Mace is heading back east tomorrow evening."

Mace said, "If you need to get hold of me, you can reach me through my secretary. I'll be traveling down the Hudson Valley but in phone contact. Got a lot of work to do." He raised his black eyebrows. "I dread what my desk will look like."

"Troubles?" Decker asked.

"Never troubles," Mace insisted with a smile. "Just issues to be worked out. As much as my heart grieves, someone has to keep an eye on our East Coast operations."

Grant said, "We decided that Mace can handle Greenridge while my brother and I work out the final burial and the details of running the company. I'll stay out here at the helm to calm everyone down."

"Kaffey Industries will go on," Mace said. "The company isn't a one-man operation."

Grant said, "My father was smart enough to delegate a lot of the management to his sons." He looked at Mace. "The three of us."

Decker nodded. "Any estimate on how long you're staying on in California?"

"I need Gil to be at full capacity, and that may take a while." Grant swirled the ice cubes in his highball glass. "I've decided that the best thing to do is to move my family out here. We'll be staying at Wind Chimes until everything's back on track. This is why I wanted to talk to you, Lieutenant." His eyes met Decker's. "I'd like to know when your people are leaving Coyote Ranch."

"I wish I could tell you. We've got a lot of material to sort through, plus now that Denny Orlando was found buried on the property, things will have to be gone over again." When Grant winced, Decker said, "Is it a problem for you? That my people will be there for a while?"

"It might be soon. For now the estate is being assessed by Dad's lawyers. I don't know the exact contents of the will, but I assume most of my parents' assets will go to Gil and me."

"Do you know that for a fact?" Decker asked.

"I'm reasonably certain that's the case. We'll not only inherit their fortune but a big, fat estate tax bill. Neither Gil nor I want the ranch. We would like to sell it. The money realized from the sale would help defray the estate tax."

"I'll do the best I can, but we don't want to overlook anything that might be crucial in the investigation. I'm sure you understand that."

"How do you know whether something is crucial or not?"

"That's the point, Mr. Kaffey. You never know. That's why we're meticulous."

Silence. Then Grant asked, "How about a guesstimate? A week? A month? A year?"

"Not a year," Decker repeated. "Probably not much more than a month."

Grant said, "As soon as the assets are allocated, the ranch is going up for sale. I've already contacted a real estate agent."

"Actually you can't do anything with the property until we've cleared it, but I'll try to be timely. I'm sure we can work something out even if we're still there."

"As long as you don't get in my way, I'm fine. There are not that many people who can afford a property of such magnitude, especially in this economic climate. If we get a buyer, we're going for it. I don't want anything to scare someone away."

"The murders were publicized. Any buyer who wants Coyote Ranch would know what went on."

"Still, there's no sense in being obvious."

"I'll try to be timely," Decker reiterated.

But Grant didn't appear to hear him. "On the other hand, the murders may attract other kinds of buyers. Lots of ghouls out there. You wouldn't believe the phone calls that have been screened by my secretaries. We're hounded by the press! All of them want details:

about the crime, about Gil's progress, about our business, about Mom and Dad's will for God's sakes. What is wrong with this world!"

Decker shrugged. "We're living in a time of instant everything, courtesy of the electronic highway. It creates a community of toddlers. When they don't get immediate gratification, they get petulant and sulky."

"Amen to that," Grant agreed.

The man didn't realize that Decker's pointed comments had included him in the petulant and sulky category. That was probably a good thing.

DRIVING NORTHWARD TOWARD L.A., Decker was happy that Rina was in a talkative mood, telling him about the paintings she saw and liked, what she might want to trade, and how much she thought they could get for some of their premium artworks. Even Decker raised an eyebrow. "Maybe it'll cover a year's tuition at college for Hannah."

"Stop pleading poverty, Lieutenant, we're doing fine. How did your day go?"

"It went as anticipated. Nothing illuminating, but I didn't come down with expectations."

"So why did you come down?"

"To be on the open road with you."

"That's very sweet." She leaned over and gave Decker a kiss. "I had a good time. I'm sorry it didn't go well."

"It's not that." He thought a moment. "You don't talk to these guys with the idea of getting a confession. And I certainly didn't get that."

Rina studied his face. "You look bothered."

"I need to interview Mace Kaffey alone, but he's leaving tomorrow night for home, which is back east. I've got to be quick. I should have arranged something, but I didn't want to do it in front of Grant."

Decker recounted his interview of the previous night with Milfred Connors. He also went on to explain all the embezzling charges leveled against Mace, the lawsuit between the brothers and how everything was eventually settled, but with Mace Kaffey getting demoted.

"It's a movie starring Mace as Robin Hood," Rina said. "Stealing from the rich to give to the poor."

"And taking a little for himself," Decker said.

"And that's what caused the lawsuit between the brothers?"

"I'm still not sure about that," Decker said. "This is the problem. Connors claims that he wrote phony checks for about two hundred grand, and Mace returned around one hundred and twenty grand. That leaves eighty grand in Mace's pocket. It's a lot of buckaroos, but it's a far cry from five million."

"But it's not eighty grand, Peter, it's two hundred grand."

"Yeah, you're right. But even if Mace did the same thing with every accountant there, it would be maximum four million, not five. And honestly I doubt that Mace pulled the same stunt with everyone in accounting."

"So what are you thinking?"

"That Mace was telling the truth when he said that Guy also skimmed off the top. When the IRS opened the books, Guy was just as vulnerable as Mace." Decker paused. "I'm just wondering if the entire lawsuit was a screen."

"What do you mean?"

"It was primarily Guy's business. What if he was doing the majority of the skimming and he got caught, owing a big fat bill to the IRS plus fines and jail time? I could see Guy promising Mace something if Mace would take the heat for the embezzlement."

"But Mace didn't take the heat. You just told me that the case was settled between the brothers, with the IRS, and then Mace was demoted big time."

"Making Mace look guilty."

"He was guilty," Rina said.

"But maybe not as guilty as Guy. Think of it, Rina. Mace is accused of embezzling yet Guy keeps him on and transfers him to the

East Coast and gives him Greenridge, one of the biggest projects ever handled by Kaffey Industries. Is that really a demotion?"

"Isn't Grant in charge of Greenridge?"

"He was, but with Guy Kaffey gone, Grant is here and Mace is handling Greenridge all alone."

"You're saying that Mace killed his brother and his sister-in-law and tried to kill his nephew so he could be put in charge of Greenridge?"

"What if Guy was going to pull the plug on Greenridge. Where would that leave Mace?"

"Except that if Mace took the fall for Guy, then that would imply that Mace had dirt on his brother. Then why would Guy deliberately rile up Mace?"

"I don't have the answers, just the questions." Rina laughed and so did Decker. "Lots of questions, and no leads except for Harriman's eavesdropping. I'll check out the guys you IDed. But even if one of them took part in the murders, I'm sure he was just a hired hand."

"You think Mace set everything up?"

"I don't know, Rina. You always look at the family and who has what to gain. Mace may have gotten Greenridge for helping out Guy with his IRS problems, but if the parents die, it's the sons who will inherit. Grant is already talking about selling the ranch to pay estate taxes. They're still number one on my list."

"But Gil was seriously shot. How could you suspect him?"

"True. The bullet took out some of his liver and that's a nasty injury. But he didn't die, whereas the others were slaughtered. Even if what Harriman said is true, that José ran out of bullets, there had to be someone else there with a spare piece of lead to shoot into Gil's brain. What if Gil set himself up to look innocent and the shooter accidentally nicked a vital organ?"

Rina said, "I've seen that on *Forensic Files*. How common is that?"

"Not common, but I've seen it before. So why did I come down besides wanting to be with you?" He thought a moment. "It's this way. You never let up. You don't badger anyone, but you keep coming back. A phone call, a surprise visit, an e-mail, one more question. If you do it long enough to someone who's involved, you start making the guilty party antsy. The person makes a phone call or two. The person starts receiving a phone call or two. People act impulsively and things get flushed out. Big cases like this one . . . you almost never start at the top dog even if the top dog is guilty."

"Too many layers of protection."

"Exactly," Decker said. "You start with the lowlifes who did the shooting. It's easier to get a bead on them because they're almost always involved in something illegal. You pull them in for drugs and then you bring up the murder. Next thing you know, someone starts rolling and you slowly work your way up until you get to the top." A pause. "If they're involved. It could be that they're innocent."

"I'm not putting your statement in the paper," Rina said. "You don't have to qualify yourself."

Decker laughed. "Force of habit." They drove for a while in silence. "You know, I keep saying that the boys stand to inherit. As of right now, that's not a forgone conclusion. The will hasn't been executed yet."

"So the sons really don't know what they have."

"Correct. But Grant seemed sure that Gil and he are set to get almost everything. Maybe Guy had a talk with his sons a long time ago and told his kids that they were set to inherit everything. Or maybe Grant just assumed . . . that's what he said. He assumed that his parents left he and his brother most everything. You know what they say about 'assume,' don't you?"

"Yes. It makes an 'ass' out of 'u' and 'me.'"

"Exactly."

"So what happens if Grant is wrong about the will?"

"I think he'll be sorely disappointed."

"That could get interesting."

"Interesting is good. Lots of things happen when the case gets that kind of interesting."

SEVENTEEN

DECKER BROUGHT IN two platters of home-baked cookies. Oliver complemented the sugar rush with two dozen doughnuts. Messing and Brubeck toted in two bags filled with fresh bagels and cream cheese, and Wynona Pratt graced the table with an assorted fruit platter. Lee Wang's addition was orange juice with plastic cups, and Marge and Wanda were responsible for the paper products and the coffee. By the time the table was set, it looked like breakfast for a corporate retreat.

The spontaneous potluck had been the collective brainwork of Marge, Wynona, and Wanda. They made the assignments and the phone calls because they knew that no guy would ever organize something so froufrou. Their idea of participating would be to eat. But the women were insistent.

"Camaraderie," Marge told Oliver as they set their goodies on the paper-cloth-covered table.

"I had to go ten blocks out of my way to find a doughnut shop."

"There's a doughnut shop three blocks from here. Next time use the Internet."

"There's something wrong with my computer. It keeps freezing."

"I have no answer. Ask Lee."

Wang was busy compulsively arranging the forks, knives, and spoons. Every time something got a millimeter out of alignment, he went back to the beginning.

Oliver said, "Why is my computer freezing all the time?"

"Because it's probably a piece of shit or it's old or maybe both."

Wynona said, "Your utensil design, Lee, although breathtaking in its compulsivity, is taking up too much room." She scooped up the spoons and put them into a cup, repeated it for the forks and knives.

Wang was perturbed. "Anything else that doesn't meet your standards?"

"No. And don't look so pissed. Now you have room for your origami napkin folding."

"First of all, that's Japanese and I'm from Hong Kong. Second, being compulsive is an excellent trait in our line of business."

"If I've offended, I apologize. Just trying to fit everything on a card table."

Brubeck dumped the bagels on a plastic platter. "Coulda fit easily if we didn't buy so much. We got enough for the entire squad room."

"That was the idea," Wynona answered. "To include everyone."

"Can't be looking too elitist," Wanda added.

Marge brought over an urn of coffee and made the announcement to everyone's delight. "Breakfast is served."

Thirty detectives crowded around the table and began to pile food on thin paper plates that began to sag under the weight. At eight-thirty Decker came out of his office, cup of coffee in hand. He said, "Kaffey task force meeting in ten minutes, interview room number three." He met Marge's eye and beckoned her over with a wiggling index finger. This morning she wore a blue sweater set and navy pants with flat rubber-soled shoes on her feet. "How's it going, Rabbi?" she asked him.

"I need to talk about something personal. You have a minute?"

"Yeah, sure." After Decker closed his office door, she said, "Is everything okay?"

"Everything's fine." He smiled at Marge to prove it. "Remember Brett Harriman—the blind guy who overheard two men talking about the Kaffey murders?"

"It was three days ago, Pete. I'm not senile yet. What's going on?"

"After I spoke to him on Friday, he called me late in the evening to tell me he remembered something." Decker tried not to pucker his lips. "He recalled speaking to a woman next to him, asking her to describe the men to him."

"Really?"

"It gets better. The woman didn't want to do that until she found out why he wanted to know. The upshot was that he felt silly and told her to forget about it. When I asked Harriman the woman's name, he said he didn't know it."

"So he has no idea who he talked to?"

"Not quite. He recognized the woman's voice from a voir dire on one of the cases he'd been working on."

"Did he tell you the case?"

"No, but he didn't have to." Decker finished his coffee. "At a voir dire, one of the standard questions asks the prospective juror if any member of the juror's family is involved in law enforcement. Harriman remembers this woman saying that she was married to a police lieutenant."

Marge's eyes got wide. "Wasn't Rina on jury duty last week?"

Decker nodded.

Marge looked at the ceiling. "Did you talk to her?"

"I did. I tried to convince her that she had nothing to offer me, but she insisted on coming down and looking through some mug books. Since she seems to recall an XII or a BXII as one of the tattoos these men were sporting, I gave her a book of the Bodega 12th Street gang."

"Oh my goodness. That is serious." Marge licked her lips. "It's also consistent with what Gil thought he saw."

"I realize that." Decker grimaced. "She picked out a couple of individuals. If you have a free moment, maybe Oliver and you can find these guys and see if you can nail their asses on something legit. Then I'll ask Harriman to come down and see if their voices match the guys he heard in the courtroom."

Marge rubbed her hands. "Can we arrest someone based on a voice identification?"

"I don't know, but we can certainly ask about the crimes. If you pick either of them up for . . . let's say drug dealing . . . maybe we can use those charges as leverage to find out what he knows about the Kaffey murders."

"And are we sure that Harriman can pick out the correct individual just from hearing his voice again?"

"No, which is why I'm going to set him up with a couple of stooges. Harriman said the accents pointed to someone from Mexico and someone from El Salvador. I'll voice print a couple of guys here who come from Mexico and El Salvador. If Harriman picks them out, then we'll know he's not reliable as a voice witness. That way, if you arrest either of Rina's guys from the mug book, we'll have a control group already in place."

"I'll talk to Oliver. We'll work something out."

"We've also got to find Joe Pine. He lives in Pacoima."

"I know that. We can't find him."

"His family may be from Mexico so maybe he's there. Try the name José Pinon. Work on this even if it means overtime. I'm sorry, but this case is just too important for a nine-to-five stint."

"Don't worry about it. Vega's not home anymore, and Oliver isn't the stud he used to be. We both have some empty slots on our calendars. You know how it is. Sometimes a night of surveillance is better than a night home alone with nothing but the idiot box for company."

AFTER BEING FED and caffeinated, the group looked sharp. Decker started by recapping the interview that he and Willy Brubeck had with Milfred Connors. "Before we get into the lawsuit between the brothers, I'd like to know about the financials now. Lee, why don't you start?"

Wang paged through his notes. "Kaffey Industries has current book value of around 600 million dollars, down from its high at 1.1 billion at the height of the real estate boom. It was delisted from the New York Stock Exchange about five years ago when the family bought back the outstanding shares."

"Around the time of the brothers' lawsuit," Brubeck noted.

"Makes sense," Wang said. "From my reading, I got the feeling that Guy didn't want anyone peeking into the books. He had made statements in magazines, saying we're now doing it our way and we no longer give a damn about anyone else's opinion."

"Who in the family holds what?" Marge asked.

"Guy has 80 percent of common stock, each son has 9.5 percent, and Mace has 1 percent."

"So Guy controlled everything," Oliver said.

"It was his baby and he was always in control."

Drew Messing broke in. The southern boy's hair was slightly mussed up, his suit just shabby enough to give him that TV detective's contrived down-and-out but handsome look. "I'd like to point out from *my* reading that Guy was one feisty fellow. His sudden outbursts were legendary. He blew up at anyone who he felt was disrespecting him. I found this article on the Web where Guy got into an altercation with a parking valet that resulted in fistfights. There was a lawsuit, but it was settled."

Oliver said, "You have copies of that?"

"I'll make you a copy."

"What about blowups within the company?"

"Didn't find anything that came to blows, but he certainly screamed a lot," Messing said. "On the flip side, he was the darling of the charities. He gave away millions to all sorts of charities."

"Including ones that rehabilitated gang members," Decker pointed out. "The man had odd tastes in alms."

Wynona said, "Is it just me or does anyone else find it interesting that Mace still has 1 percent of the stock? You'd think he wouldn't get anything if Guy seriously thought he was embezzling from the company."

"My thoughts exactly," Decker said. "I'm sure Mace was embezzling, but I bet Guy wasn't squeaky clean either."

Wang checked his notes. "When the company first went public, Guy had 56 percent of the shares with the rest of the 20 percent shared equally between his sons and Mace and the rest sold in common stock. Then there was the lawsuit. Guy accused Mace of embezzling funds. Mace countered by saying that Guy had made some poor investments and was trying to hide his screwups by pinning the company's downturn on him."

Lee paused.

"No mention of Mace saying that Guy embezzled, but it certainly appears that both had something to hide because they settled and were still working together."

"But Mace was demoted," Brubeck pointed out.

"True," Wang said. "Mace resigned from the board of directors and agreed to give Guy 5.33 percent of his stock in exchange for the suit being dropped. But Mace also retained his current salary and was given the title of executive vice president. He was also allowed to be present at all the board meetings even if he wasn't part of the board."

Decker said, "Mace lost the most, but not everything. Maybe Connors was right. Maybe Guy was embezzling also."

Oliver said, "Is the company in trouble?"

"They're not public so it's hard to get information," Wang said. "They're property heavy. In this downturn, that's not a good thing. And I've read that their cash flow is extremely tight because of the Greenridge Project. Mace and Grant were hoping to get a new influx of money by raising some municipal bonds—some redevelopment agency. The problem is that in order to get a decent credit rating, the bonds have to be backed by something tangible. With land and property values plummeting, there have been some innuendos that their assets aren't enough to carry the size of the debt.

So either they have to raise the interest rate or shrink back the offering."

"Meaning the Greenridge Project is in danger?" Brubeck said.

Wang said, "Some say it's better to finish up the project, others say cut the losses and sell the land. Plus they've had to make a lot of concessions to win over the naysayers. Every time that happens, it's money taken out of the profit till."

Decker asked, "What's the bottom line?"

"It's hard to put a bottom line, Lieutenant. Kaffey's doing well in some areas, but Greenridge is taking a bite out of the profits. Whether it'll ultimately be a boon or a boondoggle, who knows?"

"What about Cyclone Inc.?" Marge asked. "Mace made a point of telling the lieutenant and me that the CEO—Paul Pritchard—was out to get him."

"He's very small time compared to Kaffey," Wang said. "His competing mall—Percivil—is old and downscale, with stores like Bizmart and Dollars and Sense. It's about five miles from Greenridge and while it's true that Greenridge would have an impact on that mall, it certainly wouldn't be in the same class."

Decker said, "So the rivalry might be a convenient invention on Mace's part."

Wang said, "Maybe, but maybe not. I found an article quoting Pritchard, who says that the Greenridge Project was overkill. He went on to say that he wasn't worried. To me that means he is worried. I haven't connected with him yet, but I'll keep at it."

"I'm still back at the brothers' suing each other," Brubeck said. "Any way to find out what was in the court documents?"

"Not officially, but there are often unnamed sources who leak out information," Wang said. "If we're looking for someone who held a grudge against Guy, I guess Mace is as good as anyone. But Mace is still with the company. Something happened behind the scenes."

"Both of them were taking money off the top," Oliver said.

"At least Mace was giving some of it back to his employees," Brubeck added. "If Connors is believable."

"Connors definitely had a warm spot in his heart for Mace," Decker said. "While I'm sure Mace likes his money, I bet he also enjoyed being the darling to the employees."

"Yeah, didn't Connors say that he went to Mace because he had a soft spot that Guy didn't have?"

"Or maybe Mace was biding his time," Oliver said. "Nursing a grudge can be fun stuff."

"That's always a possibility," Messing said.

"What about the sons?" Wanda Bontemps asked. "Any sense of rivalry between the sons and the dad?"

"Nothing overt," Wang said.

Marge said, "From your reading, does it appear that Mace would lose the most if Guy put a stop on Greenridge?"

"I wouldn't say that," Wang told him. "Grant is in charge of the project. If it folds, he'll have egg on his face."

"How are Mace's personal finances?" Wynona asked.

Wang said, "He owns a house in Connecticut, a pied-à-terre in Manhattan, and a fifty-foot yacht; and he has money in the bank. Estimates put him at around thirty million dollars, but that was before the economy tanked. He's doing fine, but he isn't a billionaire."

Decker said, "Which brings us to a very good point. We're focusing on Mace, but it's Guy's sons who will probably inherit. Six hundred million buys a lot of motive. Mace is a slimy guy, but let's not lose sight of who really stands to benefit from Guy's death."

"I'll see what I can dig up on the boys," Wang said.

"Good idea," Decker said. "What's happening with our guard list?"

Brubeck spoke up. "Drew and I have cleared about half of them. Going alphabetically: Allen, Armstrong, Beltran, Cortez, Cruces, Dabby, Green, Howard, Lanz, Littleman, Mendosa, and Nunez. Alfonso Lanz, Evan Teasdale, and Denny Orlando were the three guards on duty who were slain. Rondo Martin is still missing."

"And you've rechecked all of the alibis?"

"Gone through it once, but I'll do it again," Brubeck said. "Rondo Martin's a cipher. I called up the Ponceville Sheriff's Department.

From what I was told, he was a decent deputy sheriff. He wasn't real social, but he'd drink a round with the guys and the locals now and then. He could be pretty hard on some of the farmers if the mood hit, but mostly he'd look the other way."

"By looking the other way, you mean illegals?"

"It happens."

"Any indication of shaking down farmers?" Decker asked.

"You never know. My father-in-law never had any problems with him, but you can't say things over the phone. I'd get more out of him if I talked to him in person."

"I'll get the funds for you, Willy. When could you leave?"

Brubeck winced. "I was supposed to get a few days off for the missus and me for our anniversary. I think I told you about it when you asked me to join the task force."

"You did," Decker said. "I forgot."

"I wouldn't care about canceling, Lieutenant, but I booked this Mexican resort about six months ago. I'll lose my deposit."

"Don't cancel, Willy, it's fine." Decker looked at Marge. "Can you go tomorrow?"

"Sure." Marge paused. "Unless you have another thing you want me to do."

That's right. He has asked her to spy on Rina's two IDs from the mug books. He was throwing out feelers in so many directions, he was losing track. "Nothing that can't wait a day or two." He regarded Oliver. "You go with her."

"Where is Ponceville?"

Brubeck said, "You fly into Sacramento and it's about two hours from there."

"Don't tell me." Oliver made a face. "You take Southwest."

"They still give you free peanuts," Brubeck said. "I'll set everything up with my father-in-law. You might even get more outta him than I would. He has a great deal of respect for the police if it ain't me he's talking to." To Decker—"Are you sure it's okay if I go?"

"As a matter of fact, Willy, I have an assignment for you south of the border. Rumor has it that one of the guards, Joe Pine going as

José Pinon, may be hiding out in Mexico." He brought the detective up to date on his conversation with Brett Harriman.

"We haven't cleared Joe, so he could be involved," Messing said. "He doesn't have a record as far as we could tell."

"He's a local boy from Pacoima. Call up Foothill Juvenile and ask someone if he's ever been in trouble. We could use a set of his prints." Decker looked at Marge and Oliver. "Rondo Martin was a sheriff. Surely we could get a set of his prints."

"I've called T in Ponceville," Brubeck said. "He can't seem to find Martin's print card."

"You're kidding," Decker said.

"Things move very slowly up there. I'm beginning to doubt if T ever printed him."

Decker threw up his hands. "Ask him again, Willy. And while you're in Mexico, try to make contact with the local law. See if they know anything about José Pinon."

"As long as someone here has my back. Mexican jails make me nervous."

Decker said, "Stay in contact and we'll keep tabs on you." He spoke to Marge and Oliver. "While you're up north, swing by Oakland and get a little background on Neptune Brady. He was in Oakland with his dad when the murders happened, but that doesn't mean he wasn't involved."

"What would he gain by killing his boss?" Wanda asked.

"I don't know. But I do find it odd that Mace and especially Grant is keeping Brady on as a bodyguard. If my parents were murdered under someone's watch, he'd be the last one I'd want guarding me."

"How far is Oakland from Sacramento?" Oliver asked.

"An hour's drive," Brubeck told him.

"You can leave from Oakland Airport—Southwest. Moving on, I had a nice little chat with Riley Karns yesterday." He summarized their conversation. "He said he was sleeping when the murders occurred. That means he was also sleeping when the horse grave was dug and Denny Orlando was thrown into the pit. We don't know if he's being truthful or not. What we do know is that he was on the property the night of the murders and he knew about the horse grave. Two strikes against him." He turned to Drew Messing. "While your partner is in sunny Mexico trying to find José Pinon, you dig into Karns. I think Gilliam Kaffey hired him from one of her horse clubs, so start there. Also, see if you can't talk him into a polygraph test."

"Why would Karns want Guy and Gilliam dead?" Messing asked.

Decker shrugged. "Maybe someone bought his silence. Find that motive and we'll have three strikes against him. Who's been checking up on Ana Mendez and Paco Albanez?"

Marge raised her hand. "Her story checks out. So does the time frame. So far as I can tell, she wasn't involved with any crazies. Paco Albanez—like Riley Karns—claims he was sleeping until Ana woke him up. But if he knew about the horse grave, maybe he should be interviewed again in Spanish."

"I'll do it," Decker said.

"What's happening with the surviving son?" Wynona asked.

"Gil Kaffey is doing fine and might even come home in a few days. His ex-boyfriend, Antoine Resseur, is going to move in with him until he's fully recovered. I think Grant has hired a nurse to look after him as well."

Oliver grimaced. "If I were Gil, I'd move far away and surround myself with my own personal bodyguards."

"Come to think of it," Decker said, "Grant and Mace didn't mention any bodyguards."

"Maybe they plan on using Neptune Brady for the job."

The room fell silent. Decker verbalized what everyone else was thinking.

Having Brady guard Gil was like the fox guarding the henhouse.

EIGHTEEN

THE RANCH WAS a contrast between nature and nurture. The back area was raw land with high desert chaparral, sage, cactus and other wild succulents, and a lot of dirt and gravel. The acreage in front had been controlled and manipulated, turned into garden rooms with towering trees, fountains, flowers, herbs, and beds of roses, their colors glistening in the noonday sun.

As Decker twisted through the driveway, he spotted a man stooped over yellow and orange marigolds set into emerald boxwood squares. He wore a long-sleeved khaki uniform and a big floppy hat tied under his chin. Decker pulled the car over and parked, leaving just enough room for any other vehicles to pass around his unmarked. He got out and walked through a knot garden. The area was in full sun, and the afternoon heat was relentless.

Paco Albanez turned when he heard shoes scruff against the loose rock and when he saw Decker, he slowly unfolded upward, his left gloved hand grabbing his hip as he arched his spine backward. His face was tanned and lined. He dropped his hands to his sides as Decker came closer and gave him the courtesy of a nod.

"*Buenas tardes,*" Decker said. "*Está caliente hoy.*"

"*El verano es caliente.*"

"*Verdad.*" When Decker told him how beautiful the flowers looked, Albanez smiled. Beyond that, the face remained a cipher. "If you have a moment, I'd like to talk to you about the other night," Decker told him in Spanish.

Albanez wiped his damp forehead with the back of his glove, leaving a streak of dirt. Dark eyes looked down at his shoes. "I have nothing new to say."

Decker slipped out his notebook. "Just need a few more details."

Albanez's gaze fell somewhere over Decker's shoulder. "I'm trying to forget the details." He bent down and pulled out a weed. "Terrible to remember."

"Could you just"—Decker swatted a fly from his face—"go over that night one more time?" When Paco was silent, Decker said, "Maybe it's time for a break. Someplace with shade possibly?"

With reluctance, Albanez left his post and took Decker into a glade of *Agonis* trees, where there were several stone benches. Decker sat on one side and the groundskeeper took up the other. He stared straight ahead, his face sweating profusely.

Decker said, "Just go over the night one more time."

Albanez's recitation was mechanical. Señor Riley woke him up. It must have been around two in the morning and Señor Riley was very upset. He couldn't understand Señor Riley because he was talking too fast. Finally, Paco realized that something happened to Señor and Señora Kaffey. Señor Riley took him back to his bungalow. Ana was already there, crying and shaking. She told him what happened, that Señor and Señora Kaffey were dead. There was blood was everywhere . . . that it was horrible. The two of them waited in Señor Riley's bungalow until he came back with the police. Then the police took them into the main house and separated them.

The smell was horrible inside. Several times, he had to go back outside to get some fresh air. He wanted to go back to his bungalow, but the policeman told him to wait until the boss came.

"Then you came and talked to me and finally I get to go back to my house."

His memory squared with Ana's account. Still, Decker didn't quite get why Ana went to Riley's bungalow before she went to see Paco. Although it was true that Riley's place was closer than Paco's, Decker had seen the physical layout. The two bungalows weren't all that far apart and because Ana was primarily Spanish speaking, Decker would have thought that she would have taken the extra steps.

Then again, the woman was panicked.

Paco's recitation had turned him a shade paler. Decker said, "Did you know that Gil Kaffey was still alive?"

"No." Albanez licked his lips.

Decker looked him in the eye. "What do you think happened?"

"Me?" Deep furrows sat between his eyes as he wrinkled his forehead. "I don't know. It was horrible."

"Why do you think Gil wasn't killed?"

"*Suerte.*"

Luck.

"Has anyone talked to you about the future of your job?" When Paco shook his head no, Decker said, "You're still working here."

"The garden still grows."

"Who is paying you?"

His eyes narrowed. "Señor Gil will pay me."

"How do you know? Did he tell you he'd pay you?"

"No, but he is alive." His voice was resolute. "He will pay me to keep the garden."

"How do you know he won't sell the ranch?"

Albanez looked confused. "Why would he do that?"

"For money."

"Then what about his plans?"

Decker hoped he kept his face flat and his voice casual. "Tell me about the plans."

"Growing the grapes for the winery. It is why Señor Kaffey bought the land. He and Señor Gil have been working on it for over a year. They draw many designs. I've seen them."

Keep your voice calm. "They wanted to build a *winery*?"

"Yes. Señor Gil and Señor Kaffey talk a lot about wine."

Decker thought of Grant Kaffey, about how anxious he was to sell the ranch to help pay estate taxes. He said, "I heard that the ranch was going up for sale."

Albanez looked at the ground. "If so, I will find work somewhere else."

"Do you think now that Señor Kaffey is gone, that Señor Gil will continue with the plans?" All Decker got was a shrug of the shoulders. "Was he here a lot? Señor Gil?"

"He was here, yes. But he doesn't live here."

"Do you think that he might want to live here now that Señor Kaffey is gone?"

"I don't know, Señor. To him, it has bad memories."

"But you think he will continue on with the plans?"

"I hope so. I like him very much. I like this job very much." He lowered his head. "I liked Señor Kaffey very much. He had a big mouth, but also a big heart."

"I heard that he often raised his voice. Did he yell at you a lot?"

A small smile played on his lips. "Yes, he yelled. 'Why is this dying? There are too many weeds. Trim this, cut that. You are lazy. You are crazy.'" Another smile. "The next moment, he would give me money for no purpose. Twenty dollars every time he yelled. One time he gave me a hundred-dollar bill. He'd say, 'Here, Paco. Take out a girl for a nice dinner.'"

"What about Señora Kaffey?"

"We speak very little. She only talks to say, 'plant zinnias or plant cosmos or plant tulips.' But she wasn't a mean woman. She loved her horses and her dogs. I take her dogs in the back for exercise when Señor Riley was too busy. She talks a lot to Señor Riley. And she always served lemonade and cookies at four in the afternoon for everyone. Very good cookies."

"I want to talk just a moment about Señor Riley." When he didn't get a response, he said, "Did you know that we found one of the guards on the property buried in the horse grave?"

"Yes, I know. You were here digging for many hours."

"Señor Riley dug the hole for the horses, but he said that he had help. Did you help him dig the hole?"

"Yes."

"Anyone else besides you help Señor Riley?"

Again the eyes narrowed, more in concentration than in suspicion. "I think one or two maybe helped. Maybe Bernardo, maybe José."

"Could you give me their last names, please?"

"Bernardo . . . I don't know. José . . . he is Joe Pine. I think he helped us."

"How well did you know Joe Pine?"

"He is young, I am old. I don't know him well."

"But he helped you and Karns dig the horse grave."

Albanez just shrugged. "He says dig here, I dig here. His uniform is clean, mine is dirty."

The underlying message was that Albanez didn't like him. Decker moved on. "Did Señor Gil ever talk to you about the winery?"

"They both talk to me about the winery. They say, 'Paco, you will be busy for years.' But now you say they sell the ranch so maybe not." Albanez got up from the bench. "I need to go back to my work."

"Thank you for talking to me. Did they tell you what kind of grapes they wanted to grow?"

"Chardonnay and cabernet. They have special men come to the ranch to talk to them about it. How to plant the grapes, how to care for the grapes, how to harvest the grapes. That's even before they make the wine."

"Wine making is complicated."

Albanez shrugged and started walking back to the flower beds. Decker said, "Thanks again for taking the time to talk to me."

"It's okay but no more. I don't know who alive is a good person and who is a bad man. If bad person is watching me, I don't want them to know that I talked to the police."

He was correct in his assessment. Still, Decker had a job to do. "I have one more question. You told me that Señor Kaffey bought the ranch to make wine. I was told that he bought the ranch for Señora Kaffey's horses."

There was silence. Then Albanez stopped and regarded the land-scape. "I think, Señor, there is enough room for both."

MARGE GRABBED HIM as soon as he walked into his office. She was kind enough to bring a fresh cup of coffee with her and set it on his desk. The woman knew the best way to a lieutenant's heart was a good, black cup of joe. She shut the door. "I got a fix on one of Rina's IDs. Fredrico Ortez, known as Rico."

"That was fast."

"Computers are wonderful things. Unfortunately, he's in jail and has been for the last three months."

"Cross him off the list. What about the other one? Alejandro Brand?"

"Checked him out as well. No record as an adult. He's nineteen and lives in Pacoima."

"So what was he doing in the mug book?"

"Probably was put in there by CRASH when they did a gang sweep."

"Isn't Joe Pine from Pacoima?"

"Yes, he is. Pine's older than Brand, but not by much. I'll look into him as well."

"Any idea what nationality Brand is?"

"No idea."

"Let's see if we can get something on Brand. Haul him in and have Harriman listen to his voice. Maybe something will click. Before you leave for Ponceville, get hold of Oscar Vitalez. We'll set up a phony interview with Oscar and get Harriman in here to see how he reacts to Vitalez's voice."

"I'll do that today."

"Are you all set for tomorrow's excursion?"

"Yep. Willy took care of everything. My only reservation is flying with Oliver and listening to him kvetch the entire time. What are you up to, Pete?"

"I just got back from Coyote Ranch." He recapped his conversation with Paco Albanez. "I wanted to see if he admitted knowing about the horse grave, and I came away finding out that Guy and Gil were planning to build a winery."

"I thought you said that Grant was planning on selling the ranch."

"That's what Grant told me. Maybe Grant didn't know about Gil's plans."

Marge said, "Or he does know and Gil doesn't want it anymore after what happened."

"Or that Grant is speaking for Gil." Decker paused. "You know Oliver said something interesting at the meeting this morning. About if he were Gil, he'd move away and surround himself with his own bodyguards. The fact that he isn't doing that makes me wonder."

"About what?"

"Shouldn't Gil be more concerned about his safety?"

"Or it could be that he's too out of it to make proper decisions. He's still in the hospital, Pete. Maybe once he gets out, he'll realize that he needs more than a nurse and an ex-boyfriend. Speaking of which, shouldn't we talk to the ex?"

"Already done. His name is Antoine Résseur and we're meeting tonight at eight at his apartment in West Hollywood."

"Why don't you meet at the Abby? I hear the food is terrific."

"Being kosher, it would be wasted on me anyway. By the way, I offered to talk to him at a public place of his choosing, but I suspect that he doesn't want people seeing him talk to the police."

"Or maybe you're not his type."

Decker smiled. "He hasn't seen me yet. How would he know that?"

"There's a stereotype that goes along with being a cop. You may just be too macho for his blood."

"Then he'd be prejudiced," Decker announced. "And that would be too bad for him because he'd never get to know my sensitive side."

NINETEEN

RINA RECOGNIZED THE sunglasses first: chic, dark, expensive. Wearing a blue jacket, khaki pants, and a red tie, Harriman leaned against the wall, eating a power bar, his stance relaxed although his jaw suggested tension, muscles bulging with each chomp. Rina knew the reason why. He was eavesdropping on the same two cholos. Now that she knew what was going on, his actions seemed heroic and reckless at the same time.

It took all of her willpower not to stare at them.

No, that would not be smart.

Instead she blended into one of the nearby crowds. With only around five minutes before the courtrooms opened after lunch, she racked her brain to form a plan, weighing her options. Harriman's face was leaning slightly in the men's direction, and one of them glanced up at him. She thought about going over and leading him away, but that might draw more attention to him than if she just left him alone.

One of the bailiffs was already calling roll for the jury in the courtroom next to hers. She figured she had a couple of minutes left.

At a standstill about what to do with Harriman, she spent the time trying to memorize the men—their size, their features, their distinguishing marks. The tattoos were her best friends—a snake, a tiger, a shark, the B12 and the BXII and XII in Roman script. The smaller man, the one who was doing most of the talking, appeared to have a scar next to his left ear. Without warning, he turned his head, looked upward, and glared at Harriman.

Then he said something to him.

Harriman's face darkened. He spoke a few words, then walked away without exhibiting any nervousness. The smaller man with the scar kept glaring at him, watching Harriman go inside the men's room. Rina's heart started racing when the smaller man got up and headed in the same direction.

But then someone called out the name Alex and the man stopped.

Rina thought to herself: *Alejandro Brand—the guy with the scar.*

Alex, aka small man with snake and tiger tattoos, turned and came toward a man in a wrinkled suit and a comb-over—probably a P.D. The two of them, along with the bigger man whom Alex had been talking to, walked into one of the courtrooms.

She intercepted Harriman just as she heard her own group being called to order by the bailiff. She whispered to the blind man. "You must be careful. He was glowering at you when you went into the bathroom."

Harriman took a half step back. Without missing a beat, he said, "Which one?"

"The shorter one."

"That does me no good. The Mexican or the El Salvadorian?"

"I have no idea. I don't speak Spanish. I think someone called him Alex."

"Then you know more about his identity than I do. You should talk to the police."

"I do on a daily basis. I've got to go. I'm keeping my jury waiting."

"So Decker is your husband?" Harriman said.

"You shouldn't be asking personal questions. But I do know that Lieutenant Decker speaks fluent Spanish. So maybe he can help you out."

"We need to talk."

"No, we don't. If you're needed, Lieutenant Decker will call you." Rina hurried off to her proper line. She wasn't the last one to show up, so technically she didn't hold up anything, but she was late enough and breathing hard enough for Joy to make a wisecrack.

"You look disheveled." She lowered her eyes and stared at Rina. "Just what did *you* do during your lunch break?"

Cheeky girl. "I wish." Rina hoped she was being casual. The case would probably conclude this afternoon and she would never see any of them again anyway. She hoped this would end the conversation, but Ally had been more observant.

"She was talking to Smiling Tom," she remarked.

"You were?" Joy's eyebrows arched. "What were you and Smilin' talking about—again?"

"Since he can't see, he asked me the time." Rina rolled her eyes and tried to act annoyed. "Ah, Chronically Late Kent is here. I think we're ready to go into the courtroom."

Ally asked her, "Do you know him?"

"Who?" Rina asked.

"Mr. Smiles."

"No, I don't know him." She turned to Ally. "Why would I know him?"

"I guess you wouldn't," Ally told her. "Too bad. I thought maybe you can introduce him to me."

"What?" Rina said.

Ally pinkened. "It's hard meeting people these days and I think he's kinda cute."

WHEN DECKER SAW his wife's cell number flash, he picked up immediately. "It's over?"

"It's over."

"Thank God. Did you fry the guy?"

"How do you know it was a guy?"

"Fifty percent chance of being right. More than a 50 percent chance. Most of the defendants are men. I don't really care about the case, but I do care about who hangs around the halls of justice. Did you see them again?"

"Yes, I did."

"Shit! Sorry. Tell me they didn't notice you."

"This time I made myself very scarce. I was well hidden."

"Thank you, Rina, for saying that."

"But there's more. Harriman was eavesdropping again. This time one of the cholos caught on and the two of them exchanged words. Harriman went to the men's room and the cholo started in that direction, but someone called him back before anything happened. Peter, I'm a little concerned."

Decker felt a sour taste ride up in his mouth. "I'll give him a call."

Rina took a deep breath. "The cholo had a scar and a snake tattoo. Someone called him Alex."

As in Alejandro Brand. Decker said, "Thanks."

"I got a better look at both this time. I'd like to look through the books again."

The sour taste turned bitter. What choice did he have? "All right. I'll set something up. When do you think you'll be home?"

"If you wouldn't mind, let's go out for dinner. Hannah is at Aviva's studying for finals so she won't be home. Let's take advantage."

"Great. How about if you go visit your parents and I'll come into the city. I have to meet someone at eight anyway."

"Great idea. Where should we go?"

"As long as I can get a steak, I'll be happy."

"I can arrange that."

"You can even invite your parents. It's been a while."

"That's nice of you."

"I like your parents." He really did. After all these years, he felt there was mutual respect. "And tell your dad that I insist on paying this time."

Rina laughed. "You know he won't let you do that."

"Ah, gee, then," Decker said. "If it makes him happy, I'll let him pick up the check. And if it makes him deliriously joyful, he can even leave the tip."

THE APARTMENT WAS on the border between Hollywood and West Hollywood in a beige French Regency–styled apartment building with blue-patina mansard eaves. The lobby gleamed with mirrors and marble decorated with new brown velvet furniture and black coffee tables. The uniformed doorman directed Decker to a set of brass art deco elevator doors and told him to take it to the seventh floor.

Antoine Resseur had a Christmas lights southern view of L.A. from two picture windows, giving punch to the boxy living room. Red leather sofas complemented bird's-eye maple tables and shelving units. The black granite floors melded into a fireplace hearth. The recess lighting was dim and soft, and there was classical music on the stereo.

Dressed in jeans, a blue oxford button-down shirt, and boat shoes, Resseur was holding a glass of red wine. He was short and slight, with propositional features, dark hair, and hazel eyes that looked like agate marbles. "Can I get you something, Lieutenant?"

"I'm fine, but thanks. I appreciate your talking to me."

Resseur's voice was low and soft. He sat down and pointed for Decker to do the same. "This has been a nightmare."

"You're still close to Gil?"

"We're the best of friends." He took a sip of wine.

"It was very nice of you to offer to look after him."

Resseur looked down. "I'm the only one who Gil trusts right now."

"Not his brother?"

"Grant wasn't shot, was he?" Resseur sighed. "That sounds horrible. Gil's being a little paranoid, I think."

"Once you're shot, there's no such thing as paranoia. Is that what Gil told you? He doesn't trust Grant?"

"What he told me is that he doesn't trust anyone except me."

Decker took out a pen and a notepad. In the back of his mind, he never trusted the hero of the story and that's how Resseur was presenting himself. "How long were you and Gil an item?"

"About six years."

"That's a long time. What broke you two up?"

Resseur swirled the wine in his glass. "Gil was a very busy man. His dad made sure of that. He didn't have a lot of time for personal relationships."

Decker nodded.

"Always busy, busy, busy." Another swirl, then Resseur took a sip. "But things got frenetic once Guy and Mace started suing each other. I thought things would quiet down once the lawsuit was resolved, but it just got crazier."

"How so?"

"Mace was shipped back east, and a huge truckload of work was dumped on Gil. It was terrible for him."

"Could we talk a little about that? Like why Mace was kept in the company when he was caught embezzling funds?"

Resseur rolled his tongue inside his cheek. "How should I say this? There isn't anything about Kaffey Industries that Guy didn't know about."

"Guy *knew* that Mace was embezzling?"

"It's not embezzling if the boss knows about it, is it." A shrug. "That's what rich people do for pocket change . . . dip into the slush fund and why not. It's their money."

"Okay," Decker said. "So why the lawsuit?"

"Kaffey got into trouble with the IRS. Mace took the brunt of the fall. On the surface, it looked like Mace got hammered, but actually he was rewarded by Greenridge." Resseur took a sip of his wine. "I talk too much when I drink."

Decker assured him that the information wouldn't be used against him, but it got him thinking in another direction. Though still high on the list of suspects, Mace dropped from the top spot. "How did Mace and Guy get along?"

Resseur rubbed his chin. "As well as can be expected. Guy had a temper. And Grant's not far behind in that department."

"Have you experienced Grant's temper?"

"Not directly, but I've seen it. Gil is much more even tempered—like Mace. That's why it was hard on him after Mace left. It was just Gil and his father without an intermediary."

"I heard that the two of them were very close."

"If you call working twenty-four/seven with a person close, then the two of were very close."

"Weren't they planning on turning Coyote Ranch into a winery?"

"They were?" Resseur seemed genuinely surprised. "That's a new one, but I've been out of the loop. Good idea though. Gil had a fabulous wine palate. It's certainly a good use of that monstrous place."

"Monstrous?"

"That's not a home. That's a national park."

"You seem to have a lot of insights into the family." Decker put down his notebook. "What do you think happened, Mr. Resseur?"

"Me?" He pointed to his chest. "I don't know."

"But you've thought about it."

"Of course." He went over to his picture window and studied the view. Then he turned and faced Decker. "Nothing too profound. To get through all that security, it must have been an inside job. Isn't one of the security guards missing?"

"Yep. But do you see just one person pulling this off by himself?"

"No, but that's not how it happened. Someone hired thugs to do the murders. Gil remembers seeing people with tattoos before he crumpled and blacked out."

"Any candidates for the mastermind besides Rondo Martin?"

"I'd check out the head of security: Neptune . . . something."

"Neptune Brady. Why do you suspect him?"

"He was supposed to keep Guy and Gilliam safe. And now they're dead."

"Grant is keeping Brady on as a security guard. What do you think about that?"

"That speaks to Grant's stupidity or Gil's paranoia about Grant."

"He really thinks his brother was in on the murders?"

"Gil has said a lot of things. But he's delirious and doped up. His brain is scrambled right now."

"Have you arranged for any type of security once Gil leaves the hospital?"

Resseur tapped a nearby end table. "I've broached the subject. Gil is disinclined to talk about it. He keeps harping on being released because he thinks the doctors are trying to poison him. That's why I can't take his talking against Grant too seriously."

"For the record, Grant told me he thought you were a good guy."

"He said that?" Resseur finished his wine. "That's good to hear. There was always . . . tension whenever I was around Gil's family. Whenever there was a big public party, I always asked my very attractive sister to come along. Not that we were fooling anyone. Gil's mother was always cordial to me, but his father was . . . let's just say uncomfortable."

"Did Guy ever say anything to you about your relationship with Gil?"

"No." Resseur got up and poured himself another glass of wine. "Gil was always very protective. He took care of me, and I was happy to go along with whatever he wanted."

"You didn't feel resentful?"

A forced laugh. "Resentful? Not at all." He attacked his wine again. "What care I if we vacation in Monaco or the Spanish Riviera?"

Decker smiled. "I see your point."

"That's the way it went. Gil told me where we were going so I could either pack my tux or my Speedos. I didn't see the point of making a fuss, especially because my time with Gil was so limited."

He studied his wineglass as if reading tea leaves. "Now it looks like we're going to have lots of time to catch up."

"It sounds like that's okay with you."

Resseur's eyes got teary. "I love Gil. I always have. I'll take what I can get."

TWENTY

I'S HIM." RINA pointed to the mug shot of Alejandro Brand. "This guy is definitely the shorter one who the man called Alex. I recognize the face, but also the tattoos—the snake and the tiger—and the scar. This is definitely the man I saw Harriman with this afternoon."

"Okay." Decker checked his watch. It was almost eleven in the evening and he was tired. But he soldiered on, inspired by Rina's enthusiasm. "Let's see what we're dealing with." He typed the name into his computer, but the machine froze. "The computer's down. It'll keep until morning. Let's go home."

"Would you like me to look for the bigger one? If you give me a little time, I could pick him out."

"Let's call it a night."

Rina's eyes swept the empty station house and landed on her husband's face. Although it had been a long day for her, it had been an even longer day for Peter. She had been caught up in the excitement of discovery. "You're right. I would probably do better anyway if I had some rest."

Decker shut the mug book and helped her on with her sweater.

The two of them left the station house, zooming out of the police parking lot in Decker's Porsche. "After you're done trying to ID man number two, your involvement in the case will be over."

"Don't worry. I'll be happy to bow out. I won't have anything more to add."

"Having just said that . . ." He tapped his fingers on the steering wheel. "I'm going to be a total hypocrite and ask you another question."

"You're not being a hypocrite. You're just wavering between wanting to know versus thinking about my safety. Stop worrying. They didn't see me. I was very careful. The men had already left for the courtroom by the time I got to Harriman."

"What if they had spies?"

"They didn't have *spies,* Peter." Rina softened her voice. "I know that the Bodega 12th Street gang is filled with bad guys, but they're not the CIA. Now what did you want to ask me?"

Decker had lost his train of thought. "Oh yeah. You're sure that Harriman didn't tell you *anything* about the words he exchanged with Alex."

"He didn't say *anything* about the conversation. He did say that we should talk."

"That's not going to happen. Not only do you two have nothing to talk about, if you two did powwow, a clever lawyer could say that you two colluded against the client."

"Good point, Counselor; your law degree did not go to waste." Rina sat back in the seat. "I told him I didn't have anything to say to him. I said if you needed to talk to him, you'd call him."

"Good answer. He doesn't have your phone number, does he?"

"No."

"That's good. The man twangs my antennas."

"Harriman? Why? You can't think he's making it up?"

"No, he's on to something, but why is he putting himself in harm's way by eavesdropping on dangerous guys?"

Rina thought a moment. "Sometimes people jump into situations without realizing the consequences. Harriman has worked for the court system for a while so he's probably been around lots of unsavory people without any problems. Also, he's blind, so he can't pick up on nonverbal cues. And you know the lure of fame. Maybe this is Harriman's one chance to be a star witness instead of a drone translator."

MAKING FREQUENT TRIPS from L.A. to Santa Barbara, Marge often passed through miles of rural farms in Oxnard and Ventura, endless acreage of green grids featuring just about everything in the salad alphabet, from artichoke to zucchini. Along the roadways were fruit and vegetable stands advertising recently picked organic produce and locally grown flowers. Many times, Marge would arrive at her boyfriend's place with bags of heirloom tomatoes, red carrots, candy stripe beets, red onion scallions, and a sack of microgreens.

But within a few minutes of driving the rental car from the airport parking lot into the town, Marge realized that Ponceville didn't grow for the "farmers' market" clientele. This place was stone-cold agribusiness with acres upon acres of commercial plots fenced and confined with NO TRESPASSING signs. No cute roadside stands here. Instead she and Oliver traversed fields and groves of crops and cultivation. There were canopies of avocado shading unripe citrus, the silver-green leaves of olive trees, rows of stone fruit trees—apricots, peaches, plums, and nectarines. The area had patchwork quilts of vegetables, and with each one she passed, a different sensation would tickle her nose: cilantro, jalapeños, onions, green peppers.

Street signs were next to impossible to find, and there were no distinguishing landmarks other than a barn here and a plow there. She and Oliver rode on two-lane asphalt streets surrounded by the breadbasket of America, trying to follow Willy Brubeck's arcane directions to his father-in-law's farm. The rental had come with a broken GPS and after a half hour, it was clear that they were lost.

"We could call up and ask for help," Marge suggested.

"We could," Oliver answered, "but I have no idea where we are."

Marge pulled the car onto the shoulder of the street. "Call him up and tell him we're at the corner of cantaloupes and habañeros."

Oliver smiled. "Give me the number."

Marge recited the digits and Oliver punched them in. "In case his wife answers, her name is Gladys."

"Got it . . . Yes, hello, I'm Detective Scott Oliver from the Los Angeles Police Department and I'm calling for Marcus Merry . . . Yes, exactly. How are you, ma'am? Your husband was gracious enough to see us today and . . . Yes, we are lost. We're at the corner of two fields. One has cantaloupes and the other has habañeros if that helps . . . Oh, it does . . . He doesn't have to do that . . . Yes, it probably would be very helpful. Yes, thank you. Bye." He turned to Marge. "The old man's coming down to fetch us. She's got a little something for us to eat when we get there."

"That probably means a big spread in farmer language."

"That's all right by me. I didn't eat any breakfast. Man, I didn't even get my coffee this morning."

"Yeah, the airline was pretty skimpy with the food and drink."

"What food and drink? By the time the beverage cart came to us, all they had left were water and peanuts. I felt like a damn blue jay. Man, even *prison* does a better job of feeding its people."

"If you like starch and sugar."

"Those penitentiary wardens ain't no dummies. All that starch and sugar puts their charges in diabetic comas. They, unlike the airlines, know how to keep the masses happy."

THEY SAT IN the living room on chintz-covered chairs, the area painted a cheery lemon yellow. The floors were knotted pine, and the walls held dozens of family photos—black and white as well as color—along with a good-sized canvas of dripping abstract art that looked completely out of place.

A little something to eat included ham, cheese, fresh fruit, sliced cucumbers, tomatoes, onions, avocados, and a variety of dark and whole wheat breads. Mustard was served in a yellow crockery dish.

At first, Oliver tried to be polite, but when Marcus Merry made himself one honking sandwich, Scott let his stomach do the talking.

Willy Brubeck's father-in-law could have been anywhere between midseventies and midnineties. He was stout with white kinky hair and pale mocha skin. He had on a denim work shirt, overalls, and rubber-soled boots. His hands and nails had been scrubbed clean.

Gladys seemed pleased by everyone's appetite. "I have some cake."

Marcus's wife was petite with gray kinky hair cut close to her scalp. She had round brown eyes and a round face. Gamine-like, she could have been a tanned older version of Audrey Hepburn. She wore jeans with a white shirt tucked into her pants and white tennis shoes, and there were small diamond studs twinkling from her earlobes.

Marge said, "Honestly, Mrs. Merry, this is just terrific."

"So cake will make it even more terrific. You two go ahead and do your talking with Marcus. I'll get the cake."

"I don't need cake," Marcus complained. "I'm fat enough as it is."

"Then don't eat it."

Discussion over.

Marge said, "Have you always been a farmer, Mr. Merry?"

"It's Marcus, and the answer is yes. I can trace my relatives way, way back." He spoke with a combination of southern drawl and black patois. "The name Merry comes from my great-granddaddy's owner. After he was emancipated, Colonel Merry gave him fifty dollars and his name." Merry took another bite of his sandwich. "I think the colonel must have been my great-great-granddaddy. You see how light we are."

Marge nodded.

"Comes from both sides. My daughter . . . Willy's wife . . . everyone wanted to marry her. She was a real beauty . . . like my wife. Damn, I miss that girl. Willy ain't so bad, either. Don't tell him I said that."

He laughed.

"It was my grandfather who picked up stakes and decided to come to California from Georgia. Back then, the state was filled with all different kinds of people: Mexicans, Chinese, Japanese, Indians . . . a couple of extra black men didn't bother no one too much. Later on when Dr. King started talking about a dream . . . that's when the tension started."

"Is there still tension around here?" Oliver asked.

"No, sir. We do our job and mind our own business. Now we even got a black man in the White House." He waved his hand dismissively. "Why am I telling *you* this? You see tension all the time." A pause. "Willy tells me his area don't have much crime."

Marge said, "Not too bad."

"Well, then that's good." Merry took another enormous bite. "No sense having my boy in danger. Don't tell him I said that, either."

"Your secret is safe with me," Marge told him. "So how did your daughter meet Willy?"

"At church."

"Willy isn't from around here," Oliver said.

"No, but he served in Vietnam with a boy who grew up about three farms to the north of here. Willy came out for a visit and I was impressed that he bothered going to church." He shook his head in fatherly consternation.

"What happened to Willy's friend who grew up on the farm?" Oliver asked.

"Oh, he went back to his roots. He grows corn and is making money off biofuel. Me, I don't grow crops for no cars. I grow crops for people." Another bite. "Is that cake comin'?" he shouted out loud.

"Just hold your socks!" When Gladys came in with the cake, everyone oohed and aahed. It was chocolate with chocolate frosting and several layers of fresh berries in between. When she handed Oliver a slice, he noticed he was salivating heavily.

"Thank you so much."

"You're very welcome. And I'll give you both a slice to take home. He certainly don't need the whole thing."

"If you don't want me to eat it, why do you bake it?" Marcus asked his wife.

"I do it as an artistic project," Gladys countered.

"Then donate it to a museum." He finished his slice in four bites. "I know you came here to talk to the sheriff. He won't be able to see us for another half hour. In the meantime, you can watch us bicker."

"Oh, you're so silly." She gave him a gentle slap on the shoulder. "Coffee?"

"I'll have some," Marcus said.

"I'm making up a fresh pot." She went back into the kitchen.

Marge said, "How well did you know Rondo Martin?"

"Or did you even know him?" Oliver added.

"I knew who he was. Can't say I knew him well. Did I ever have any business with him? Is that what you're asking me?"

"Just anything you can tell us about him," Marge said as she took out her notebook. "You know why we're interested in him, don't you?"

"Yes, I do. He was the guard in those murders and he's missing."

Oliver said, "What can you tell us about him?"

"Nothing much. We didn't talk other than an occasional nod. I felt he might have kept his distance because of my skin color, but after talking to others around here, he just wasn't the neighborly type. Not too many neighborly types anymore. Most of the farms here are run by big business."

Marge nodded.

"There are still several holdouts like myself. I've been approached a few times about selling my land. It's my children's inheritance. Anyway, you don't want to talk politics, you want to talk about Rondo Martin." Marcus cleared his throat. "There were a couple of times when I stopped at the Watering Hole for a beer, he'd be there drinking whiskey, talking to Matt or Trevor or whoever was tending bar. We farmers work sunup to sundown when the days are long and the weather's good. In the wintertime, it can get cold. That's when the tavern does its business."

"Is there a lot of crime around here?" Oliver asked.

"Sheriff would know more than me," Marcus said. "Reading the daily sheet, I think that most of the crimes come from the migrants getting drunk on the weekends and whopping on each other. There's not a whole lot to do around here. We've got a general store, a church, a movie house, a lending library, a couple of family restaurants, and a street of taverns. That's about it."

"Do the migrants go to the same church as you do?"

"No, they do not. We're all Baptists. Migrants are mostly Catholic or Pentecostal. We don't have any Catholic or Pentecostal churches. They must have their own."

"Where do the migrants live?" Marge asked.

"In the outlying areas. We call them the *ciudads,* which means cities in Spanish. Ponceville is built like a square. Smack in the middle is the town, then the farms, and on the perimeter is where the migrants live. Their living quarters, provided by the big businesses that hire them, are pretty primitive. They got their running water and electrical lines, but it's still very basic. Don't matter how basic it is, though, they just keep coming. And they'll keep on coming as long as conditions down in their countries are poorer than conditions up here."

"Are they legal?" Oliver asked.

"The businesses get them their green cards. All my workers have green cards. Can't do it any other way. Otherwise the INS will shut you down. We're not talking about Martin very much."

"My partner and I are just trying to get a feel for the town," Marge said. "Maybe it'll help us understand Rondo Martin better. Do you know if he spoke Spanish?"

"Anyone living here for some time speaks Spanish."

Marge nodded. "So . . . what about you and Rondo Martin . . . getting back to the original question."

Marcus smiled. "I never said much to him, honestly. Occasionally, he'd show up at church. I sing in the choir. My wife does as well. He showed up once when I had a solo and told me I had a good voice. That was about as personal as it ever got." He checked his watch and managed to hoist himself out of his chair. "Well, we'd better get going if we want to be on time."

At that moment, Gladys walked in with the coffee.

Marcus looked at the tray of mugs. "We can be a few minutes late, I suppose."

"You certainly can." She smiled. "We have a . . . fluid concept of time here."

Her husband passed out the coffee cups. Gladys said to help themselves to cream and sugar. The detectives thanked her profusely.

Marge said, "I like your photos, Mrs. Merry."

Gladys smiled. "That's what walls are for."

"I also like the artwork."

"Really?" Gladys said. "I don't care much for it. It was given to my in-laws by the artist. His father was a farmer in Chino and I think he was a family friend . . . Did I get that right, Marcus?"

"Something like that. Paul was a weirdo. My mama only kept it because she didn't want to hurt his feelings." Marcus laughed. "Turned out he became real famous."

"Paul Pollock," Gladys said. "Have you ever heard of him?"

"No," Marge said, "but he paints like Jackson Pollock. Are they related?"

"That's him," Gladys said. "Jackson Pollock. Paul was his real first name."

"Uh, he's pretty well known," Oliver said. "His father was a farmer?"

"Yes, Detective, he was."

"The painting's very valuable, Mrs. Merry," Marge told her.

"Oh yes, it is. And please call me Gladys."

"And you're not worried about theft?" Marge said.

Gladys shook her head. "The people around here who see it think it was done by one of my grandchildren." She stared at the painting. "I don't bother to correct them."

TWENTY-ONE

THE LAST KNOWN address of Alejandro Brand was in Pacoima, part of Decker's old hunting ground in Foothill. The place was a burb of about a hundred thousand people. Its major claim to fame—besides a horrendous airplane crash in 1957 that killed children in a schoolyard—was its junior high that had once schooled Ritchie Valens, a rising pop star in the 1950s. The poor boy's career had come to an abrupt halt when he, along with Buddy Holly and J. P. Richardson, aka the Big Bopper, had died in a heartbreaking small-craft crash in Iowa in 1959. Pacoima Junior High had been changed to Pacoima Middle School, but that was just about the only thing in the town that had evolved. It was still a working-class Hispanic neighborhood pocked with violence.

The area was rife with industrial plants and warehouses for the trades, but there was some local shopping: discount clothing stores, liquor stores, convenience marts, fast-food chains, launderettes, used-car lots, and the occasional ethnic bodega. Around here, money was tight unless it was Friday night. Then the bars did bang-up businesses. As Decker cruised down the wide streets, he slowed down to study the bad boys who populated the sidewalks or the weed-choked lots. They eyed him back with defiant looks and aggressive stances.

Brand's address was an apartment building constructed in the 1950s out of glittery stucco with an aqua blue sign that bore the name The Caribbean. It was two stories of depression with laundry hung from the balconies. Decker found parking easily and walked up to an outside locked gate. It was short enough for Decker to extend his arm over the top and reach the doorknob on the other side. The courtyard had a small clean pool that was currently in use by a slew of elementary-aged children. There were several women in swimsuits reclining on plastic-strap lawn chairs, yakking with one another as they worked on their tans. The ladies looked at Decker with suspicion.

He picked a woman at random—a Latina of around thirty with short black hair, dark eyes, and a voluptuous body that was pouring out of her bikini. He told her in Spanish that he was the police—a show of his badge—and looking for Alejandro Brand.

The woman responded with a purse of her lips. "He's bad news."

Her friend, overhearing the conversation, broke in. She was older and heavier, wearing a halter top and cutoff shorts. "Very bad news," she concurred. "Raul, stop playing so rough with your sister. Let go of her now!" Back to Decker. "He sold drugs upstairs from his mother's apartment.

"After Mrs. Cruz died, it got much worse. We called the police, but every time they tell us there's nothing they can do unless someone wants to press charges.

"Finally the apartment caught fire. The building almost burned down.

"But the fire department was quick, *gracias a Dios*." She crossed herself.

Decker thought about a meth lab and all its flammable components. "Did you smell anything funny coming from the apartment?"

"Who got that close?"

"What about the trash? Did you find a lot of antifreeze containers, Drano, lye, iodine maybe?"

"I don't look at other people's trash," Lady 2 said. "I don't know what he was doing and I don't care now. All I know is we have more peace."

"Although there is funny business with Apartment K," Lady 1 told him.

"Not as bad as with Alejandro. Many bad men come in that apartment. I had to watch my daughters like a mother hen. He had lots of spending cash and had a pretty face—a bad combination for teenaged girls."

"Any idea where he lives now?"

"No, and I don't care."

"*Gracias a Dios,*" said Lady 1.

"Let him be someone else's problem."

Decker said, "Did anyone else besides his mother live upstairs?"

"Who knows?" Lady 2 said. "So many people going in and out . . . Raul, next time you hit her, you're getting out!"

"Did Brand have any sisters and brothers?"

Lady 1 said, "I think Alejandro was the only child. Mrs. Cruz was very old."

"It was his grandmother," Lady 2 said.

"She used to call him *mi hijo.*"

"He called her *abuela* once. She was the grandmother, maybe even great-grandmother. She was very old."

"So you have no idea where Alejandro went?"

"He's somewhere in the neighborhood," Lady 1 told him. "I see him at the market from time to time. I pretend not to notice him."

"Good idea," Decker said. "What market?"

"Anderson's warehouse food and grocery. It's about three blocks away."

Decker wrote it down. "How many months would you say it was between when the old lady died and the apartment caught fire?"

"Maybe three months."

Lady 2 concurred. "Finally he's gone. Now we have peace and security. We all got together and put in the iron gate." Suddenly, she nar-rowed her eyes and glowered at Decker. "How'd you get in here?"

"I reached over and opened it from the inside."

"Hmmm, that is a problem. We put the gate up for protection. If you got in so easily, maybe we need to think of other things."

"How tall are you?" Lady 1 asked.

"Six four give or take."

"How many men do you know who are six four?" Lady 1 asked Lady 2.

"None."

"Me, too. It's not a problem." She looked at Decker. "Make sure the gate is closed on the way out. Next time, use the bell. That's what it's for."

"HARRIMAN JUST LEFT." It was Wanda Bontemps on the phone.

"What did he want?" Decker tried to keep the acid out of his voice.

"We asked him to come in, Loo."

Hunched over the steering wheel, it took a couple of beats before Decker processed the words. He had been so focused on Rina's safety that he forgot that Harriman was actually serving a purpose. "Yeah . . . right. The phony interview with Oscar Vitalez. How'd that go?"

"Harriman said it wasn't him. We tried to convince him that he was the guy based on Rina's ID, but he didn't take the bait. He said emphatically that it wasn't the guy. So I've got a couple more guys lined up for him to listen to. We've set up another meeting at five this afternoon."

"Good job, Wanda, thank you. Alejandro Brand—the guy who Rina did ID—doesn't live at his listed address but he's still in the neighborhood. I'm going to hunt around. Any luck locating Joe Pine?"

"I haven't heard from Messing. Want me to give him a call?"

"Yeah, do that. I'm getting another call, Wanda, could you hold?"

"Just take it. Nothing more to say. I'll talk to you later."

Decker loved the efficiency in Wanda. The call was from Rina.

"I've got some time this afternoon if you want me to look through more mug books."

Decker knew there was no stopping her. "Sure. How about . . . three?"

"Great. Do you need anything?"

"No, darlin', I'm fine. I'm in Pacoima now. I'll talk to you later."

"What are you doing in Pacoima?"

"Looking for Alejandro Brand."

"When you find him, let me know."

"Why would I do that?"

"So I can ID him in person."

"Your ID doesn't mean anything because you didn't hear him talk about the Kaffey murders. Harriman needs to ID him, not you."

"Why not both?"

"Because he overheard something suspicious. You didn't."

"I can tell you if he's the guy that Harriman was eavesdropping on."

"I'm sure Harriman eavesdrops on many people. That's what got him into trouble in the first place. Look in the mug books, but nothing more. Please be considerate of your weary husband's feelings and do not get involved any deeper, okay?"

"Stop worrying, Peter. I'm just trying to help."

The road to hell, et cetera, et cetera. "I know, darlin'. I'll see you at three."

"We've got a date. I'm bringing a cake for the squad room. If you behave yourself, you can have a slice."

"And if I don't?"

"Then you don't get a piece and can use it to jump-start your diet for the seventy millionth time. Either way, it's a win-win situation."

MARCUS MERRY DROVE them in his 1978 Ford Bronco Ranger with 102,000 miles on it, the three of them crammed into a cabin designed for two. He announced that he was making a stop first and took them across open fields until he pulled up in front of a barn in the middle of nowhere. He cut the engine.

"Just gotta unload some stuff."

"Need help?" Marge asked.

"Got six crates of produce in the back. If you want to carry one in, I won't object."

Oliver whispered to her, "You had to ask."

"It'll get us to the sheriff quicker." She got out of the car and slid a crate of onions over the tailgate. "Where are we, Marcus?"

"Local food cooperative. Although everything grows out here, no one farmer grows everything. This way we just swap for what we need." Marcus moved quickly for an old guy. Within five minutes, six crates of onions and garlic had been unloaded and Marcus received credit for his produce. "I was running a little low on points. Now Gladys can shop."

When everyone was stuffed back into the cab, Marcus drove into "town." Main Street was two lanes sided by storefronts: general clothing, general feed, one grocery mart, a store for fabrics, a bank, a used-car and tractor lot, and an auto parts store with a big sign that said TRACTOR PARTS. There were also two hardware stores, a movie house, couple of family restaurants, and several drinking man's bars.

The local courthouse and county jail was the last stop on Main. It was a Federalist-style building fashioned in white plaster, not very large by courthouse standards, but it dwarfed its competition down the road.

The sheriff's office was on the third floor and overlooked green rows of flat fields. The receptionist was an ancient woman with blue white hair partially covered by a jaunty red beret. The red was echoed again in the woman's dress and her fingernail polish. She looked up and held out a long, liver-spotted hand. "Edna Wellers. You must be the detective friends of Willy."

Marge smiled. The way Edna said "detective friends" made it sound like they had come to Ponceville for a play date with Brubeck. "Yes, we are. Nice to meet you."

Edna looked at Oliver. "Well, you're a handsome young man. Are you married? I got a daughter. Divorced but her kids are grown."

Oliver said, "Thank you, but I'm currently seeing someone."

She gave him a once-over. "You look like you can juggle more than one at a time. Don't he, Marcus. Back me up on this."

"Edna, enough out of you. They got business to do. Go get Sheriff T out here so they can make their plane in time."

"When are you leaving, handsome?"

"This evening," Oliver answered.

Edna's face fell. "Well, that stinks!"

"Where's T, Edna?"

"He hasn't come back yet." To Oliver she said, "You can't stay another day?"

"Not at the present time."

"So you'll come back."

Marcus said, "He's not coming back, Edna. They're working on a very important murder case down south."

"Those rich people, right? The ones that Rondo worked for. You should be talking to me. I've been here longer than anyone. Back me up on this, Marcus."

"I back you up."

"What can you tell us about Rondo Martin?" Oliver brought out his notebook.

"He wasn't as good-looking as you, handsome."

"Few men are."

Edna smiled. "He dated my daughter, Shareen, for a couple of months. It didn't work out. Shareen is a talker. Rondo wasn't much of a talker—no man is—but he wasn't much of a listener, either. I think they were both in it for . . . well, you know why. I don't have to get specific."

"I can figure it out," Marge said. "Was it just a casual thing or did Shareen have hopes of something more?"

"Nah, just casual." A pause. "Rondo was a loner, didn't talk much to anyone. Back me up on this, Marcus."

"I hardly knew the man."

"Just what I'm talking about. He did his job but wasn't friendly. Even when he got a little tipsy, his lips were mostly sealed."

Marge asked, "Did he ever slip up?"

Edna said, "Once he talked about his family."

"Yeah, I was there," Marcus said. "It was around Christmas. Man, it was cold and dry and just all around bone chilling. Bars did lots of business."

Edna said, "It wasn't good what he had to say about his folks."

Marcus said. "Yeah, he was bitchin' about his father . . . what a mean son of a gun he was. The old man used to whack him until one day he whacked back. I remember it because it was an odd thing to bring up around the holidays."

"Yeah, he had some bad memories," Edna said.

"Anything else?" Oliver asked.

Both of them shook their heads. Edna's beret slid to one side.

"Where was Martin from?" Marge asked.

Edna said, "Missouri, I think. Back me up, Marcus."

Merry said, "I thought it was Iowa."

At that moment, T the sheriff walked in. He was around five six, 140 pounds, with a seamed face and milky blue eyes. His lips were so thin that they faded into his face. He gave a surprisingly strong handshake—not exactly bone crushing but strong enough to let Oliver know he could take care of himself. He wore a khaki uniform and a Smokey the Bear hat, which he doffed, displaying a crew cut and ears that stuck out of the sides of his face. "Tim England. Sorry I took so long. We had a little problem down in the ciudads . . . something about stolen money. Turns out the boy just didn't remember where he hid his stash. Probably drunk when he did it."

"That's where all the migrants live," Edna said. "We call it the ciudads. That means cities in Spanish." She turned to the sheriff. "Hey, T, maybe you can solve a mystery for us. Where was Rondo Martin from? Missouri or Iowa?"

"First he told me Kansas, but then later he said he was from New

York. He said he thought he'd fit in better if he was from the Midwest. He told me his old man was a farmer in upstate."

"Was it true?" Marge asked.

"Who knows?" T shrugged. "I always felt the man was hiding something, but never could find out what. He didn't have any kind of arrest record. He had a good work history."

Marge asked, "Where did he do his law enforcement training?"

"I don't reckon I know that. He came to us from Bakersfield Police Department . . . worked there for a few years. His record was clean—no absentee problem, no record of undue force or brutality, no IA investigations. The day watch commander said he was always on time, took his notes, but didn't talk much. A good, clean cop was how he put it."

"Why'd he leave the force?" Oliver asked.

T thought a moment. "He said something about wanting a small town. He was tired of the big city."

"Bakersfield's a big city?"

"It isn't L.A., but it's going on four hundred thousand. That's a lot of people. He certainly got small here in Ponceville."

Marge said, "Then why did he leave Ponceville to do private security in L.A.?"

"Don't really know, ma'am. I think Rondo was a restless sort. It takes a certain type of person to live here if you're not a farmer. You don't got a lot of choices—it's either the bars or the churches. Rondo couldn't make up his mind. Sometimes he'd show up at church, sometimes he'd show up at the tavern. He didn't fit in anywhere."

"Back me up on this, T. I remember Shareen saying he spent some time at the ciudads." She lowered her voice to a whisper. "That's where the whores are."

"Cut it out, Edna." T rolled his eyes. "But she's got a point. If you're lonely and don't feel like praying, going to certain places is an alternative."

"Where are these ciudads?" Oliver asked.

"They surround the farms," T said. "There are four of 'em— north, south, east, and west."

Marge said, "Would Shareen know who Martin visited in the ciudads?"

"Maybe," Edna said.

"Could you call up your daughter and ask her?"

"Now?"

"Yes, now, Edna," T said. "They have work to do."

"Well, all right then." She called up her daughter and five minutes later she hung up the phone. "Shareen thinks he spent a lot of time in the north district. Who lives there, T? Lots of Gonzales, right? And the Ricardos and the Mendez, the Alvarez and the Luzons. I think they're all related."

"They are." T regarded the detectives. "I never ask my men what they do on their off hours. Isn't my business. Do either of you speak Spanish?"

Marge and Oliver shook their heads no.

"Then no use going down there. You won't understand a thing they say." T's cell phone started ringing. "Excuse me."

He took the call and when he hung up, he said, "Another problem at the ciudads. South district. Wanna come and see what I deal with? You can follow me in your car."

"I drove them here," Marcus said. "I gotta get back to work."

"Could we ride with you?" Oliver asked.

"Sure, but it'll take about an hour. What time is your plane out?"

"We've got time," Marge said.

"Sure," Edna said. "Enough time to see whores but not my daughter."

"Now stop that, Edna. This isn't a dating service. Let them do their job." T picked up his hat. "Boy oh boy. That's four calls in four hours. That's what happens when it gets sweltering out there. The natives get restless."

TWENTY-TWO

THERE HAD BEEN a lot of remodeling since Decker worked Foothill Substation some fifteen years ago, but it still smelled and sounded familiar. Detective Mallory Quince—a petite brunette in her thirties—played with the keyboard until Alejandro's face flashed on the computer screen. "Oh him . . . the meth maker. He almost burned down an apartment building. That was a close call."

"So I've heard."

"From who?"

"The tenants. I talked to them this morning. I thought about a meth lab but the tenants didn't know anything about that. How bad was the fire?"

"His unit was completely burned out. The two units on either side were a mess, too, but the FD saved the building. We picked up the sucker a couple of days later. He claimed he had nothing to do with the fire and he hadn't been there since his grandmother died. A pack of lies, but no one contradicted him. I think they were all afraid of retribution."

"The women said they called the police many times about him. Any record of the calls?"

"I'll check it out, but it's probably bullshit." Mallory rolled her eyes. "We'd investigate crack houses and meth labs, you know that."

Decker did know that. "So nothing on Alejandro Brand?"

"Nope."

"You have his fingerprints?"

"Let's see if there's a card." She clicked a few buttons. "Sorry. We didn't arrest him." She printed out the picture on the computer and handed the paper to Decker. "I'll keep a lookout for him. Pass the word around."

"I'd appreciate that." He shook the woman's hand. "Thanks for your time."

"You miss it around here?"

"Not too different from where I am geographically, but my district's more affluent. There's less violent crime."

"So you don't miss being in the action?"

"Sometimes I miss being in the field, but I'm happy where I am. It's good having an office with a door that closes."

THIS WAS NOT the sunny side of Mexico inhabited by margarita-drinking American expats lying in the white sands next to warm lapis waves. This was the Baja California of Oliver's childhood memories: a land steeped in poverty and have-nots with its shacks and lean-tos and tin-roof hovels. Tijuana was just a step across the border yet it had seemed light-years away. When he grew older, he and some army buddies would often visit the underbelly to cop cheap liquor and old whores—a rite of passage. The ciudads here were row upon row of makeshift houses plunked down in the middle of nowhere. Like Tijuana, the Ponceville ciudad residents had tried to liven up the neighborhood by painting the exteriors bright colors: aquas, lemon yellows, kelly greens, and deep lilacs. For Oliver, these Day-Glo colors had been so exotic at eighteen. Now it made him sad.

There were few landmarks, but Sheriff T knew his way around. The official vehicle was a thirty-year-old Suburban and as T maneuvered the tank along the dirt roads, the three of them bounced on none-too-padded seats. He stopped in the middle of the lane in front of a one-story orange shack.

The three of them got out. T strode up to the door and gave it a hard whack. A teenaged girl not more than thirteen answered, a plump baby on her hip and a stick-thin toddler tugging her skirt. She was pretty—dark hair, smooth coffee complexion, wide-set eyes, and high cheekbones. She was sweating profusely, drops on her brow and nose. She swung the door wide open and Marge, Oliver, and T came inside.

A four-year-old boy was sitting on an old sofa, watching cartoons on an old TV perched up on boxes. Besides the TV and the couch, furniture included a dinette set, two folding chairs, and a playpen with toys. A worn rug covered an unfinished floor that looked like it had been constructed from old crates. There was one sagging shelf with a few books, a few DVDs, and an American flag mounted in an empty coffee can.

It was barebones but clean with the sweet-smelling aroma of something baking. The heat also added about twenty degrees to the already sweltering day. Marge immediately felt her face moisten. She took out a tissue and gave one to Oliver.

The young girl put the baby and the toddler in a playpen and gave each of them a cookie. The two tiny ones sat among a sea of old toys, eating their cookies without a fuss, staring at the rapid-fire animated cells of color occupying the little boy's attention.

The teenager's face was grave. She mopped up the sweat with the back of her hand and immediately started speaking Spanish, her tone clearly agitated. She bounced her leg up and down as she talked, kneading her hands together as well. The sheriff nodded at appropriate intervals. Their conversation was brief, and within minutes T stood up and placed a hand on her shoulder. At that point, her eyes became teary as she repeated "gracias" over and over.

After they left, T said, "She lives with her parents who are both in the fields. She's the oldest of seven. The three others are in school but someone has to stay home to watch the little babies."

Marge said, "What about her schooling?"

"Her birth certificate says she's sixteen, which means she doesn't have to go to school anymore."

"She looks about twelve."

"She probably is, but I don't do her family a favor by asking too many questions."

"What was the problem?" Oliver asked.

"Some twenty-year-old punk out in the fields keeps bugging her, sneaking away from work and trying to come inside and have sex with her. Ignacias Pepe, whoever the hell that is. There's just too many of them for me to keep track. Just as I get to know who lives where, one moves out and another comes in to take his place. She told me that Ignacias is picking strawberries at the McClellans' farm. I'll go over and have a talk with the jerk. Tell him to keep his pecker in his pants unless he wants it pickled in a jar."

The three of them loaded back into the Suburban.

"I'll pass Marcus's place on the way to Ardes McClellan's farm. I know you've got other business to tend to so how about if I drop you off."

"That would work out," Oliver said. "Edna, your secretary, said something about Rondo Martin hanging out in the northern area. Is that different from where we were?"

"Interchangeable. Wish I could tell you more about the man, but you know how it is. If no one's making trouble, you don't go looking for it."

Marge said, "Thanks for bringing us along. We didn't find out too much about Rondo Martin, but we certainly got a good feel for the town."

T said, "This place is not much more than two spits in the wind, but I love it. Wide-open fields and a big blue sky. I can do my job without the brass-ass boys above me telling me what to do."

Oliver said, "You've got that one pegged."

"Not that I don't answer to someone," T said. "There's the mayor and the city council, but for the most part, they mind their own business and let me keep the law."

"Good for them and good for you," Marge said.

"Yeah, you always answer to someone unless you're God. I suppose he don't answer to no one, but I've never met him, so I couldn't say for sure."

THE WOMAN HAD tenacity and would have made a fine detective. She looked up at Decker and said, "This isn't coming as easily as Brand. No face just pops out at me."

"Then maybe he isn't there."

"He had a BXII tattooed on his arm."

"He's a member of the Bodega 12th Street gang but that doesn't mean he made the mug book. Don't force it, Rina. It's after five. Maybe it's time to quit."

She closed the book. "I'm sorry."

"What for? You've certainly done your bit." Decker checked his watch again. "I've got a couple more things to finish up here. I'll be home in an hour."

"Okay." She stood up and gave him a kiss. "See you then."

"I'll walk you out."

"No need. I know the way. Go finish up."

"Thanks for the cake, Rina. The Dees really enjoyed it."

"It's my pleasure. After all these years of baking, it's hard to wean me away from the oven. Making cakes for the squad room prevents me from going cold turkey."

"Anytime you want to feed your jones, it would be welcomed here."

Rina smiled. Just as she stepped out of the door to the substation, she saw Harriman coming her way. She told herself to keep moving and when he wordlessly passed her, she felt a twang in her gut—as if she were impolite.

Don't get involved, she told herself. She didn't always listen to her gut, but images of all that spilled blood gave her pause.

THE DETOUR THROUGH the ciudads put Oliver and Marge behind schedule. With the drive from Ponceville to Oakland eating up another couple of hours, an actual dinner was out of the question. They ate tuna sandwiches on the way, arriving in the Bay Area with a little over an hour to call up Porter Brady and arrange an interview with him. The detectives figured that after bypass surgery the man would stick close to home, so they weren't surprised when he answered on the third ring.

"Why do you want to talk to me?" Porter sounded annoyed. "I already told the police that Neptune was with me. We have phone records to prove it."

Marge said, "It would be helpful if we could talk to you in person."

"Why's that? I never had an ounce of trouble with the boy." A pause. "Does my son know you're coming here?"

"No, he doesn't." Marge was matter-of-fact.

"I don't have much to say to you about Neptune. He's a good boy." Another pause. "I suppose I wouldn't mind some company."

"Then we'll see you in a few minutes."

Porter lived in an apartment not far from Jack London Square—a waterfront tourist attraction made up of old warehouses converted to shopping malls. Brady's unit was two bedrooms and two baths and was furnished with original 1950s furniture. It hadn't been pricey at the time but the color of the maple had mellowed to a fine tawny port, and the clean lines transferred nicely into the twenty-first century.

The old man had greeted them in pajamas, bathrobe, and slippers. He was stick thin with an unhealthy-looking gray pallor. He had a long face topped with white kinky hair, brown eyes, and thick lips. At present, his skin color could have belonged to any race, but his hair pointed to black. What was even more surprising was his age. Neptune was in his thirties, and the old man appeared to be in his seventies. The mystery was cleared up within a matter of seconds.

"I'm his grandfather but I raised him. That makes me his father."

Marge sipped a mug filled with sweet tea. "This is good. Thank you."

"My own brew."

"Delicious." She took out a notepad. "Are you Neptune's maternal grandfather?"

"Paternal," Porter told her. "His daddy, my son, was murdered before Neptune was born. Eighteen years old. He ran with the wrong crowd."

"What about Neptune's mother?" Oliver asked.

The old man sat back on his divan, his robe falling open to reveal a sunken chest. He closed it back up. "She's from a white family across the bay. She worked as a teacher's pet . . . no, not pet." He laughed. "What do they call those helpers?"

"Teacher's aide?" Marge said.

"Yeah, an aide. That's right." He nodded. "That's right. She wasn't but a year older than the students. Erstin—that was my boy—was in her class. He was a good-looking boy. Tall and strapping and a charmer. My wife died when he was five. I tried, but I couldn't be both a daddy and a mommy. I had to work."

"What work did you do?" Marge asked him.

"Longshoreman. I spent my life loading and unloading docks. Good pay, but long hours and backbreaking work. Still, I paid all my bills and never owed anyone a red cent." He sipped tea. "You want some more brew, missy?"

"No, thank you."

Porter looked at Oliver. "What about you, sir?"

"I'm fine, sir," Oliver said. "So your son didn't have your work ethic?"

"Pshaw." Porter waved his hand in the air. "Erstin had a work ethic for one thing only. He made himself a daddy when he was fifteen, then again at sixteen. By the time he got around to Wendy, Erstin was an old pro."

"That's a lot of babies," Marge said. "Do you keep in contact with your grandsons?"

"One of 'em is in prison." Porter rolled his eyes. "The other one loved cars from the get-go. He moved to St. Louis and sells Porsches. He's a good kid."

Another sip of tea.

"Erstin was shot about two months before Neptune was born. The girl's parents wanted to put the baby up for adoption, of course. But when I got wind of it, I put up a fight. I wanted the boy especially since I lost my own son . . ." His eyes got pensive. "A judge saw it my way. The girl relinquished claim on him."

Oliver said, "Do you have the girl's full name?"

"Wendy Anderson . . ." He held up his hands and let them drop into his lap. "She called me out of the blue one day . . . just like you did. She wanted to visit the boy and I said fine. Neptune was a good-looking boy—tall like his daddy but he looked like his mommy. He was a charmer like his daddy."

The detectives waited.

"The next day, Wendy and her parents show up at my door, all sweetness and light. One minute they want nothin' to do with the boy, the next minute they're trying to play with my sympathies. Wendy . . . she's crying and crying. I believed that she really cared. But the parents. Hah! The boy could pass . . . that's all they cared about."

Marge nodded.

"They had no legal grounds to get the boy back. But then there are moral grounds. I felt for that little girl. I lost my son and she had feeling for her little boy. I wouldn't give up custody—no sirreebob—but I did tell the judge that maybe we could work something out."

He finished his tea and smiled with yellow teeth. "And we did. She wound up taking him alternative weekends and every Wednesday night. When he had to go to school and couldn't sleep over in the city no more, she'd drive all the way out here, take him for dinner, and then drive all the way back. Tell you the truth, as he grew up, he became a handful. I didn't mind the relief. When the boy was eight, she married, became a lawyer, and had kids of her own. But she still kept it up with Neptune. Every other weekend and every

Wednesday, that girl was there like clockwork. I was the boy's daddy, but she molded herself into one fine mommy."

"Where does she live now?" Oliver asked.

"When Neptune was eighteen, she and her husband moved back east. I get a Christmas card every year from her. She calls me on my birthday. She's a real good woman." His eyes were misty. "You never know about people. That's why there's something called a second chance."

Marge flipped a page on her notepad. "What did Neptune do after he graduated from high school?"

"I thought he had a chance at college. Instead he became a cop for the Oakland Police Department."

"So that was right out of high school?"

"Yes, it was."

"Do you know how he got his job with Mr. Kaffey?" Oliver asked.

"No idea. He never said nothing to me, but I suspect that he moved to L.A. because he wanted to be an actor. He certainly had the looks for it."

Marge and Oliver nodded.

Porter said, "Neptune was happy with the position. He made money. Bought himself a little house and a new Porsche—from his half-brother in St. Louis." A smile. "He's living the good life." The old man shook his head. "I feel for my boy. He's a bundle of nerves, although he tries to hide it from me."

"Has he spoken to you about the murders?" Oliver asked.

"Nothing much. Something about an insider messed him up."

Marge tried to hide her excitement. "Did he mention a name?"

"Martin something . . ."

"Rondo Martin?" When Porter nodded, Marge said, "What did he say about him?"

"Lemme think." Porter was quiet as he drank tea. "Just that Martin messed him up and that he was missing. He said once the cops found him, they'd know who did this."

"When did Neptune tell you this?"

"I don't know . . . maybe right after it happened." Porter slowly started to rise from the couch. When it was clear he was having trouble, Marge stood and lent him a hand.

"What can I get for you?"

"Well, if you're asking, you could get me more tea with a little milk."

"I could do that." She poured him a fresh cup. She set the mug down on an end table. "On the night of the murders, do you know what time you received the phone call with the news?"

"I was sleeping, missy. Next thing I know, Neptune's shaking my shoulder and telling me that there's been an emergency and he has to leave right away."

Oliver said, "Would you mind if we looked at a copy of your phone records?"

"You can have a copy, but it won't do you any good. Neptune always used his cell phone. Kept the damn thing glued to his ear even when we were watching the game."

"You're probably right," Marge said. "He probably didn't use your phone. But my boss likes us to be thorough."

"You can have a copy as soon as I get it."

"We can just call up the phone company," Marge said. "You don't have to bother as long as I have your permission and your account number."

"I don't know my account number, but I just paid my bill. The receipt is still on the kitchen counter in the mail slot."

Oliver got up. "I'll get it."

"Thanks." Marge turned her attention back to Porter. "Anything else we can do before we leave?"

"Yeah, find this Martin guy. This whole mess is weighing real heavy on my boy."

"We're doing what we can." Oliver proffered his hand. "We have a plane to catch. Thanks so much for your time."

The old man took the hand and gave it a dead-fish shake. Probably not so long ago, the man had an iron grip. Oliver handed the old man a card. "Here's my office number at the station house and here's my cell number."

"Here's mine as well," Marge said.

"What are these for?"

"If you think of something you want to tell us," Oliver said.

"Or even if you want to talk," Marge said.

"Call you up just to talk?" Porter gave her a wide grin. "I'm an old man and spending a lot of time alone. Be careful what you offer, missy. You might not know it, but I'm the king of gab."

TWENTY-THREE

AS SOON AS the plane took off, Oliver reclined the seat and stared out the window. He and Marge were the only ones in the row, so they had some privacy. Still, Marge kept her voice low. "The younger Mr. B's phone records are clean, right?"

"Yes. And since B is not a stupid man, I don't think the old man's phone records will show anything. But we should look at them just in case."

"Agreed," Marge said. "What about Mr. B's childhood? Is it even relevant?"

"How about a black who can pass as white who hates rich white people?"

"But according to the grandfather, the mother did a good job," Marge said. "Besides, what makes you think that B is trying to pass? He was up-front about using his black grandfather as an alibi. And he went up to Oakland to take care of him."

Oliver nodded. "Point taken."

Marge took out her notebook. "I just thought of something."

"What?"

"Tell you when I find it."

Oliver rubbed his head. "Man, what a depressing day. The ciudads were one ugly place after another."

"You're still there?"

"I never left."

She scanned her scrawls as she spoke. "Still it must be better than where they came from. Otherwise people would be going the other way."

"Sometimes they do."

Marge looked up. "Someone stretching their retirement dollar or buying a second house on the beach doesn't count as going the other way. Last I heard there wasn't a plethora of Americans trying to sneak across the border."

Oliver said, "Hard ass."

"Bleeding heart." Marge patted his knee. "Actually I find your empathy very touching."

"I keep seeing that young girl . . . looking after her brother and sisters while trying to fend off a hormone-driven idiot. What kind of life is she going to have?"

"Don't even go there." Marge returned her attention to her notes. "She reminded me of a hundred cases I saw when I worked Juvenile with the rabbi. All those beautiful little faces saying help me, and there wasn't a damn thing I could do. Homicide is crushing, but juvenile is day in and day out of heartbreak."

A flight attendant came by with the beverage cart. "What can I get for you today?"

Marge looked up. "Diet Coke, please."

"One dollar."

Marge's eyes got wide. "You *charge* for soft drinks?"

The woman's eyes glazed over. "Water and orange juice are complimentary."

"Orange juice," Marge said.

"Pretzels or peanuts?"

"Are they free?"

"Yes, ma'am."

"I'm paralyzed by such choice. How about pretzels. What do you want, Scott?"

"OJ and peanuts. Do you think the department will reimburse me if I add a little vodka to the OJ?"

"Probably not," Marge said.

"Department?" the flight attendant asked.

Marge pulled out her badge. "Official business. Do we get any perks?"

The flight attendant didn't hesitate. "Don't tell anyone I did this." She opened up a can of Diet Coke and gave it to Marge. "My dad was a cop." She turned to Oliver and handed him OJ with a tiny bottle of Skyy. "On the house."

"Thank you very much," Marge said. But the woman was already on down the aisle. "I do believe that's the first time my badge ever got me a freebie."

Oliver poured the vodka into his OJ. "Wow, that's good. Want a sip?"

"In a minute . . . Okay, I found it!" Marge dropped her voice to a whisper. "Edna's daughter said that Mr. RM used to go down to the northern district of the ciudads for a little R and R?"

"More like Puss and Cee, but why quibble."

"Edna asked T who lived there and I wrote down the names: Gonzales, Ricardos, Mendez, Alvarez, Luzons. Any of those names sound familiar?"

Oliver sat up. "Paco Alvarez?"

"It's Albanez. But how about the maid—Ana Mendez?"

Oliver nodded. "Her alibi checked out, but that doesn't mean anything." A pause. "Neither does her name. There are lots of Mendez surnames in the Hispanic world."

"Yeah, for sure, but picture this. RM and Ana meet in Ponceville. They come down to L.A. together. Certain ideas start hatching. We both feel it's an inside job. Why not those two? Someone knew the layout to move so quickly."

"I'm sure Mr. RM knew the layout."

"The layout of the main house but not the layout of the servants' quarters. It doesn't look like there was forced entry. It looks like the shooters came busting in from down below. Ana said that the help was usually locked out of the kitchen by twelve, right? It was set up that way so that the help couldn't enter the house through the servants' quarters while everyone was sleeping. But someone breeched that point of entry.

"Say that Ana comes home but she's not alone. She opens the servants' quarters for the shooters, they kill whoever is down below, then they go upstairs to the kitchen door where Mr. RM lets them in. He tells the guys where everyone is and the shooters do their thing. Then they all leave via the servants' quarters and Ana fakes like she just came home."

Oliver shrugged. "She was at the church. People remember her. But maybe she left earlier and no one noticed."

"Or, Scott, it could be that she gave RM the code to get in. Then her alibi would be righteous and no one would think she was involved."

"That would work." He sipped his spiked OJ.

"It's a long shot. There are zillions of Mendez families. But what would it hurt if someone went to the ciudads with a picture of Ana?"

Oliver said, "How do we do that? If she does have family there, they'll alert her. I don't want her bolting south."

"Neither do I. And I don't want to involve Sheriff T in what may be nothing more than speculation."

"Agreed," Oliver said. "We send another team up to the ciudads without telling the sheriff."

"How about Brubeck and Decker?" Marge said. "Deck is fluent in Spanish, and Brubeck has the local connections."

"A black and a Jew." Oliver finished the last of his drink. "Who says LAPD isn't multicultural."

UPON LANDING, MARGE turned her cell phone back on. The window instantly lit up with message waiting. The first call was from Vega wishing her a meaningful and productive trip. Marge smiled. It took a Herculean effort on her daughter's part to engage in the banality of human intercourse. The girl was half Vulcan.

The second call was more alarming.

Call as soon as you get the message.

"Oh boy." Marge punched in Decker's cell number. "The Loo sounds upset and that's never good."

Decker picked it up on the third ring. "Are you back?"

"We're at the airport. We just landed."

"I'm at St. Joseph's hospital. We have a crime scene. Get here as soon as you can."

"What's going on?"

"Gil Kaffey was released at five this evening. As they were wheeling him to the car, someone opened fire—"

"Oh my God!" She brought the phone up to Oliver's ear so that he could listen in. "Who was with him?"

"Grant, Neptune Brady, Piet Kotsky, Antoine Resseur, and Mace Kaffey, who was supposed to leave yesterday but the memorial service was changed so he stayed for another day. The bullets missed Gil and Grant because of Brady's quick action. He and one of his guards fell on top of the brothers. Neptune took one in the shoulder, and Mace got hit in the arm. They're in surgery now. All told, it could have been a lot worse."

"Did Brady return the fire?"

"No, he did not, and that was smart. Too many people around."

"Where are Gil and Grant now?" Oliver asked.

"That's a big problem. They, along with Resseur, took off in the waiting limo. Brady might know where they went, but he's in surgery. West Hollywood P.D. has already checked out Resseur's apartment. No one's there and we don't have a warrant to get inside, so that's a dead end right now."

"What about the shooters?" Marge asked.

"Brady was sharp enough to glance at the car as it sped away. He and Kotsky said it was a red sedan, Japanese model—either Honda or Toyota. About fifteen minutes ago, a local cruiser found an abandoned car a half mile from the hospital: a maroon Honda Accord with the plates removed. I've sent Messing and Pratt out there to secure the scene. How far are you from St. Joseph's?"

"We're just walking out of Burbank. We should be there in fifteen minutes."

"Come up to the tenth floor. Don't bother calling because my cell will be off. Hospital rules. We'll talk later." He cut the line.

Marge pulled out the handle on her wheelie. "You drive." She tossed Scott the keys. "Another long night."

"After a very long day," Oliver said.

"Been a lot of those lately . . . twenty-four-hour shifts. If I'm gonna work that hard, I should have gone to medical school and made money."

"I was dating a doctor. She constantly whined about how hard she worked for how little money. But that's women. They whine about everything."

"Shut up, Oliver, you complain as much as anyone."

"But that's my given persona: the chronic curmudgeon."

"How come you get the curmudgeon persona and not me?"

"It could have been your persona, Margie, but instead, you chose perky, optimistic, and cooperative. So I took curmudgeon. Now you regret it, but it's too late. Don't blame me for your bad decisions. That won't get you anywhere."

THE CRIME SCENE was in the parking lot, but the action was on the tenth floor. It overflowed with men in uniform—hospital security guards in khaki, Kaffey's personal security guards in khaki, and about a half-dozen LAPD officers in blues. Decker was talking to Piet Kotsky—the big man with the jaundiced complexion—and when he saw Marge and Oliver, he motioned them over.

"We need to get a post schedule pronto," Decker ordered. "There are too many people in some places and none in others. Coordinate with hospital security to make sure that our people are involved."

"Any luck on finding Gil and Grant?" Oliver asked.

Decker's expression was sour, and his eyes went to Kotsky. "There may be people who *do* know where they are, but they aren't telling."

"What you want from me?" Kotsky had his arms folded over his chest. "I don't hide anywhere. I wait instructions of Mr. Brady."

Decker was trying to keep his temper. "I've been trying to tell Mr. Kotsky that Gil Kaffey's life may be in danger."

"He's with his brother," Kotsky said.

"Grant is still a suspect, Mr. Kotsky. I could subpoena you to reveal his location but by the time I do that, Gil Kaffey may be dead."

Kotsky waved him off. "I don't believe that Grant would hurt his brother."

"Can I quote you if Gil winds up dead? Maybe the shooters are hunting them down at this very minute."

"What for?"

"What do you mean, 'what for'?" Decker was aghast. "To kill Gil off and complete the job. Maybe this time the shooter will get lucky and kill all the men."

Kotsky was imperturbable. "I wait for Neptune Brady. He is the boss. He is out of surgery. Doctor says we can talk to him in maybe half hour."

It came out "maybe khef hour."

"What happened?" Marge asked Decker.

"Ask him." Decker cocked a thumb toward Kotsky. "He was there."

Kotsky said, "Somebody's make shots. Mr. Brady jump on Gil and Grant and bring them to the ground, I pull Mace down, but still he is shot in the arm. I feel bullet . . . the wind." He brushed his hand across his right cheek. "I hear it like a bumblebee go past my ear. I am lucky."

"And the shooters?" Oliver asked.

"I don't see much," Kotsky said. "When I look up, I see red car sedan. I think it is Toyota or Honda."

Marge said, "What about Antoine Resseur?"

Kotsky said, "He not get shots. He's gone, too."

Decker regarded Kotsky. "Excuse us for a moment."

"Sure. I no go nowhere."

Decker led Oliver and Marge into a secluded corner. "Rina identified Alejandro Brand as one of the guys that Brett Harriman overheard talking about the murders. I've called up Foothill and asked them to put a couple of men on him. I also assigned Messing and Pratt to hunt around. I'd like to know where Brand has been for the last few hours since he seems to be the only lead we have."

"Who's looking for the Kaffeys and Resseur?" Marge said.

"I've put out an APB on them."

"Maybe it's a setup, Loo, with the three of them in it together," Oliver said. "Gil and Grant to get the money and Resseur to get Gil back. You told us he was pissed that he broke up with Gil and that he blamed the parents."

"That's extreme measures to get back your boyfriend."

"When passions get high . . ." Oliver said. "And why would the men run if someone was really trying to whack them? You'd think they'd be too scared not to be protected."

"Protection hasn't done anything to help them," Marge said. "Maybe they're too scared to stick around. Maybe they don't trust anyone except each other."

"Okay . . . then assuming the shooting is legit," Oliver said. "Who's the target?"

Marge said, "Who knows? The only Kaffey who hasn't been shot is Grant. He's worth looking at a little closer."

"I'm still thinking about the embezzling uncle," Oliver said. "How serious is Mace's gunshot wound?"

Decker said, "Far from life threatening, but it's still a bullet in the arm. We still have a missing guard, guys. What's going on with Rondo Martin?"

Marge said, "The man was a cipher even in Ponceville. No one is even sure where he came from."

Oliver said, "Martin wasn't overly social—an occasional beer or two. In his off hours, he used to hang out at the field-hand houses.

They're called the ciudads and they surround the farms. The areas look like Tijuana on a bad day."

"It's more shantytown than city," Marge said. "And the area probably houses prostitutes."

"Not much else to do up there," Oliver said.

"Rondo Martin used to frequent the northern district of the ciudads."

"They're divided into four quarters?" Decker asked.

"I believe so," Marge told him. "The sheriff is a guy named Tim England, but everyone calls him T. His secretary rattled off some of the families who live in the northern district. One of the surnames was Mendez."

Immediately, Decker said, "As in Ana Mendez."

"You got it," Marge said. "We had to leave before we could nose around. There may be nothing to it. Mendez is a common Hispanic surname. The simplest thing to do would be to ask Ana about it, but we don't want to scare her away."

Oliver said, "We thought that maybe you and Brubeck would want to go up and see the ciudads for yourselves."

Decker smiled. "You're giving me an assignment."

"Brubeck is local and you speak Spanish," Marge said.

Oliver said, "I would leave Sheriff T in the dark. I think he might not like you poking into his territory."

Decker said, "You don't like Sheriff T?"

Marge said, "He is a flat guy. He wasn't self-revealing, but why would he be?"

"All right," Decker said. "Sounds like a good day's work. What about Oakland? Did you make contact with Neptune's dad?"

"It's actually his grandfather," Oliver said. "Porter Brady. Neptune's father was black, but his mother is white. That explains his perpetual tan."

"What does his race have to do with the Kaffey murders?" Decker said. "Displaced anger or something?"

"According to Porter, Neptune didn't hate his mom." Oliver gave him a recap on what they had learned.

Marge said, "That explains why Brady's in his thirties and the old man is in his seventies."

"Brady's phone records put him in Oakland when the shooting went down," Oliver said. "Do you still consider him a strong suspect, Rabbi?"

"He hasn't been ruled out. No one has, including that guy."

Decker was referring to Kotsky. The man hadn't moved, still standing in the same spot with his arms across his chest. He would have made a dynamite beefeater.

"I guess we'll just have to wait until we talk to Neptune. He seems to be calling the shots." Decker shrugged. "Maybe more shots than we think."

BECAUSE DR. RAIN had met Decker previously, he allowed him contact with Brady. But only he could go in and only for a short time. Neptune's face was gray and his skin was mottled. There was an oxygen tube up his nose and an IV in his arm. His lips were cracked but his eyes were open. Bedsheets were covering his lower body. His upper torso, swathed in bandages, was exposed. He was semi-upright, and when he noticed Decker, he gave him a dazed look. "I know you."

"Lieutenant Decker. How are you feeling?"

"I'm flying, man . . . don't want to crash. Ever been shot?"

"A couple of times."

"Like being stuck with a hot poker. Fuck, it burns."

"Yes, it does."

"But now all is mellow."

"I'll keep the questions short."

"Short is good . . . not in dicks though."

"Neptune, do you know where the Kaffey boys are?"

"Nope! No idea."

"They just jumped in the limo and disappeared?"

"I told them . . . get the hell out of Dodge."

"What about Antoine Resseur?"

"What about him?"

"Did he go with the Kaffey boys?"

"Did he?"

"I don't know," Decker said. "I'm asking you."

"Fuck if I know."

"Where do you think they might have gone?"

"To go where no man has ever gone . . ." He gave the *Star Trek* V sign. Index and middle finger together on one side of the V split with the ring and pinkie finger on the other. Decker knew that this was a ritual gesture given by the Jews' priests—the Kohanim—when blessing the congregation. It was two thousand years old.

"Maybe you can guess within earthly boundaries?"

"No idea." Another silly smile. "I redeemed myself. I got shot, but not the Kaffeys."

"Mace got shot."

Brady was thinking hard. "Yeah . . . that's messed up." A pause. "Demerol is great. I should become an addict. They tried to send me to rehab but I said no, no, no."

"Neptune, who besides Kotsky and you knew that Gil was coming out?"

"Gil came out a while ago . . ." A wide smile.

Decker said, "Knew that Gil was being released from the hospital."

He coughed and winced when he did. "Shit, that burns."

"Do you need the nurse?"

"I need more drugs."

Decker pushed the nurse's call button. He decided to simplify further. "You knew when Gil was going to be released from the hospital, right?"

"Right."

"So did Grant, Mace, Antoine Resseur, and Piet Kotsky, correct?"

"Correct."

"Anyone else know?"

"Know what?"

"When Gil was coming out of the hospital." Decker tried another way. "Did you hire anyone else besides Piet Kotsky to guard the Kaffeys?"

The question stumped him. "I don't think so . . . it's a little foggy . . . my brain."

"So far the only one who wasn't shot was Grant and Resseur," Decker said. "What do you think about that?"

"I did my job. Otherwise his brains would have been splattered on my bomber jacket."

"Was a man named Alejandro Brand ever employed by you?"

He blinked several times. "Doesn't sound familiar. Who is he?"

"You look in pain."

"I could use another shot of happiness."

Decker depressed the button a second time. He decided to pull one out of the hat. "Did you know that Rondo Martin and Ana Mendez were an item?"

Brady said, "Ana the maid?"

"Yes. Ana Mendez. I heard they were dating."

"Hmmm . . ." Brady appeared thoughtful. "Once time, I came into the guards' quarters." He inhaled and exhaled, slow and steady. "Rondo was there in his civvies . . . he was eating a plate of Mexican food." He closed his eyes. "Tacos and enchiladas, rice and beans. No roach coaches on the ranch."

"I wouldn't think so. Did you ask him about it?"

"Yep. He told me he could cook and offered me some. I told him no thanks and he said, suit yourself. Then he got up and threw the plate in the garbage. He told me he was going to get dressed for his post." Another spasm of pain.

"Did Ana cook the meal for him?"

"Don't know. The hot plate and the microwave were clean. He didn't heat it up there. And it sure didn't smell like frozen shit. . . . I'm tired."

"I know. But I'd really like to find Gil and Grant. I'm worried about them."

"Go get rapists and robbers . . . they'll show up."

The nurse came in and consulted the chart, then the IV line. "How are we doing?"

Brady said, "Don't know about you, but I'm doing shitty."

"I'll add a little more medicine to your drip," the nurse said. "It'll make you a little sleepy."

"Sleepy is fine," Brady told her. "Just get rid of the fucking pain."

TWENTY-FOUR

MACE'S ROOM WAS down the hall from Brady's. His injury required an overnight stay, but if all went well, he'd be discharged the following morning. He was sitting atop the bed, his arm in a sling, watching TV, dressed in pajamas and a robe. He was gray around the eyes set in deep, dark circles. His lips were blanched and dry. His black hair was shiny and a shade off of greasy.

"I can't wait to get out of here," he told Decker. "This place is a loony bin."

"When are you leaving?" Decker asked him.

"Soon as I can travel, even if I charter a private jet." He clicked off the TV. "Guy was always getting me into fixes. In life and in death."

"I read about that," Decker said. "The lawsuit."

Mace waved Decker off with his good hand. "A misunderstanding. I could have pursued it, but the only ones who'd have gotten rich would have been the lawyers. In the end, I got what I wanted and so did he. And no, I don't care to elaborate."

Decker said, "I'd like to ask you about what happened in the parking lot. Did you see anything?"

Mace shook his head. "It happened so fast."

"Brady and Kotsky remember a car peeling rubber after the shots."

"Good for them. I can't say that I remember anything except thinking I was going to die. I knew I got hit. Blood was everywhere. I was so confused, I thought I took it in the chest. Thank God, it was only my arm."

"Could you go over the sequence? Like you walked out of the hospital and then . . ."

"Okay, let me think." Mace closed his eyes. "Gil was in a wheelchair. Antoine was on his right, Grant was on the left. Brady was in front of us, whatshisname was in back." He paused. "Where was I?" Another pause. "I was between Gil and whatshisname."

"Kotsky?" Decker said.

"Yeah, him. I was walking ahead of Kotsky, but behind Gil, Grant, and Resseur. I heard a popping noise and Kotsky . . . he pushed me to the ground. Next thing I remember is shaking like Jell-O. My first thought was: please God, don't let me die and don't let me die in L.A."

"Looks like God answered your prayers."

"Maybe." Then under his breath, Mace added, "At least for the moment."

Decker gave him a card. "If you need anything or remember anything . . ."

Mace took the card, and then clicked back on the TV.

Interview over.

"THE LATEST PRINTOUTS on Greenridge." Lee Wang set a stack of papers on the Loo's desk. He brushed black hair from his face and sat down without being asked. His brown jacket had padded shoulders but was an inch too short in the sleeves. The clothing salesperson must have been on crack.

Placing aside a pile of phone messages, Decker picked up the papers and stifled a yawn. Last night, he'd slept four fitful hours, and even with a couple of cups of morning coffee, he had to think about focusing.

"What am I reading, Lee?"

"The top ones are recent articles on Paul Pritchard of Cyclone Inc."

"Greenridge's nemesis. Can you summarize it in ten words or less?"

"Pritchard thinks Greenridge is a bust. The project as proposed isn't feasible. I know, that's a dozen words but it's the best I can do."

"Could his sentiments be sour grapes?"

"Sure, but read the articles, Loo. Pritchard talks about how Greenridge's costs have skyrocketed to the point where the project is dead. He's just waiting for the official burial."

"How does he know so much about Kaffey's finances?"

"It's not Kaffey Industries that's naked in the wind, it's the Greenridge Project specifically. Their projected costs analysis was in a prospectus that they gave the bond insurers in order to underwrite municipal debt. But with the recent market destabilization, the Kaffey group has been hit hard. Plus Greenridge has been socked with additional costs due to delays in construction and necessary improvements that had to be made in order to win local approval. Finally, because of terrible equity market conditions and cost overrun, Greenridge's initial offering that was supposed to come out at an A1 rating was lowered to almost junk bond status. That means to get people to buy Greenridge bonds, the Kaffey group has to offer a very high interest rate."

"More added costs."

"Exactly," Wang said. "I'm going to go out on a short limb and say that a man as savvy as Guy Kaffey would have pulled the plug on the project. But now that Guy's gone, who knows?"

"Any information on who's going to take over Kaffey Industries?"

"Most of the articles predict near-equal inheritance between his sons."

"What about Mace? Initially, didn't you tell me he has a tiny stake in the company?"

"I believe he does."

"If Gil and Grant have a difference of opinion, Mace's tiny stake could be worth a lot. Theoretically, Grant and Mace could side against Gil and keep Greenridge alive."

"If the sons inherit an equal amount of stock with Mace having a percentage or two, that would be true."

Decker sat back in his desk chair and smoothed his mustache. "Lee, what do you think about the murders? Was Gil supposed to be killed along with his parents?"

Wang gave the question some serious thought. "Grant Kaffey is the only member of the Kaffey group who hasn't been shot."

Decker made a tent with his fingers. "Right now, Grant, Gil, and Antoine Resseur are missing. Could Grant be using the situation as the perfect opportunity to get rid of his brother?"

"It would look suspicious if Gil suddenly wound up, dead. Plus, if Resseur was with them, Grant would have to kill him as well."

Decker nodded. "Just a thought."

The phone rang. Decker picked up the receiver. "Hey, Willy, welcome back . . . That's okay, Will, we didn't expect you to find him. It was a pig in a poke. But I do have another assignment for you when . . . No, you don't have to come in today. Enjoy your vaca—" He smiled. "Well, if she's driving you crazy, you can tell her that I need you to come in right away, all right? Sure. See you in a bit."

Wang smiled. "His wife?"

"As long as Willy still has a couple of days left, she wants him to retile the bathroom floor." Decker's mind was still on the former conversation. "Let me play devil's advocate for a moment. Guy Kaffey was an over-the-top kind of guy. Just look at his ranch. It's the size of a small European country. He also loved winning and by all accounts, he was a risk taker, even manic at times in his business practices."

"All true from what I've read," Wang said.

"You don't think that he might have allowed Grant and Mace to see Greenridge to its conclusion rather than throw up his hands and admit defeat?"

"I could see that if Greenridge was *Guy's* idea. But Greenridge was Grant's brainchild—Grant and Mace. Loo, this is a project that should have been killed in an exuberant market. In times of recessions and cutbacks, Greenridge is a dinosaur."

Wang thought a moment.

"Maybe Guy would build Greenridge on a smaller scale. But even if he did that, he'd still need to siphon off some money from other parts of Kaffey Industries."

"Let's take this one step further," Decker said. "If Grant and Mace want to see Greenridge to completion, would Guy and Gil have to go?"

"Gil would be an obstacle, sure. But whoever did this can't kill everyone." Wang stood up. "I have some free time in the afternoon. You want me to hunt around for Grant, Gil, and Antoine?"

"I've got people on that. Why don't you get a judge to issue a couple of subpoenas for them, demanding that they appear as material witnesses to the shootings. It's kind of ass-backward, but at least let's have all the pieces in place when we do locate them."

Decker's phone rang again. Wang gave a wave as he walked out of the office.

"Hi, Mallory Quince here. We've got Alejandro Brand in custody."

"Wow!" Decker sat up. "That was fast. Great job. How'd you bust him?"

"He busted himself. His meth lab blew up."

THE VIDEO CAMERA in the interview room showed a man of around nineteen in an oversized white T-shirt and baggy green shorts that hung down to his knees. He had a Dodger cap on his head, the visor casting a shadow over his eyes and nose. Decker could make out a thin mouth and a long chin adorned with a soul patch. The skin on his arms and neck was blued with ink. There were two anaconda snakes running down his arms, and a B12 was visible on the back of his neck.

Mallory Quince stared over Decker's shoulder at the video screen while clucking her tongue. "Rumor has it that Narcotics isn't happy shaving time off the charge based on some blind guy's hearing voices. The only reason they've agreed is that you're a lieutenant and the scope of the Kaffey murders."

"That's two reasons. And I say what harm will it do to let the dude hear the tape? The blind guy's ear is very acute."

Mallory straightened up and folded her arms across her chest, pulling on the shoulders of her pumpkin-colored jacket. Her hair was short, dark. Her voice was tense. "How do you know that the blind guy isn't going to say 'yes, it's the scumbag I heard' just to feel important and to get a reward?"

"Because I told him that the eyewitness had picked out four possible suspects. Harriman has already discarded two Spanish-speaking Mexican officers."

"Maybe he knew you were setting him up with shills."

Decker shrugged. "Tell Narcotics that I'm not offering Brand anything. All I want him to do is speak Spanish for voice identification."

"Will that hold up in court?"

"We're not accusing Brand of anything. We're only trying to find out what he knows about the Kaffey murders. It shouldn't take long. I really don't even want to broach the murders until Harriman identifies his voice."

"So what's the plan?" Mallory's voice had softened.

"I tell him the current charges against him . . . get him talking. His grandmother's apartment in Pacoima was burned out. I want him to think that I'm trying to pin an additional arson charge on him."

"Did he do it?"

"Probably. Who knows? Maybe I'll even get a confession. I'll be sitting right here." On the monitor, Decker pointed to the empty chair across from Brand. "That way the camera picks up my good side."

DECKER INTRODUCED HIMSELF in Spanish and shook hands with the kid.

Brand scratched a scar near his eye and said, "I know English."

Decker kept his face flat although he was inwardly cursing. He switched to English. "However you're comfortable, Alejandro."

The gangbanger folded his hands and laid them on the table. The hairs on his forearm smelled like barbecue ash. That must have happened when the lab blew up. Maybe that's how he got the first scar.

Decker said, "Do you know why you're here?"

"No."

"Your apartment exploded."

"So what? I didn't have nothing to do with it."

"Why don't you tell me what happened?"

"I can't tell you 'cause I don't know." He switched to Spanish. "*Estallado* . . . Boom. *Comprende?*"

"*Sí.*"

He said, "I think it was a gas line. It smelled like gas was leaking, you know?"

In Spanish, Decker said, "How long had you lived in the apartment?"

"*Posible seis meses.*" Six months.

"And how long were you inside before the apartment exploded?"

"Hmmm . . . *posiblemente viente minutos.*"

Maybe twenty minutes. He wasn't much for long sentences, but at least they were conversing in the right language. Decker said, "And you smelled gas?"

"Yeah, I did." Sensing an out, Brand was running with the story. "It stank."

"So why didn't you call the gas company?"

" 'Cause it all happened too fast."

"You were just sitting there . . . *usted acaba sentarse alli y* . . . boom?"

"*Sí, sí. Exactamente.*"

In Spanish, Decker said, "The police found antifreeze containers in your garbage."

In Spanish, "It gets cold in the winter."

"It freezes like once every six years in Southern California."

"My car isn't so good."

"They also found containers of acetone, paint thinner, Freon, battery acid . . . those materials are very explosive."

"Yeah, I found out the hard way."

"There were empty pop bottles, tubing, lots of matches, and a hot plate—"

"I need a hot plate 'cause I don't have a stove. Talk to my landlord."

"C'mon, Alex." Decker leaned in. "What were you doing with all that stuff?"

"It's a crime to have stuff?"

"It's not a crime to have paint thinner if you're an artist. It's not a crime to have antifreeze if you're going to drive to Colorado in the winter. It's not a crime to have acetone if you own a nail salon. It looks suspicious when you have all those things and you don't paint, you're not driving in cold weather, and you're not doing your nails."

The gangbanger shrugged.

"You have some heavy-duty charges against you, son. You can help yourself if you tell us what was going on. Judges like honesty."

Another shrug.

"If you tell us the truth, we might even be a little more lenient with the arson charge in your grandmother's apartment."

He yanked his head up. "What arson charge?"

"Alex, c'mon!" Silence. "Everyone saw you running away. We have dozens of eyewitnesses."

"I say they're liars and I say you're a liar. You don't have nothing."

"Look, Alex, you're in trouble. You have stuff in your apartment that makes you look like you were doing something illegal . . . like you're not only dealing, but also manufacturing. That's twenty years minimum."

The kid's eyes were doing a little dance in their sockets. "It wasn't even my stuff."

Excuse number two. "So whose stuff was it?"

"La Boca."

The mouth. "That's a person?"

"Yes, yes."

"Tell me about La Boca and how all that stuff got inside your apartment."

It began in fits and starts. How La Boca had friends who were out of business and they needed a place to store their stuff. How he volunteered to keep his stuff 'cause he's a nice guy. When Brand saw that Decker wasn't interrupting, he elaborated further. It didn't matter because it was all a pack of lies. But once the kid started talking, he couldn't stop.

And that's exactly what Decker wanted: Brand's voice speaking Spanish and recorded on tape.

TWENTY-FIVE

EVEN IF IT wasn't an actual legal breach, showing up at the house certainly was unethical. Rina studied Brett Harriman through the peephole to see if anyone was with him, but he appeared to be alone. He was dressed in a blue T-shirt and jeans.

"What do you want?" she asked through the closed door.

"Can I come in? I just want to talk to you for a few minutes." A pause. "It's awkward to speak through a barrier."

Rina opened the door, but kept the security chain on. "It's awkward for you to show up at my house. We don't have anything to talk about."

"I identified the voice of the man I overheard at the courthouse." A pause. "Maybe now you can come down and identify him."

Rina was silent. She resented the intrusion.

Harriman said, "We should feel good about the teamwork. I think the ID might have helped your husband." A pause. "I mean I feel good about it."

It was nice to do one's civic duty, but it wasn't worth uncorking the champagne. Unless he was after the Kaffey reward. But then why bother her? Maybe if she continued the silent treatment, he'd take the hint.

Sure enough, Harriman gave up. "Sorry to have bothered you."

Rina felt bad. Inhospitable wasn't a word in her vocabulary, but the man was odd and she was alone. She watched him make his way down the steps, feeling the dips of the cement with the point of his shoe. When she couldn't see him anymore through the peephole, she went to the window and pulled back the curtains just in time to see him slide into the passenger side of a newer-model black Honda Accord. Of course he hadn't come alone. He couldn't drive.

Her eyes swept along the empty street.

Well, nearly empty.

Directly across the road was Addison Ellerby's twenty-five-year-old white Suburban. A few feet away from the truck was a dark blue Saturn sedan with tinted windows. She didn't remember ever seeing that car in her neighborhood, but she didn't pay much attention to cars. Automobiles were just background pieces, bits of color that dotted the landscape like a tree or a rosebush.

As soon as the Honda pulled away, the Saturn sprang to life and drove off behind it. Rina was positioned to catch the license plate.

An exercise in futility. There were no plates, just a framed piece of paper where the license plate was supposed to be, stating AN-OTHER SATURN SOLD FROM POPPER MOTORS.

DECKER SPOKE WITH surprising calm, making his threat all the more ominous. "I'm going to kill him!"

Rina unwrapped a roast beef sandwich and handed it to him. They were sitting at his desk. Peter once told her that since he had an office—as opposed to a cubicle—he felt as if he had arrived. The area wasn't much bigger than a walk-in closet. "I'm sure he didn't mean anything."

"I don't care." He took a bite. With a bulging cheek, he said, "His showing up is out of line and just plain creepy."

"Yes, it is. Potato salad?" She passed him the carton before he could answer. "Not that I'm Xena the warrior, but even I could take on a blind man."

Decker said, "Maybe he's not blind. Maybe he's one big con."

Rina laughed. "He's faking his blindness?"

"He's obviously an attention seeker. Have you ever seen his eyes? Maybe he's perfectly sighted and just wants to get into your pants."

"Now you're being ridiculous."

"If he shows up again, call me immediately."

"That would be about the last thing I'd do. You carry a gun."

"And I know how to use it. Now tell me about the Saturn."

She took a nibble of her turkey sandwich. "I told you everything. It was navy with tinted side windows, maybe two, three years old and didn't have any regular plates."

"Sedan, SUV, or coupe?"

"Sedan."

"That would probably be an Astra or an Aura. And there was no license plate . . . just paper saying the car came from Popper Motors."

"Exactly. It took off as soon as Harriman left."

"And you didn't see who was inside?"

"I didn't even know someone was inside until it left. The windows were very dark. The Saturn made me more nervous than Harriman."

"Why's that?"

"Because I couldn't see who was behind the wheel. You should call up Popper Motors."

"Marge is doing it right now. Do you think that the car was watching the house or watching Harriman?"

"I couldn't say. If I had to guess, it would be Harriman. Or maybe no one."

"Did the Saturn have a view of the window you were looking through?"

"I don't know."

"So not only did this schmuck show up at our house, potentially tainting any useful information he gave me, but he also possibly dragged you into something dangerous." Decker was trying to control his temper. "I don't want you and Hannah to stay in the house if I'm not there."

"That's ridiculous."

"A strange car with tinted windows and paper plates was parked across the street, and I'm working on a very high-profile murder. Maybe it didn't have anything to do with Harriman. Maybe it has something to do with me."

"But then why did it leave when Harriman left?"

"I don't know, Rina. But until I do know, it pays to be careful. Just do me a favor. Stay at your parents' when I'm not home."

"My parents are almost an hour away in traffic and Hannah has school."

"She can stay with friends until I get home. You stay at your parents'. Agreed?"

"Aye, aye, Captain." A broad smile. "But you won't be getting any home-cooked meals for a while. What about Shabbos?"

"Call up friends and we'll get us invited out."

If Peter was willing to be that social, he was serious. "And you don't think you're overreacting?"

"No, I'm not overreacting, and even if I was, better to be safe." Peter was still angry. "I can't believe he showed up at the house. What an idiot! Or maybe he's just deranged. I'll kill that bastard!"

"Please don't do that, Peter." Rina took his hand and smiled. "Cops generally don't do well behind bars."

But he didn't laugh. Rina took another stab at humor. "If I weren't so trusting, I would think you're trying to get rid of us. If I drop in and find you in the middle of a lap dance, your goose is cooked."

"The only lap dance I want right now is one with Ms. Beretta. You mess with my wife, you mess with me."

THE CALL TO Harriman was brief. Stay away from his house, stay away from his wife.

"I didn't mean anything." He was contrite. "I just wanted to make sure she knew—"

"That's *not* your business, Mr. Harriman, it's *my* business. Your part in this investigation is done! Over! Finished! Get it?"

"Lieutenant, I know you think I'm a weirdo, but I'm not. I've worked for the courts for five years and I don't get a lot of opportunity to do novel things. I suppose I overestimated the worth of my participation. If you need me, call."

"Good," Decker said. "We've reached an understanding. Before you get off, I want to ask you a couple of questions. Starting with who drove you to my house?"

"My girlfriend, Dana. You want her phone number?"

"I do."

Harriman rattled off some numbers. "She's at work. I just spoke to her a few minutes ago. I'm sure you can reach her."

"Brett, did you notice anything unusual when you left my house?"

"Did I *notice* anything unusual?" A slight chuckle. "I'm blind."

Okay. So he didn't fall into that one. "Did you hear anything unusual when you left?"

"Like what?"

"You tell me."

"Unusual?" Harriman was silent, trying to re-create the moment. "I walked back to the car . . . your wife closed the door to the house . . ."

"She told me she didn't open the door."

"I'm sorry to contradict you, but she did open the door. Probably not all the way because her voice still sounded a little muffled. Do you have a security chain on the front door? Maybe she opened it as far as the chain."

Decker didn't answer. "Go on. You heard her close the door . . ."

"Uh . . . I didn't hear any footsteps nearby. I heard a dog bark. Sounded like a golden or a lab—something medium to large. I didn't hear voices. There was some distant traffic. We took off . . ." A long pause. "I think there was a car behind us. Ask Dana."

"I will. What's Dana's last name?"

"Cochelli. I've got to go back to court. I apologize for being overly zealous."

"No problem." Decker hung up. He was about to call up Harriman's girlfriend when Grant Kaffey burst through the doors of the squad room. His eyes were wild and his hair was messy, as if it had been raked by nervous fingers. Decker bolted up and attempted to usher him into his office, but the man was too agitated.

"He's *gone!*" Grant said.

Decker said, "Who's gone?"

"Gil! I went to the market to pick up a few staples and when I came back, he'd disappeared!" Grant grabbed Decker's arms. "You've got to find him!"

"Let's go inside the office and talk about—"

"What's there to talk about!" Grant screamed. "He's gone! Just find him! Isn't that your fucking job?!"

Decker kept his voice even. "If you all hadn't disappeared in the first place, this might not have been necessary. If you want me to find your brother, let's go into my office and you can tell me what happened. And if I find you credible, then I'll think about an APB. Right now, buddy, from my standpoint, you look like suspect number one!"

The color drained from Grant's face. "You think I hurt him?" Then his face turned crimson. "You think I'd hurt my own brother!"

Decker flung open the door to his office. "After you."

Kaffey weighed his options, then stormed across the threshold of Decker's office.

Score one for the lieutenant.

Decker closed his office door. "Did you call 911?"

"I called the police," Grant said. "They told me that an adult missing for an hour wasn't a crime. I tried to explain the situation, but the guy was an asshole." He was pacing on whatever little floor space there was. "I hung up and came out here."

"Where were you staying?"

"Somewhere in the Hollywood Hills. One of Gil's buddies owns the place. He told my brother we could have it for the month."

Decker said, "You drove all the way from Hollywood?"

"I was panicked! I didn't want to stay alone in the house and I didn't know what to do. You're the enemy I know rather than the enemy I don't know."

"We're on the same side, Mr. Kaffey. I need the address of the house."

Grant was still pacing. "I don't know it, but I could point out the house. It's near a big street with lots of little cafés. Gil and I had dinner there last night."

"Hillhurst?"

"Yeah, Hillhurst. Right."

"Are you staying east or west of Hillhurst?"

"West . . . between Hillhurst and Tower."

"Gower?"

"Yeah, Gower. If we ride down Hollywood, I could probably direct you."

"How'd you find your way here?"

"I used the navigation system." Grant stopped moving and regarded Decker. "We need to go now."

"Where is Antoine Resseur?"

"Antoine?" Grant was confused. "At his apartment. Why? Where should he be?"

"I thought Gil was going to stay with Antoine Resseur. What changed his mind?"

"Resseur felt that Gil's place and his place were targets. So Gil picked out another location. Why are you bringing up Antoine?"

"He's missing. I was under the impression that he left with you two."

"He did, but then he left and went back home, I thought." A pause. "Do you think Antoine had something to do with it?"

Decker sidestepped the question. Resseur hadn't been in his apartment for the last two days. That marked him as either a suspect or a scared man. "Do you know the name of the driver who took you to the house? We could call him and get the address."

"No." His face turned red with fury. "Why aren't you making calls to your people?"

"To make calls to my people, I need an address. Hold on. Let me think." Decker picked up the phone and called up the Hollywood station, asking for Detective Kutiel. It was a stroke of luck that his daughter was at her desk. "It's your favorite Loo. I've got Grant Kaffey in my office. Apparently his brother is missing."

"Not *apparently*!" Grant shouted. "He's *missing*! Why don't you believe me?"

Over the phone, Cindy said, "I heard that. How long has he been missing?"

"About an hour, maybe a little longer," Decker said.

"An hour?" Cindy said. "Maybe he took a walk."

"He just got out of the hospital, so I don't think so. It could be that someone came by and picked him up—"

"Impossible!" Grant yelled.

"Picked him up to get away from his brother?" Cindy asked.

"The thought crossed my mind," Decker told her. "Antoine Resseur—Gil's ex-partner—has been missing since the shooting at the hospital. It could be the two of them ran away—"

"He didn't run away with Antoine!" Kaffey interjected. "Someone fucking kidnapped him!"

"Hold on!" Decker covered the mouthpiece with his hand. "Excuse me while I finish up the conversation. I'm not cutting you off, but if you want help, we've got to get a plan going." To Cindy he said, "The Kaffeys were staying in your territory. Somewhere between Gower and Hillhurst but I don't know the address—"

"Beachwood!" Grant said triumphantly. "Is there a Beachwood street or boulevard?" When Decker nodded, he said, "We're staying on Beachwood."

Decker related the information to Cindy. "We're on our way over. He can point out the house. Do you have time right now?"

"What do you want me to do? Hop in the car and hunt around the street?"

"That would be a start."

"And what exactly am I looking for?"

"Start with Antoine Resseur's car. It's a 2006 red BMW 328i." He gave her the license number. "If Gil was picked up by anyone, I'm betting it was him. Could be they just went out for lunch—"

"Jesus fucking Christ!" Grant shouted. "Gil was in no shape to go out!"

"Why not?" Decker countered. "You two went out for dinner last night."

"And it took me about twenty minutes of helping him in and out of a wheelchair. Besides, if he had gone out, he would have left me a note."

Not if he wanted to get away from you. Out loud he said, "Is the wheelchair still in the house?"

He didn't answer right away. "I don't remember."

Decker went back to the phone. "If you could put out a call to the cruisers to look for Resseur's car, that would be helpful."

"Not a problem. I'm just about done here anyway. I don't mind driving around the area. It's a good way for me to unwind and besides, Koby's still working. Call me when you're in the city, okay?"

"I will. Thank you, Detective." He hung up. "Mr. Kaffey, think hard. Where might your brother have gone?"

He slumped into one of the chairs across from Decker's desk. "I don't *know!*"

"Have you called Neptune Brady yet?"

"No." He hesitated a moment. "Honestly, I don't trust him. At least you're neutral."

"How'd you get over here?"

"I drove. Gil had set up a rental at the house."

"Gil set it up?"

"Maybe it was Antoine." Grant flew from the chair and started to pace. "I don't know! That's why I'm here. Because I don't fucking know!"

"Where's your uncle?"

"Mace?" Grant made a face. "I don't know. I thought he left to go home."

"Was he well enough?"

"I don't know. I haven't spoken to him. I don't know if I trust him. I don't know who to trust. I just want my brother to be okay."

Tears in Grant's eyes. His voice broke. "Can we go now?"

Decker picked up the car keys. He had more questions to ask, but he figured he could do that on the way to the house. Grant might be more amenable to talking then.

Nothing as sweet as a captive audience.

TWENTY-SIX

THE HOUSE THAT Grant pointed out was a 1960s modern perched on the crest of a mountain: low slung and built into the rocky crag. The exterior was glass, steel, and white stucco and was ringed with large camellia bushes in full pink bloom. Grant's identification was confirmed when his key opened the door.

The first thing Decker noticed was a vertigo view of the entire L.A. basin. It was all glass with no seams, giving the space a green-house look. It was one story and sprawled from room to room: handy for someone who was wheelchair bound—as long as the person didn't crash into the glass. The wood floors were stained ebony but the rest of the house, including the vaulted ceilings and walls, were painted a deep taupe.

The furniture was also 1960s in style but looked too new to be original. There was a low-slung gray velvet sofa, a love seat fashioned from multicolored leather polka dots framed with aluminum tubular molding, a red plastic chair fashioned into the shape of a hand, and a psychedelic area rug.

Decker and his daughter exchanged glances. A quick once-over told them immediately that nothing appeared out of place. There was no obvious sign of a struggle. Vases and knickknacks stood upright on tables and shelves. The dining room chairs were neatly spaced around the table, and the kitchen counter with all its appliances and accoutrements looked undisturbed.

Off an open area that contained the living room, the dining room, and the kitchen were two long hallways—one to the left and one to the right. Grant was already seated on the couch with his eyes closed. He was wan.

Decker said, "When was the last time you ate?"

"I don't remember."

"Go eat something. You'll need to keep up your strength. Where's Gil's room?"

"To the left, all the way down. The house has two master suites, which is why Gil liked it."

To Cindy, Decker said, "I'll take the left, you take the right."

"You're going to go through my things?" Grant asked Cindy.

"Briefly."

"Maybe I should come with you."

"Go eat something," Decker said. "Let us do our job."

Surprisingly, Grant acquiesced with a nod.

"Come in when you feel better," Cindy told him. Although she dressed for comfort, she still managed to look stylish: brown pants, a gold sweater, and an orange jacket that matched her flaming ginger hair. She had pulled back her mop into a ponytail and it swayed as she walked. Pearl earrings were her only concession to adornment. When she and Decker met back in the living room, twenty minutes later, the Los Angeles sky was tumbling in pinks and oranges.

Grant was on the phone. He quickly excused himself and hung up. "Anything?"

"Nothing seems out of place to my eye," Cindy said. "You're very neat. I tried to disturb your order as little as possible."

Decker said, "Did you find the wheelchair?"

Cindy shook her head no.

"Neither did I." He turned to Grant. "Your brother doesn't have a lot of clothing. Three shirts, a couple pairs of pants, two pairs of pajamas, two robes, a pair of slippers, and a pair of loafers."

"How many robes?"

Decker consulted his list. "A white terry robe hanging in the bathroom, and a silk maroon robe in the closet."

"Gil had way more silk robes than that. That was his preferred mode of dress. Silk robes over silk pajamas except when we went out."

Decker shook his head. "There were some spare hangers." He took a seat next to Grant. "You're not going to want to hear this, Mr. Kaffey, but to me, it seems that your brother packed up and left in your absence."

"He wasn't in good shape." Grant appeared truly baffled. "Why would he do that?"

"You tell me."

"Maybe someone had a gun to his head."

"That's a possibility." Decker paused. "But everything in his room looked very neat. You'd think if he were packing while his life was being threatened, he'd drop a hanger or the drawers would look a little messier." He turned to Cindy. "Did you find anything that indicates a kidnap, Detective?"

"Quite the opposite. Everything is really neat."

Grant faced Cindy, his eyes wet with tears. "But why would he just leave like that? Without telling me? Without leaving me a note?"

Decker raised his eyebrows. "This may also be what you don't want to hear, but it could be he doesn't trust you."

"That's ridiculous," Grant sputtered out. "We're not only brothers, we're best friends. If anyone should be suspicious, it should be me. He left me all alone. That's what you do when you're trying to set someone up."

Decker held out his hands and shrugged. "Until we know what's going on, it's smart to take precautions. Get a bodyguard. If you don't trust Brady, find someone yourself. And you should probably move out. Wherever you end up, tell me, okay?"

"Do you think Wind Chimes in Newport would be okay?"

"If you stay at Wind Chimes, you'll need a staff of bodyguards. If I were you, I'd go smaller."

Grant said, "What do you think about Neptune? Should I trust him?"

"How about if we talk about it on the way back to the station house. Why don't you pack up a few things and then we'll go?"

"Is it safe for me to do that?"

"I'll come with you," Cindy said. "There are a lot of windows with no treatments. Just in case something's lurking."

It took Grant twenty minutes to pack his belongings into two suitcases. By that time, the view outside had faded to charcoal with starlight sitting above the twinkling city lights. Outside the air was mild with crickets chirping. The roadside was nearly black, with streetlamps being few and far between. Grant struggled to get the key into the lock, the sole illumination a yellow-tinged porch light. Because it was so quiet, Decker heard the pops and because it was so dark, he saw the blinding orange flashes. Without thinking he pushed Cindy into the camellia bushes on the right while falling on top of Grant Kaffey, rolling the both of them into the shrubbery on the left. As he lay sprawled out on Grant, he managed to extract his gun, while screaming to Cindy to ask if she was all right.

"I'm fine, I'm fine, I'm fine," she screamed back. "I got my gun."

"Don't shoot!" Decker screamed.

And then the night turned deathly quiet.

He dropped his voice to a whisper. "Can you hear me?"

"Loud and clear."

"Don't shoot. Let your eyes adjust."

"I'm with you, boss."

His own eyes were intensely focused, staring through the bushes, seeing whatever he could make out: some pinpoints of light but mostly shadows. Houses . . . parked cars . . . trees. Nothing in human shape appeared to be moving. To Grant he whispered, "You okay?"

"Yeah. My leg hurts."

Grant was grunting. Not surprising because Decker must have outweighed him by fifty pounds. "Bad?"

"I think I scraped it. I'm okay."

Decker's ears suddenly perked up to the sound of receding footsteps, but he couldn't see any shape or form. Within a moment, an ignition fired followed by the screech of tires laying down rubber. The noise grew softer as the seconds ticked on.

"Can you reach your phone?"

"Yeah . . . I think so . . ."

Decker waited stock-still while his eyes continued to look for a change in the shadows. "Call 911 and hold it up to my ear, okay? You still there, Cin?"

"I'm still here with my metallic friend in hand."

The crickets had started up again. After what seemed like an eternity, he finally felt the cell upon his ear, an operator saying those beautiful words.

"911. What's your emergency?"

In a calm whisper that belied his rapidly beating heart, Decker explained that he was from LAPD, that shots had been fired, that one person may be hurt, and they needed immediate backup. He gave the address and the street to the operator and told her to tell the cruisers to stop any vehicle they met coming up the mountain. "Use extreme caution. The driver of the car may be armed."

She repeated the address back to him.

Decker told her yes. He wasn't even aware that he had memorized the street numerals. But such was the force of habit after thirty-plus years on the job. He had always made it a point to know where he was, had done so unconsciously.

Five minutes later, Decker could hear the wail of the approaching sirens. Using Grant's cell phone, he pinpointed his location to the uniformed cops. It took a while to secure the area and extract them from the foliage.

All around were blinking black-and-whites. Curious neighbors stood behind yellow crime tape. As the three of them brushed dirt off their clothes, Grant discovered that his pants were torn and he was bleeding from his leg. Decker took a flashlight from a uniformed officer, knelt down, and carefully parted the torn cloth on Grant's pants leg.

Could be a nasty scrape or it could be a graze wound. In better light, he could have discerned if the skin had been burned or not. He could see that it was oozing—wet and shiny—but it wasn't spurting. He looped his arm around Grant's waist and asked Cindy to help him carry Grant to a cruiser. The best thing to do was to keep him settled and let the professionals handle this one.

As soon as Kaffey was seated in a black-and-white, Decker radioed for an ambulance.

"I'M HUNG UP at work." Decker was trying to keep his voice neutral. "Do me a favor and stay overnight with your parents."

"How late are you going to be?" Rina asked him.

"I don't know. I'm at a crime scene. Maybe pretty late."

"What crime scene?"

"Can't go into that right now. I'll talk to you later, okay? Call me when you get to your parents'."

"Peter, you sound very tense. What aren't you telling me?"

"I can't get into that."

Rina could hear voices in the background. One of them sounded like her stepdaughter. "Is Cindy there?"

"What makes you say that?"

"Obviously I hear her. What are you doing in Hollywood?"

"Maybe she's in West Valley. I've got to go."

"Not until you tell me what's going on. I've been a cop's wife for seventeen years. I'm not going to melt. Tell me right now!"

Decker gave her the abbreviated version, hoping that would satisfy her.

"But you and Cindy are okay?"

Her voice sounded shaky. "Rina, we're both fine. My face got scratched a little, but other than that, I am completely whole."

"Baruch Hashem. I'll bench Gomel for you."

The prayer for surviving a dire situation. "Do it for Cindy as well."

"I will." Now her voice sounded teary. "What are you doing right now?"

"We're trying to find all the bullets and reconstructing the trajectory."

"So you can know how lucky you were."

Decker smiled. "I just wish I could have seen something. You know how dark it is in the hills, and I was literally hiding in the bushes."

"Could you hear anything?"

"Receding footsteps and a car peeling rubber. I've called in a tech to see if we can lift a tire print from the skid marks. Maybe we'll catch a break."

Rina didn't answer.

"Are you still there?" Decker asked.

"I was just thinking about the blue Saturn that was parked across the street."

"The one with the tinted windows and Popper Motors license plate. I had Marge check it out. They do sell new and used Saturns. Marge spoke to a salesperson named Dean Reeves. They're checking the records. If it came from them, they have a record of the tires on the car."

"It would be interesting if the treads matched your skid marks."

"It would be more than interesting, it would be downright scary. I've got to go. Call me when you're at your parents."

"I will. You're not so far from them. Maybe you'll get off earlier than you think."

"I'll come over whenever I can."

"Good to hear," Rina said. "I'll keep the night-light on and the sheets warm."

TWENTY-SEVEN

THE PAIR LOOKED like Marge and Oliver. The woman had on a gray sweater with the sleeves hiked up at the elbows, dark blue trousers, and sneakers, but the man's dress was a giveaway—a spiffy blue sports jacket, khaki slacks, and oxfords. As they came closer, their faces took form.

"What are you *doing* here?" Decker said.

"I called up Marge," Cindy said. "I thought she'd want to know." To Oliver, she waved. "Hello, Scott, how have you been?"

"I've been dandy, Cynthia. How's married life?"

"So far, it's an excellent fit."

"I'm glad to hear you're well."

"Thank you."

Marge said, "Now that we got the pleasantries over with, you wanna tell us what the hell happened?" She looked at Cindy. "Either one of you."

Although there was no reason for them to have come down, it was good to see friendly faces. Decker said, "As we were leaving the house, someone took aim and fired. We're here, we're whole, but Grant went to the hospital with a gash in his leg."

"He was shot?" Oliver asked.

"I don't know. It was dark and I couldn't tell. Maybe his leg was ripped open when I fell on him."

"Did you discharge your gun?" Oliver asked.

"Nope."

"That's good," Marge said. "Less paperwork."

Cindy said, "They came, they shot, they left—"

"They?"

"They, he, she . . . I couldn't see a thing," Cindy said. "Last thing the Loo wanted was to accidentally pop a neighbor out walking the dog."

Marge said, "If Grant was shot, that means every single Kaffey has had a close encounter with molten lead."

Decker rubbed his forehead. "I was thinking the same thing. We've run out of family suspects."

"And maybe that's the point," Marge said. "To confuse us. Because all three Kaffeys are all alive."

"Maybe all three were in on the hit together," Oliver said.

"Could be," Marge said. "It appears that Grant got away with the least damage."

"Mace's wound was minor as far as shotgun wounds go," Decker pointed out. "And don't forget Antoine Resseur is still missing."

"Why would he shoot Grant?" Oliver asked.

"To have Gil all to himself." Decker held up his hands. "You asked for a motive, I gave you the first thing I thought of."

Cindy checked her watch. It was almost ten. They'd been at the scene for three hours. "Luckily, I was off duty, and I didn't discharge my weapon thanks to Papa's instructions. Instead of doing extra paperwork, I get to go home."

"That sounds like a good idea." Decker kissed his daughter's cheek. "Until we know who the good guy is and who the bad guy is, keep an eye over your shoulder."

Cindy pointed to her chest. "We're the good guys." Then she swept her hand across a twinkling L.A. basin. "Those are the bad guys." She kissed Marge and Scott. "Take care of the Loo in my absence."

Decker watched his daughter slide into the driver's seat of her car and kept staring until her taillights faded into nothingness. "I'm ready to pack it in."

"I told you we shouldn't have bothered," Oliver said to Marge.

"And I told you, you didn't have to come with me," she countered.

Decker said, "Since you two were nice enough to drive all the way out here, come to Beverly Hills with me. We can kick around a few ideas." He exhaled forcefully. "My brain is still in overdrive, and I could use some fresh input."

"What's in Beverly Hills?" Oliver asked.

"Rina's parents. We're spending the night there." He gave them the address. "It's about twenty minutes from here."

Oliver made a face. "You're voluntarily sleeping at your *mother-in-law*'s?"

"I'm sleeping *at* my mother-in-law's, not *with* my mother-in-law," Decker told him. "I like Magda. She provides us with room service and first-class food at any hour. Plus, the accommodations are spacious and cheap."

Oliver thought about it. "Does she need any borders? Maybe she'd like a handsome police detective to protect her."

"She already has that. It's called a son-in-law."

MAGDA'S SPREAD INCLUDED finger sandwiches, vegetable crudités with onion dip, fresh fruit, slices of pound cake, slices of chocolate cake, almond cookies, potato chips (for a little crunch), mixed nuts, and mint candy.

"I'll go make a fresh pot of decaf if anyone wants," she said.

The woman was on the dark side of eighty, as thin as linguini, and never appeared in public without makeup. Her blond hair was meticulously coiffed—teased and sprayed for maximum volume. Rina often said that her mother was the night person while her father, Stephan, got up with the sun. He was sleeping while she was in her element playing hostess. She wore knitted black pants that hung on her clothes-hanger hips and a red cashmere sweater.

"If you're having some, I'll take some," Oliver told her.

"I'll have a cup," she told him. "What is cake without coffee?"

Rina said, "I'll do it, Mama."

"No, no," Magda insisted. "I like to make coffee. You sit and eat, Ginny." She smiled at Oliver. "By the way, my granddaughter made the pound cake."

"Obviously Hannah learned from the best," Marge said.

Magda patted Rina. "I don't know if you mean me or Ginny, but we both take the compliment." She disappeared into the kitchen.

To Decker, Rina said, "You made her very happy when you said you're a little hungry."

The Loo smiled. "Do I know my mother-in-law or what?"

"This is really good," Marge said as she bit into an egg salad sandwich. "I feel like we should be having high tea."

"If you would have given her a little more time, I'm sure she would have baked scones." Rina stood up. "I'll keep her company. You two keep an eye on him. He's out of my sight for a couple of hours and he gets shot at. I am not pleased."

As Rina was walking out, Decker said, "It wasn't planned, you know."

She turned and looked over her shoulder. "Unlike last time?"

"How many times do I have to apologize . . ." Decker was talking to the air. "That woman has a gigabyte worth of memories, most of them infractions that I've committed for the last nineteen years."

"That's the point," Oliver said. "You exist so she can tell you what you did wrong."

"That is neither just nor fair," Marge said. "And Rina is certainly not like that. The situation was unusual."

Decker said, "We can change the subject now."

Oliver complied. "What do you guys think about all the Kaffeys having war wounds? Do you think it's possible that there's actually someone out there who wants to annihilate the family or is it collusion?"

Decker popped a cashew into his mouth. "Who'd want to hurt the family?"

Oliver took another piece of chocolate cake. "What about the guy back east who's in competition with the Greenridge Project?"

"Paul Pritchard of Cyclone Inc." Decker took a mint from the candy bowl. "Lee Wang gave me some articles that quote Pritchard. He says he isn't worried at all about Greenridge. He thinks the project is a big lox. Now that could be bravado. But even if Pritchard was worried, do you think he'd be worried enough to murder an entire family?"

"Far-fetched, but not impossible." Marge picked up another egg salad sandwich. "Is there another family member who'll inherit if the rest of the family is murdered?"

Oliver spoke with a mouthful of chocolate cake. "Doesn't Mace have a son?"

"He does," Decker said. "His name is Sean."

Marge said, "Even if all the principal Kaffeys were dead, Sean Kaffey wouldn't inherit everything. Grant has a kid. And would Sean be stupid enough to gun them all down within a ten-day period?"

Oliver said, "What would be the harm if I looked into him? It sounds stupid, but greedy people act stupid all the time."

"Sure, look into Sean, but don't forget basic police work. We need to find Gil Kaffey and Antoine Resseur."

Marge took out her notepad. "You want me to make that my personal mission?"

"Priority number one," Decker told her. "Find out everything you can about Resseur. Grant said the breakup between Gil and Antoine was friendly, but maybe it wasn't."

Marge said, "Maybe their breakup was staged to keep Resseur out of the picture while Gil knocked off the rest of the family. It still strikes me as odd that whoever blasted Guy and Gilliam to smithereens didn't bother to finish off Gil."

"Agreed." Decker took another handful of nuts. "But we all know that if Gil contracted for the hits, he didn't do the actual shooting."

Everyone agreed.

"Oh, we got some good news today," Decker said. "Sheriff T

from Ponceville finally sent us a copy of Rondo Martin's prints via FedEx. We found a match with a bloody print at the scene." Amid high fives, Decker said, "Now we can prove that Rondo Martin was at the scene. We need to find him."

"I'll mark that as priority number two," Oliver said.

Decker smiled. "Then this is number three. Brett Harriman identified Alejandro Brand's voice as one of the voices he overheard at the courthouse. Unfortunately that's not enough to indict Brand on murder charges."

"You think he did it?" Marge asked.

"He knows something." Decker shoved the nuts in his mouth and chewed. "Foothill picked up Brand on meth manufacturing charges so I got a copy of his print. Nothing in the system and no match from the unknowns at the crime scene."

"That's a bummer," Oliver said.

"It should be that easy," Decker said. "Brand is in jail and isn't going anywhere soon. I'd like to dangle a carrot of a reduced sentence to get him to talk about the hit."

"And you still think Harriman's information is reliable?"

"He picked out Alejandro Brand's voice after rejecting two other tapes. Plus, Rina identified Brand as the guy she saw at the courthouse. Also, if Harriman was making things up, how would he know about Joe Pine?" Decker paused. "On the other hand, he's a weird guy. He showed up at my doorstep this afternoon."

Oliver made a face. "Why?"

"He just wanted to talk to Rina. He asked if I had set up a lineup for her to identify Brand."

"The P.D. would have a field day with that."

"She sent him away," Decker asked. "But as she watched him go, she noticed a car following Harriman."

Marge told Oliver the story. "I'm checking out Saturns with Popper Motors."

Decker said, "Be interesting to see if any of the skid marks from tonight's getaway matched the treads on any of the Saturns from the dealership."

"But first we have to find the car," Marge said. "If the guy at Popper Motors can tell me some names, I can drive by the addresses and see if any of them own a navy Saturn with tinted windows."

Decker eyed a piece of chocolate cake and then decided to wait for the coffee. "Willy Brubeck and I are going up to Ponceville to see if we can't get a better fix on Rondo Martin. While we're there, we'll check out the Mendez family and a possible connection to Ana Mendez. While I'm gone, you two double-check Riley Karns and Pablo Albanez. Both the men knew where the horses were buried, so both the men could have dumped Denny Orlando."

"I'll take Karns and you can have Albanez," Marge told Oliver.

"Sounds good."

Decker said, "And last, we need to find Joe Pine or José Pinon."

"Are they definitely one and the same?"

"That's a good question. Start with José Pinon because that's who Harriman mentioned."

Marge said, "We're still trying to get a copy of his prints. Brady doesn't have them on file. We're trying to push Juvey at Foothill to get us a copy because he had some teen offenses. Those records have been sealed unfortunately, but we're trying."

Magda came back, Rina in tow carrying a tray with a silver coffee service and five mugs. Decker jumped up. "I'll take that."

"Thank you," Rina said.

"Who wants decaf?" Magda announced.

"I'm game." Decker took a piece of chocolate cake and ate it in four bites. "Delicious. Who made this one?"

"I did." Magda beamed. "Your wife made the almond cookies."

"Those are great," Marge said. "I'm a disaster in the kitchen, and you have three women who could open up a bakery."

Decker debated, then took a second piece. "It's an XX conspiracy to keep me fat and happy."

He patted his burgeoning stomach.

"One out of two ain't bad."

TWENTY-EIGHT

T HAD BEEN Decker's hope that County Jail might make Brand more amenable to talking. Instead, he appeared as if he had just spent a few days at Sandals. The soul patch was gone, along with the acne, and his skin glowed bronze and clear, making him appear more college student than goon. When Decker commented on his appearance, Brand attributed it to "good living."

"Three meals a day and lights out by ten," Brand told Decker in English. He was dressed in dark blue scrubs. "I used to wake up at four in the afternoon." A pause. "Maybe sunlight is good."

"I'm glad you find your living conditions so pleasant."

"I didn't say that." A pause. "I don' expect to be there forever."

"You won't be in County for long," Decker told him. "Your charges carry prison time. Your next stop is Folsom."

"I don' think so. You come here to talk. That means I got somethin' you need." He leaned forward, his breath reeking of tobacco. "You come to talk to me *twice*. That's one more time than that shit head lawyer they give me." He sat back. "But I can't give you nothin' if I don' know what you want."

Decker took a smoke out of a pack of cigarettes and lit it up. "You're a smart kid."

"That's wha' my *abuela* always said."

"Smart but you make some bad decisions."

"She said that, too. Why you talkin' English to me now?"

Decker gave the cigarette to Brand who thanked him by way of a nod. He switched over to Spanish. "Either one is fine with me."

Brand sat back and inhaled deeply. "You speak like a Cuban."

"Good ear, Alex, I'm originally from Florida. Tell me about some of your amigos."

"I have lots of friends." A lopsided grin. "I'm a popular man."

Decker took out a pen and a notepad. "Talk to me about La Boca."

Initially, Brand's eyes registered blanks, but then they livened up. "Yeah, you gotta find him, man. All that shit belonged to him."

"We've been looking," Decker lied. "So far nothing. Where would we find him?"

"I dunno. He just hangs in the area."

"Tell me what he does?"

For the next ten minutes, Brand spun some yarn about La Boca being a master dealer. He said, "He's a piece of work. You be careful, man."

"You seem to know a lot of pieces of work, Alex. Anything else you want to tell me about La Boca?"

"That's it, man." Brand crushed out his cigarette. "How about another smoke?"

Decker lit another cigarette and inhaled deeply, blowing a fine stream of smoke into Alex's face. "Maybe you'll get enough nicotine from secondhand smoke."

Brand's eyes grew dark. "I don' have to talk to you."

Decker said, "Is La Boca a Bodega 12th Street gang member?"

"I dunno."

"Sure you do."

"Why should I tell you anything?"

Decker had been talking to Alex for about a half hour but not much rapport had been established. The kid was as cold as brain freeze. "Tell me about your amigos in the Bodega 12th Street."

"No gang, man. We're just a bunch of guys who hang."

"I hear you're real tough dudes."

"You got to take care of yourself."

"I agree," Decker told him. "Sometimes that works okay . . . but then sometimes things go wrong . . . things get real fucked up, know what I'm saying?"

Brand didn't answer.

"Like when your apartment blew up, that was a bad fuckup. But I really don't care about that, Alex. That's between you and your shithead lawyer. I'm not a drug cop."

"I'm not sayin' no more until you tell me what you can do for me."

"I'm not from Narcotics, Alex, I'm from Homicide. I deal with murders."

Brand appeared baffled. "So wha' you want with me. I don' kill nobody."

"Did I say you killed anyone?" Decker gave Brand his half-smoked cigarette. "I didn't say you killed anyone. I mean maybe you did, but I didn't say you did."

"I didn't kill nobody." Brand inhaled the smoke and seemed to relax with each inhalation. That was good. Keep him in nicotine and maybe they'd get somewhere.

"I work in the West Valley, working on a very bad double homicide," Decker said. "It was supposed to be a triple homicide, but one of the victims lived so it's a double homicide and attempted murder. Guy and Gilliam Kaffey. Know anything about that?"

"Everyone knows about those two dudes," Brand said. "It's all over the news."

"The victim who lived . . . he saw things. He told what he saw. There was more than one killer, Alex. There were several men and they spoke Spanish. They had Bodega 12th Street tattoos."

"Not me! I don' have nothin' to do with that!"

"You've been identified by the victim."

"That's bullshit! I wasn't there. I can prove it."

"So where were you?"

Brand immediately launched into his alibi. He spoke quickly—Spanish is a language that rolls off the tongue—and he slurred his words. Decker had to pay attention to keep up with him. This was his alibi.

He was with his girlfriend the entire night. They went to the movies. Then they went out for a hamburger. Then they went back to his apartment and had sex. Then they went out again.

"What time was that?" Decker asked.

"Around one, maybe a little later." His leg started shaking up and down. "We caught up with some of my friends on the street."

"Where?"

"Just around . . ."

"Around where?"

"Pacoima." He named a street corner. "We was just hangin'."

"What do you mean by hanging? Be more specific."

"You know . . ."

"Scoring dope?"

Silence.

Decker said, "You're already in trouble for manufacturing, Alex. A few more pills won't make or break your case."

"No big deal." The leg was going full force. "Just a little weed."

"Were you smoking it or selling it?"

"Why you asking so many questions if you're not a narc?"

"Just trying to get a picture. Were you smoking it or selling it?"

Brand switched to English as if to emphasize the point. "Just a little weed."

Decker answered back in English. "You already said that."

"A million people saw me there all night."

"A million people?"

"Not a million, but you know . . . I was there all night. People saw me. I saw people. I didn't kill nobody."

"You know, Alex, I can't even remember what I had for dinner a couple of nights ago." Decker regarded him with intense eyes. "How do you remember a week ago so clearly—in pretty good detail?"

"The killings was big news, man. I hear about it the next day."

"Why don't you tell me what really happened and I'll see what I can do. Because I'm betting you knew what went down before any-one else knew what went down."

"I *wasn't there,* man! If someone told you I was there, that's bullshit!"

"I believe you. Maybe you weren't there, but some of your 12th Street amigos were there."

"Nope." He shook his head for emphasis.

"Now you're lying."

Back to Spanish. "I swear I don't know!"

"Then why did the victim ID you?"

"'Cause he's probably a dumbshit white boy and all cholos look alike to him. I don' know why he'd identify me. I wasn't *there.*"

Decker persisted. "But I know that you know who *was* there!"

"No, I don't." But the blinking of his eyes was as good as yes.

They went back and forth for another twenty minutes. By that time, Decker had been at him for almost two hours. Beads of sweat had coalesced on Brand's face, chest, and arms. His anaconda tattoo now looked as if it was swimming in the river.

Decker gave the kid another cigarette, hoping that would calm him down. "One of the victims lived, Alex. He saw things—"

"Not me."

"You could do yourself a world of good. All you have to do is tell me what *you* know about it."

"I wasn't there!"

"I didn't say you were there." A beat. "I said that all you have to do is tell me what you know about it."

His eyes were on his lap. "I don' know nothin'."

"Alex, that's not true. You know all about José Pinon and that he fucked up because he didn't kill the surviving victim. You know all about Rondo Martin and El Patrón. People have heard you talk."

Brand's expression appeared stunned and confused. He shut his lips together as if that would take back his words.

"Tell me about El Patrón."

Brand shrugged, but he didn't make eye contact. His leg was still bouncing.

"C'mon, Alejandro. You don't want it getting back to El Patrón that you were yapping about him."

More silence.

"We also have people looking for José in Mexico," Decker lied. "What's Pinon going to do when he finds out that you've been talking about him?"

"Look, man, I tole you the truth! I wasn't there!"

"I believe you," Decker said quietly. "I believe that you weren't there. But you do know who *was* there."

"No, I don' know." He squirmed. "I just hear some things. I don' know what's true and what's not true. Why you bustin' my cojones, man?"

"Tell me what you've heard."

No response. Decker waited him out. Finally, Alex said, "You work for that guy with the sunglasses?"

It took a few seconds before Decker realized he was referring to Brett Harriman, and that was definitely not good. Luckily, Decker was a more seasoned liar than Alex was. "Who are you talking about?"

"The faggy guy in the courthouse. I could tell he was spying on me. I shoulda dealt with it when I had the chance."

"I don't know what you're talking about, Alex. I told you, I'm from Homicide."

"I knew he was a motherfucker. I could tell how he was lookin' at me."

"Alex, let's try to keep on topic." Decker made a mental note to contact Harriman. "Tell me what rumors you've heard."

"What do I get if I talk to you?"

"You get a Homicide police lieutenant who's on your side along with your shithead lawyer."

"You tell the Narcos that the shit wasn't mine?"

"No, I can't do that. But if you cooperate, I'll talk to the judge who'll be sentencing you. If he's impressed enough, he could knock off some time."

"How much?"

"I don't know. But what do you have to lose?"

"I don't want people findin' out I talked to you."

"So tell me what you know and I'll see what I can do."

Brand thought about it. "I just hear what you said. That José fucked up and that El Patrón was looking for him."

"Just to make sure that we're on the same page, let's make sure we're talking about the same El Patrón. Tell me about him."

"I dunno his name." Brand averted his eyes. "He does a lot of business with Bodega Twelve, if you know what I mean."

"Drugs?"

"Yeah, he gets the shit from the big guys. Everyone says he ordered the hit."

"Describe him to me."

"Just that he's some white dude who flashes a lot of cash. I never seen him." The cholo's smile deepened as the seconds ticked on. "You don' know who he is."

"How do you know that he ordered these hits?"

"That's just what I hear from my amigos."

"Which friends?"

"I don' remember . . ." Brand looked at Decker. "That's the truth, man. I just hear from around."

"How did you hear about José Pinon fucking up?"

"José is a loser."

"How do you know José?"

"He was a righteous Twelver when I was a kid, but then he started going to someplace called Go-karts or something. It's where rich *vacas* in suits 'rehabilitate' gang members." He chuckled. "I don' see him for a while. The next time I see him, he tells me that some rich guy hired him as a guard. I thought it was a joke."

Decker nodded.

"What a stupid fuck!"

"José or the man who hired him."

"Both," Brand said. "The idiot gave him a *uniform*. He gave him a *gun*. He gave him a *title*. José thought he was hot shit . . . above us, know what I mean? I hope El Patrón finds him and burns his balls with cigarettes."

"Describe El Patrón to me."

"I already tole you, I never seen him." Brand crushed out his cigarette. "Now whatchu gonna do for me, man?"

"Well, Alex, the point is you haven't told me anything good. I knew about José Pinon and El Patrón. I need a *name*."

"I don't know his name."

"So give me the name of the shooters."

"I tole you. José Pinon was there."

"Who else?"

Brand fell quiet.

Decker said, "It's only a matter of time before the surviving victim identifies everyone who was there and your information will be useless."

"Then let him do that."

Decker switched tactics. "Did José ever talk to you about the people he worked with on his job?"

"I don' talk no more to José. He stopped hangin' once he got his fancy fuck job."

"So he never mentioned any names to you?"

A long sigh. "I think he tole me that most of them were Hispanic. Once José tole me I was smart—the only smart thing he ever said—and that if I could get my shit together, he could probably get me a job. But he had to talk to his boss first. I said I wasn't interested."

"Who was his boss?"

"I dunno. Some dude."

Decker pulled out his list of guards. The first name he read was Neptune Brady. Brand's eyes lit up.

"Yeah, that was the dumb fuck who hired him."

"Did you ever meet him?"

"No."

"Could Neptune Brady be El Patrón?"

"Could be if he's a white guy with a lot of cash."

"I'm going to read some more names. Tell me if they sound familiar." When Decker got to Denny Orlando, Brand held up his hand.

"That guy sounds familiar. He works with José."

"Yes, he does. Or did. He's dead."

"José whacked him?"

"Somebody did."

"Figures. He turns his back on Bodega 12th Street, he can turn his back on anyone."

Decker mentioned Rondo Martin and Brand didn't react. "That name doesn't sound familiar?"

Brand thought a moment. "You name a lot of people. I get them mixed up."

"He's a tough white dude. Could he be El Patrón?"

Brand was dismissive. "I don' know what El Patrón's name is, but I don' thin' it's somethin' stupid like Rondo Martin."

TWENTY-NINE

OME WHITE DUDE who flashes a lot of cash?" Marge said. "Boy, he really went out on a limb."

"Like they say in the electronic world: GIGO." Oliver smiled.

"How very techie of you."

"I also know LOL and IMHO."

"You don't have a 'humble opinion,' Scott."

Oliver said, "No, it means 'in my highest opinion.'"

"Or 'in my honest opinion.'" Decker exhaled aloud. "Wow, this is a lot more fun than talking to bullshit cons who feed me crap."

The three of them were sitting in Decker's office, kicking around ideas. Oliver had on a black suit, Marge had on a gray suit, and Decker was wearing a brown suit. They were appropriately dressed for a funeral, an event that would have dovetailed nicely with their sagging spirits.

Gil was missing, Resseur was missing, Grant was nursing wounds at the Kaffey compound in Newport, and Mace was somewhere . . . not exactly missing, but he wasn't answering Decker's phone calls.

Neptune Brady and his crew had been unceremoniously axed. The leads were thinning, and the case was growing frosty.

Decker smoothed his mustache. "I am concerned about Brett Harriman. You should have seen the look in Alejandro Brand's eyes when he talked about him."

"He's behind bars," Oliver said. "He's got other things to worry about."

"He's a Bodega Twelver," Marge said. "He knows people on the outside."

"Exactly," Decker said. "I've talked to a few of the jailers in County. They'll keep their ears open. But someone needs to talk to Harriman, tell him to be careful."

"He can't exactly look over his shoulder," Oliver said. "Well, he could, but it wouldn't do him any good."

"Maybe he has his own way of discerning if someone is around him. In the meantime, he shouldn't be out and alone until we get a better handle on Brand."

"I've got some news about the Saturn, but don't get excited." Marge flipped a couple of pages of her notepad. "The lead was a bust. The Saturn was used and sold to a rental car service called Cheap Deals. It was rented to Alyssa Mendel and on the day that Harriman showed up at your house, Mendel was visiting her eighty-five-year-old aunt Gwen. She lives across the street and a few doors down from you."

"Well, that's good for me, but bad for the case." Decker paused. "Rina's going to have a field day when she finds out that the Saturn was nothing. I bought all this security equipment because I was so nervous." A beat. "I might as well install it. I'm still a cop, Brand is still a Bodega Twelver, and I still got two nasty homicides."

"I have three locks on my condo," Marge said. "If I ever have a heart attack, no way the paramedics will be able to get in."

"What are you doing to the house?" Oliver asked Decker.

"Updating the alarm, adding a couple extra horns, video cameras, motion sensors, rekeying the locks, checking the window locks . . . basic stuff that couldn't stop a professional, but it might give pause to an amateur." Decker flipped through his notes. "Oh yeah . . . this may be important. When I mentioned the name Rondo Martin, Brand appeared as if he didn't have a clue who he was."

"He could have been lying," Oliver said.

"In my opin—" Decker smiled. "IMHO, Brand wasn't faking."

Marge said, "That doesn't say anything about Martin's involvement. Maybe Martin's involvement wasn't common knowledge—in contrast to Joe Pine or José Pinon."

"Exactly. Brand admitted knowing Pinon and said Pinon was a former Bodega 12th member who apparently went through rehabilitation at a place called Go-carts. I had Wang look up community centers for gangbangers and there's a government and privately funded community service group called GOCOTS."

"Get Our Children Off the Streets," Marge said. "When I was looking for Jervis Wenderhole on the Bennett Little case, I came across the name."

"Guy Kaffey was on the board of directors. I had Wang go down the list of personal bodyguards as well as company security guards. Guy hired quite a few ex–Bodega 12th members."

Oliver said, "He might as well have given Pinon a gun. Oh, wait. He did give Pinon a gun."

Decker said, "Brand told me that Pinon was not only involved but that El Patrón was pissed because Pinon had fucked up by not finishing off Gil Kaffey."

"So what do we think about Gil Kaffey?" Oliver asked. "Suspect or victim?"

"My first thought was victim. But then he went missing and I was shot at. That could have been a setup on Grant's part. Or on Gil's part. Or on Resseur's part. Or none of the above." Decker blew out air. "When we find Gil and Resseur, hopefully we get some answers."

"I just thought of something," Marge said. "Brand told you that El Patrón deals drugs."

"Gotta deal drugs if you're El Patrón," Oliver said.

"Yeah, it does sound like a lie, but hear me out. Rondo Martin policed an agricultural community. I bet there are some sneaky-ass farmers who might plant some . . . marginal crops."

Decker thought about it. "Martin developed contacts with marijuana growers and took the business to L.A.?"

"Just a thought."

"Did you get any indication that illegal stuff was being grown in Ponceville?" Decker asked.

"No, but we're not going to get that kind of information from talking to the sheriff. Maybe Willy Brubeck's father would know about things like that."

"More likely someone in the ciudads knows about those kinds of things," Oliver said.

"We're off to Ponceville tomorrow at ten," Decker told them. "I'll not only inquire about Rondo Martin the shooter, I'll also ask questions about Rondo Martin the dealer."

"Be careful, Pete," Marge told him. "A dealer who's good with a gun is a formidable enemy."

RINA REGARDED THE video camera set under the roof of the porch and aimed at the door. "It's beginning to look like a fortress."

Decker was up on a ladder, adding a few finishing screws. "You can't even see it from the street."

"So how does it act as a deterrent if you can't see it?"

"The point of the camera is to give you a bird's-eye view of what's going on out there."

"So I can see my neighbor's niece drive away?"

"The Saturn turned out to be harmless, but it was a wake-up call to update our security. Why are you giving me a hard time when all I want to do is protect my family?"

"You're right."

Decker stopped hammering. "What did you say?"

Rina smiled. "You heard me." She regarded the sunset—a stunning display of golds and violets. The day had been hot, but the evening was balmy. She had changed into a short-sleeved white blouse and a denim skirt. Her black hair was covered by a colorful silk scarf that hung down her back. "Can I help out to speed things along?"

He readjusted the arm on the camera. "No, thanks. I'm good . . . almost done."

Hannah walked out. She had put on her pajamas and wore fuzzy slippers. "When are we eating?"

"As soon as your father's done."

"In about fifteen minutes," Decker said.

She huffed and stormed back into the house.

"We're hungry," Rina said.

"I want to do this right. Why don't you set up the table and by that time, I'll be done."

"I've already set up the table."

"Then drink a glass of wine or something."

"The wine will mellow me out, but it will do nothing for our progeny."

"Give her a snack."

"She doesn't like to eat snacks right before dinner."

Decker looked down at his wife. "Just start without me. I'm a fast eater anyway. Besides, the less time I spend with her, the better she likes me."

"She loves you."

"So you keep saying. Cindy was always nice to me."

"Cindy didn't live with you."

Silence. Decker hammered away for a few more minutes, then climbed down the ladder. "Done." As the two of them walked into the house, he said, "I'm going to shower first. Start eating and I'll be there in a little bit."

It seemed like a good idea. Hannah was already at the table, eyeing the chicken in predator/prey fashion. Rina poured herself a half glass of Herzog petite sirah. "You can start."

"Finally." She grabbed the two drumsticks, then heaped her plate with a mound of broccoli and a half-baked potato. "Why is he so paranoid all of a sudden? It's not like he suddenly joined the police squad."

"The case involves members of the Bodega 12th Street gang. One of them is in jail and I identified him. Your father's a little nervous."

"But you didn't put that guy in jail."

"I don't even think he knows I exist, but your father is just being cautious."

"It's really inconvenient staying at Oma and Opa's. I have to wake up a half hour earlier."

"It's only for a few days."

"Yeah, but it has to be the day before I take my SATs. And no, I don't want to sleep over at a friend's house."

Rina reached over and squeezed her daughter's arm. "You're very smart. You'll do fine."

Hannah speared a piece of broccoli and chewed vigorously. There were tears in her eyes. Decker showed up a minute later, his wet hair slicked back.

"You look like Dracula," Hannah told him.

Decker started to laugh. "I suppose that's a compliment. He was a count."

Hannah giggled. "I'm sorry. I'm nervous."

"SATs," Rina said.

"When are you taking them?" Decker asked.

"Tomorrow, as I have previously told you."

"I'm old. I forget things. I'm sure you'll do fine." He paused. "You'll certainly do better than I did. If they hadn't given me points for filling in my name, my score would have been negative. Not that it mattered. I never intended to go to college."

Hannah stopped eating and studied her father. "Why's that? You're so smart."

"Thank you," Decker said with sincerity. "Education didn't matter much to my parents. I'm sure that sounds pretty good to you now." That got a smile out of Hannah. "Grandpa worked with his hands. I figured I'd do the same."

"Yet you chose something that requires a lot of brain work."

"It was all serendipitous. After I came out of the army, the police academy was looking for people. Gainesville was . . . is a college town and I detested all the protesters because they were my age and having too much fun. The police hated the students as much as I did. My enemy's enemy is my friend."

Hannah appeared thoughtful. "You could have quit."

"It turned out to be a good fit." He chewed thoughtfully. "I can't believe I've been doing this for almost thirty-five years."

"I hope I find something I'm passionate about. The only thing I love besides you guys and boys is listening to music."

"So be a music critic," Decker said.

"Yeah, you'd love that."

"Why would I care? As long as you live it honestly, do what you want."

"Abba, you can't make a living out of that."

"Pumpkin, if you work hard enough and do what you love, you'll make a living. You may not make a lot of money. You may have to do without certain things. But there's nothing better than doing work that you like. I don't like my job every day, but I wouldn't consider anything else." Decker poured himself a glass of wine and toasted with Rina. "You can't put a price tag on everything."

"You really wouldn't care if I became a music critic?"

"No. Why should I? It's your life."

"So I should forget about college and pursue my dreams?"

"Excuse me?" Rina said.

Decker laughed. "I'd like you to finish college to keep your options open. Other than that, I have no expectations."

Hannah pushed her plate away. "I've got to go pack for Oma's."

"Hannah?" Rina said. "If it's important to you, we can sleep here. The Saturn turned out to be nothing."

"*Now* you're telling me?"

"I didn't want to cancel on my parents. They seemed excited to have us over. But that's thinking about them and not you. I'll call them up."

"No, no," Hannah said. "I have my own room over there and my computer's transportable. It's fine, Eema. Honestly, I won't sleep much anyway." She got up from the table and hugged her father. "Thank you for talking to me. It really helped."

She skipped off to her room.

"Good job, Abba," Rina said. "Pat yourself on the back."

Decker had a smile on his face. "Once in a while, I get it right."

"C'mon, Decker, give yourself some credit. That was incredibly sensitive."

"Wasn't trying to be. I meant every word. I'm no shining star. I'm just a government employee."

"You're my shining star," Rina told him. "You've always been a hero to me."

Decker looked down at his chicken. "Thank you. You're my hero, too." He kissed her hand and held it for a moment before letting go to pick up his wineglass. After all this time, he still had trouble expressing himself: how nice his daughter's words had made him feel and how lovely Rina's comment was. Instead he toasted with Rina again while basking in the moment.

It was great to feel adored.

THIRTY

THE LANDSCAPE OF channels and furrows brought back memories of childhood, when Decker was a kid and the family used to drive to visit his grandparents in Iowa. They did it twice a year—Easter and Christmas—traveling from Florida through miles of flat, endless terrain. Christmastime presented an ocean of brown or white, but Easter was a time of renewal: verdant fields glistening with morning dew and the perfume of blossoming trees. The trips were indelibly etched because of the promise at the end of the rainbow. Family reunions and gargantuan feasts, lights, decorations and pageantry, cousins to play with, and of course, presents. No matter how big or small, it was a thrill to open a wrapped package. Traveling through the fields, Decker knew it was a very different time for a very different reason, but the scenery evoked a primal excitement.

Perhaps they'd catch a break.

Brubeck drove like a native, whipping through the agrarian countryside. The dirt roads were uneven, and the lumpy topography gave the rental's axle a run for its money. One rut sent them flying off the ground, coming down with a spine-breaking thud.

"Sorry about that, boss." Brubeck reduced his speed. "Damn roads. You'd think after all this time, the town would do something about the potholes."

"We can't change the roads, but we can slow down. A couple of minutes saved isn't worth paralysis."

"Damn roads," Brubeck muttered again. He wore a short-sleeved navy shirt and a black pair of jeans, his gut peeking over his belt. Decker had opted for a brown polo shirt and denims. Sneakers rounded out the look.

Decker pulled out the partial list of northern ciudad families, given to him by Brubeck courtesy of his father-in-law, Marcus Merry. There were over a dozen surnames. "Did you contact your father-in-law?"

"Daisy would kill me if I didn't drop in for a visit. I told him we'd meet him for lunch around two . . . which is more like dinner for him. The man is in bed by eight." Brubeck paused. "Dad isn't comfortable with us doing police work and T not knowing about it. He has to work here, and Lord knows he's already at a disadvantage."

"I thought about that," Decker said. "Despite what Oliver said, I called T up and left him a message that we were coming."

Brubeck turned his head in Decker's direction while he was driving. "You did?"

"Eyes on the road, Brubeck."

"I can see. Why'd you call him up?"

"So your father-in-law wouldn't take any heat if T got mad. Also, if we got into a fix, we'll need his help."

The car skipped over a dip, landed like a clumsy dancer. Brubeck said, "You think T's trustworthy?"

"I don't know, but it makes sense to have the local law on your side."

"If he's on our side."

"That's why I told him that we'd be here in the afternoon and we'd meet up in town at around four. That way we can go about our business without him."

"What if we run into him at the ciudads?"

"I'll tell him that we managed to get an earlier flight, tried to call him, but he wasn't in."

"Makes sense. And if he does show up at the ciudads, that'll tell us something."

"Exactly. Have you ever been out there before?"

"Just in passing. Never been any reason for me to stop."

"How's your Spanish?"

"Not great, but I can follow a simple conversation," Brubeck said. "I'll do the driving, if you do the talking."

"Sounds good. Just get us there in one piece."

MIGRANT FARM WORKERS were a fact of life in California. They came over on work permits and were allowed to live and toil doing very specific labor for a very specific amount of time. The temporariness—along with the smothering poverty—was reflected in the living conditions. It wasn't shantytown because there were some wooden houses with stucco walls, but there was no permanence to the areas. The houses were meant to be erected in a day's time and razed with the single push of a Bobcat.

"Every so often that happens," Brubeck told Decker. "Some social activist raises a hue and a cry about workers' rights and then the area's leveled. Next week, it starts all over again. It's not like the old days when the hands would live on the ranches. Not enough money to feed a staff and pay them wages. Something had to go."

Decker noticed electric lines jerry-rigged to the houses so at least some of the places could sustain a modern convenience or two. Most of the structures shared walls, making them look like tenements. A cheerless and depressing chunk of nothing; the only exuberance was the paint color on the exteriors—bright yellows, electrifying oranges, deep purples, kelly greens, and rose reds. Instead of address numerals, the units were identified by letters, and in the northern district the rooms were A through P. The Mendez families lived in H, I, and J. As Brubeck approached the huts,

Decker noticed a recently washed twenty-year-old Suburban parked outside.

"Stop the car, Willy." As Brubeck braked, tires churned up the loose gravel. Decker said, "Any idea who drives the Suburban?"

"No, but it's a visitor. The car's old, but it's too clean to belong to one of the tenants."

Decker opened the rental's door. "Let's take a peek."

Quietly, they slipped out and tiptoed up to the Suburban. Inside was a leather jacket, a paper cup of coffee, a cop's radio and mike, and an empty shotgun rack. The two of them exchanged glances and tread softly back to the car.

"It's outfitted with a police scanner," Brubeck said.

"Yeah, I noticed. Also the gun rack is empty."

"I noticed that, too. Let me call up Dad and find out what T drives." He got off the phone a minute later. "It's T's official vehicle."

Neither spoke for a moment.

"I don't think sneaking up on the sheriff would be a good thing," Decker said.

"I agree with that."

They sat a few more moments.

"Maybe I should tell T that we've just arrived here and we're headed for town."

"What good would that do?" Brubeck asked.

"We could wait for him to drive away and then go inside." A pause. "Unless someone inside has guns."

"Out here everyone has guns. And once he figures out we duped him, he's gonna be pissed."

A good point. "Then how about if we watch him as he comes out the door . . . see if he's traveling with his shotgun."

"Then what?" Brubeck laughed. "You're not saying we should jump him, right?"

Decker shrugged. "Back up and hide the car so it's not so visible. I'm going to give him a call."

Brubeck put the rental in reverse and slowly backed up, hiding the vehicle behind a pink and green shed that housed a red Toyota

Corolla—the paint job new and not professionally done. The two men regarded the car until Decker scratched the surface with his nail. There was navy paint underneath.

"Martin drove an '02 blue Toyota Corolla."

"Now what?" Brubeck asked.

"I'm not quite sure. Let me call up the local law, and at least no one can say we didn't try."

Edna, the secretary, told him that T wasn't in. "He wasn't expecting you until this afternoon."

"We got an earlier flight."

"Oh . . . but the call just came in a half hour ago."

"Must have been the delay of my cell going through." It made no sense whatsoever, but Edna didn't challenge it. "Any idea where T is?"

"No, sir. Just that he's out on official business."

"Does he have a cell phone?"

"He sure does, but I'm under strict orders not to give out the number. I'll call him for you, if you want."

"That would be great."

"Where are you now?"

"We're just picking up our rental at the airport."

"It'll take about a half hour to get over here. You need directions?"

"No, I'm with Willy Brubeck. He knows the area."

"Willy Brubeck? Marcus Merry's son-in-law?"

"Yes, ma'am, he works for me."

"Call me Edna."

"I'll see you in a half hour, Edna." Decker cut the line. They were about a hundred feet from unit J, but there was no clear view of the front doors from where they had parked. "You stay near the car, Willy. I'm going to move a little closer."

"Are you crazy? We're naked in the wind."

"I didn't say I was going to confront him. I just said I was going to move a little closer. Just stay with the car. And if I get plugged, don't tell my wife how it happened."

Before Brubeck could protest, Decker was out of the automobile.

Sneaking up, he got within striking distance from unit J's front door.

Five minutes later, T came out, garbed in a plaid shirt, jeans, and scuffed leather boots, toting a twelve-gauge shotgun. It looked like a Remington 1100—an old sucker, not at all state of the art. T was a small guy, but sometimes that made an armed man especially dangerous.

The sheriff glanced around, then opened the Suburban's door and got inside. There was no visibility through the windshield of the vehicle because of the glare from the sun, but T had made the tactical error of not closing the driver's door. Decker crept around until the sheriff's arm came into view. He waited until T had secured the gun into the rack, and then caught him by surprise.

"Good morning, Sheriff, I'm Lieutenant Decker from the LAPD."

T's head spun around, his hand instinctively reaching for the gun rack. Decker, anticipating the move, caught T by the wrist, causing the car keys to drop to the floor. He said, "Don't do that."

T's arm was in an awkward position. To break free, he would have had to wrench a socket. "Are you fucking insane?"

"No, I just don't want to get shot."

"Then don't sneak up on a man, for Chrissakes! Let go of my arm or I'll throw your fucking ass in jail."

"Get out of the vehicle and we can talk about it."

"I can't do nothin' because you're holding on to my arm."

Decker eased him out of the car and let go of T's arm. Being almost a foot taller and a hundred pounds heavier, it was clear who had the advantage. As the saying went, size mattered. A moment later, Brubeck was at his side. "You okay, sir?"

"Is *he* okay?" T was shaking his arm up and down. "Jackass nearly broke my wrist. What the fuck is your problem?"

"I'm not armed," Decker said. "I like a level playing field."

"Why the fuck would I shoot you?" T's eyes were daggers. He

was still shaking out his wrist. "I should throw your ass in jail." He suddenly noticed Brubeck. "Willy, how could you let him do that to me?"

"Sorry, T, but he's my boss."

"He's crazy!"

"I don't deny that, T, but I got to work with him."

Decker took out his ID, but T swatted it to the ground. "Why the fuck did you sneak up on me . . . nearly gave me a heart attack."

"I identified myself."

"And that was supposed to impress me?"

"I'm sorry, Sheriff," Decker said.

"You're a fucking idiot."

Decker suppressed a smile but T caught it. "Your supervisor will hear from me."

"Why are you here?" Decker asked him.

"I live here, idiot!"

"I don't mean here in general, I mean at the Mendez house. You knew I was going to interview the families. Is it just coincidence that you paid them a visit a half hour after I called you?"

For the first time, T didn't curse him out. His eyes darted back toward the house, then at Decker's face. "Just get the fuck out of my jurisdiction before I bring you up on assault charges."

"Are you going to do that before or after I bring you up on tampering-with-justice charges? Or maybe the charges should actually be harboring a fugitive?"

"Fuck off." Again, his eyes involuntarily went to the door. "You're insane. I'm not harboring anyone."

"There's an '02 Toyota Corolla that looks suspiciously like Rondo Martin's car. How long is it going to take me to check the VIN number?" When T didn't answer, Decker said, "If you've been giving Rondo Martin a place to crash because you feel some kind of loyalty, hey, I'll turn a blind eye. All I want is Rondo Martin, and you've got to help me bring him to justice."

"Don't mess yourself up for him, T," Brubeck said. "Let's do it the easy way."

The sheriff shook his head. "It isn't what you think. I ain't hiding no killer." He flapped his wrist up and down. "Shit, that smarts!"

"I'm really sorry about your arm. I'll pay for any of your doctor bills—"

"I don't need no doctor. I'm no fucking wussy."

"We need to go inside, Sheriff."

"You don't understand a rat's ass."

"So explain it to me."

T said, "I dropped my keys in my car. On the ring is the lock to the gun rack. Take down the shotgun if you want. I trust you won't use it on me."

"I apologize for sneaking up on you." Decker held out his hand.

After a few seconds, T shook it. "Give me a minute, then I'll come back outside." He nodded to Brubeck. "It still don't make him any less of a jackass." He stomped back.

Decker blew out air. "I didn't handle that optimally."

"No, you didn't," Brubeck said. "I didn't want to say nothing, but what the fuck did you do that for? Why didn't we just let him drive away and then go inside?"

"And let Rondo Martin mow us down? Maybe we were walking into a trap."

"Then we still could be walking into a trap."

Decker said, "Wait in T's Suburban, Willy. I'll call for you when it's safe."

"I'm not letting you go in alone," Brubeck said.

"I'm giving you an order."

"You're crazy."

"We've already established that. If you hear shots firing, get the hell out of here. That's an order, too."

Willy shook his head. "You don't have to tell me twice."

THIRTY-ONE

IKE T HAD said, it wasn't what Decker thought.

Rondo Martin lay atop a twin mattress placed on a wood/dirt floor, his pale face bathed in sweat, his torso enveloped in miles of bandages. The dressing seemed fresh, but something underneath was oozing, darkening spots from white to ash. The room stank with a fetid odor—infection mixed with antiseptic. Martin's eyes were probably blue but dulled with illness, gray and sunken with deep circles giving him the look of a raccoon. His long face was enveloped in gray stubble quickly turning to a beard. His hair was pewter and greasy.

Ana Mendez was on his left, wiping his face with a damp washcloth. Paco Albanez sat on his right, attempting to feed him some soup. Martin winced as he pursed his lips, sucking hot liquid into his throat. His eyes went from his nursemaids to Decker.

Decker's own gaze volleyed between Paco and Ana. Because he hadn't seen them together, he hadn't realized how much they looked alike. Father-daughter? Uncle-niece? There were also two other women in the room and who they were was anyone's guess.

Bottles of medicine were everywhere, mostly antibiotics and painkillers. The labels said Pet Time. It was far easier to access needed drugs for Fido than it was trying to get prescriptions from a licensed physician. Rondo Martin was going to need a lot more than canine Cipro and a pet Vicodin derivative if he had hopes of recovery.

Decker said, "He needs to go to the hospital."

"You don't think I've tried?" T said.

Martin's eyes fluttered. "You find Joe Pine yet?"

Ana Mendez said the name José Pinon and then spat at the floor.

"No," Decker told him. "He's still missing."

"Then I'm not going nowhere. He's gunning for me." Willy Brubeck walked in with the rifle. His eyes swept across the room and then onto Decker's face.

To Willy, Decker said, "Rondo just told me Joe Pine is gunning for him."

"Looked me in the eye and pulled the trigger," Martin said.

Decker said, "Then you need to be somewhere safe. If I found you, he'll find you."

T said, "That's what I've been trying to tell him."

Ana talked in Spanish. "Where were the police when the Kaffeys were killed? Where were the police when my Rondo was shot full of holes?"

T said, "You understand that?"

"Yeah." Decker took out a cell phone. "I'm calling 911."

T put his hand over the keypad. "It's quicker if we take him in the truck. An ambulance will take about a half hour to get here."

"Not going nowhere," Martin said. "I'll die here."

"That's going to happen unless you take care of those wounds"

Brubeck said, "Is Joe the only person you recognized?"

"The only one I remember . . ." Martin winced in pain.

"He's got to get to a hospital," Decker reiterated.

T nodded, and the women began to gather blankets for the Suburban. Ana insisted on staying next to Martin. "Who has the keys?"

Brubeck tossed them to T, who gave them to one of the ladies. "Let's get you better, Rondo."

"You put me in a hospital . . . I'm dead . . . I saw too much."

"What did you see?" Decker asked.

"At least four of 'em . . . maybe more."

"And you didn't recognize any of the others?"

"I don't know . . . Joe got to me real fast."

"How'd you escape?"

"You work at a mansion . . . with people who have money . . . eventually, they're gonna get hit . . . robbery, I mean . . . I made a plan."

"How'd it go down, Rondo?" Brubeck asked.

"Heard noise in the library . . . ran in and saw Joe with the gun. I got hit and hit again and again and again. Noise brought Denny in. Someone blasted him. I took off."

Decker said, "Where'd you go?"

"Locked myself inside a cabinet. I was bleeding bad." He took a few minutes to get his breath back. "Lots of gunshots, then it was quiet. So I waited . . . I might've passed out. I heard Joe ask someone if he had more ammo."

He paused for a long time.

"He didn't."

"Is that why they didn't finish off Gil Kaffey?"

"Don't know why, but that makes sense. Didn't hear any more firing. Eventually, I managed to get downstairs . . . saw what they did to Alicia. Then I passed out."

No one spoke. Tears were streaming down Ana's face. Paco sat stoically, soup spoon in his hands.

Martin said, "Alicia was Paco's niece . . . Ana's cousin."

Decker turned to the groundskeeper. "I'm sorry."

Paco nodded.

Ana's voice was choked with emotion. "When I saw him, I thought he was dead. When I saw he wasn't, I went to get Paco."

Martin said, "They hid me until Paco's son came down from Ponceville and brought me up here."

Brubeck said, "Where'd you hide?"

"In one of Riley's horse trailers."

"How are Ana and Paco related?" Decker asked.

"*Mi tio, tambien,*" Ana told him.

Paco was her uncle as well.

Decker said, "Is Paco's last name Albanez or Alvarez?"

"Albanez," Martin said.

"Edna told my guys that the family name in this area was Alvarez."

T said, "That's Edna being Edna."

Martin licked his cracked lips. "Ana's my woman. We're working on getting married. INS has been a bitch."

The women came back, telling T that the car was ready.

Martin said, "I told you I'm not going nowhere."

"Not up to me no more, Rondo." T cocked a thumb in Decker's direction. "He's in charge. You might as well cooperate."

"Who's gonna protect me?"

Decker said, "I'll be at your side until we can organize twenty-four-hour police protection."

"Where are you gonna find the policemen? This ain't the big city."

"I'll borrow from my staff if I have to. How many times did you get shot, Rondo?"

"Don't know . . . more than once. I still got lead inside me."

T said, "We're going to put you in the Suburban now. Can you walk?"

"Not without help."

"That's not a problem," Decker said.

There were four strong men, but Martin was a big guy and getting him upright from the floor without hurting him was a strain on the back. Slowly, they guided him until he was on his feet. Rondo's breathing was labored and his body was ripe with infection. Had they not interfered, Martin would have died in a matter of weeks, maybe days.

Inch by inch they led him to the Suburban. When they got to the back, four men—Decker, Brubeck, T, and Paco—each to a limb, lifted him up. He screamed out in pain as they secured him in the back of the van. When the task was finally finished, Ana climbed into the back of the vehicle.

"You can't go, baby," Martin told her. "You'll get arrested and deported."

She answered him in Spanish that she was not leaving him. The two of them bickered for a minute, and then Martin said, "Stubborn girl. Let's just get this over with."

Before Decker closed the hatch, he said, "Do you know who set you up?"

"No. Only remember Joe."

"Did he give the orders?"

Brubeck bit back agony. "I think someone else."

"Who?" Decker asked. "Someone familiar?"

"Possibly."

"One of the Kaffeys' sons, maybe?"

"Can't say nothing, for sure."

But Decker detected some hesitation. The man was a thread away from dying. He'd press the issue once he was hospitalized and, more important, stabilized. He closed the hatch to the Suburban. To T, he said, "Want me to sit shotgun or follow you in our rental?"

"You sit shotgun, for real this time," T said. "Who knows who's out there."

HOT AND SMOGGY, the afternoon didn't lend itself to gardening. Even the greenhouse seemed weighted down by the heavy air. Rina decided to call it quits. She had planned to be out for a couple of hours, but it was just too muggy. Had she kept to her original schedule, she wouldn't have heard the frantic knocking at the door.

She looked out the peephole and couldn't believe her eyes. She checked the newly installed video camera, and his face was very clear. She probably should have ignored it, but he seemed to be panicked. "What do you want?"

"Your husband isn't in his office. Is he here?"

"No."

"I need to talk to him."

"He's not here. Go back to the station house and someone will contact him for you."

"They think I'm crazy."

So do I, Rina thought.

"Please! I need his help!"

Again, Rina opened the door but kept the chain on. "What is it?"

"I'm pretty sure someone is following me. I want to know what I should do." He thought a moment. "I'm sorry. I must seem like a whack job, but I'm not."

Within a moment, Rina made a snap judgment. It wouldn't have been what Peter wanted, but he wasn't here right now. She opened the door. "Come in."

He was breathing hard and sweating profusely. Gone was the Tom Cruise smile, replaced by tension and anxiety. He wore a light-weight tan jacket over a white shirt and brown slacks. He walked haltingly across the threshold, and Rina closed the door. "Thank you . . . thank you so much."

"Would you like a glass of water?"

"Yes, please."

"I'll be right back." When she returned, he hadn't moved from the front door. "How about if we sit down?"

"Okay."

His expression was hard to read without the eyes, but he still seemed tense. When she touched his arm, he jumped, knocking the glass in her hands, water and ice sloshing over the lip. "I'm trying to guide you to a chair."

"Yeah . . . sure. Sorry."

Rina took him to the settee and he sat down stiffly. She put the glass in his hand; he gripped it and brought it to his mouth. "Why do you think you're being followed?"

"I keep hearing footsteps in back of me . . . the same footsteps."

"You can differentiate between footsteps?"

He nodded and took off his sunglasses to wipe his face. Glass eyes rolled in their sockets—pale blue with no light behind them. Like marbles spinning across the floor. He put his glasses back on. "I was out with my girlfriend. We heard popping noises. She said it sounded like a car backfiring, but I know what gunshot sounds like."

"Did it hit the car?"

"No, thank goodness."

"Were you driving through a rough area?"

"We were at the downtown interchange."

"Freeway snipings aren't unheard of. Did you contact the police?"

"I can't see anything, the car wasn't damaged, and Dana thought it was a car backfiring." He was agitated. "Everyone in your husband's department thinks I'm crazy except maybe him. I need to talk to him."

"He's not available, but I'll call him and leave a message."

"When will he be available?"

"I don't know, Mr. Harriman."

"Brett. I'm so sorry to barge in on you, but I know when something's wrong, Mrs. Decker. I can hear it. More than that, I can smell it! It's the same smell! Someone is stalking me!"

"Is your girlfriend waiting outside?"

"No, I took a cab. She already thinks I'm going off the deep end."

She ain't the only one.

Harriman said, "I don't know what to do. That's why I came here."

"If someone is really stalking you, you shouldn't be here. You should be at the station house."

He sighed. "They're not going to believe me."

"That may be, but they won't throw you out on the street." She considered her options. "How about if I take you there? They'll give me some credence."

"That's very kind of you . . . I'm so sorry to drag you into this. I just didn't know where to turn. When they told me over the phone that Lieutenant Decker wasn't in, I figured he was at home."

"He's not here."

"I realize that. I'm sure I seem crazy to you."

"Fear can do that."

"I've been translating in the courtrooms for years. I've been used in some very bad murder cases. But no one has ever bothered me before."

"Let me get my keys."

"Yes. Where should I put the glass?"

"I'll take it." She went back into the kitchen and returned with her keys. She was about to guide him to the door, but then her eyes rested on the video monitor. The front porch was blank, but there was a strange car across the street. The white sedan appeared with a sizable dent on the rear passenger door. It could be another relative for the elderly woman who lived down the street, but Harriman's paranoia was infectious. She couldn't make out the license plate and something told her not to go outside.

Harriman said, "I caught a whiff of something that wasn't there a second ago. Like tension or fear. What's going on?"

"Maybe I'm nervous to be alone in a car with you."

"That's not it." He stood up. "What is it?"

"There's a car across the street—"

"What kind of car?"

"A Toyota or maybe a Honda. I have trouble telling them apart. Just calm down. I'm going to call up someone and have her drive by the house."

"Is anyone in the car?"

"I can't tell. Excuse me." Marge was in the field, but she answered her cell. Speaking softly over the line, Rina explained the situation.

Marge said, "I'm with Oliver. We're walking to the car. We'll be right over."

"It's probably nothing—"

"That nutcase is in your house, that's something."

"He's blind."

"Are you sure about that?"

"I saw his eyes. I'm sure." She paused. "I might be a little unnerved by him, but I can't say I'm scared by him."

"You still have your gun?"

"Yes. I'll get it out of the safe, although I'm probably overreacting."

"I have to be honest with you. The Loo had some concerns about Harriman dragging you into something bad."

"I opened the door voluntarily. It probably wasn't smart."

"Not smart, but a human thing to do. You know what they say."

"What?"

"To err is human, but to shoot the son of a bitch is divine."

THIRTY-TWO

AS MARGE APPROACHED the white Accord from the rear, its motor sprang to life and the sedan crawled away from the curb. She followed it for a block or two, before the car turned on to Devonshire, one of the main drags of the West Valley. Oliver read off the license plate numerals to the RTO and it came back with no wants or warrants. The vehicle was registered to Imelda Cruz, age thirty-four, with an address in East Valley.

"Maybe Auntie Gwen had another visitor," Oliver said.

"I don't think so." Marge's eyes were glued on the Accord as it signaled a lane change. "From the back, the driver looks like a he." Another signal, another lane change. "Joe fucking model citizen."

"We're driving a cruiser. He knows we're tailing him."

Marge's cell rang. Oliver fished the phone out of her purse. It was Rina.

"The car's gone, Scott. Where are you?"

"Tailing the car."

"Oh . . . okay," Rina said. "In that case, I'm going to take Harriman to the station. Neither one of us wants to stay here right now."

"Rina, let me call in an escort for you."

"What's going on?" Marge said.

"She wants to take Harriman in." Into the receiver, Oliver said, "Just wait for a cruiser to show up to follow you."

"As long as you make it quick. I'm getting creeped out."

"Got it." Oliver hung up the phone and called in for a cruiser. "He looks like he's headed for the freeway. If we're going to pull him over, do it before the on-ramp."

Marge turned on the siren. A moment later, the Honda signaled and pulled to the curb. Every time cops made a stop, there was that potential for violence. The Kaffey double homicide just made them all that more cautious.

"This is a case for ye olde bullhorn." Oliver instructed the driver and any of the passengers to step out of the car with hands in the air. The seconds that followed were infused with tension, waiting for the unexpected.

The passenger door swung open and a scarecrow-thin kid emerged, wearing a wife-beater undershirt and saggy shorts. His arms were bony, and his hands were in the air. His skin was covered with tattoos.

Oliver said, "Put your hands on the trunk of your car."

When the kid complied, Oliver told him not to move and the two of them descended quickly, Marge on one side, Oliver on the other. It was clear he wasn't carrying weapons, so Oliver told him to turn around. The kid was around five five with a face filled with zits. He barely looked old enough to drive. His eyes were dull and brown. His expression was an utter blank—neither aggression nor fear.

"Anyone else in the car?"

"No, sir."

"Where's your ID?"

"In the car."

Marge said, "Mind if I go inside your car to look for it?"

"No, ma'am."

"What's your name?" Oliver asked him.

"Esteban."

"Esteban what?"

"Cruz."

Probably a relative of the owner. Oliver said, "How old are you?"

"Seventeen."

"Where do you live?"

"Ramona Drive."

"Do you have an address?" The number he gave put Esteban living in the East Valley. "You're a little far from home."

"Yes, sir."

"What are you doing here?"

"Hanging around."

"You shouldn't be here, hanging around. That doesn't look good."

"Yes, sir."

"You should be in school."

"I dropped out of school."

"So what do you do now that you're not in school?"

"Hang around."

"That's not a very healthy way to live, Esteban. Who owns the car?"

"My mother."

"And she gives you the car to drive just to hang around?"

"Yes, sir."

"So if I called her, she wouldn't be upset that you have the car?"

"No, sir."

The boy seemed basic, and in this case that made him smart. He didn't ask why he was pulled over, he wasn't belligerent, and he didn't volunteer any information.

"Do you have a number for your mother?"

Esteban gave Oliver a phone number. He made the call on his cell phone and a woman came on the line. "Is this Imelda Cruz?"

"*Sí?*"

When Oliver identified himself and told her that he had her son in custody, the woman answered with a "no speak English." Knowing that Marge's Spanish wasn't much better than his, he mumbled a *"muchas gracias"* and cut the line.

He studied Esteban. "You've got a lot of number twelves tattooed on your skin."

"Yes, sir."

"Bodega 12th Street gang?"

"No, sir."

"Then why the tats?"

A simple shrug. "It looks good."

"So you have all the tats, but you're not a gang member."

"No, sir."

Oliver said, "That doesn't make a lot of sense."

The boy didn't answer. Marge had finished her search and was walking toward the two of them. She gave Oliver a slight shake of the head.

Approaching the boy, she said, "What are you doing in this area?"

"Just hanging, ma'am."

"Esteban, what were you *doing* in your car in the middle of a residential area about twenty miles from home?"

The boy picked at one of his pimples. "I can sleep here and not get shot."

Marge and Oliver exchanged glances. "You sleep in the car?"

"Sometimes. Sometimes I listen to my iPod. Sometimes I read."

"Did you find reading material inside the car?" Oliver asked Marge.

"Two comic books and a graphic novel." She studied Cruz's face. Portraits in the museum held a lot more life than he did. "You shouldn't be hanging around. It makes you look like you're doing something bad."

"Yes, ma'am."

"You should be in school."

"I dropped out of school."

"You like to read," Marge said. "Why'd you drop out of school?"

Esteban didn't answer right away. Finally, he offered an opinion.

"It's not a school, it's a zoo." A flash of anger had abruptly emerged from his face: frightening in its intensity, but within seconds it had faded into nothingness.

"If you like reading, you should go to the library," Marge told him.

"You can't sleep in a library," Esteban told her. "They kick you out."

"Well, find a better place to read," Marge said.

"Yes, ma'am."

She handed him back his wallet. "The reason we pulled you over is that your taillight doesn't work very well. Get it fixed."

"Yes, ma'am."

Silence.

"You can go," Marge told him.

"Yes, ma'am."

After the kid had driven off, Marge regarded Oliver. "Did you notice the anger when he talked about the school? A flare-up in an otherwise monotone conversation."

Oliver rolled his eyes. "That's one cool demon spawn. I could see him shooting you in the face and not blinking an eye."

"Which reminds me . . ." Marge called up Rina. "Where are you?"

"We're almost at the station house. Is everything okay?"

"Everything's fine. We'll be there in a few minutes." She hung up the phone and looked back at Oliver. "There weren't any weapons in the car. If the kid was hired to hit Harriman, he was scouting his target with an objective eye."

Oliver nodded. "That would make Mr. Politeness even scarier."

DECKER WAS IRATE. "What do you mean you *opened* the door! Why'd you *do* that?"

Rina said, "Because he was outside all alone and he seemed vulnerable."

"You didn't know that he was alone. He could have brought in a posse of killers."

"Since someone bothered to install a video camera, I had a bird's-eye view of the street." She took in a breath and let it out. "Harriman went to the police, Peter, and asked to speak with you. Someone told him that you'd be contacted and you'd call Harriman back. Didn't anyone deliver the message to you?"

Decker didn't answer. No one bothered to contact him because they thought Harriman was psycho. "I'm a busy person, Rina. I've got better things to do than to check up on some weirdo."

Rina said, "So you're completely discounting his fears. No wonder he feels marginalized, especially after he helped you by identifying Alejandro Brand."

"You're not his shrink, you're my wife. The idiot put you in jeopardy." Decker had a burning urge to punch something. "If the bastard was being followed, he led the bad guys to your doorstep. Now you have no choice. You've got to move in with your parents until we know what's going on."

"How do you know that the kid in the Accord was after Harriman? You're the lead detective on the Kaffey case. Maybe he's after you."

"If he's after anyone, it's Harriman. Stop arguing with me and listen for a change—"

"For a change? That is not fair! I've done everything you've asked of me."

"You answered the door! Why the hell did you do that?"

"Because Harriman seemed distraught. I wasn't going to throw him to the wolves. You're not the only one with intuitions. And, I repeat, if Harriman had felt that someone in the department had taken him seriously, maybe he wouldn't have had to *resort* to trying to track you down. And stop yelling at me!"

Decker took a deep breath. "Move in with your parents, all right?"

"Fine." She hung up the phone, her hands shaking from adrenaline. The cell rang again. She blew out air and answered it. "Yes?"

"You hung up on me!"

"There's nothing left to say."

Decker spoke in a measured voice. "I'm nervous."

"Peter, I'm sorry that I made you anxious. I'll pack up and move in with my parents. I'll see you whenever you get home." A pause. "When are you coming home?"

"I was planning on coming home tonight, but something's come up and I have to stick around in Ponceville." A pause. "I mean I don't have to stick around but—"

"Do what you need to do. I've got to go."

"Rina, I'm sorry I yelled."

"And I'm sorry if I used bad judgment, but since you weren't around for guidance, I did the best I could."

"I should have had someone dealing with him before it got to this point."

Shoulda, woulda, coulda, she thought. "I'll be careful. You be careful, too."

"I'll call you later."

"If I'm not there, don't worry. I'm going down to the range to practice."

"Good idea."

"It's not because I think I'll need to fire a weapon. Right now, I need to attack something and so far as I know, a bull's-eye doesn't fire back."

MARGE KNOCKED ON the door to Decker's office, then came inside. Rina's face was a mixture of anger, frustration, and weariness. She got up from the desk chair, smoothed her denim skirt, and adjusted the scarf that covered her hair. "You need to use the office, Marge?"

"Whenever you're ready."

She stood up. "You probably think I'm an idiot. It was dumb to open the door, but it's the way I'm made. I look for the good in humanity, Peter looks for the kinks."

"You're a very kindhearted person, Rina. And you have good instincts. In this case, it worked out fine. Just be careful from now on until we get some answers."

Rina sighed. She couldn't expect her husband to be as empathetic as Marge, but a girl could dream. "Thanks for all your help."

"Anytime." Marge placed a hand on her shoulder. "And don't pay attention to the Loo. He's been snarling at anyone who comes near him. He's just worried about your back." The desk phone rang. "That's him. Should I tell him anything for you?"

"Tell him to watch *his* back." Rina waved a bye. "His is a lot bigger than mine."

With the desk chair vacated, Marge took up the empty seat. It was close to three in the afternoon and she hadn't eaten all day, but basic drives would just have to wait. "Hey, Rabbi. This is what I found out about Esteban Cruz. Are you ready?"

"I'm ready," Decker answered.

Marge said, "No wants, no warrants, no priors. Just an average high school dropout. Oliver and I are going to drop by his former high school . . . try to find out who he associated with. You don't have that many B12 tattoos on your skin without making a few friends with the homies."

"Did you run the name by Henry Almont or Crystal McCall in Juvenile at Foothill?"

"Yes, I did. Also showed them his DMV picture. No recognition." She thought a moment. "Even if he was camping out, both Oliver and I decided he was creepy. His placidity . . . like he'd shoot you while bopping to the music on his iPod."

"I trust your instincts . . ." His voice faded.

"You still there, Pete?"

"I'm here." Decker hit his forehead. "I've been so caught up with Rina, I've been ignoring the obvious. The kid's name is Esteban *Cruz*?"

"Unless he has a fake ID, yes."

"Alejandro Brand's grandmother was named Cruz."

Marge sat up in Decker's desk chair. "A cousin?"

"Does he look like Brand?"

"I don't know. I've never seen Brand."

"Brand was going on about Harriman . . . saying that he was an asshole who was out to get him. What if he hired a relative to do it for him?"

"Why would Brand think that Harriman IDed him? The guy is blind."

"Brand doesn't know that, and I didn't correct him. I figured it would prod him to talk about the Kaffey murders if he thought that we had an eyewitness against him."

Marge said, "Okay. What's the next step?"

"A good question." Decker's brain was firing with ideas. "First of all, I want someone at my in-laws' house full-time."

"Already done."

"Second, keep someone on Harriman twenty-four/seven until we figure out who Esteban Cruz is."

"Done as well."

"Third, let's see if there's a connection between Esteban and Alejandro."

"You got it," Marge said.

"Give me an update on what's happening down there."

"Gil and Resseur are still missing. Pratt and Messing are checking out their old haunts. Oliver checked out Sean Kaffey. He seems to be the smartest of the bunch. He's a junior partner in a big law firm, making his own six figures. He doesn't look like a good candidate for El Patrón. His dad, on the other hand, is an elusive guy. He flew back east on a private jet and is already back at the office working like a dog according to his secretary. She said he'd call me when he had a spare moment."

Decker said, "Is it possible that he took Gil and Resseur with him?"

"I can try to locate the jet company that took him back home. See if they'll let me peek at the airline manifest to see who's on it."

"Do your best. Could you also call Cindy and make sure she's okay?"

"I'll called her this morning. She's fine." Marge shifted the phone. "What's happening up there with Rondo Martin?"

"I'm waiting in front of the ICU. Martin came out of surgery about an hour ago. I'm hoping to be able to talk to him in a bit."

"That would be great . . . I mean, how do we know that Martin's telling the truth?"

Decker paused. "What do you mean?"

"Martin is painting himself as an innocent bystander like Denny Orlando. But he also could have been a participant."

"He's in terrible shape. Why do you think he was involved in the murders?"

"It's not what I think. It's what Harriman said in his statement. I've got it in front of me. He mentions Martin a couple of times . . . that Martin was really pissed about José running out of ammo."

Decker shifted the phone to the other ear. "That's a good point."

"Maybe Martin was riding Pine about fucking up. Maybe Pine got super pissed and shot Martin full of lead. Maybe that's why Joe didn't have enough ammunition to finish off Kaffey. Just because Martin was shot doesn't mean he wasn't involved."

Decker exhaled. "That's very true."

The nurse peeked her head out of the ICU. "Mr. Martin is up. Please be brief."

"Thank you very much," Decker told her. Into the line, he said, "Martin's conscious. I've got to go."

"Good luck."

"Keep a watch over the station house for me. Brubeck and I will be here for a while. Neither of us is going anywhere until we get some answers."

ALTHOUGH MARTIN SMELLED a lot better, he looked a lot worse. Tubes were feeding him, medicating him, and plying his lungs with additional oxygen. Machines monitored his heart rate and his breathing. The obvious infected areas had been cleaned, but the lapsed time without proper care had taken its toll. Rondo wasn't out of the woods yet, and Decker acted as if this was his one and only shot at the medal.

Martin acknowledged him with a slight nod. That was the best he could do.

"You're a strong man, Rondo. You're in good hands now. You'll be all right." There was no response. But the eyes were still open.

"I'm keeping watch over you until we arrange for something perma-
nent. Brubeck and me. We'll take shifts and watch over you personally."

Another slight nod.

"Do you mind if I talk a little?" Decker asked. "I'll tell you
what's going on from my angle. If I'm wrong about something, you
can correct me. I'll go slowly, okay?"

A nod.

Decker kept the recitation short. Gil Kaffey had survived. He
heard the murderers speaking Spanish, but that's all he could remember. Later, by sheer coincidence, someone overheard two men
talking about the case. One of them seemed to have an insider's
knowledge. That man was Alejandro Brand.

"Does the name sound familiar?" Decker asked him.

Martin closed his eyes and then opened them. Decker thought he
detected a shake of the head.

"Is that a no?"

A nod.

Decker said, "It could be that he also goes by the name Alejandro
Cruz. How about that name? Familiar?"

"No . . ." he whispered.

"Okay, you don't know Alejandro Brand or Alejandro Cruz.
The guy is a member of the Bodega 12th Street gang. So was Joe
Pine. Did you know that?"

A nod.

"You knew Joe was an ex-gangbanger?"

A nod.

"Did you know that Guy Kaffey hired other ex-gang members—
supposedly rehabilitated gang members—as guards?"

A nod.

"I think that's crazy."

Martin muttered something. Decker leaned in close.

"Few . . ."

"A few what?"

The response was delayed. "A few gang . . ."

Decker put the pieces together. "There were only a *few* gang members in the group?"

A nod.

"We found more than a few with felonies." Decker checked his notes. "This one guy, Ernesto Sanchez, was also a former Bodega 12th gang member. He had been arrested and served time for two assaults. Did you know him?"

A nod.

"Rondo . . . if you close your eyes . . . and think about the other people who invaded the Kaffey house . . . close your eyes and picture the scene."

He cooperated, wincing as some vision coursed through his brain.

"Could one of those men at the scene be Ernesto Sanchez?"

A shake of the head. That made sense because Sanchez was at a bar. Messing had talked to several people who remembered seeing him. So far, Martin appeared credible.

The woman in scrubs walked in. She stopped and folded her arms across her chest. Her name tag identified her as Chris Bellows, MD, surgical resident. Her eyes were intelligent and annoyed, but she managed a fleeting smile. "You need to wrap this up. It's time for Mr. Martin to receive his medications. He needs to sleep."

"Five more minutes?"

"How about one?" Her face told him that she wouldn't brook any argument. She glanced at her watch. "Starting now."

Decker sighed. "Okay. This is what I'm going to do, Rondo. I'm going to read a list of the guards who worked for the Kaffeys and you tell me by nodding if I should be investigating them."

A nod.

"There are about twenty-two names. I'll have to go a little fast because I have to leave soon."

"Thirty seconds," the doctor told them.

Decker said, "I'm reading them off in alphabetical order."

A nod.

"Doug Allen."

Nothing.

"Curt Armstrong."

No response.

"Javier Beltran."

Nothing from Martin.

"Time's up."

"C'mon. All he's doing is nodding. How about Francisco Cortez?"

There was no response from Martin.

"You're not only stressing him out, you're stressing me. Goodbye, Detective."

"When can I come back?"

"Tomorrow, if he's doing better."

There was no sense bucking authority. He almost got himself shot with that approach this morning. As Decker started to put away his notes, his eyes swept over the next name on the list. His brain suddenly leaped into overdrive.

Decker spoke a final name aloud.

Martin's eyes got very wide. His blood pressure skyrocketed and machines started beeping.

The doctor glared at him. "Leave now!"

"I'm out of here," Decker said.

But he was smiling.

He had found his missing link.

THIRTY-THREE

THE LOS ANGELES Unified School District was a dinosaur: a brain in its head as well as in its tail. The head part was the wealthier districts—Bel Air, Holmby Hills, Westwood, Encino, and Pacific Palisades—while the caudal portion administered to the less-endowed schools in East L.A., South L.A., and the poorer sections of the San Fernando Valley. Pacoima definitely qualified as a tail.

"The dropout rate is probably higher than the graduation rate," the guidance counselor told them. Her name was Carmen Montenegro, a woman in her midthirties with mocha skin, almond-shaped brown eyes, and a wide mouth with her lips painted deep red. She wore a red shirt under a black suit with no stockings. "We do the best we can with what we have, which isn't much."

Marge and Oliver followed Carmen as she trotted down a hallway lined with lockers, her heels clacking on yellowed, institutional floor tiling. School had let out a half hour ago, but students were still milling around, heavy backpacks dragging on their sloping shoulders. The teens were dressed in baggy jeans or sweats for the boys, and jeans, sweats, or short skirts for the girls.

Carmen took a sharp right into the admissions office, pushing past a saloon door that almost caught Marge in the stomach. Her office was tiny and looked out over the school's parking lot. A computer was surrounded by stacks of papers on her desktop with more piles spilling on the floors. Overflowing bookshelves lined two of the walls.

"Sorry about the mess." The administrator began hunting through yearbooks. She pulled one out. "This is from two years ago. He would have been a freshman, right?"

"Right," Oliver answered.

"Esteban Cruz . . . Esteban Cruz . . . Esteban . . . Here he is." She showed the picture to Marge. "Looks like the picture you showed me."

Marge said, "He hasn't aged much."

"Yeah, he looks kinda small. You want a copy of the picture?"

"Yes, that would help."

"Hold on." She whisked past them and came back a few moments later with ten copies. "Here you go . . . Anything else?"

Marge said, "Would you mind if I looked through the book to see if he was involved in any activities?"

"No problem." Carmen handed her the book. "Sit at my desk. Makes it easier to sift through the pages." The administrator's eyes skipped over Oliver's face. She gave him the briefest of smiles. "Probably, he wasn't involved in much. The ones who drop out are just marking time."

Oliver's eyes went to her hands. No wedding ring. "Do you have any recollection of him?"

She looked at the picture again. "We have so many kids going in and out of the system. I don't remember him as being a troublemaker."

"He told us he likes to read a lot," Marge said. "Do you have a record of his grades and his teachers?"

"I can get both for you, but I need my computer."

Marge stood up, yearbook in hand. She showed it to Oliver, and the two of them studied the pages as Carmen looked up the former student. "Esteban Cruz . . . here we go. He was passing . . .C's, a few B's even. He did get an A in English. His teacher was Jake Tibbets. Want me to see if he's still around?"

"That would be great," Oliver said.

Again Carmen gave him a quick smile. "Don't go away. I'll be back."

After she rushed out of the office, Marge said, "She's a bundle of energy."

"Nothing wrong with that."

"She was definitely giving you the eye." When Oliver returned a Cheshire cat grin, she nudged him in the ribs. "Since when have you ever been discreet?"

"I'm trying to be less obvious. So do me a favor. Ask for a card with the phone number—in case we need to talk to her again."

"If I ask for the card, she'll think you're not interested."

"So you think I should ask for the card?"

"Yes . . . shhhh . . . I hear her."

Carmen returned with a smile. "He's in the teachers' lounge and he'll be happy to talk to you about Esteban."

"Thanks," Marge said. "Ms. Montenegro, I am also curious about two other men: Alejandro Brand, who would be around nineteen, and José Pinon or maybe Joe Pine. He'd be in his early twenties. Would you know if they attended high school here?"

"I can look that up for you . . ." She pushed some buttons and tapped the monitor. "Wow! Brand did attend here, and he was a troublemaker: a banger with the Bodega 12th Street homies. Multiple suspensions until he was expelled four years ago. He also had Mr. Tibbets as an English teacher. No success story there. What was the other name?"

"José Pinon," Marge told her.

"Uh . . . Pinon, Pinon . . . I have Maria Pinon who was in Brand's grade. Probably a sister, so . . ." Click, click, click. "Uh, he lasted through ninth grade . . . actually he repeated ninth grade, and then he flunked out."

"Was he a troublemaker?"

"Uh . . . not really." She looked up from the monitor. "Just your average dropout."

"A gangbanger?" Marge asked.

"They all are." She stood up. "Let's go to the lounge . . . which is sort of misnamed. It's a room with used furniture and a coffeepot. I think someone brought in doughnuts today. They're probably stale by now, but if you need a sugar fix, they'll do the trick."

IN HIS SIXTIES or even older, Jake Tibbets was tall and as limp as a noodle. He had salt-and-pepper hair, deep crow's-feet at the corners of his eyes, and a nice-sized wattle under his neck. His eyes were algae colored and twinkled with mischief. He wore a yellow paisley shirt, black slacks, and orthopedic shoes. He was sitting on a futon, drinking something hot, the veins in his hands blue and thick. Carmen made quick introductions.

Tibbets's voice was moderate in pitch and youthful sounding. "Have a seat. Want some tea?"

The detectives passed. It was around ninety degrees outside and the school's air-conditioning was tepid at best.

"So you want to know about Esteban Cruz." Tibbets sipped his beverage. "What's the boy done now?"

"We don't know that he's done anything," Marge told him. She pulled up a mismatched chair, leaving Carmen and Oliver a love seat. "We're just gathering information. Do you remember him?"

"Sure. Not because my memory is so great. I'm at that stage where I have to write everything down. Except Shakespeare. I know Shakespeare by heart. That's mostly what I teach. Believe it or not, when you frame Willy in modern turns, it strikes a resonant chord with the kids. Murder and jealousy and greed and naked ambition." His voice had risen to an orator's pitch. "Romeo and Juliet is the greatest love story ever written, with gang warfare to boot. What could be more modern?"

The three of them nodded.

Tibbets said, "Yes, I remember Esteban Cruz. Smart kid. I gave him an A. An A at Pacoima High isn't the same as an A at Boston Latin, but it did mean that he took the quizzes and tests and handed in his homework on time."

"So he did well on the material."

"Decent. Plus, we give a lot of credit to anyone who shows up."

"Then why do you remember him as being smart?" Marge asked.

"Everything is relative," Carmen broke in.

"That's the truth," Tibbets said. "We're just trying to keep the kids enrolled. Try to convince them that if they stay another year or two and do a minimum job, they can walk away with a diploma that'll give them more options. Or for the real bright ones, there's community college. I thought that might be an option for Esteban, but he left about a year ago. I did try to contact him . . . left my number with his mother."

"Did he call back?" Oliver asked.

"Nope. My Spanish isn't perfect, but I can make myself understood. So I'm left to think that he never got the message or he wasn't interested in what I had to say."

"He got an A in your class," Oliver said. "That must have stood out."

"It did. That's why I remember him."

"That A must have provided him with some encouragement," Marge said.

"If it did, he never said anything to me about it. He didn't talk much." Another sip of tea. "Whenever I talked to him, he was polite. He just wasn't much on conversation. Some kids . . . you give them an ear to listen, they'll spill their guts. Esteban wasn't a talker. Like he'd given up a long time ago. Story of this community, my friends."

"He has gang tattoos," Oliver said.

"The area is swarming with Bodega 12th Street gang members." He turned to Carmen for verification and she nodded. "The boys get the tattoos even if they aren't hard-core gangbangers."

"They pay allegiance money to the heads of the local gang to be able to wear the markings," Carmen said. "It gives them protection . . . not against other gangs but against other Bodega 12th Street bangers. If the smaller kids sport the proper tattoos and have paid their fees, the bigger ones won't bother them as much."

Tibbets said, "Of course, once you've got a gun, height doesn't matter too much."

Carmen said, "In this area alone we have three different Bodega Twelve gangs, each one with its own turf. That means three heads who report to some other guy who reports to some other guy. I don't know who the leader of the leaders is. It changes all the time because the leaders get shot and killed so often."

"So do the runners," Tibbets said. "But the whole thing runs efficiently because it's very easy to find drugs. Every other corner is a drop and pickup spot."

Marge asked, "Do you remember any of Esteban's friends?"

"No . . ." A shake of the head. "But he's a Cruz. That's a big family."

"Isn't Cruz a common Hispanic name?" Oliver said.

"Yes, it is," Carmen answered, "but around here, they all seem to be related."

"Interesting," Marge said. "We're curious about Alejandro Brand. His grandmother was named Cruz. Would the two boys be related?"

"Alejandro Brand." Tibbets smiled. "Is he incarcerated yet? He should be."

"He is currently behind bars," Marge told him.

"What for? Drugs? Assault? Murder? All of the above?"

"Sounds like you've had experience with Brand."

"I have and it's all been negative. If you suspect the kid of something, he's probably done it."

Oliver smiled. "Would you know if Cruz and Brand were related?"

"Not by temperament, but if Brand is a Cruz, he and Esteban share some common ancestry."

"Do you ever remember the two of them talking or hanging out together?" Marge asked.

"I think Alejandro was gone when Esteban got here." The teacher frowned. "Esteban was a queer duck. Couldn't tell what he was thinking. Couldn't tell what he was feeling. His eyes were flat. A body without a soul."

"That would be a zombie," Oliver said.

"I wouldn't call Esteban a zombie," Tibbets said. "But if he had emotions, if he had hopes or dreams or aspirations, he was very skilled at not letting them show."

THE PALM OF his right hand kept hitting his forehead. The way Decker felt, there was no gray matter inside to harm. He couldn't use the cell phone inside the hospital, and it would be another two hours before Brubeck would come to relieve him. He got up and went to the nurses' station, manned by Shari Pettigrew according to her ID tag. Decker gave the sixtyish woman his most boyish smile. "I need to call one of my detectives."

"You can't use your cell phone inside the hospital."

"I know that. That's why I'm talking to you. I can't leave the ICU right now. Could I possibly borrow one of your lines? It should only take a few moments."

Shari punched a line. "Number?"

Decker gave her the digits, and she handed him the receiver. "Willy, I need you down here right away. I've got to make some calls and I can't do it and watch the ICU at the same time. . . . Thanks. Bye." He handed the phone back. "Thank you very much."

"Why are you watching the ICU?"

Again, Decker graced her with a smile. "Eavesdropping, were you?"

"You're an inch away. Why are you watching the ICU? Is it because someone tried to kill the sheriff?"

"How'd you find that out?"

She rolled her eyes. "I can see you've never lived in a small town."

"Gainesville, Florida."

"That's New York City compared with Ponceville. We're all

concerned about one of our own." She looked down. "I sure hope he makes it."

"Were you close to the deputy sheriff?"

"Not really, but we drank at the same place . . . the Watering Hole. Not too many bars around here so you run into the same people. Rondo kept pretty much to himself, but he seemed like he was one of the good guys." She laughed. "Good guys . . . bad guys, what the hey. Mostly it's just people being people."

OVER THE LINE, Marge said, "Stop battering yourself. We just made the Cruz connection a couple of hours ago."

"Martin Cruces was right in front of our faces."

"It makes sense *now,* but only because we found Rondo Martin near death and have pushed him down the suspect list." Marge said, "Martin Cruces was looked into and cleared right away."

"What was his alibi?"

"Oliver's paging through the file. Talk to Brubeck and Messing. They're the ones who checked him off. We did run him through NCIC. He doesn't have a record. He's in his midtwenties—older than Brand and Esteban, not exactly prime age for a gang. He still may have nothing to do with it."

"Is he Bodega Twelve?" Decker asked.

"I don't know."

"See if Neptune Brady has a set of fingerprints for him. Usually they do something like that before guards are hired."

"If he didn't do it for Joe Pine, he probably didn't do it for Cruces, but I'll check it out anyway. Hold on. Scott's reaching for the phone."

"Okay," Oliver said. "This is the story. Messing and Brubeck cleared him. The night of the murders, he was at his local bar—Ernie's El Matador. He routinely comes in about two to three times a week, usually after dinner. The bartender, Julio Davis, confirmed that Cruces came in around nine, drank beer, and shot the breeze with the regulars."

"How late did he stay?"

"Until closing: two in the morning. That pretty much put him out of the time frame. Messing also says that Cruces gave a cheek swab and was cooperative."

"Means nothing."

"I know, but you know how it is. You concentrate on the obvious." Oliver said, "I just checked with the lab. No matches yet, but not all of the biological material has come back. We'll go back to the bar and interview Davis again."

"Good. Also, bring Cruces in again. Tell him it's a routine reinterview."

"Got it."

Decker said, "What did you learn about Esteban Cruz?"

"He wasn't much of a talker, but he wasn't a troublemaker. We did find out that most of the Cruzes in that area are related, so maybe Brand and Esteban are kin. I don't know where that puts Martin Cruces. Maybe the Cruz family is different from the Cruces family. I've called up the guidance counselor at Pacoima High to find out if Cruces went there."

"And?"

"She's checking into it. If he did attend, it was about seven years earlier than Alejandro Brand. I also had her check a little deeper into Joe Pine who was José Pinon. She said she could pull all the written records, but it'll take a little time. We've arranged to meet later tonight, and she'll give me whatever she has on him."

"That could be taken care of with a phone call. Why are you meeting her in person?" The line fell silent. "How old is she?"

"I dunno . . ." Oliver smiled. "Maybe around thirty-five."

"Uh-huh. Are you meeting her for dinner?"

"I haven't had time to eat, Loo. And with Marge and me going back to Ernie's El Matador to interview the bartender, I'm going to be famished." Oliver was grinning. "If we were to have dinner, it would be a business meeting."

"And that would mean you're putting it on the department tab?"

"You know how it is with sources. You get a good one, Rabbi, you treat her right."

THIRTY-FOUR

THE FIRST STEP was to locate Martin Cruces.

Apparently the former guard felt comfortable enough to stay in town—and why not? The papers had moved on to the "puzzling" disappearance of Gil Kaffey and Antoine Resseur and there was no reason for him to think that the police were even close to a solve. Decker had assigned Messing and Pratt to track Cruces's activities, which included hanging out in his house and with his B12 street buds.

Cruces was older than most of the Bodega clan—in his midtwenties and he seemed to be respected. He appeared to be constantly on the watch, and Messing and Pratt had to keep enough distance between the bangers and the car so that their cover wouldn't be blown.

Step two was to find forensic evidence that would put Cruces at the murder scene. He had given a DNA swab, but since genetic profiling was an expensive undertaking and he had been initially cleared, his material hadn't been sent to the lab. That was rectified an hour ago, but it would take weeks to get back the results.

Cruces's prints hadn't been on file when Messing ran him through

AFIS. Lee Wang went over to Foothill and asked about his activities as a teen. His youthful indiscretions had been sealed, so Wang assembled the paperwork to unseal both Martin Cruces's and José Piñon's records. Dozens of bloody fingerprints had been lifted from the murder scene and if Wang could only get a fingerprint card, maybe they'd have something forensically to link them to the scene. With evidence and eyewitness testimony from Rondo Martin, Wang felt sure the police could nail Joe Pine.

The third step involved clarifying the information from Rondo Martin, who was currently in a drug-induced sleep. His eyes had widened at the mention of Cruces's name, but the specifics were yet to come. Maybe he could provide something crucial.

The last step involved breaking Cruces's alibi, which would give the cops an excuse to bring him in again for questioning.

AT THREE IN the afternoon, Ernie's El Matador was doing business. Salsa music was blaring from the speakers, and a soccer game flashed on a sound-muted flat screen mounted on the wall just above a neon Corona clock. Five men were sitting at the bar and two more were playing pool. The place was dark. Marge couldn't see well enough to avoid the sticky spots on the floor.

Oliver was the first one to show his badge although he didn't need to. He and Marge were made as soon as they walked in. No one there was wearing a seersucker jacket and a pair of linen slacks. The preferred dress was jeans with some kind of T-shirt top and sneakers. The place was warm, a shade off from uncomfortable.

The bartender was in his late twenties with dark brown eyes, café au lait skin, and black hair slicked straight back. He had an iron pumper's body with thick biceps and oven-mitt hands. He regarded Oliver's badge, his eyes attempting disinterest.

"How are you doing?" Oliver asked him.

Muscleman gave a shrug. "No complaints."

"I'm Detective Scott Oliver and this is my partner, Detective Sergeant Marge Dunn. We're looking for Julio Davis."

"He's not here." He picked up a rag and began wiping down the bar.

"Could I get your name?" Marge asked.

"*My* name?"

"Yeah, your name." Marge regarded the man's face—lined and seamed and scarred from an old knife wound.

"Sam Truillo." He stopped wiping the bar. His English was un-accented. "What do you want with Julio?"

"Just want to talk to him," Oliver said.

"He works here, doesn't he?" Marge asked.

A grizzled patron in the corner asked the barkeep for something in Spanish. Truillo popped the top from a Corona, stuck a lime in the mouth of the bottle, and placed it in front of the man on a nap-kin. He said, "I haven't seen Julio in over a week."

"Something happened to him?"

"I don't know. The boss told me to call him, but his cell was dis-connected."

"That doesn't sound promising," Marge said. "What did you do after that?"

"Nothing. He doesn't want to work, what's it my business?"

Oliver asked, "How long had he worked here?"

"Four . . . maybe five months."

"How long have you worked here?" Marge asked.

"A year." Truillo shrugged. "Are we done?"

"And you work here full-time?" Marge smiled again. "I mean you look like you should be a spotter in a gym."

For the first time, the bartender cracked a smile. "This pays better."

"So you *do* work in a gym," Marge told him. "Am I a detective or what?"

"I work as a personal trainer, but things are tight now. I lost a few clients and the gym lost membership. The boss was going to cut my hours, but then he told me I could work here part-time to make up for my salary cut."

Another patron spoke up. Truillo placed a shot of tequila in front of him.

"I'm always looking for a good gym," Marge said. "Where do you work?"

"It isn't your type of gym," Truillo said. "It doesn't smell very nice."

Marge grinned. "Neither does my job."

"Your boss owns the gym and the bar?" Oliver said.

"Maybe." Truillo's eyes narrowed. "What do you want with Julio?"

"Do you know where he lives?"

"Nope."

Oliver said, "Your boss asked you to find him and you don't know where he lives?"

"My boss asked me to call him, not find him. And he wasn't my buddy so why would I know where he lived." His expression became flat. "Anything else?"

Marge took out her card and slid it across the bar top. "If he comes in here, can you give me a call?"

Truillo picked up the card and stowed it in his pocket. "If I remember."

"I hope you do. By the way, who's the boss?"

Truillo's eyes narrowed. "I'll give him your card. If he wants to talk to you, he'll give you a call."

Marge shrugged it off. "Hey, maybe I'll check out your gym."

"I didn't tell you where I worked."

"No, you didn't, did you?" She winked. "Are you going to make me figure that one out or are you going to tell me?"

"Let's see how good a detective you are."

"Sure. Thanks for your help."

"I didn't give you any help."

"That's not entirely true," Marge said. "You never know what's going to be helpful." She turned to Oliver. "Let's go."

When they were in the car, Oliver said, "You've got that look in your eyes, Dunn."

"Did you notice that Truillo said I don't know where Julio *lived*—like in past tense?"

"Actually, I didn't. You think he's dead?"

"I think he's definitely not around the neighborhood. Let's take a trip downtown." She glanced at her watch. "We need to move it, Scotty."

"What's the rush?"

"The offices close at five. Too bad. I could use a shot of caffeine, but I suppose it'll have to wait."

"You're not going to find a Starbucks in this area anyway."

"I actually prefer McDonald's coffee, but I don't want to waste the time."

"I repeat, 'What's the rush?'"

"He doesn't want to tell me who owns the bar. I want to check out business licenses."

"Aha." Oliver looked at his watch. It was almost four. "This can't be done online?"

"I suppose we can find out who owns the building online through the assessor's office, but that's not necessarily who owns the business."

"Can you get the name of business owners online?"

"Don't know. And it is getting late. That's why I think it's simpler to go downtown."

"So let's just leave it until tomorrow."

"Scotty," Marge said, "Truillo kept referring to the owner of the bar as the boss . . . which in and of itself doesn't mean too much . . . except that . . . I mean, maybe I'm just grasping, but El Patrón means The Boss in Spanish, right."

Oliver didn't answer. As he entered the on-ramp of the 5 freeway, he put the magnetic red light atop the unmarked and turned on the siren. In this traffic, it was the only way that they were going to make it before closing time.

OVER THE PHONE, Marge said, "Calling your boss 'the boss' doesn't mean anything, but since Julio isn't around right now, I figured it wouldn't hurt to know who owns the bar. At the very least, we could call him or her up and ask about Julio Davis."

"Do you have an address for Davis?"

"Wanda is working on it. Lee's still doing paperwork to unseal Cruces's and Pinon's juvenile records. If we can't unseal the entire file, we're hoping that a judge will let us look inside and pull out the prints. We've got Marvin Oldham on call to do comparisons. If we get a match, we'll pick up Cruces immediately."

"And Messing and Pratt still have him in their sights?"

"Absolutely."

"What about my wife?"

"We've got a black-and-white on Rina, and one on Harriman, too. We're also keeping tabs on Esteban Cruz. No activity."

"That's good. Anything on Gil Kaffey or Antoine Resseur?"

"No." Marge glanced at her watch. They were stuck in terrible traffic and even with the siren, it was slow going. "If we discover something interesting, I'll buzz you back. Oliver is meeting Carmen Montenegro for dinner. Maybe Pinon's school records will tell us something. She's also checking to see if Martin Cruces went to the same school. If downtown turns out to be a bust, I've got some time. What do you need from me?"

"Our main focus is on Cruces. If we get lucky and place his prints at the scene, we'll take him in. He'll need to be interviewed. You want to do it?"

"Sure."

"Just keep track of everyone, Marge; Harriman, Martin Cruces, Esteban Cruz, and Alejandro Brand—he's a real loose canon. Make sure he stays put in jail."

"He isn't going anywhere."

"Hold on a sec, Marge." Decker placed his hand over the receiver. The floor nurse, the same sixtyish looking woman who had loaned him the phone, said that Rondo Martin was up and wanted to talk to him.

"Don't tax him too much. Otherwise the doc will give us both hell."

"I promise. Thank you." To Marge he said, "I've got to go. Martin is up. Let me know what's going on." He cut the line, washed his hands, and went into the ICU.

Rondo Martin appeared more awake and in a lot of pain. He lifted a veined hand with an IV needle taped to his wrist and managed to point to the chair by his bedside. Decker sat and as the former deputy sheriff shifted his position to move a little closer, his face contorted. Sweat trickled down his forehead.

"You need something for the pain, Rondo?" Decker asked.

"Demerol helps . . . but it knocks me out." A slight smile. "Didn't die before . . . ain't gonna die now."

"Tell me about Martin Cruces."

"Cruces . . ." A nod. "He was there."

"You're sure?"

A nod. He closed his eyes. Under the lids, his orbs were moving rapidly. "It was Denny . . . he said . . . Denny said, 'Martin' . . . I thought he meant me." He paused, his eyes quivering. "I turned around . . . he exploded . . . Denny did." He opened his eyes, weary and bloodshot. "It was Cruces. I'm positive."

"Weren't the shooters wearing masks?"

"No . . . not Joe . . . not Cruces. Wish they did. I see their ugly mugs every time I close my eyes."

"And you're sure that it was Cruces who shot Denny Orlando?"

Again, he closed his eyes. "I . . . I don't know who fired . . ." A pause, then he opened his eyelids. "But Cruces was there." He readjusted his position, but he was still in pain.

"That would make sense," Decker told him. "Someone overheard a gangbanger talk about the murder. He mentioned Joe Pine, calling him José Pinon, and said that he ran out of ammo, that he didn't kill Gil Kaffey. He said that Martin was pissed. Logically, I thought he meant you since you were missing."

"Who's the banger?" Martin asked.

"The kid named Alejandro Brand. His grandmother is named Cruz, so he might be related to Cruces. Are you sure you don't know him?"

Martin shook his head no.

"Brand is a member of Bodega 12th Street gang. So is Pine. We think Cruces is as well. I can't understand why Guy would hire thugs to guard him or his property."

"Guy . . . he wanted to . . . to give back."

"By hiring thugs?"

"He hired all kinds . . . like Paco . . . to give back."

"Is that how Ana got the job?"

He nodded.

"And you got the job with Kaffey through Ana?"

A shake of the head said no. "Through Paco."

"You met Paco before Ana?"

"No. I met Ana here . . . in Ponceville. She told me about . . . her uncle. He worked in L.A. and could get her a paying job as a maid. She was working in the fields before . . . stoop labor. I told her to take it."

He took in a deep breath and when he let it out, he winced.

"Hard to get work if you're illegal. Later, Paco set me up with Neptune Brady . . . so Ana and I could be together . . . no one knew about us. I didn't want Brady to find out . . . Ana to get deported."

"I understand."

"Guy wanted to give back. It bit him in the ass."

"Neptune Brady said Guy hired thugs because they were cheap."

He thought about it. "Maybe that, too."

"So you don't know Alejandro Brand?"

"No."

"How about Esteban Cruz?"

"Another Cruz? What does he look like?"

Decker tried to remember Marge's description. "Scrawny kid around seventeen."

Martin thought about it. "No . . . don't sound familiar."

"Joe Pine was young."

"Twenties—not seventeen."

"What about Cruces?"

Martin grimaced in pain. "Twenties, too. Don't know any teens."

The nurse came in and signaled five more minutes. Decker said, "I'm waiting for backup protection to watch the room. Brubeck, Tim England, and I are rotating shifts. England's also looking for some volunteers in town, but I've requested professionals from

Fresno. Willy and I won't leave until we've got a system in place, Rondo."

"That's good, but I got my own system." A smile formed on his lips as he pulled a hunk of steel from under his pillow. "Your protection is good, but a gun is even better."

THIRTY-FIVE

AFTER REACHING THE hallowed Halls of Records at twenty minutes before closing time, Marge and Oliver rushed from floor to floor until they reached the correct department just as the door was closing. Their pleas fell on the ears of Adrianna Whitcomb, a forty-year-old, good-looking blonde.

"I can't thank you enough," Marge told the clerk.

They were talking in the anteroom of a basic government space: three teller windows with glass partitions, an institutional table holding brochures that no one ever read, and a floor of green and black terrazzo.

"You caught me at a good time." She smoothed out the hips of her black pants suit. "I have a dinner date at six with nothing to do until then. Well, not exactly a date. What's the street address of the business?"

Oliver gave her the address of Ernie's El Matador. "Where do you eat around here?"

"Tonight we're going to A Thousand Cranes. My girlfriend and me. She's an assistant district attorney." Her smile turned sly.

"Would you care to join us, Detective? You two might have a lot in common."

Oliver smiled back. "I'd love to join you two, but I have a meeting in the Valley. If you wouldn't mind giving me your number, we'll make it another time."

"She might not be available."

"We could work something out."

"Well, we'll see about *that*." A pause. "Wait here. I'll see what I can dig up."

She disappeared behind the door and the area fell silent.

"You're having a good day," Marge whispered.

Oliver grinned. "Hey, when you sink enough shafts, you're bound to hit oil."

Adrianna returned a few minutes later and handed a printout to Marge. "Wish all my work was that easy. Anything else I can do for you?"

Oliver took out his business card. "In case you have the sudden need to contact a detective."

Adrianna took it. "You never know."

"And do you have a card in return . . . in case I have to come back?"

"Just call the office," she told him.

Oliver tried to hide his disappointment. "Thanks."

"Call the office if you want the office," Adrianna said with a crooked smile. "But if you want to call me, my cell is on the top of the printout."

"RONDO PUTS CRUCES at the scene," Decker said over the phone. "Pick him up."

"If you think the timing's right, absolutely," Marge said.

"What does that mean?"

"Do we really know if Rondo Martin is reliable? He still could be involved, Pete. It could be a conspiracy between him, Ana Mendez, Paco, and Riley Karns."

"Why would they conspire to murder the Kaffeys?"

"Same reason you think Cruces and Pine did the killings. Someone paid them to do the hit. I'm looking at how defense would spin it. The bloody prints taken from the scene matched with Rondo Martin, Ana Mendez, and Riley Karns. Sure, they admit being at the scene, but in what capacity? If we had something, anything, to back up Martin's story, I'd go for it. But since we don't, maybe we should wait until all the forensic evidence comes in."

Decker said, "I don't want to lose this guy. Surveillance isn't foolproof."

"You're certainly right about that. I'm just worried that if we bring him in without forensics, it'll alert him and we'll be more likely to lose him. Because we don't have anything to keep him other than Rondo Martin's say-so. How strong is that?"

"How far is Lee from unsealing Cruces's juvenile record?"

"I don't know. We're headed back to the station house now."

"Okay. We'll give it another twenty-four hours to round up a set of prints. By that time, I'll be back home. Keep a watch over Cruces. If it looks like he's taking evasive action, grab him."

"I hear you. I'll tell Messing to beef it up."

"Good. What's happening with Ernie's El Matador?"

"The bar is owned by the Baker Corporation."

"Who the hell is that? And what kind of corporation owns a seedy bar? Sounds like a dummy corporation to me. Did you check if it's a DBA?"

"Doing Business As? We didn't have time to check it out. I bet Lee could do that kind of search on the computers in the squad room."

"Keep me informed. And whatever you do, don't lose Cruces."

"Hopefully, we'll get a set of his prints. I'm just trying to keep egg off our faces."

"If Cruces rabbits, it won't be just egg, Margie. It'll be a whole damn soufflé."

WANG SAID, "BAKER Corporation is a subsidiary of Kaffey Industries."

"You're kidding!" Marge opened and closed her mouth. "Kaffey owns Baker?"

"Read for yourself, but don't get too excited. I'm sure Kaffey owns a lot of different businesses."

"And among the businesses is the bar where Martin Cruces got his alibi." She skimmed through the pages. "Does this make sense to you, Lee? That Kaffey Industries—a major development corporation that's responsible for malls nationwide—would bother buying a seedy bar in Van Nuys?"

"Someone bought the bar using Kaffey money—or Baker Corporation money."

Marge said, "Does the Baker Corporation have officers?"

"If it's a DBA, probably not. Let me do a little more digging. Or you could just call Grant Kaffey and ask him about it."

"I'm not calling Grant. He's still a major suspect."

"How's he doing?"

"He's back in Newport Beach. We don't have to check in on him because he calls every two hours and asks about Gil. If he's truly a concerned brother, I admire him. If he's faking concern, let me tell you something. He's a lousy actor."

CARMEN MONTENEGRO HAD changed into something black and sexyish without going over the edge. She had put on just a dash of makeup and had drawn her hair into a knot allowing little curls to frame the side of her face. She was every high school boy's fantasy: a TILF—Teacher I'd Like to Fuck. The only giveaway that the dinner had some business content was her briefcase-like purse.

Oliver had chosen a blue blazer and khaki pants. As they walked to the table, he held out the chair for her. "You look lovely."

"Thank you." She scooted the chair closer to the table and took the menu offered by a waiter who introduced himself as Mike. He asked if either of them wanted a cocktail and both opted for a glass of house red wine.

"Excellent," Mike extolled.

After he left, Carmen said, "It's nice to get dressed up once in a while. Thank you for taking me out here. I couldn't afford it otherwise. I hope the department is paying."

Oliver smiled. "I'll send in some kind of voucher, but usually the department frowns on these kinds of places. I'm taking you out here just because you're you."

"Don't you know how to charm a woman." Carmen opened the menu and her eyes widened. "Did you check this place out beforehand?"

"Order from the left side," Oliver said. "The duck is great, but I'm having the Black Angus. And thank you very much for helping us out this afternoon."

"You're welcome. I have the copies of the files." She opened her purse/briefcase and peered inside. "I hope you can read them, because I had to photocopy the papers. A lot of this stuff was forwarded material from elementary school."

"Whose files did you get?"

"I've got Esteban Cruz, Alejandro Brand, Martin Cruces, and José Pinon. I hope I didn't miss anyone."

"Wow. That's complete. Thank you very much. Are they related?"

"They all went to Pacoima High, and they all dropped out." She shut her purse. "Not our success stories, I'm sorry to say."

"Were Cruces and Pinon troublemakers?"

"I don't know personally, but their records don't show either as being a thug."

"They're Bodega 12th Street gang members."

"That says nothing. The school is crawling with Bodega 12th Streeters."

The waiter came back with the wine. "Are you ready to order?"

Carmen's smile looked frozen. "I guess I'll have the duck."

"Excellent choice," Mike told her.

"Black Angus, medium rare."

"Excellent," Mike repeated. "Would either of you like a side vegetable. Our creamed spinach is excellent."

"Sounds good," Oliver said.

"Excellent." Mike took the menus and left.

"As a former English teacher," Carmen said dryly, "I would tell him to look in the thesaurus for another adjective."

Oliver burst into laughter. "Indeed. At least he's pleasant."

"Yeah, I hate snooty waiters. They make me nervous, like I'm not good enough."

"That would never be the case."

Carmen lowered her eyes. The next few minutes were spent in idle chitchat about their respective fields. But Oliver was antsy. He really had arranged the dinner for business purposes. When the time seemed right, he said, "Carmen, would you be offended if I took a peek at the records?"

"Uh . . . sure."

"Why the hesitation?"

She put up a forced smile. "I don't know if I was really supposed to copy the files and give them to you."

"Ah . . . I'll wait. No problem."

Carmen slid her purse under the table. "You're here for a purpose. I respect that. Take a peek, Detective." She leaned over and wrinkled her nose. "Just be subtle."

"It's Scott, and thanks for being such a good sport. I owe you a dinner where we don't conduct business."

"You don't owe me anything."

"Then I'd like to take you out again."

"Are you sure about that?" She grinned. "The evening's not over."

"I'm sure." Oliver thought about Adrianna Whitcomb and decided she'd have to wait. At his age, he just couldn't handle more than one at a time. He lifted one of the files from the briefcase on the floor and set it on his lap. Esteban Cruz; he flipped through the pages, but he couldn't really make out the type because the lighting was so dim.

Then something stopped him cold.

Carmen said, "What's wrong?"

"Nothing . . . nothing." He put the file back and took out another one. This one was José Pinon. Again he paged through the sheets.

"You look like you've seen a ghost."

"Sorry to be abrupt." He stared at his date. "Where'd you score a copy of José Pinon's fingerprints?"

"It came with their elementary school records. We have this pro-gram where we routinely print the kids in elementary school. We say it's for kidnapping, but what it's really been useful for is identi-fying bodies. We've got a lot of gang shooting where often the bod-ies are dumped without ID and—"

"Do you have the original fingerprint cards on file or do you just have copies?" He realized his voice was breathless.

"We have the originals."

"With their names on them . . . just like the copies."

"Yes, sir."

"It's Scott. I need them, Carmen. Like as in right now. Do you have a key to the high school?"

"I have a key to the school, but I don't know if I can give you the cards, Detective . . . Scott. There may be some invasion of privacy issues."

"Yeah, you're right. I'll get a warrant."

Someone of lesser rank appeared to serve the entrées. Apparently Excellent Mike had bigger fish to fry. Carmen smiled as the waiter placed the duck in front of her. "Thank you very much." To Oliver, she said, "Shall we ask them to wrap it to go?"

"Uh . . ." Oliver regarded his steak. "Uh, no. Just let me make a phone call to my partner and have her prepare the papers."

"It's really okay. I'm kind of an eat-and-run kinda gal anyway."

"Give me five minutes, Carmen, and I'm all yours." He tried to look charming. "Please. It's going to take a little while anyway to get the paperwork. Why waste a steak?"

"Okay." She nodded. "I'll wait. But if you don't make it quick, I just may eat your steak. I don't even understand why I ordered the duck."

"Eat mine. I insist." He excused himself and stepped outside. Marge came on the line a moment later. "I hit the jackpot. The school files have fingerprint cards for Martin Cruces, José Pinon, and Esteban Cruz."

"Holy shit! That's amazing! I'll call Oldham for print analysis right now."

"Hold on, Margie, there's a rub. Carmen Montenegro gave us the files on the sly. She doesn't think that it's totally kosher to remove them from the school. We need a search warrant to get us into the original files. Rondo Martin identified Cruces and Pinon as being at the scene. That should be enough probable cause."

"I would think so. Scott, I don't want to get the lady in trouble. You don't think a judge is going to be suspicious about us having to do this at eight in the evening?"

"Uh . . . good point." Oliver was pacing. "I don't want this to wait until tomorrow."

"How about if I say that Rondo Martin just IDed Cruces and the suspect is in our sights now. That we don't want him to flee like Pine did."

"That's good, that's really good," Oliver told her. "As soon as you get the warrant, I'll meet you at the school with Carmen."

"Where are you right now?"

"Still at the restaurant. We'll finish up, and she'll meet us at the school in her own car. It'll look a little less suspicious."

"So you're still with the lovely lady?"

"Lovely indeed. And she just got a whole lot lovelier."

THIRTY-SIX

MAN!" DECKER EXCLAIMED over the line. "That just saved us hours of work."

"You ain't kidding," Oliver said. "Marge just got the warrant signed so we're off to Pacoima High. Here's to hoping that the fingerprint cards match our unknown prints."

"Amen to that." Decker's cell phone beeped for a call waiting. "You put the dinner with Montenegro on your personal credit card, right?"

"Of course. I didn't want it getting back that Carmen did anything improper."

"Exactly. Is Marge with you?"

"She's meeting Carmen and me at the high school. Carmen took her own car."

Decker's phone beeped in a second time from call waiting. He looked at the window. Restricted number. *If you aren't gonna trust me with your number, you can leave a message, bozo.* "Call me when you have the fingerprint cards."

"I will," Oliver said. "Where are you now?"

"Just outside the hospital. Willy Brubeck is watching Rondo Martin, but reinforcements are coming up soon. Did either you or Marge find out anything else about the owner of Ernie's El Matador and Baker Corporation?"

"Marge sent a team out to the bar, to press Sam Truillo for the name of El Patrón. I think it was Wanda Bontemps and Lee Wang."

"Is Truillo tending bar there now?"

"I don't know, but whoever is pouring tap should know the boss's name."

"If Wanda gets any kind of resistance, tell her to haul the son of a bitch in."

"I couldn't have said it better."

HARRIMAN PUSHED THE end call button on his phone and plugged it into the cord for recharging. Lying in his bed in cotton pajamas that were too heavy for the weather, he felt sweat trickle down his neck and onto his back. The days were getting hotter and his air-conditioning didn't seem to be working too well. He had cranked up the fly fan to max whirl, but he was still hot. It could be a psychological heat. Who didn't sweat when nervous?

For the last ten minutes, his ears had perked up . . . heightened to every little nuance of sound. Foreign sounds. Sounds he shouldn't have been hearing at eleven at night. The noises lasted about ten minutes, and then seemed to fade.

Precisely why he didn't leave a message. He felt silly.

Take a chill pill. Relax and read a book. He had four of them piled up on his nightstand. What the hell was he waiting for? Because the noises were probably nothing more than his overactive imagination. If it hadn't been for that car across the street from Mrs. Decker's house, he wouldn't have given the scratches a thought.

You're safe.

He was more than safe. For Chrissakes, there was a cruiser outside his town house watching his front door. How much more security could a person ask for?

But the sounds weren't coming from the front of his unit. His place was on ground level, and there was a back entrance. That's where he heard the scratching. True, that entrance had three locks on it, but still . . .

It wasn't just that he heard things. He smelled things, like the odor of male sweat. And then there was that kid in the parked car across from the Decker house. Nowadays, it seemed that everything was making him nervous.

So why hadn't he bothered to leave the lieutenant a message?

That was an easy one to answer. He felt uneasy about being anxious. It reminded him of his childhood, his feelings of being a 'fraidy cat. It took him years to get over his fear of darkness, and damn if he was going to let it get to him again.

Thinking back over his youth, he recalled how terrified he had felt every time his mother dropped his hand. He was little—five or six or seven—but too old for boys to cry. His father castigating his tears; the old man believed in him, though. He had psychologically and physically pushed him to his upper limits. By the time he was twelve, he could use a cane to expertly navigate his way around anywhere.

His mind jumped from topic to topic.

How many times had he tripped and fallen as a youngster?

How many things had he bumped into?

How many times had he felt like an imbecile or a clod?

People treating him as if he was subhuman?

Even now it was painful to think about it.

The old man had been rough but only because he had known the world that his son had to face as a blind man. Harriman had been grateful to his father, but he had always sensed two primates on his back—the monkey of his sightlessness and the much bigger gorilla of his father.

One of his proudest moments had been the day that he had reconciled with the old man, the two of them great friends in adulthood up until the old man's heart exploded.

Harriman thought of his father as his ears continued to listen for intrusion. Sometimes, he doubted his own sanity. He was glad he didn't leave Decker a message. God only knew what the lieutenant really thought about him, but Harriman must have been believable enough for the lieutenant to send out a black-and-white to watch the front door.

Finally, he was sufficiently calm to get comfortable in bed. He took off his pajamas and felt the cool air of the fan wash over his body. He had to go to work tomorrow—a carjacking/murder case— so he'd better get some shut-eye because he needed to be alert in the morning.

He turned his iPod to his classical mix of symphonies. The grandiose nature of the music was usually enough to lull him to sleep. He positioned himself on his right side . . . his favorite side. Closing his eyes.

No need to turn out the light.

THE NEWS CAME into the station house just as the clock struck the witching hour.

Cheers soon followed.

After comparing the fingerprints from the cards located inside the high school files of Martin Cruces, José Pinon, Alejandro Brand, and Esteban Cruz against the unknowns taken from the murder scene, Oldham found a number of hits. Next came the painstaking process of evaluating whorls, swirls, and lines and he was magically rewarded when Cruces's index finger and Pinon's thumbprint proved to be a five-point match to two previously unidentified images lifted from a cabinet and a table.

An eyewitness plus physical evidence: Decker was in seventh heaven.

"Who's picking Cruces up?"

"We've got a group from CRASH on its way to Cruces's apartment. Messing and Pratt are going to the scene as well. Oliver and I are sticking close to home. As soon as they nab him, we'll go in for the kill. I'm doing the interview. You want to talk strategy?"

"Sure. Get a confession."

"Thanks, boss, I wouldn't have thought of that."

"Find out who ordered the hits."

Marge said, "You know, Pete, I figured out that one as well."

"Find out where Joe Pine is."

"We're three for three, Rabbi. Mi strategy es tu strategy."

Decker smiled. "It would also help if Cruces implicated Alejandro Brand and Esteban Cruz in something bad. I'd love to get those psychos off the streets. How're my wife and kid doing?"

"Haven't heard of any problems. Anything else?"

"Actually, yes there is. How much time do you think you'll have between now and the Cruces interview?"

"How much *time*?"

"Yeah . . . like supposing all goes smoothly and they pick him up. How much time between now and before he's ready to be interviewed?"

"They have to pick him up and process him . . ." She did mental calculations. "He should be ready for interviewing in about an hour."

"Then do me a favor, Margie. I got a missed call the last time I spoke to you. It was from a restricted number and no one left a message. It could be a number of people, but I know Harriman has a restricted number. Could you swing by his place?"

"Isn't there a cruiser outside his unit?"

"So swing by and talk to the officers on watch."

"Why don't you call up the officers? Better yet, why don't you call up Harriman?"

"I don't have his number on me, and besides it's close to midnight."

"I can swing by, no problem." She paused. "Are you worried about something?"

"Not worried. I just want to make sure everything's okay." Decker switched ears. "Even if we nail Cruces tonight, I don't know where Joe Pine or Esteban Cruz is. Harriman is vulnerable. Just drive by, okay?"

Marge stood up and slung her sweater over her shoulder. "Okay, I'm on my way. I'll call you if anything's up. Will I be able to reach you?"

"Call the hospital because my cell won't be working. While Brubeck's babysitting Rondo Martin, I'm going to try to grab some shut-eye. I'm sure there's an empty bed somewhere in these corridors. If not, there's always a slab in the morgue."

IF THE COPS out in front of the place weren't bad enough, the gringo had three locks on the door. But that was rich dudes for you. Thinking that a single piece of metal could prevent a pro from coming in and stealing the gold. The facts were that anything you owned could be taken if the stakes were high enough.

The first barrier was a piece of shit that could be flipped with a flick of a credit card. The second was a dead bolt, a little more challenging but nothing that couldn't be taken care of with a good set of lock picks. The last obstacle was a chain—a snap once he finished off the dead bolt. He could have cracked the locks sooner except that the policia had nothing better to do than to search the rear area, shining their flashlights over the backyard. On a brick patio was a barbecue and a set of patio furniture—table and stackable chairs. If he had more time and a bigger truck, he would have helped himself to the set, but he had a job to do.

The first time the policia had come in the back, he'd been caught off guard. Didn't even hear them until they were almost on top of him. He'd been one kissed cholo because he'd been kneeling, rifling through his bags to get his tools. He was dressed in black, too, making him hard to see. And he'd been extra lucky because he had just taken out the lightbulb over the back door. Even the cops said something about it, that the light must have gone out. But the two fat asses had been too lazy to investigate. They looked around for a minute and then went back to their cruiser, sitting on their butts, probably stuffing their ugly faces with coffee and doughnuts.

He had to work quickly in case they returned a second time. His only illumination came from a penlight. Couldn't see too well, but that was okay. Most of the work was done by feel. The scratching of the tools seemed to make more noise than usual, and he was a little worried about that because the neighborhood was quiet. Maybe the dude heard something. But now, the apartment seemed dark and still. All was right.

As he worked, he thought about how far he had come. He was a fucking *pro* now, not some shitty, dime-bag drug runner for some other little fuck who was a step higher on the ladder. No more of that shit: *he* was one of the big boys. And like all pros, he had done his homework, scoping the layout of the place and checking the mark. The gringo was protected and that was a pain in the ass, but he had taken down bigger marks. Being closer to the top meant he had to deliver. The fuck if he was gonna let a few dumb cops stop him.

So far, he hadn't even broken a sweat.

When he was sure that all was clear, he tiptoed into his spot at the back door and pulled out his lock picks: a set of sixteen manufactured in the highest quality of stainless steel. He liked the feel of the sharp points and the heft of the handles.

He sandwiched the penlight between his chin and his chest, trying to aim the beam at the keyhole. There was enough light for him to see the sweet spot and with a single swoop, he inserted two picks inside the keyhole. Jiggling them around, he tried to feel the click of the tumblers.

He jiggled and jiggled and jiggled. But nothing happened.

Huh!

Well, maybe it was going to be a little harder than he thought.

He let the picks dangle from the keyhole and shut off the penlight. Then he worked by his sense of touch only. It was smart to be in darkness anyway. With the sky being black with no moon out tonight, a penlight could give him away as easily as a spotlight. After a few minutes, he decided that he needed a different set of picks. He carefully chose another set of steel points and put the first two picks in the leather holder.

Scratching and scratching inside the keyhole, trying to feel the tumblers. Yeah, this time, things were working better. He heard the first click of a tumbler falling into place, then the second, and finally the third. As the dead bolt gave, he slowly opened the door.

The chain was connected, but getting that puppy off was no big deal. You insert the tool, move the door until it was just about closed, then slide the lock over the . . .

His ears perked up.

Someone was talking . . . a woman with a couple of guys.

He heard the beep of a walkie-talkie.

It was cop talk.

He didn't like that at all.

Hurry up, hurry up.

For the first time tonight, he began to sweat. It wasn't supposed to happen like this. He always had a plan, and he usually had time.

His hands began to shake.

Concentrate, motherfucker, concentrate!

Sliding the lock past . . . hearing the chain drop. Not the most elegant of jobs but it was over. Within seconds, he had slipped inside.

He flipped the dead bolt back into place and replaced the chain.

The cops could talk as much as they wanted now. He was safe inside—exactly where he wanted to be.

THIS WASN'T A dream.

The scratching sounds were real. The smell was real—sweat and fear from a man.

Harriman knew he was in trouble.

As perspiration poured down his face and back, he sat up, his hands shaking as he reached over to his nightstand and groped for his cell phone. In the process, he knocked over the remote control to the TV. It fell to the ground with a muffled thud.

Did he hear it? Hopefully not. Thank God for carpets.

More fumbling until there it was in his hot, wet hands, the metal feeling cool and sleek. Depressing the button to turn it on. The man was getting bolder, walking around, not even bothering to tiptoe, his footsteps easily perceived.

He heard the phone's jingle as he turned it on. It seemed to take forever. He spoke into the autodial.

911.

A moment later, the voice on the telephone.

911, what's your emergency?

Talking as calmly and clearly as he could, but his voice sounded foreign to his ears.

Someone's broken into my condo.

What is the address, sir?

His mind went momentarily blank.

What was *his address?*

One breath, two breaths . . . ah, yes.

He told the lovely 911 lady his address.

Someone will be out right away.

Hurry, please! I'm blind!

When he hung up, he remembered the cops in front of his unit. Then how did this happen? Were they asleep? Did Decker lie and pull them off the job without telling him?

How the fuck did this break-in *happen?*

Do something, you wimp!

Think, think!

He kept his phone in his hand and silently eased himself out of bed, dropping to the floor and sliding under his bed. He was naked and shivering, but it wasn't from cold. He was sandwiched between the carpet and the mattress so he was warm enough, but he couldn't get rid of the internal chill of dread. He tried to concentrate on what was happening inside his condo, but his breathing was so loud it was as if he was listening with cotton in his ears.

Steady, steady.

Concentrate.

The enemy was in the kitchen. Harriman could hear him clicking the light switch on and off. The bastard wouldn't get any help

there. Harriman never bothered to put any bulbs in the ceiling fix-
tures.

Why pay for electricity that you're never going to use?

THE BEAMS FROM the flashlights crisscrossed the yard.

"I still don't understand why you had to come down." It was Bud
Rangler talking. "Why not just call us up?"

He was clearly miffed, but so was Marge. The man was giving
her attitude that she didn't need at 12:30 in the night. Rangler was a
punching bag on legs—a big barrel chest with short, muscular limbs.
In his late twenties, he'd been on the force for five years. He seemed
to regard Marge's personal appearance as an affront to his compe-
tence.

"When the boss says go, I go." Marge added, "Not a bad thing to
remember, Officer."

The second uniform on watch, Mark Breslau, was the older of the
two and more seasoned. He was an eleven-year vet, and time had
mellowed his machismo. "You're the boss, Sergeant. I think Bud just
wanted you to know that we're doing our job. We've been checking
out the back every couple of hours."

"You can see for yourself, Sergeant," Rangler said. "Nothing's
been disturbed."

"Dark back here." Marge followed the ray of light with her eyes.
"How well could you see if something was disturbed?"

"The lightbulb over the porch just burned out," Rangler said.
"Before that, the place was pretty well lit up."

"Burned out?" Marge turned around and faced him. "Why didn't
you replace it?"

Rangler said, "I didn't think replacing lightbulbs was part of the
job description."

"If it helps you see what's going on, it sure as hell is." She turned
to Breslau. "Do you have a lightbulb in the car?"

"No, ma'am."

"There's a twenty-four-hour place just around the corner." She tossed him the keys to her car. "Go down and get one. I'll stay with Officer Rangler until you get back."

"Yes, ma'am."

Marge could hear the young cop chuckle. "Something funny, Rangler?"

"Not at all, Sergeant."

"I thought I heard laughter. Must be imagining things, huh?"

Rangler was silent. Marge walked over to the back door and focused the flashlight on the socket over the entrance. "C'mere, Officer."

Rangler complied, stopping about a foot away from Marge.

"Take a look up there." She shone her beam on the light fixture. "How could a bulb burn out . . . when there's no bulb in the socket? Want to explain that to me?"

Rangler started to speak, but then wisely stopped himself.

Marge swept her flashlight over the ground until she found the molded piece of glass resting in the grass. She picked it up and screwed it back into the socket, bathing the back area in welcomed yellow light.

"Call in for backup, all units in the area." Standing off to the side, she pounded on the back door and shouted out to Harriman. Did it again and when she got no response, she hooked her flashlight onto her belt and took out her service revolver.

"Cover my ass, Rangler, we're going in."

IT WASN'T GOING like he planned.

None of the fucking lights worked!

They were pounding at the back door.

There were the two cops watching the front door.

Sirens in the background.

You're not a stupid guy, he said to himself. *Don't start being stupid now!*

With desperation, he looked around for a way to get out undetected. But both doors were guarded. He was a cornered animal about to be hunted down.

Think, you asshole, think!

He took out his piece and held it in his hand. It would give him some leverage, but in the end he was badly outnumbered. A shoot-out wasn't the answer.

There was no place to run; he might as well hide.

THIRTY-SEVEN

HARRIMAN COULD HEAR the banging at his back door. His heart, already galloping, almost flew out of his chest. If he yelled from under the bed, could they even hear him? Would he give himself away to the intruder?

Wait until they were closer.

Patience, patience.

Like they say, silence is golden.

WITHIN MOMENTS, BRESLAU had returned and was breathless. "I heard the call go out."

"What call?" Marge pounded the door again.

"911 from the inside of this address."

"Good God!" Marge exclaimed. "If Harriman called 911, someone's inside. The door's bolted. I don't want a hostage situation, but I don't want to ram the door without vest protection. Guy could have a gun."

Her eyes made a frantic search around the yard and landed on the patio chairs. She stacked the four of them together, picked them up, and brought them to her chest, using them as a shield.

"This'll have to do," Marge said. "Cover me."

"I'll ram the door, Sarge," Rangler said. "I got a lot more weight on me."

"This isn't Kevlar, Rangler. A bullet could rip through this like it was snow."

"We all signed up for the job." Rangler held his arms out. "I got more weight on me. Whoever can do it the easiest, you know?"

"Can't argue with that." Marge would remember the good attitude as she passed the chairs to Rangler. He hefted them as if they were a pile of blankets. Taking two steps backward, he rammed the door.

Once.

Twice.

By the third time, the frame splintered and the back door swung open. In the background, the three of them could hear the sounds of approaching sirens.

Marge peered inside: dark and silent.

"Harriman, are you here?" When Marge didn't get any response, she pulled out her semiautomatic issue. "Rangler, you take the flashlights and shine the beam inside so I can see. Breslau, you're my cover. Let's go."

There was not nearly enough illumination to discharge a weapon. Marge flattened herself against the wall and inched her way inside, groping for the light switch. When her fingers finally found it, she steadied her breath and lifted it up.

Nothing happened.

She did it again and again and then remembered the obvious.

The guy was blind.

Marge wondered if there were *any* active lights in the entire unit. She thought for a few moments. Brett had mentioned something about a girlfriend driving him to Rina's. She must visit sometimes at night. There had to be artificial lighting somewhere. Assessing her surroundings, Marge was standing in the laundry room, which led directly into the kitchen.

The kitchen!

Maybe there was a hood light over the cooktop with a working bulb. She said, "Throw some beams into the kitchen with your flashlights."

The area looked unoccupied, but someone could be hiding. Slowly she moved toward the cooktop. She reached under the hood, felt for the switch, and turned it on.

Voilà!

The illumination was better but far from adequate. She saw a duplex switch on the tiled backsplash. The first one operated the garbage disposal, but the second one turned on a system of under-the-counter lighting. They could see enough to clear the kitchen and move forward.

Harriman's condo sported an open floor plan: living room, dining area, and kitchen bleeding into one another. The good news was that nothing appeared disturbed. There was no upended furniture or other signs of a struggle, but there was just something off about the place.

Too quiet? The smell?

Sirens continued to wail in the background.

Marge said, "Rangler, call in our position to the RTO and tell all units coming to the scene to approach with extreme caution."

Her eyes skittered around in the dimness. Off the open public area was a hallway that probably led to the bedrooms.

"Cover me," Marge told the officers.

She plastered herself against the wall and inched her way down the foyer until she came to the first closed door. She knocked hard on the door, announcing herself as the police, telling anyone inside to come out with their hands in the air. When the door remained shut, she threw it open and pointed a gun forward.

Nothing happened.

With caution, Rangler shined the flashlights inside the room and it appeared to be empty.

"Police!" Marge shouted again. "You're surrounded! Come out with your hands in the air!"

They waited . . . one second . . . two seconds . . . three seconds.

They entered the room. The small space was set up as a gym with a stationary bicycle, a treadmill, and a weight machine. The pole lamp inside worked and bathed the area in soft light. Marge pointed to a closed door—probably a closet. Pressing herself against the wall, she turned the knob and tossed open the door.

Nothing happened, and that was just the way she wanted it.

As Breslau kept watch at the door and Rangler provided the spotlight, Marge rummaged inside the closet, pushing away clothes and weights just to make sure that no one was hiding.

She jumped when she heard a pounding at the front door. Rangler let the backup officers into the living room, turning on as many lamps as they could find. Good mood lighting but no romance was in the air. When everyone was safely inside, Marge took a head count—eight including herself.

"I want one at the front door, one at the back door, one guarding the first bedroom and two of you clearing that closed door, which is probably a bathroom." She turned to Breslau and Rangler. "We'll check out the last closed door, which is probably Harriman's bedroom."

Heart hammering in her chest, Marge pounded on the door and yelled, "Police. Come out with your hands up."

The response was a male voice that screamed out a "Help!"

"Harriman?"

"Yes! Help me! I'm under the bed."

"Don't move. Are you alone?"

"I have no idea."

"Are you hurt?"

"No."

"Don't move!" Marge repeated. "We'll come in and get you." Speaking loudly, she said, "We found the occupant. We're going in. I need a couple more bodies."

The two officers who had cleared the hallway bathroom came to help. Marge said, "This could be a setup. Everyone take a position of safety, and I'll open the door when we're all ready."

When she got the nods, she flattened herself against the wall, turned the knob, and flung open the door.

Flashlights lit up the dark room, darting around the blackness like giant fireflies on a moonless night.

"We're inside, Brett," Marge said. "Stay put. We're going to clear the room. Are there any lights that work in this room?"

"Try the bed lamp on the nightstand. I think that's what my girl-friend uses."

Marge worked her way to the nightstand lamp and turned it on. The space was a decent size with a king bed and two flanking night-stands. Across from the bed was a dresser. One wall had a closet with sliding mirrored doors and opposite that was a closed door, which Marge guessed opened to the bathroom.

Using standard procedure, she opened the bathroom door. Empty but the shower curtains were drawn.

"Police!" Marge screamed, pointing the gun at the tub enclosure. "Come out with your hands in the air!"

The shower curtains didn't appear to hear because they didn't even ripple. With great care, she pulled them back and revealed an empty tub.

"Clear!" She went back to the bedroom. "What about the closet?"

"Clear," Rangler told her.

"Harriman?"

"Still here."

"You can come out now."

"I'm naked."

"Somebody get a robe or something."

Harriman crept out from under the bed and stood on shaky legs. He was trembling all over as they handed him a terry cloth robe. He was breathing as shallowly as a panting dog. "Did you find him?"

"Not yet."

"I'm not crazy!" Harriman said. "I swear I heard something."

"We're not done searching, Brett. We've got the place surrounded. As soon as we get you out of here, we'll finish up." Marge offered him her arm. "I'll guide you out."

When they reached the front door, Harriman started shivering. "He's here!" he whispered to Marge. "I can smell him!"

"Then we'll find him."

"Please don't leave until you do. I know he's here!"

"Officer Fetterling is going to escort you to a police car. He'll wait with you until we've cleared the area."

He grabbed Marge's arm. "Thank you."

"You're welcome. That's what we're paid to do." When he was gone and safely ensconced inside one of the cruisers, Marge looked around.

"We've cleared everything but the hall closet." Standing off to the side, she pounded on the door. "Police! Come out with your hands in the air!"

Nothing. What was the likelihood that this last search would yield anyone?

The door had been locked from the inside. Was Harriman putting everyone on? Was he a drama king? But then how did the back porch light become unscrewed unless the blind man did it himself.

She thought about all the possibilities as she flattened herself against the wall. Then her brain shifted into pure focused energy. Hand on the knob, she shouted, "Take positions!"

Throwing open the door.

Nothing happened.

"Hold your positions!" Marge was still squashed against the wall, and something told her not to move. It was the smell of sweat . . . the smell of fear.

The air became very quiet. Her breathing was amplified in her brain, as if listening through a stethoscope. Heart pounding in her chest.

Breathe in, breathe out.

Slow it down, Marge.

"Hold your positions!" she repeated.

Listening carefully, she finally heard it; inhalations and exhalations that didn't match her own breathing rate.

Someone was definitely inside, hiding.

"Police!" she shouted. "You're surrounded! Come out with your hands in the air!"

Again, no one stirred.

"I'm giving you to the count of three and then we're going to shoot—"

"No, don't do that!" a voice pleaded.

"Get out, get out, get out," Marge ordered.

Something rose from the corner, and Marge caught a glint of metal. "Drop the gun! Drop it! Drop it! Drop it!" When she heard something hard fall with a thud, she said, "Hands up, hands up, hands up!"

As the creature from the black lagoon emerged, Marge told him to hit the ground. As soon as he did, he was pounced on by four officers while two others searched the closet. The gun was a .32 Smith and Wesson, one of the weapons used in the Kaffey shootings.

What were the chances that it matched anything? She supposed it depended on who was lying spread-eagle on the floor. She shined a light on the face, seeing if he looked familiar while Rangler rifled through the man's back pockets. He pulled out a wallet and then a driver's license and showed it to the sarge.

Marge grinned. "Well, hello, Joe. Welcome back to the USA."

THIRTY-EIGHT

THE PACING SERVED a twofold purpose. It kept Decker warm and it shook off some nerves. At three in the morning, the hospital loomed like an electric ghost as he held the phone to his ear. He was shaking, but from excitement. "You got *Cruces and Pine* in custody?"

"Not bad for a day's work—a very full day. I've been up around twenty hours."

"Who's down at the station house besides you?"

"Oliver, Messing, and Pratt. Who should interview whom?"

Decker thought a moment. "Okay, here's the thing. The optimum would be that neither Pine nor Cruces gets a deal, but we may have to flip one against the other. With Pine, we've not only got fingerprints, we've also got Rondo Martin's eyewitness testimony. He mentioned Pine before I did. With Cruces, Rondo Martin remembered him, but only after I mentioned his name. His memory with Cruces is less clear. It makes more sense to have Cruces flip on Pine. So you and Oliver take Pine. If you don't get anywhere, bring in someone else for a fresh perspective."

"That sounds good. Where are you at up there, Rabbi?"

"There's a team from Herrod P.D.—which is the next town over—that's taking over our positions at the hospital in about a half hour. Tim England—Sheriff T—said he'd drop in in the morning. Martin's in good hands."

Marge said, "Now that Pine is in custody, maybe Martin can breathe a sigh of relief."

"Maybe a little sigh, but not a big one until we find out who El Patrón is. Did anyone go back to interview Truillo, the bartender, at Ernie's El Matador?"

"By the time Bontemps and Lee reached the place, it had closed for the night. I'll make sure someone's there when it opens tomorrow. Maybe it won't be necessary once we talk to Cruces and Pine."

"Rechecking is always necessary. Willy and I are taking the first flight down in the morning." Decker checked his watch. The plane was set to leave at six-thirty—four hours from now. "We'll see you at around eight in the morning."

"Get some sleep, Pete."

"Too wound up. Any word from Gil Kaffey or Antoine Resseur?"

"Nope."

"No idea where they are?"

"Not a clue, but if they're like most people at this time of night, they're sleeping." Marge paused. "Unless they're dead. In that case, nothing's gonna wake them up."

THE FIRST THING Marge did was check Joe Pine's fingerprints against José Pinon's school fingerprint card. When it was confirmed that Joe/José was the same person, Marge and Oliver steadied themselves for a long night. Watching from the video camera, they saw Pine go through a series of nonverbal gesticulations almost as meaningful as speech. There was the pacing, then plopping in the chair with the head in the hands, then laying the head on the table, then pacing again. There was one quick swipe at the eyes, wiping away tears, crying for no one but himself.

Pine had on a lightweight nylon jacket over black jeans and a black T-shirt and the usual B and E ski cap. He was built on the small side, around five seven with wiry arms. His face was long, and his complexion was mocha with cream. His dark brown hair had been snipped a few millimeters shy of a crew cut. His round brown eyes gave him a boyish expression mitigated by a strong, masculine cleft chin.

When Marge and Oliver came into the room, Pine was sitting, his eyes at his feet. He glanced up and then looked back down. The room was around eight-by-six feet with a steel table pushed up against the wall and three chairs. Pine occupied the chair on the right side, the one farthest from the door. Marge took up the seat closest to him while Oliver sat opposite.

"Detective Scott Oliver." He placed a cup of water in front of Pine. "How're you doing?"

Pine shrugged. "Okay."

Marge introduced herself and placed her clipboard on her lap. "We're a little confused," she told Pine. "What was going on back there, Joe?"

"What do you mean?"

"What we mean is we found you hiding in a closet with a gun." Marge tried to make eye contact, but his focus was elsewhere. "What was that all about?"

"No big deal."

Oliver nodded. "How's that?"

"Just what I said . . . no big deal."

Oliver said, "To the guy living there, it was a big deal."

Marge said, "Tell us why you were there."

"In the closet?"

"In the closet in the condo that didn't belong to you."

Pine said, "I heard you banging on the door and I knew you'd take it the wrong way. So I hid."

"Okay," Marge said, writing down notes. She stopped and regarded his face. "How would we take it wrong? What *way* were we supposed to take it?"

"It isn't like you think. It was just a game, you know?"

"A game?" Oliver repeated.

Marge said, "Explain it to us."

"You know . . . a game." Pine leaned his head against the wall until he couldn't move any farther. Beads of moisture were forming on his forehead. "To get in with the right people, you gotta play the game."

"Which right people?" Oliver said.

"My bros, you know?"

"Which bros?"

"In Bodega 12th." Pine shrugged. "It's all a big game."

Marge said, "I thought you were already a member of Bodega 12th."

"To move up."

Marge nodded. "How does that work? Moving up?"

Pine snickered. "Hey, you been in your business for a while, no? You know how it works."

"So tell me anyway."

"You gotta prove yourself. If you don't, there are plenty others who will. So that's what I was doing."

"You committed a breaking and entering to get into a higher position in the gang?"

"Exactly."

Oliver said, "So what were you supposed to do when you got inside the condo?"

"Just like . . . take something . . . to prove you were there, you know?"

"Then why the gun?"

"Just in case . . ."

"In case of what?" Marge said.

"In case things get like . . . you know . . . complicated."

"How would things get complicated?"

"What if he had a gun?" He smiled and sipped water. "A guy's gotta protect himself."

"So you knew who lived in the condo you were breaking into," Marge said.

"Uh . . . no." Pine shook his head. "No, I didn't know."

"You said in case *he* has a gun."

"He . . . she. I'd only use the gun for protection."

"Joe, you're confused about something," Marge said. "If you break into a person's house and he uses a gun against you, that's protection. If you use the gun against him, that's called a home invasion and that's a felony."

"I wasn't gonna use it," Pine told her. "It was for protection, man."

"You're still committing a crime," Oliver said. The two of them went back and forth on the gun until Marge broke in. "Why did you choose that condo?"

"What?" Pine answered.

"Why did you choose to break into that *particular* condo?"

"I dunno." Pine's eyes went to the floor. "It was on the ground floor. It was easy."

"So to prove that you deserve a . . . promotion in the organization, you chose to do an easy B and E?"

Pine narrowed his eyes in anger. "It's never easy . . . things can happen."

Marge said, "And things did happen. You committed a felony, and because you were packing, now you could go away for a long time."

"No one got hurt."

"Your security guard days are over," Oliver told him.

"That's okay with me." Pine sat back and folded his arms across his chest. "Who needs that shit?"

"The Kaffeys gave you shit?"

"Not the Kaffeys . . . that motherfucker Brady . . . reaming out my ass for being a minute late. I don't need that shit."

Marge noticed he hadn't broached the murders. He spoke as if he had been merely fired. "What else didn't you like about Neptune Brady?"

Her question unleashed the furies. For the next half hour, she and Oliver heard a litany of complaints about "that motherfucking, half-nigger, asshole Brady." And while she didn't feel any warmth for the Neptune, the punishment Brady had given Pine for his infractions fit the crime.

1. Neptune docked his pay whenever he was late.

2. He docked his pay if his uniform wasn't cleaned and pressed.

3. He docked his pay if he heard inappropriate language.

4. He docked his pay if he'd miss a day without twenty-four-hour notice.

Oliver said, "So why'd you keep working at the job?"

The question momentarily threw him. "I dunno. It was steady money. Just not enough of it, know what I'm saying?"

"What'd you think of the Kaffeys?" Oliver asked him.

"I dunno."

"It's not a trick question," Marge told him. "Did you like the Kaffeys?"

"I didn't know them enough to like them."

"But you guarded them," Marge said.

"Yeah, but that don't mean we were bros. It was just like . . . yes ma'am, no ma'am. The guy never talked to me. I coulda been a piece of furniture. Once he reamed my ass for talking to the wife."

"What were you talking to her about?" Marge asked.

"I said I liked her new Vette or something like that. He put his hand on my shoulder and said, 'Don't talk personal to the lady.' From then on, it was good morning, ma'am, and nothing else."

"Sounds like you didn't like them."

Pine shrugged. "I was furniture to them, but they were furniture to me."

Making them that much easier to blow away, Marge thought. "I heard it was Guy Kaffey who brought you onto the staff."

"News to me." Pine frowned. "Why you asking me so many questions about Kaffey?"

"That's kinda obvious, Joe," Oliver said.

"Uh-uh, no way. I didn't have nothing to do with that!" Pine slapped his arms across his chest. "I've been out of town."

"Yeah, I know," Marge said. "We've been looking for you."

Pine tightened his grip on himself. "So I'm here."

"You were out of town when it happened?" Oliver said.

"I was in Mexico," Pine told him.

"What were you doing there?"

"I got family there. Hey, you wanna arrest me for the B and E, hey, what can I do? But I didn't have nothing to do with the Kaffeys."

"Joe, we're in Homicide, not CAPS." Marge gave him a moment to digest that. "We've been interviewing all the guards who worked for Guy and Gilliam Kaffey for the last few weeks. We've been looking for you, then you just happened to be in the closet of a guy that the cops were protecting. That makes us curious."

"Yeah, Joe, about that," Oliver said. "Why'd you break into a condo where there were cops in front?"

"They were out front." Pine shrugged. "I was in the back."

"But it didn't bother you that the cops were out front?"

"Makes me a bigger man with the bros, you know?"

"Do you know why the cops were out front?"

"No idea," Pine said. "I've been outta the country for a while."

"How'd you feel when you found out about the homicides?" Oliver said.

Pine shrugged. "Shit happens."

Marge said, "When did you go to Mexico?"

"I don't remember the exact date, just that I went before it happened." Again the arms crisscrossed his chest.

"How'd you find out about the murders?"

"My cousin called me. I thought, man, that's real messed up. Then I was happy it wasn't me doing the shift. I heard they all got whacked."

He looked at them expectantly. Neither Marge nor Oliver responded. His knee started to bounce up and down. "Then I thought, I'm out of a job. So I stayed in Mexico a little longer."

"Who's the cousin?" Marge asked him.

Pine looked confused. "The cousin?"

"The one who called and told you about the crime," Oliver said.

"Why you want to know?"

"So he can give you an alibi," Marge said.

"Oh . . . okay. He's not my real cousin, but we're like brothers, you know?"

"His name?" Oliver asked.

"Martin Cruces. He worked for the Kaffeys, too."

Marge willed her face to remain impassive. "Yeah, we know. He's on our list."

"Yeah . . . he's the one who got me the job."

"Martin did."

"Yeah."

"And he called you and told you about the murders?" Oliver said.

"Yeah, he told me all about it. Sounded real gory, man."

Marge said, "Martin's in deep trouble, Joe. Did he tell you that as well?"

Pine's face momentarily froze. "That's bullshit. I just talked to him, man. He don't say nothing about that."

"Yeah, you just talked to him, but we just *arrested* him," Marge said.

Oliver said, "He's right next door, talking to another set of Homicide detectives."

Marge said, "So if you have something to tell us, now's the time."

"I don't have nothing to tell you." Pine's eyes darted back and forth.

"That's weird," Oliver said. "Because Martin has plenty to tell us."

Marge said, "We found your fingerprints at the Coyote Ranch, Joe."

" 'Course you did," Pine said. "I worked there."

Marge clarified. "We found bloody prints, the kinds that were made by someone who was there when the murders went down."

"You're in deep doo-doo," Oliver said. "Martin is in the building, talking to us . . . this may be your only chance to explain what happened."

"Don't let Martin tell the whole story for both of you," Marge said.

Oliver said, "Yeah, we want to hear your side."

Pine refused to be baited.

"Hey, Joe, maybe it wasn't supposed to go down like it did," Marge said. "You just brought along the gun for protection."

"Or maybe all you wanted to do was scare them," Oliver said. "If it was an accident, then we can make a case for you."

"I wasn't there," Pine insisted.

"Your fingerprints, Joe," Marge said. "Fingerprints don't lie."

"Yeah, but the cops do," Pine snapped back. "You're trying to get me to lie."

"No, Joe, that's not what we want. We want the truth, Joe. That's it."

"You wouldn't know the truth if it bit you in the ass," Pine said. "I bet you don't even got Martin in custody."

"Well, then, hold on a moment." Marge stood up. "We'll see if we can take you to the video room." She and Oliver left and returned a few minutes later. Marge placed six Polaroid pictures of Martin Cruces, dressed in jacket and jeans, being questioned by Messing and Pratt. "Look at the date on the pictures."

Pine glanced at them and tried to shrug them off. "You can fix those up. You guys got all sorts of stuff so you can trap me into saying lies."

"But that's just it, Joe," Oliver said. "We don't want lies. We want the truth."

"Martin is telling us the truth," Marge said. "We're just curious if his truth is the same as your truth."

"I wasn't there."

"You were there. We have witnesses saying you were there. The guy whose house you broke into. He heard people talk about it," Marge said. "He overheard people talking about *you*. How Martin was pissed at you because you didn't finish off Gil Kaffey."

"I *wasn't* there!"

"Your fingerprints say you were there."

"You're lying. I wasn't there."

"No, *you're* lying. You *were* there," Marge said. "You can keep lying or you can help yourself by telling the truth."

Something finally got to Pine, and he started sweating in earnest. Still, it took another couple of hours, several cups of coffee, and a half-dozen nutrition bars before Marge and Oliver noticed his psyche cracking. They excused themselves and went out of the room, leaving Pine alone to weigh his options.

The two of them stared at Pine in the video camera for a minute or two. Then Marge looked at the clock. "Decker's due back in two hours. I'd love to wrap this up before he comes."

"He's coming apart," Oliver said. "Now's the time to bring up Rondo Martin."

Marge took a swig of water and regarded Messing and Pratt going after Cruces. She turned up the volume, hearing Wynona trying to seduce Cruces into talking about the murders.

But we have your fingerprints at the scene, Martin. We also have witnesses who heard you talk about it. Plus, we have Joe Pine in the other room. He screwed up tonight. He got caught. He's telling us things. We want to hear your side of the story.

Marge turned the volume down. "Let's go."

They returned to the interview room. Marge said, "I just checked in with Martin Cruces, Joe. I'm telling you that this is your one chance to tell *your* side of the story."

"I wasn't . . ." He sighed and leaned back in his chair. "I need sleep, man. Maybe after I sleep, I'll talk."

"We have your fingerprints in the Kaffeys' blood, Joe," Oliver said. "We have an eyewitness who told us everything. Just tell us what happened."

Pine's eyes darted from side to side. "What eyewitness?"

"Joe . . ." Marge leaned over and spoke softly. "You think we'd come down on you if we didn't have your fingerprints at the scene? You think we'd come down on you if we didn't have an eyewitness who said that you looked him in the eye and then pulled the trigger? You think we'd arrest you for murder if we couldn't deliver the goods?"

"You're lying," Pine answered.

Marge moved in close to him and spoke softly. "We're not lying, Joe. Martin Cruces is talking. It's not right for you to take all the shit when you were just part of the plan. Now's the time to man up. You gotta start thinking about yourself. Because you can't explain away fingerprints and eyewitness testimony."

"You don't have an eyewitness," Pine insisted. "That jackass mighta heard things, but he never saw me before in his life!"

"Which jackass is that?" Marge asked.

"The court guy."

"The court guy whose condo you broke into?"

Pine didn't answer.

"Joe, we know you didn't pick his condo at random. Who sent you there?"

"Okay . . ." Pine took a deep breath. "Okay, I'll tell you this, okay. Martin sent me over to scare him. That's the only thing I'll admit to, okay?"

"Why did Martin Cruces send you over to scare the court guy?" Marge asked him.

" 'Cause he overheard his cousin talking about the crime." Under his breath, Pine uttered, "Fucking idiot!"

"Tell us about it," Oliver said.

Pine sighed. "Can I get something to eat around here?"

Marge got up and came back with an assortment of candy.

Pine unwrapped a Snickers bar and ate half in a single bite. "Cruces said that the court guy overheard his moron cousin talking about the murders. He told me to break into the court guy's house and scare him."

"So why were you assigned to scare the court guy?" Oliver said. "Why didn't the moron cousin scare him?"

" 'Cause he's an idiot and can't do anything right. He got arrested before he could get to the court guy."

"What's the cousin's name?" Oliver asked.

"Alejandro Brand."

Strike one! Marge thought triumphantly. "The court guy overheard Brand talking about the murders?"

"Yeah."

"What did the court guy overhear Brand say?"

"Hell if I know, but it made Cruces nervous. So he tole me to take him . . . to scare him."

Marge went in for the attack. "Martin Cruces didn't lie to you, Joe."

Oliver said, "The court guy did hear Brand talking about the Kaffey murders."

Marge said, "The court guy overheard Brand talking about Martin Cruces . . . and the court guy overheard Brand talking about *you.*"

"That you screwed up by not whacking Gil Kaffey," Oliver said.

Pine finished his candy bar. "That's a lie, man. I wasn't there. The court guy's lying."

Marge said, "Since Brand had the big mouth, Martin Cruces told Brand to take out the court guy?"

"That's the first true thing you said in the last four hours. Cruces told *Brand,* not me. He gave the assignment to Brand. But then Alejandro screwed up and got arrested. So Cruces asked his other cousin, Esteban Cruz, to take out the court guy."

Marge said, "And when Cruz screwed up, he told you to get your ass back from Mexico and finish the job, or he'll fuck you over good. That's what's happening right now, Joe. Martin is screwing you over. Cruces told you to break into the court guy's condo and finish him off."

"Why go down when it was Cruces's order?" Oliver said.

"Yeah, it was Cruces's order." Pine pushed sweat from his eyes. "But all I was supposed to do was scare him."

Strike two! They now had collusion: Cruces and Pine working together against Brett Harriman. Marge said, "So we have the court guy's testimony, we have your bloody fingerprints . . . why don't you just tell us what happened?"

Oliver told Marge, "You forgot something."

Marge said, "What did I forget?"

"Our eyewitness." Oliver leaned back in his chair. "Joe, you told us a couple of hours ago that all the guards were whacked. But the truth is . . . not everyone died."

Pine was quiet.

"Rondo Martin survived," Marge said. "And he's talking."

Oliver said, "So we have Martin Cruces telling his side of the story, we have Rondo Martin telling his side, we have the court guy telling his side of the story."

Marge leaned forward. "Why don't you tell us your side?"

Oliver said, "Joe, it's real simple. Just tell us exactly what happened."

A few seconds passed and then Pine began to talk.

He talked and talked and talked and talked and talked.

Though she kept a straight face, inside she was grinning.

Strike three and you are so out!

THIRTY-NINE

HE UNOFFICIAL TRANSCRIPTS were dozens of pages long. Marge handed them to Decker and said, "These were taken off the audio portion of the tape by the computerized voice recognition system. Then Lee programmed the system to put whoever was talking in front of the statement. There are lots of mistakes, but I think you can grab the gist of the interview."

Decker skimmed through the paper. "What's happening with Martin Cruces?"

"Messing and Pratt are still working on him."

"How long have they been going?"

"About seven hours. We all figured as long as you're here, maybe your title would make an impression on him."

"Seven hours and he hasn't asked for a lawyer?"

"Not yet," Marge said. "We're keeping our fingers crossed, giving him just enough hope to think that he can weasel out of the forensics. The noose is going to tighten. Because at the end of the transcripts, Joe named names."

Oliver let out a big yawn. "We'll get him eventually."

"Have you two gotten any sleep?"

"Not yet."

"Want to go home?"

"Not on your life," Oliver said. Marge seconded the sentiment.

Decker stifled an oncoming yawn. "Okay. Just let me review this to bring me up to speed. Then I'll deal with Cruces."

"Sounds good," Oliver said. "Want some coffee? We've been living on caffeine."

"That would be great."

A few moments later, mug in hand, Decker went into his office, closed the door, and buried his attention in a stack of papers. There were tons of typos, but his brain was mostly able to correct them. The first two-thirds of the interview was Oliver and Marge cajoling Pine into confession, using everything from sympathy to lies.

In the last fifth of the interview, things got interesting. Although the dry printed words lacked emotion, maybe that was better. It was only Decker's eyes and the text.

SCOTT OLIVER: Start from the beginning, Joe. How'd you get involved in the murders?

JOE PINE: It wasn't supposed to happen like that.

MARGE DUNN: So how was it supposed to happen?

JOE PINE: No one was supposed to get hurt. It was supposed to be a robbery.

MARGE DUNN: How'd you get involved in the robbery?

JOE PINE: It was Martin Cruces. He had the plan.

MARGE DUNN: The plan to do what?

JOE PINE: You know. To get the money. Martin planned it for a long time.

SCOTT OLIVER: How long had Martin Cruces been planning this robbery?

JOE PINE: A long time.

SCOTT OLIVER: Weeks? Months?

JOE PINE: Maybe six months.

MARGE DUNN: That is a long time.

The same speaker in a row must indicate a pause, Decker decided.

MARGE DUNN: You mentioned money. That he planned it to get money. What kind of money? Cash? Jewelry? Valuables?

JOE PINE: Martin said that the old man kept a giganto wad of cash in a safe. I never seen the safe, but Martin said there was a safe so why should I think he was lying?

MARGE DUNN: Did you find the safe?

JOE PINE: No, things messed up pretty quickly.

MARGE DUNN: Did you take anything from the house?

JOE PINE: We found a little cash and rings and shit, but we didn't have time. Cruces wanted us to bury Denny so we took what we seen around and got out.

SCOTT OLIVER: If it was a robbery, why kill anyone? And why take the time to bury Denny? You already had other dead bodies. Why not just get to the safe and split?

JOE PINE: Now that the old man and old lady was dead, it

was gonna be a problem. Cruces said they'd come checking every guard. He said that if we buried Denny and no one could find him, it would look like Denny did it and ran away.

SCOTT OLIVER: Then what about Rondo Martin?

JOE PINE: Cruces said that he'd take care of him, personally.

SCOTT OLIVER: Joe, it looked like the burial site was planned in advance. It looks to our eye like the murder was planned from the beginning.

JOE PINE: It was supposed to be a robbery, but things messed up real quick.

SCOTT OLIVER: Joe, you had a place all picked out—the horse grave.

JOE PINE: Cruces said get rid of the body. I started digging, but the soil was like concrete, man. Then I thought of the dead horses. I figured it would be easier to dig up a grave than start from nothin'.

MARGE DUNN: But you buried the body way below the horses. That took time, Joe. How'd you have that much time?

JOE PINE: I guess I worked fast. Things were fuzzy that night.

Decker stopped and analyzed the words. Their line of questioning was excellent. It was clear that this had been a carefully planned execution by the use of the horse grave. They were just trying to get Pine to admit it. Decker continued to read.

MARGE DUNN: If I had planned to murder Denny and Rondo,

I would plan to murder everyone around to eliminate witnesses, including Guy, Gilliam, and Gil Kaffey.

JOE PINE: Yeah, well as soon as Rondo bolted, that's what Cruces decided to do. Just whack everybody. But that wasn't the original plan. It was supposed to be a robbery and that's why we had the guns. To scare the old man and convince him that we were serious. That's why the son had to be there. That's why the old lady had to be there. With guns to their heads, the old man would be more like . . . cooperative. No one was supposed to get hurt. That's why we had a lot of people. To show that we were serious and to make sure no one got hurt.

SCOTT OLIVER: But people still got murdered, even if you didn't plan it that way.

JOE PINE: I wouldna done it if I thought people would get hurt. It was supposed to be a robbery.

(Decker felt his eyes roll into the back of his head.)

MARGE DUNN: How many people were involved in the plan?

JOE PINE: I think there were six.

JOE PINE: Yeah, six.

SCOTT OLIVER: Why six?

JOE PINE: One for Denny, one for Rondo, one for the wife, one for the son, and two on the old man.

MARGE DUNN: We need names.

MARGE DUNN: Joe, if you want someone to help you out, you've got to help us out. Cooperation is your best friend right now. Cooperation is your only friend.

(But Pine still was hesitant to rat out the others. So Scott tried a different tactic.)

SCOTT OLIVER: You had six people: one for Denny, one for Rondo, one for the wife, one for the son, and two for the old man.

JOE PINE: Yes, sir.

SCOTT OLIVER: What about the maid?

JOE PINE: See, that's how things got fucked up. She wasn't supposed to be there. She was supposed to be at church. We knew how to get into the house through the maid's quarters because we knew that shit. Or Martin knew that shit. I dunno. Anyway, we were supposed to go through the maid's bedroom. But we didn't know that there was another one. She started screaming and then it all went south.

MARGE DUNN: What happened?

JOE PINE: Gordo tried to knock her out, but that didn't work. 'Cause the bitch kept on screaming. So Martin just plugged her.

MARGE DUNN: Joe, we need the names.

MARGE DUNN: Joe, if you don't help us, how can we possibly help you?

SCOTT OLIVER: It's survival, man. Either you roll on them or they'll roll on you.

SCOTT OLIVER: You seem like a decent guy. I know you never

meant to hurt anyone. Why should you take all the blame when there were others involved?

MARGE DUNN: Start out with just a name. Gordo. Gordo who?

JOE PINE: Gordo Cruces.

MARGE DUNN: See how easy that was. Gordo Cruces. Is Gordo Cruces a relative of Martin Cruces?

JOE PINE: I think he's a cousin. Martin's got a lot of cousins.

SCOTT OLIVER: So we have Martin, Gordo, and you. Give us another name.

JOE PINE: You know about Esteban Cruz. You arrested him.

That wasn't quite true. The police merely stopped him. But why quibble.

JOE PINE: Cruz had two simple jobs and didn't do either one. That's what happens when you get your family involved. So Martin . . . he calls me up and tells me to get my ass back from Mexico, even though he sent me to Mexico in the first place.

MARGE DUNN: Why did he send you away?

JOE PINE: Well, he didn't exactly send me away. I just kinda left. But Martin knew where to find me. He calls me up and says if I don't take care of that crazy gringo, he's gonna take care of me and not in a good way.

JOE PINE: I shoulda never come back.

MARGE DUNN: What gringo?

JOE PINE: You know who I mean. The court guy in the condo. I didn't hurt him.

MARGE DUNN: Okay, now we've got four names. Just two more to go.

JOE PINE: Cruces also got Miguel Mendoza and Julio Davis from the Bodega 12th, know what I'm saying.

MARGE DUNN: Julio Davis is missing. Any chance he skipped with you to Mexico?

JOE PINE: What do I get if I tell you where he is?

MARGE DUNN: I don't know. I have to talk to people.

JOE PINE: Well, when you do, get back to me.

MARGE DUNN: What about Alejandro Brand?

JOE PINE: Brand is an idiot . . . a motherfucker juicehead. His big mouth fucked me up. When Brand told Cruces that the gringo heard him talking in the courthouse, Cruces told Esteban to take care of the gringo and Brand.

MARGE DUNN: He told Esteban to murder his cousin.

JOE PINE: Blood is only so thick, you know what I'm saying.

SCOTT OLIVER: So what happened?

JOE PINE: What happened was Brand got hisself arrested before Esteban could whack him. Then before he could get to the gringo, the idiot was stopped by the cops.

SCOTT OLIVER: Which idiot?

JOE PINE: Esteban Cruz.

SCOTT OLIVER: How is Martin Cruces related to Esteban Cruz and Alejandro Brand?

JOE PINE: I think they're all cousins or something.

MARGE DUNN: Who chose the people to do the murders?

JOE PINE: Robbery not murder. And Cruces set everything up.

MARGE DUNN: So Martin planned these murders—

JOE PINE: Robbery.

MARGE DUNN: So Martin planned the robbery. What did he pay you to do the crime?

JOE PINE: Not enough.

SCOTT OLIVER: How much did you make, Joe?

JOE PINE: Ten grand cash plus whatever I could steal and fence.

MARGE DUNN: Martin Cruces paid you ten grand in cash?

JOE PINE: Lotta money, right?

SCOTT OLIVER: A whole lotta money. Did he pay the other men ten grand, too?

JOE PINE: I dunno. I never asked.

SCOTT OLIVER: What do you think he paid the others?

JOE PINE: Probably something but not as much. I told Martin I needed a lotta money to do this because the police were gonna check out every guard who worked for Kaffey. So if he wanted my help, he had to come up with a lotta cash.

SCOTT OLIVER: Where did Martin Cruces get that kind of money?

JOE PINE: I dunno.

SCOTT OLIVER: You're gonna have to do better than that, Joe, if you want us to help you. Where did Martin Cruces get the ten grand to pay you?

JOE PINE: Maybe he had a good day with cards.

SCOTT OLIVER: Even if Cruces didn't pay the others as much as you, he had to get that kind of cash from somewhere. Where would a twenty-five-year-old security guard get that kind of cash?

JOE PINE: I don't know. I didn't ask him.

MARGE DUNN: That's crazy, Joe. No one's going to believe that Martin Cruces offered you ten thousand dollars in cash to do something illegal and you never asked where the money came from.

JOE PINE: He gives me a lotta cash for a robbery, I don't ask questions, lady.

SCOTT OLIVER: I don't believe that, Joe.

(Decker read on. They kept pressing the point, but it took until two pages from the end to get something out of Pine.)

JOE PINE: Okay, you want me to make something up. I'll make

something up. Cruces said that he had a sugar daddy paying for everything. He called him El Patrón, but he never did say a name.

JOE PINE: I swear he didn't say a name.

SCOTT OLIVER: Which patrón do you think Cruces was talking about?

JOE PINE: I don't know.

MARGE DUNN: C'mon, Joe. You can do better than you're doing.

(More pages of cajoling.)

JOE PINE: I swear I don't know. Probably someone high up with a lot of cash who hated the old man. Cruces never did say.

The transcript ended. Decker put down the papers and finished up his third cup of coffee. Armed with a little bit of knowledge and a fresh cup of coffee, he was ready to face the fire.

"HELLO, MARTIN, HOW are you doing?" Decker asked him.

Cruces lifted his head from the table. Despite the man's blood-shot eyes and tired face, he was decent looking. His features were symmetrical with dark eyes, dark hair, a dark mustache, prominent cheekbones, and a square chin. He said, "Who're you?"

"Lieutenant Peter Decker. Can I get you anything?"

Cruces's voice was slurry. "Are you . . . like The Boss?"

"I'm in charge of the detective squad."

"So tell your people to stop lying."

"What do you think they're lying about?" Decker sat across

from Cruces, giving him space. He'd move over later to the middle seat for intimidation or intimacy depending on how the conversation was going.

"They keep telling me I was involved in the Kaffey murders. I wasn't anywhere near the Coyote Ranch. I was at a bar, getting drunk. You checked out my alibi. I was where I said I was. Why you come back and hassle me?"

"Because your bloody fingerprint was lifted from the crime scene."

"That's bullshit."

"Forensics doesn't lie."

"But you do."

"I do lie," Decker admitted. "But this isn't one of the times."

"Why should I believe you?"

"Martin, I don't care if you believe me or not. We have your fingerprint and you, my friend, are in deep trouble. Not only do we have forensics, we have an eyewitness who puts you there." Decker leaned across the table. "I found Rondo Martin. I've been interviewing him for the last twenty-four hours. He's locked up and he's safe and you can't get to him. None of your cousins can get to him either, because we've arrested almost all of them. Rondo can't wait to testify against you."

"You don't know how many cousins I have," Cruces told him. He looked upward and closed his eyes.

"Martin . . ." Decker moved over to the middle chair. "Even if someone did manage to whack Rondo Martin, it still wouldn't do you any good. We've got everything that he told us videotaped, and we've already made copies. Help yourself and talk to us."

"I never seen no videotape."

That's because it didn't exist. Since Cruces did seem to have oodles of cousins, Decker decided that saying he had a videotape would be a good idea. He actually should make one in case something did happen. "Why in the world would I show it to you?"

"I wanna see it."

"If you cooperate, maybe I'll show it to you. So this is what we have, Martin. We've got José Pinon telling us all about you and Esteban and Miguel and Gordo and Julio Davis—the guy who gave you your alibi. We've got Joe telling us where Julio is. We have bloody fingerprints, we have an eyewitness who puts you at the scene."

"I wasn't there."

"Martin, it's over. Joe Pine told us everything because he was looking at the death penalty."

"So José tells you lies to save his skin and I'm supposed to be upset? It's bullshit."

"It's not just him, Martin. It's José and the rest of your homies from Bodega 12th. We've got them all . . . except maybe Julio." Decker liked to throw in a bit of truth. "But we'll find him. It's only a matter of time."

Cruces laughed derisively. "You got a problem, man. José is feeding you bullshit."

"But José makes sense," Decker said. "Sure, he's probably handing us some lines, but the story makes sense and the forensics back him up. He's saying that it's all you, Martin. You set up everything, and you paid each of your cousins ten grand to do it. It's all over, Martin. Help yourself out by helping us out."

Cruces was silent.

Decker said, "How'd you get that kind of money, Martin?"

"José is telling you *lies*! How many times do I gotta tell you?"

"Why should I believe you when we have your bloody fingerprints, Rondo Martin's eyewitness testimony against you, and Joe Pine talking like a mynah bird?"

"Rondo's lying, too. He hates me."

"The fingerprints don't lie." Decker leaned in close. "Martin, I know that you didn't set this up without help. From the very beginning we knew that you were paid off by someone who wanted to murder the Kaffeys. Someone who had a lot of money. Help yourself and tell us who paid you to do the murders."

"I didn't get paid off by anyone. How many times do I have to tell you? I wasn't there. And I'm gonna keep saying this until you guys let me go."

"You're not going anywhere, Martin. We've got enough to arrest you on three counts of premeditated murder, which can carry the death penalty. This crime was so cruel that I'm sure a judge would have no problem ordering the needle. Is that how you want it to end?"

"I wasn't there!"

Decker went at him for another hour, but Martin refused to budge. If this had been going on for eight hours prior to Decker's questioning, how likely was it that he was going to crack?

Patience, patience.

Decker suddenly recalled a police seminar he had about ten years ago. The lecturer spoke about a shrink who had been a master hypnotist. Sometimes instead of fighting the induction, the head doctor would incorporate the patient's resistance in part of the induction. So what would it hurt if Decker just played along with Cruces's lie?

"All right," Decker said. "You weren't there, okay?"

Cruces narrowed his eyes and stared at him. "That's right."

"You were not there. Rondo Martin was mistaken, Joe Pine was mistaken, the fingerprint was wrong, you weren't there."

"That's right."

"Okay." Decker nodded. "I believe you."

There was a long pause. Cruces said, "Good."

Decker said, "You know why I believe you?"

"Why?"

"Because we've been questioning you for a long time and you keep coming up with the same sentence. *You weren't there.* I have to ask myself: why would someone keep saying that when the evidence is so overwhelming against him? And the only thing that I can come up with is . . . it must be the truth."

"That's right." Cruces straightened his spine. "It's the truth."

"Okay, you weren't there," Decker told him. "But you know some of the people who were there."

"I don't know who was there because I wasn't there."

"All I'm saying is that you know Joe Pine, right?"

"Yeah, of course."

"And you know Esteban Cruz and Gordo Cruces. They're your cousins, right?"

"Yeah, they're my cousins."

"And you know Julio Davis. He's the one who gave you your alibi."

"Yeah, I know Julio. He wasn't there, either. I told you we were both getting drunk in a bar. About a million people saw us."

"And you know Miguel Mendoza."

"Met him a couple of times."

"That's all I'm saying. That you know the guys that Joe Pine said were involved in the murders."

"Joe's full of shit."

"Probably. But let's get back to you. If I believe you and I'm willing to help you out, you've got to help me."

"Depends on what."

"Can I be straight up with you?" When Cruces didn't object, Decker said, "We're in a little bit of a quandary. We know that the people who shot the Kaffeys were paid off by someone with a lot of money. Because Joe Pine said he got ten grand for the murders."

"Joe's full of shit."

Decker leaned forward. "We know that the Kaffey murders were an inside job, Martin. We know that it wasn't just planned by a bunch of Bodega 12th Street boys and a couple of guards. We know someone with a lot of money started the whole thing going, know what I'm saying?"

Cruces didn't say anything, but he managed a small nod.

"And whoever started it . . . he's the real bad guy. Why should your cousins take a fall for some fat cat?"

Cruces didn't answer.

"Look, you had nothing to do with it," Decker said. "So you're okay. So why don't you man up and help your cousins? Tell me who paid them to murder the Kaffeys?"

"I don't know," Cruces said. "I wasn't there."

Decker said, "But if you had to guess who El Patrón was, who would it be? You know El Patrón, right?"

"Why should I know?"

"Because you're a player, Martin. You know about these people."

Cruces didn't answer.

"Who is El Patrón?"

"Why would I know about him?"

"I'm just asking for your opinion."

"Well . . ." Cruces sat back. "If I give you my opinion, are you gonna let me go?"

"It's not up to me. But I'll tell everyone that I believe you. And I'll tell everyone that you helped me out by giving me your opinion."

"That means you ain't gonna do dick."

"What's the harm in giving me your opinion? You're not admitting to anything."

"That's right. I ain't saying anything."

Decker made a point of sighing. "I know you could help me. You're a smart guy."

"Why should I help you?"

" 'Cause I'm the only one who believes you."

"Are you really a lieutenant?"

"Yes, sir, I am. All I want is your opinion, smart guy. Nothing that's admissible in court. Just want your plain honest opinion, sir."

Cruces blinked then lay back in the chair. "Okay . . . in my opinion, if I was you . . . I would say . . . look at the brother."

"Grant Kaffey or Gil Kaffey?"

"Not the sons, dude, the hermano. Mace Kaffey. Man, he never liked Guy at all."

"Excuse me for a moment." Decker walked out of the room—a big smile on his face.

Sometimes all you have to do is ask.

FORTY

THREE WEEKS LATER, Martin Cruces agreed to turn state's evidence against Mace Kaffey in exchange for a plea of life in prison *with* the possibility of parole. But even after Decker had heard the story, Mace was not an easy fish to land. The district attorney wanted more and more, and it took months of tedious investigation to uncover the few shreds of evidence against Mace. With Cruces's testimony, a judge agreed to issue warrants that allowed the police to study Mace's bank accounts, credit card receipts, e-mail correspondence, and phone records.

Oliver and Marge were able to document two places where conversations took place between Cruces and Mace. The sides argued vociferously about what was said between the two of them.

Lee Wang uncovered a trail of one hundred and fifty thousand dollars in ten withdrawals that exited Mace's bank accounts and traveled from one dummy corporation to another until it appeared to reach Martin Cruces's hands. It was never specified what the money was for, and each side gave a different interpretation. Cruces claimed it was ten thousand for each of his drones in the hit and one hundred thousand for himself. Mace's lawyers claimed it was a pay-ment for beefed-up security after Guy received anonymous threats against his life. Why it went from Mace to Cruces was the subject of more speculation on the defense side.

Messing and Pratt were able to find about a half-dozen phone calls from Cruces to Kaffey, all of them placed on disposable cell phones that Cruces never disposed of. Particular attention was paid to two calls made on the night of the murders—one before and one after.

Willy Brubeck probably was responsible for the most damning piece of evidence: a gun registered to Mace Kaffey that was matched to the bullets pulled from Kaffey's own body as well as in the jacket taken from Neptune Brady. Why Mace chose to set himself up using his own gun was anyone's guess, but it probably had more to do with desperation measures than with common sense.

The total evidence was enough for the Los Angeles D.A. to take the case.

Immediately a warrant was issued for Mace Kaffey's arrest.

The man came into the police station armed with a posse of law-yers, all of them claiming that Martin Cruces was a lying psycho-path and his statements were fabrication. The charges were foisted upon Mace because the police needed a quick solve. The money transfer never happened. The conversations between them never happened. And the phone calls on a couple of throwaway phones? Who knew why Cruces was calling Mace? And suddenly Mace had remembered that Guy had asked Mace to borrow his gun. The thugs must have picked up the gun when they rampaged Coyote Ranch.

The defense claimed that the murders were a case of robbery gone wrong, and the subsequent shootings were the thugs trying to get rid of witnesses against them. Mace needed all the spin and help he could get. The charges against him included the premeditated murders of Guy Kaffey, Gilliam Kaffey, Denny Orlando, Alfonso Lanz and Evan Teasdale, Alicia Montoya, and the attempted mur-ders of Gil Kaffey, Grant Kaffey, Neptune Brady, Antoine Resseur, Piet Kotsky, Peter Decker, and Cindy Kutiel. It had taken almost a year to bring the case to trial. With the evidence and a star witness, the prosecution convinced a jury of twelve peers that Mace Kaffey was guilty of six counts of murder one. He was also found guilty of the attempted murder of Gil Kaffey. But the jury remained deadlocked on the charges of the attempted murder of Neptune Brady, Grant Kaffey, Antoine Resseur, Piet Kotsky, Peter Decker, and Cindy Kutiel.

It was unlikely that Mace would be tried again by the state as he already faced the death penalty.

"IT'S STINKY THAT you won't have your day in court," Rina told Decker over dinner.

"You can only die once," Decker answered.

"You're lucky I wasn't on that jury." The verdict had been announced a week ago, but it was still on everyone's minds. "That would have taken me away for months."

Decker eyed her over a glass of cabernet. "You would have been recused." They were in Tierra Sur restaurant inside the Herzog Winery, Decker's favorite place. It had a friendly waitstaff, the best kosher wine list bar none, a lovely ambience, and a killer chef who made magic with every edible thing he touched. "Do you know what you want to eat?"

"I'm looking at the lamb."

"Is it looking back at you?"

"That would be a little too rare for my taste," Rina said. "What an evil man."

"You're still back on Mace?"

"It's pretty astounding."

"He is evil."

"But . . ."

Decker took another sip of his wine. "Why do you think there's a but?"

"You just have that look in your eyes . . . that you're about to offer excuses."

"I would never offer excuses for a man who executed six people and tried to kill me because I was involved in the case. They make very good lamb. If you want it, I'll be happy to share my steak with you."

"Great," Rina said. "Let's order a side of French fries."

"Don't do that. You take two and I eat the rest."

"So control yourself."

"I have no control."

"So I'll occupy your mouth with conversation so you won't be tempted to overeat."

Decker said, "And how are you going to do that?"

"I want your opinion of Mace Kaffey. Why did he do it?"

"I don't think we'll ever know, and my opinion isn't worth anything."

"It's worth something to me," Rina said.

Decker looked in the breadbasket, then pushed it away. "Why don't you tell me your opinion. You followed the trial as closely as I did. And you have great insights."

"Thank you." Rina took a sip of her pinot noir. "But you have insider's trading info."

"You go first," Decker said.

Rina gave her words some thought. "You think of sibling rivalry—as old as the Bible. But it wasn't that the two of them were arguing and Mace killed Guy in a fit of passion like Cain and Abel. The murders were well-planned executions. Still, I don't think Mace woke up one morning and decided his only solution was to kill his family. I think it was a gradual process."

"I agree."

"I think it was a confluence of things that led Mace to do what he did. First off, Mace took all of the blame when Kaffey was on a downswing. When the lawsuit was settled, Guy came away with a lot more than Mace."

Decker said, "Mace was stripped of his board position, had his shares in the company taken away, and had his income reduced by half. But he was still making a hell of a lot of money."

"Not what he was used to making," Rina said. "We saw what happened during the trough of the recession. How the big three automakers flew to Washington on their private jets asking for billions of dollars. It's hard to get used to a reduced lifestyle."

Decker nodded.

Rina said, "I think Mace moved back east to prove himself with this Greenridge Project. But when the economy tanked and the project went way over budget, Mace saw his dreams of redemption being flushed down the toilet. It was pretty clear that Guy was getting ready to pull the plug."

"Grant was involved in Greenridge, too."

"I know. But Guy would take care of his son. No such guarantees with his brother," Rina said. "So there goes Mace's income and his moment of glory. His world was about to come crashing down, and he blamed Guy for everything. I think he was out to get Guy. Gilliam and Gil and the help were probably collateral damage."

"Hmm, I'm not so sure about that," Decker said. "I think Mace waited for a day when Gilliam, Gil, and Guy were all under one roof. Gilliam, had she lived, would have inherited a big share of Kaffey Industries. With her gone, the remaining shares would go to the boys. With Gil gone, all the shares would go to Grant. There was no way that Grant could handle the Kaffey Industries—East Coast and West Coast—by himself. Besides, Mace got along with Grant.

"I think Mace was hoping that Grant would give him the eastern division, including the Greenridge Project, and that Grant would take over the west where most of the business was."

Rina said, "Also, I suppose with Grant alive, there'd be less focus on Mace because Grant would inherit everything."

"You better believe it," Decker said. "We really didn't know who to focus on at first. Had Mace been the only man left standing, he would have been our best suspect."

Their waiter approached. His name was Vlad and he was over six seven with black hair, blue eyes, and mouth as wide as a canyon. After he took their order, he refilled Decker's wineglass.

"On the house," Vlad said. "Besides, we're at the end of the bottle."

Decker smiled. "I'm happy to take the dregs off you."

"What about you?" Vlad said to Rina.

"I'm fine with my one glass." After the waiter left, Rina said, "I do have a couple of questions about the case."

"If it's only a couple of questions, you're clearer than I am on it."

"Did Mace arrange for himself to be shot?"

"I think he arranged for himself to be shot *at*," Decker said. "The intended target was probably Gil, to finish off what the gangbangers had messed up at the ranch."

"Then why did someone shoot at Grant, you, and Cindy?"

"That remains a mystery. In my mind, Grant being alive was Mace's best excuse." He gave the question some thought. "I will say this from a professional point of view. With all of the Kaffeys being wounded or dead, we were stumped. There was no one person who we could point a finger at. We really did begin to think of maybe an outside crime—like a robbery."

"Who actually shot at you?"

"I don't know. None of the thugs owned up to that one."

"Who do *you* think shot at you?"

"It wasn't Alejandro Brand: he was already in jail. Joe Pine and Julio Davis were probably in Mexico, and Martin Cruces was probably the type to delegate. That leaves Gordo Cruz, Esteban Cruz, and Miguel Mendoza. I'd say Esteban because he seems to be the smartest."

"Esteban Cruz never confessed to doing anything."

"Yeah, he was the only gang member who was smart enough to lawyer up. The others said he was there, but we don't have definitive forensics. We do have a couple of fibers, a hair that's consistent with his hair. But that's not a fingerprint or DNA. He'll get time, but probably not life without parole. That's a shame. He seems smart . . . smarter . . . and you don't want a smart evil guy on the streets."

"Although according to Joe Pine, Esteban messed up on Harriman."

"Maybe yes, maybe no."

"And he messed up by not getting Gil Kaffey the first time."

"No, that was Joe Pine who messed up. He ran out of bullets."

"What a fiasco!"

"We may never figure all of it out, but we have enough to put the right guys behind bars."

Rina sipped her wine. "Mace must have been crazy with hatred to slaughter his family like that. Surely he could have found another project. It might not have been Greenridge, but he could have found something. And he was making good money. It wasn't as if Guy was going to boot him out of the business altogether."

"We don't know what Guy was planning to do."

"No one heard Guy say that he was firing Mace."

"No one heard Guy say that he was canceling Greenridge. But almost everyone in the company knew that it was a done deal, especially once the recession hit."

"That's true."

The waiter brought over the entrées. "More wine?"

"Any more and I'll be floating home," Decker said.

"And that's a bad thing because . . ."

"I drove."

"So give the woman your keys."

"I'm not allowed behind the wheel of his Porsche," Rina said.

"That's not true," Decker protested. "Well, it's sort of true."

Rina smiled. "It's okay. I just think of him as my handsome chauffeur."

Vlad laughed. "How about you? Another glass?"

"Sure, give her a glass," Decker said.

"Now I really won't be able to drive."

"That's the idea," Decker said.

Rina gave him a playful hit. "I'll take another glass."

After Vlad refilled her pinot noir, he said, "Anything else I can get you?"

"Nothing," Rina said. "Everything looks fantastic."

Vlad left and Rina took a few bites of lamb. "This is delicious. You want some?"

"I won't turn it down. Want some steak?"

"Just a bite."

"See, this is why you're still thin and I'm growing widthwise. I take half your lamb and you take a bite of my steak."

"You outweigh me by over one hundred pounds. I shouldn't be eating as much as you." She took a French fry. "Want one?"

"Jezebel." But Decker succumbed and ate a couple. "You want to know what I think was the final blow for Mace?"

Rina leaned forward. "Tell me."

Decker laughed. "You're my best audience."

"I'm interested."

"Okay, this is what I think," Decker told her. "Mace could have dealt with the closure of Greenridge. Like you said, it was unlikely that Mace would get canned. Demoted yes, but probably not canned. And like you said, he still would be making very good money and could have probably latched on to some other project. In my mind what really got to Mace was the ranch."

"Guy's had that ranch for ages."

"Yes, that's true. But it was a money pit. Had Guy sold the ranch, even in bad times, he could have cleared a lot of bucks and some of the money could have been put back into the Greenridge Project."

"Not nearly enough to override the costs."

"But maybe it would have been just enough money to keep Greenridge afloat until times turned around. I think Mace could have dealt with Greenridge closing. I think Mace could have dealt with Guy owning the ranch. But when Guy and Gil started making plans to turn the ranch into a winery, that's when Mace went berserk. Not only was Guy not going to give Mace money for Greenridge, Guy was going to spend millions of dollars for a vanity project."

"Interesting," Rina told him.

"I think Mace just couldn't bear Greenridge being canceled for lack of funds while millions of dollars were going into a money-losing proposition like a winery."

"Not all wineries lose money." Rina spread her arm about. "To wit."

"I will amend my statement. Small wineries rarely make money. You've got to know what you're doing."

"That's true." Rina finished her pinot. "Actually, I like that theory."

Decker brightened. "Thank you."

Rina raised her goblet. "Well, here's to you and a job well done. You deserve a good meal, and I promise I won't drive your Porsche."

"You can drive my Porsche. Just not after you've had a couple glasses of wine."

Rina giggled. "That's probably a good idea. Cheers."

Decker smiled and clinked glasses. "Cheers."

THE TRANSFORMATION WAS magical. The once hard-packed grounds had been covered by a green blanket as far as the eye could see. There were thousands of rows of netted, seedling grape vines. Replacing the guardhouses and paddocks was a spanking new industrial building that held hundreds of oak and steel barrels, several labs for the enologists and wine mixers, and a tasting room. When the place was up and operable, it would be quite a draw for the area.

The sun was trying to break through the marine layer common in L.A. springs. The sky was cloudy, but the air was clean. Decker took in a deep breath and let it out slowly. Hardscrabble turned into vibrant, verdant farmland.

Guy's dream.

"This is unbelievable." Decker zipped up his jacket. "Thanks for the invitation."

"Long overdue," Gil Kaffey said, "but I wanted it to be just right."

They walked on the tilled earth between the rows of grapevines: Gil Kaffey, Grant Kaffey, Antoine Resseur, Decker, and the well-dressed man on his right who held his arm. He could afford nice clothing with a reward of twenty thousand dollars sitting in his bank account. Harriman couldn't see any of it, but he sure could smell it.

"Cabernet grapes on the left and chardonnay on the right," he told Gil.

Gil smiled. "What a nose. Are your taste buds as sensitive?"

"Give me a taste test and then we can both know for sure."

"It'll be a long, long time before I can use any of my own grapes. I have been talking to some appellations up north. I think it might be wise to start small with premium grapes and then gradually use that experience on my own crops."

"How long do you think that will take?" Harriman asked.

"At least another couple of years," Gil said. "In the meantime, I've got plenty to keep me busy. People ask if I miss the business . . . if I'm sorry I sold out my share to Grant. And I say, what is there to miss?"

Grant said, "Well, we miss you."

Gil said, "You'd never know it by your profits, bro."

Grant said, "That's because we've laid off over five hundred people and shut down East Coast operations. You streamline anything, your revenues will go up."

"Dad should have streamlined the business a long time ago," Gil said.

"Dad should have done this a long time ago." Grant swiped an extended arm over the fields—like Moses splitting the Red Sea.

Gil blew out air. "The man could be impossible. He had his fingers in every aspect of the business and was a control freak. He could emasculate you with a few choice words or even one word. Uncle Mace deserves to rot in jail, he deserves to rot in hell. But there's this little, teeny part of me that understands him."

"I hear you, bro," Grant said.

"Dad was a force of nature." Gil surveyed the ranchland. "But he was also a visionary."

Resseur patted his boyfriend's hand. "Should I check in on lunch, Gil? I'm starving."

"We'll all head back," Gil said.

"No, no," Antoine said. "You stay here and I'll call you when everything's ready. I just want to get a head start." He kissed Gil on the cheek. "Enjoy."

The men walked along for another minute before Decker spoke. "How many people do you employ?"

"For the fields, it's mostly Paco Albanez and his family," Gil said. "When the vines start to mature, I'll bring in the experts."

"Seems reasonable."

"You know I kept on Rondo Martin, Ana Mendez, and Riley Karns even though we sold the horses."

Grant smiled. "Better to keep them under our employ than to deal with lawsuits."

Gil laughed. "Paco knows what he's doing." No one spoke. "Thank you both for coming down."

"Yes, really," Grant said. "Thank you both for everything."

"No thanks necessary," Decker said. "I just did my job. If you want to thank Brett, that's another thing."

"Not really," Harriman said. "I wouldn't have a job if people didn't testify. Still . . ." He laughed. "If I had known, maybe I wouldn't have been such a good citizen."

"We appreciate what you did," Decker said.

"We both appreciate what both of you did," Grant said. "My brother and I."

For a moment, the air was devoid of man's intrusion—just the sounds of crows expressing displeasure. Gil broke the silence. "When the place is operable, please come down again. I'll make it worth your while by giving you each a couple dozen cases."

"That's my brother," Grant said. "Giving away the profits."

"If I can break even, I'll be happy." Gil took in another whiff of air and let it out. "Although I can't be any happier than I am right now. I just wish Dad and Mom were here to share the dream."

Grant linked his arm with Gil, and the group started back toward the main house. Decker with Harriman; Grant with Gil.

In the Bible, there was Cain and Abel. But there was also Moses and Aaron—two siblings who respected and loved each other until the day Aaron died. Decker figured Gil and Grant were probably somewhere in between the extremes. Just a year ago, Gil had tearfully admitted to Grant that he had escaped with Antoine Resseur the day Grant was shot at because he really didn't trust anyone in his family, including his own brother. Grant had been shocked and angry, but eventually the two men reconciled and became closer than ever.

Brother plus brother didn't always total to brotherhood. But when it did, Decker thought, it was really nice.

RJD